The first book Matthew can recall reading was a torn, musty and yellowed paperback copy of *Ice Station Zebra* by Alistair MacLean which he'd found on an aunty's book shelf at a very young age. This set the ball rolling. Having gone from comics and picture books to a story so full of detail, character and such a believable, tension-filled environment, this book changed his world just as *Moby Dick*, *The Lord of the Rings* and *Catch 22* changed the lives of countless others when first read. Not that *Ice Station Zebra* would ever appear on a top 100 literary list but that didn't concern Matt. This book opened his eyes to a rich world that was now malleable in the right author's mind. Short stories of his own would follow each novel he consumed. He created many stories, some one page long, others epics, each different from the last and across many genres.

Currently working as a locomotive operator hauling coal trains down the Hunter Valley to the port of Newcastle, Matt has had many jobs but claims these are simply to fund his many (mostly legal) vices.

As well as being an award winning artist he is also a morbid, temperamental prick with the sense of humour of an unwanted and unhinged drunken uncle. In the eyes of others his dad jokes suck. But his two sons love 'em.

He still has that copy of *Ice Station Zebra* and inhales its aroma from time to time.

This book was written in an aluminium smelter during the quiet hours of many night shifts. At the time, I was an operator at the Tomago smelter just outside of Newcastle and in the down time whilst others played cards, watched TV or slept, I wrote. So in a way, I was being paid to write.

I would like to thank my tolerant wife for putting up with me constantly returning to the story to rework and polish and correct this or that over the last couple of years.

I thank my dad for reading it early on and offering advice on the life of a soldier in Vietnam. To this I add thanks to the Vietnam Veterans in Bundaberg that read it and offered both praise, information and encouragement.

To all those family and friends that encouraged me not to give up, I thank you.

Whilst many have helped me with the finer details, any mistakes are ultimately mine.

A DARKER GREEN

MATTHEW KEEGAN

VIVID PUBLISHING

ISBN: 978-1-925086-49-2
Published by Vivid Publishing
A division of the Fontaine Publishing Group
P.O. Box 948 Fremantle
Western Australia 6959
www.vividpublishing.com.au

Cataloguing-in-publication data is held at the National Library of Australia.

This book is available in both paperback and ebook editions.
To order further copies or to contact the author,
please visit www.vividpublishing.com.au/adarkergreen

For Ally and Roger
(Mum and Dad)

PROLOGUE

The blood that fell to the wet turf by his feet was flowing freely. The rays of a new day's sun caught each of the glossy red orbs, briefly reflecting their crimson darkness as they fell to the ground. What remained of his shattered left hand throbbed with each rapid heartbeat. The sharp, cold air of a northern January burned his lungs. War injuries obtained on the other side of the globe wrenched at his knees and his back. His legs felt weak under him. He was tired from the pursuit.

At that moment however, standing on a small hill on the border which separates the Irish Republic from the British Northern Ireland, Sean Doherty could feel no pain. It had vanished. Both pain and fear had been replaced by disbelief as he focused on the man that stood opposite him; the man aiming a rifle at him. Through exhausted eyes Sean looked beyond the barrel of the rifle and into the familiar, once friendly eyes of the other man.

Before the gunshots shattered the morning silence, Sean, a former Australian Army soldier and now Irish Republican Army volunteer, shook his head and wanted to ask the other man the simplest of questions.

Why...?

PART ONE

"The true soldier fights not because he hates what is in front of him, but because he loves what is behind him."

G.K. Chesterton

ONE

I will not die today…

It was now something of a ritual. Sort of a personal prayer. Not so much a "prayer" in the form of a divine invocation, but a promise to himself… a compulsive preparatory habit for want of a better explanation. A prayer in its literal religious meaning was of no use to him now. Sean Doherty had stopped believing in a God long ago. In his experience South Vietnam either drove men towards their God or towards reality.

But reality sucked and God was a cunt.

I will not die today…

The silent mantra echoed in his mind as he felt the giant airborne machine drop suddenly. The wind from the open door of the heavily laden Huey helicopter futilely attempted to dry his wet, torn clothing but the humidity always won in the tropics. The only way to be free of wet clothes around here was to get around naked. Hardly an option for them.

Sean watched as the upper levels of the jungle canopy beneath raced up towards him. For an instant it seemed as though the burdened Bushranger of the RAAF was going to continue plummeting down into the tree tops in a tearing collision of metal and wood mixed with the flesh of ten men, but the helicopter shuddered, levelled out and held a contour-hugging distance of several feet above the blurred green vegetation.

He removed his green cloth bush hat and used it to wipe the sweat from his drained, expressionless face. He felt the heavy stubble of two weeks growth that had camouflaged his once innocent facade and promised himself a shave back at base.

Two long weeks without a single contact, the fact mulled over in his mind. *Two weeks of silence… and not a single shot fired.* It felt like they had been out there for two months. Their only excitement had been the arrival of the resupply chopper after ten days out; a brief respite to the monotony of patrolling.

Sitting opposite Sean was Joel Copland, a full time soldier, not a Nasho, a conscripted soldier like himself. The young father of two had the most morbid sense of humour Sean had ever come across which is why they got on so well. Joel's eyes were currently shut but Sean knew he was not sleeping. Joel hated to fly. As the pilot lifted and dropped the giant Huey, Sean watched Joel flinch each time, his knuckles white around the barrel of his weapon. It wasn't air sickness; he just feared crashing out here.

Sean cradled his own rifle between his knees, the butt resting on the floor, and looked out at the vast, dense rainforest below. The hills of Long Hai rolled off into the distance, a shimmering heat haze distorting their clarity. To the south, the direction they were headed, gigantic cumulus nimbus clouds gathered into a giant frenzied thunderhead that prepared to dump its contents on the Phuoc Tuy Province of South Vietnam. Other than this one monstrous storm front there wasn't a cloud in the sky.

The tap on his shoulder finally came. He turned to his commanding officer, 2nd Lieutenant Michaels to see him hold up a finger, mouth over-emphasising as he yelled 'ONE MINUTE.' Sean nodded and gave Joel the customary kick to his boot, snapping the 22 year old out of his mental sanctuary. Instantly Joel went about preparing for deployment, glad the flight was coming to an end. Sean then cast an eye over himself. His pack straps he pulled tight, securing the seventy-odd pound bag to his back. His sleeves unrolled to their full length and his green cheesecloth sweat-rag repositioned around his neck. His webbing was checked; two fragmentation and two phosphorous grenades, machete, shovel and six full and sterilised water bottles. Eight more magazines for his Belgian designed, Lithgow made Self Loading Rifle, or SLR. Slung over his shoulders and backpack were three hundred rounds of chain-link ammunition for the platoon's two M60 machine guns.

The Huey banked sharply to the right and the starboard crewman studied the floor of the jungle through the holes in the canopy; his mounted swivelling M60 machine gun pointing wherever his bulbous impersonal helmet looked. Here and there the jungle floor would shine like the countless pieces of a shattered mirror as the mid-afternoon sun bounced off small streams, pools and puddles left by yesterday's rain.

The jungle ended and open plains of razor sharp elephant grass raced by. The pilot banked the rotors hard, the blades biting into the air as they slowed rapidly, the Huey's tail falling behind as it dropped towards the ground. Sean moved to the floor and swung his legs out over the edge. Placing his boots on the chopper's skid he turned his attention to the ground rushing up to meet him.

2nd Lieutenant Michaels looked at the men around him. 'Remember lads!' he shouted at them from behind a wry grin, 'Try not to look conspicuous! It draws fire!'

The Huey came to a stop only a foot above the brown bladed grass and Sean was the first to jump.

The words *I will not die today* resurfaced again.

Think of home. Make it home.

Private Sean Doherty hit the sponge-wet ground and ran 40 feet out to secure the landing zone, the wash of the large blades spinning above him briefly cooling his wet clothes. Sean looked to his side and watched a second, third and fourth Huey with the remainder of the platoon deploying out in similar fashion. He saw their sergeant wave back to the pilot and at once the big green Bushrangers of 9 Squadron Royal Australian Air Force began clawing their way back up the invisible ladder into the sky.

Squatting beside Joel, Sean felt a slap on his pack and turned to see Michaels kneeling beside him.

'Spud, you're on point!' the CO shouted over the deafening noise of the departing Hueys, calling the private by his nick-name. 'Two-eight-zero degrees for one click.'

Sean nodded and, with his SLR raised up to his shoulder, he trotted off towards the tree line as fast as the burden on his back would allow. The group followed, keen to get out of the open. The edge of the jungle lay only 200 feet away. Once under the cover of the trees the men set out in a line, Indian file and silently made their way into the darkness away from the LZ.

As the jungle's canopy shadows crawled over his sweat pregnant uniform he whispered in self reassurance, 'I will not die today.'

I will not die today...

TWO

Sean Doherty had been conscripted into the Royal Australian Army one week before his 21st birthday, three months after completing his trade certificate at the BHP steel mill in Newcastle. He was a boilermaker but a rolling numbered wooden marble in a small steel cage changed all that. He applied for a trade roll with the engineers but he ended up in the infantry. He was told "No one gets their first choice".

When Sean was called up it knocked his older brother James hard. James had become the youngest publican in Newcastle and managed a dodgy Toohey's pub called the Lass O'Gowrie which was only a couple of blocks from Sean's place in Wickham. James claimed the whole world was trying to rob him of everyone close to him, which was a fair call. Their mother had died from an infection caught during a short stay at the Newcastle Hospital when James was only 9, Sean 6, leaving Melanie, the eldest of the three kids at age 11, to take care of them when their father was working. Melanie, having the role thrust upon her, was their mother figure from then on.

Sean had some recollection of his mother but not much. The photos they had of her were aged and beginning to fade, worn at the edges from young hands memorising her loving face; the embodiment of the perfect mother. Sean still carried a photo of her wherever he went. The one he had taken with him to Vietnam was kept inside his wallet in his locker with his civilian clothes. The photo had been taken at Merewether beach in the mid 50's when he was just 5. It displayed his mother holding him tightly in her lap, a flamboyant set of sunglasses perched high on her head of blond hair. Her eyes were smiling, full of love for the shirtless little boy that was laughing and struggling in her arms. He liked to think she was tickling him in that shot, playing with him and knowing there was nothing more important to her in the world at that moment than her funny boy Sean. He could see himself in her face. He looked more like her than his father, a handsome young man born of a strikingly enchanting woman. His dark blond hair came from her although both he and James obtained their height and athletic build from their father.

Anna Baldwin, Sean's girlfriend, had cried for the whole day at the news of his conscription. She told him to write a letter to his local member of parliament but he knew it would do no good. She cursed the country, she cursed Prime Minister Gorton and she even cursed Sean for being born on that day before running off out of his house. When she returned the next morning she kissed him, said she was sorry and took him into his bedroom. All was forgiven. The following morning he proposed to her. Everyone was happy.

Sean didn't mind the Army once he finished basic training but he still feared going to Vietnam. He had been pretty fit before going in from years of playing rugby league but basic training took it out of everyone. He had never fired a weapon before and found he was quite good at it. He topped his class in marksmanship and proved to be an exceptional soldier. After the three months of rookie training and the three months of Corp training he joined his Regiment of 6RAR and did a further three months of specified infantry training which included the inexorable jungle course in Canungra, Queensland, which he thought was a lot of fun – something it is not meant to be.

Nine months after entering the army he stepped off a Qantas jet as a member of 4 Platoon Alpha Company 6th Battalion in the humid hell-hole known as South Vietnam.

After an hour Sean came to a stop and sat on his haunches. The platoon did the same without a single word being uttered. The jungle around them was silent, the peace occasionally being broken by the sound of a distant bird or a nearby insect. Every pair of eyes pushed into the dense surroundings looking for the slightest of movements as ears strained to hear man-made noises. The distant rumbling to the north had stopped a while ago; the impossibly high B52s were now heading back to bases in Thailand with empty bellies and cocky crews.

The seconds dragged on as the platoon waited. No wind blew to cool down the Australians, and their jungle greens, torn and rotten and in need of replacement after the 2 week patrol, looked black with sweat. Despite the conditions each waited patiently. They could go for days without talking when on patrol. Only the briefest and most essential words were exchanged face to face, inches apart, in less than a quick short whisper. The Viet Cong had come to fear the silence. Australian soldiers were known to sneak right up to within a few meters of them without any indication of their presence, something that was lost on their American allies.

At the head of the group Sean was studying the area directly in front. He could see roughly 80 feet into the jungle before the vegetation blocked out the world beyond. Knowing he was responsible for the safety of the group made him wait longer than most would have.

His patience paid off. In the valley ahead gunfire erupted but it was not directed at them. The distant, invisible battle flared with the tearing sounds of opposing rifles fighting for authority before suddenly ending in an echoed, rolling silence. Then Sean saw movement heading his way. His heart pounded as he took aim on the distant shaking leaves and branches. He let his index finger rest against the trigger to take up the small amount of slack in its operation. In his time in South Vietnam he had been in many encounters which had ranged from single shot confrontations to three day long battalion engagements involving artillery and air strikes. Regardless of their size they always started with a disgusting feeling of fear and terror at the unknown of what was about to reveal itself.

First one then two soldiers broke through the wall of distant foliage and it took a tremendous amount of will for Sean not to react on instinct and fire. A shiver ran over him when he realised the men running towards him were allies. His hand shot out instantly, relaying a silent message to his platoon mates not to fire. Lowering his rifle Sean waited until the two men were within 10 yards before giving a short crisp whistle to gain their attention. The two hurried men both raised rifles without hesitation and looked at the young Australian soldier crouched on the ground before them. Sean saw that both were dressed in the fatigues of the Australian Special Air Service Regiment and nodded to them. The two relaxed slightly as they ran towards him, dropping down by his side as several deafening shots of a shortened SLR rang out far behind them.

'You blokes need a hand?' Sean whispered through a grin.

The taller of the two smiled back and pointed behind him. 'There will be six more of us coming this way.' He turned at a sound and saw the remainder of his men trotting through the bush, all relieved to see that their numbers had grown.

By now 2nd Lieutenant Michaels had moved to the front and gave a short introduction to the newcomers before asking for the news. Sergeant Andrew Wilton, the taller SAS man, filled him in.

'We're a long range patrol. Just ran into a sizeable group of VC. We hit them hard before they could react but there's too many for just us eight. We *were* out of here. Unless you guys wanna join in the fun?'

'Seems you lads have found the mob *we* were looking for,' Michaels replied, glad to have something to finally do. 'How many of them?'

Sergeant Wilton's face was a collage of dried mud and camo face paint bound together with weeks, possibly months of heavy stubble growth. The mud cracked in places as he talked.

'A platoon size. Twenty at least.'

By now the remaining SAS men had already spread out in a defensive ambush covering the way they had come.

At this stage Sean's own Sergeant Lynch, their overly blasphemous second in charge had already organised their platoon into a similar defensive circle with the two M60 machine gunners on their flanks. Sean saw the SAS Sergeant get into firing position on the other side of the tree that he himself was using as cover. He caught the elite soldier's eye and nodded. Sergeant Wilton nodded back with his face-cracking grin smiling away.

'These nogs are in for a surprise if they think we're on the run now,' he whispered to Sean.

Sean smiled back and returned his attention to the jungle beyond his rifle sights. It didn't take long for the pursuing Viet Cong to arrive.

The SAS men all seemed to fire in unison without a call to do so. Sean's fellow infantrymen fired barely a second after. He saw the first four VC fall instantly as the rest went for cover. Dirt kicked up next to him and bark exploded from the tree above him, clumps of it raining down over his back. A grenade went off on the right flank but no one was hit. At the far right of the opposing line was a light machine gun; definitely Russian with a drum mag, its thumping sound unmistakeable.

Drawing a bead on the closest to him, Sean fired off his first few rounds, the first two being tracer rounds. The flash of the Vietnamese's rifle answered back. He couldn't see the guerrilla for the foliage, but adjusted his aim onto the flash instead. He squeezed off four more rounds, saw a rifle cartwheel up out of the shadows and then moved onto the next target. For some reason this next Vietnamese sat up to get a better look of the battlefield. Sean dropped him with two quick shots, leaving a pink cloud floating where his head had once been.

Sean's mind was racing and pulling everything into slow motion at the same time. Adrenalin made him forget about the heat. Someone on the left tried to run but Sean pegged him. He fell but was still moving. Through the ringing in his ears Sean could hear him screaming and probably cursing him in his own tongue. Before he had a chance to put a couple more into him, he crawled out of sight.

Feeling someone kick his pack, probably to get his attention, Sean risked a glance behind him but saw no one. Then it occurred to him that he had been hit. He could feel the blood spreading across his back and down around both sides of his waist. Fear spread with it.

Oh fuck. I'm paralysed!

THREE

He let go of his rifle and felt the small of his back, his hand becoming wet. Bringing it back around in front of his eyes he was surprised to see nothing but water on his fingers. The pain that he had begun to imagine vanished when the realisation came to him: a bullet had hit one of his water bottles. The thoughts of never walking again or never riding a motorbike, never dancing with his fiancée, even the thought of her leaving him for someone else, all left him instantly. Calm washed over him like a warm wave but just as quickly it left. He was still in this shit fight.

The thundering M60 to the far left went quiet. Either Macca was hit or his weapon had jammed. Whatever the reason, the enemy used this opportunity to shift its attack. Several of the black clad figures rose off the jungle floor and bolted for denser cover. They were trying to encircle the Aussies. This movement drew a lot of gunfire but none found a target.

Sean heard Sergeant Wilton call out to him. He was rolled over onto his side fitting a new magazine to his shortened SLR.

'Grenade. Willy Peter towards those trees!' he called to Sean.

Pulling one from his webbing, Sean tore out the pin and looked back at the Sarge. They both nodded and Sergeant Wilton fired a dozen deafening rounds towards the trees as Sean threw the small explosive. It went off just before it hit the ground releasing a large blinding cloud of white phosphorous – Willy Peter – in a spectacular flash. The concussion or shrapnel killed one of them outright leaving the other three screaming in pain as the chemicals burned away at their bodies like dry, sun-hot acid. One of them came thrashing out from behind cover, running in a futile attempt to escape the pain and was shot squarely in the chest by one of the SAS men, a red mist exploding from his back.

Two of the Aussies got up and ran towards the enemy, firing off several rounds into the burning victims as they came across them. They continued on beyond the area away from the phosphorous covered ground and took up a new position looking along the line of VC.

Seeing this, the Vietnamese decided to disengage. A call was heard from within their ranks and several grenades were thrown to provide cover. The first grenade went off less than 10 feet from Sergeant Lynch; his body disappearing in the flash and smoke. The second went off further to Sean's left but clear of anyone. He aimed back into the foliage and fired off several more rounds, the second last in his mag being, once again, a tracer, a red hot line of burning magnesium marking its journey for all to see. He changed out mags and waited. Soon all that was evident to them being there was the fine, dissipating haze of cordite smoke that hung in the still, humid air...and their dead.

Joel landed beside Sean in a textbook perfect running drop, eyes still looking down his sights for anything he could unload on. He fired off several rounds just to keep them running. He turned to Sean and winked, both of them feeling the buzz that came after having survived a contact.

'That was fun,' he said with his usual black humour.

It was all over. The fire fight had lasted less than a minute.

'Medic! The C.O. and Sarge are hit! We need a Dust Off!' someone called from their right. Sean and the SAS sergeant climbed to their feet and raced over to check on Michaels.

He was dead. No pulse and it was pointless trying to resuscitate him. The bullet had entered the side of the neck just above his right shoulder blade and exited his left cheek bone, taking his jaw and tongue with it. The angle of the CO's head at the time had directed the bullet to pass through the centre of his neck in a slightly upward path almost certainly destroying his spinal column. Sean knew he had died quickly. He then moved over to the Sarge's body. Lynch had been hit by shrapnel and had lost some blood but nothing major. He had been knocked out by the blast and came too as his wounds were being checked. He had two large cuts to his face and a deep gash to his right forearm that would need stitching. However most of the blood was from his forehead. As he came around he did what he did best and that was blaspheme.

'Fucken Christ Almighty! Am I still here?'

Sean smiled as he watched the medic bandage the wounds. 'Anywhere else you'd rather be?'

'Shit. Can't think of anyplace off the top of me 'ead.' He groaned with discomfort, a headache rolling in. 'Michaels?' he asked but knew the answer. He had seen him go down.

'Yeah, he's dead,' Sean said as he pulled the map from the Sarge's pocket and went back to check on the rest of the platoon. Their radioman was already chasing up a Dust Off chopper.

No one else was injured besides Brownie. Lance corporal Grant Brooks was pouring water over Brownie's left hand to wash away some phosphorous that was burning him. Corporal Shane Brown had to be the toughest prick around. He never complained when he was injured, just smiled and shrugged it off as part of the job. He hadn't cried out in pain when he had been winged only two weeks in country. A small calibre bullet had hit him in his left elbow, knocking out a decent piece of flesh and chipping his ulna. In typical Brownie fashion he had casually walked over to the hospital tent after returning from patrol and quietly waited to see a nurse. 'Sorry to bother ya love, but some bastard shot me.'

Sean looked at the burning skin on Brownie's hand. It had bubbled up a bit from the chemical reaction and looked painful, but he didn't wince at all.

'She'll be right, Spud,' he said as Grant gently emptied one of his canteens over it, 'It's not me wankin' hand.'

'Michaels is dead,' he said to them directly. There was no other way he could say it.

'Fuck,' Brownie shook his head.

Sean looked up at his Corporal. 'Do we pursue?'

'No. Fuck 'em. Let's get on home.'

'Dust off in twenty minutes!' Gazza called out.

Sergeant Wilton returned to speak to Brownie who was now in charge of the platoon. 'You lot out of here?'

Brownie nodded. 'Chopper's on its way.'

The SAS man extended a hand to each. 'Sorry about your CO. But thanks for your help. Don't know how far they would have followed us…so, glad you could lend us a hand.'

'No worries,' Sean replied. 'Just buy us a beer when we get back to base.' He tried to smile but it felt forced.

'Base? What the fuck is base?' Despite the loss of the platoon's officer, Sergeant Andrew Wilton smiled. 'We live out here.' He turned to walk back to his men but called out over his shoulder as they disappeared back into the bush once more, 'Have fun burying the dead gooks!'

Sean and Brownie just shook their head at the comment. Even though they were the enemy they did have orders to bury the dead when time permitted.

'I'll set up a perimeter,' Brownie informed him. 'You right here?'

'Yeah.'

There were seven dead Viet Cong but several drag marks. They estimated 11 dead overall. *Estimated.* Sean searched the two he believed he had shot. Both were lucky to have once stood four and a half feet tall. The first was an older man; probably in his mid thirties but sometimes it was hard to tell. As he rolled him over to search for documents or maps, he saw the holes in the top of his chest that had killed him. No guilt came to him as he rummaged through the dead man's pockets. Personally he felt no deep hatred towards the Vietnamese people unlike some of his comrades. He preferred to block out the fact they were people with families. Every time he had killed someone he had been glad he could feel a sort of neutrality which could help him carry on. He couldn't afford to think of them any other way. He didn't think of them as anything; just the enemy. Just angry targets.

He found a letter which he pocketed for the Army Intelligence lads and a photograph of a young boy. The boy looked about five or six and had a huge smile. The image of himself and his mother on a sunny Newcastle beach came to him again. Sean smiled back at the kid and placed the photo back in the pocket of the dead man. He slung the man's AK47 over his shoulder and moved on to the next body.

This one had had the back of his head blown out along with the left side of his face. Sean remembered this one looking up over the cover of the jungle floor and getting two rounds dead centre from his SLR. From what was left of his face Sean guessed he was slightly younger than himself. But he had been inexperienced in battle and it had been his downfall. Trying not to look at the pulp of brain, teeth and bone which had already become a nesting ground for flies, he searched him but found nothing.

Grabbing the kid's old German Mauser rifle, he rejoined the others to examine the intelligence found before partaking in the onerous but benevolent task of burying the bodies as soon as Gazza had finished taking a few photos and logging on a map where the burials would take place.

Ten minutes later they all doubled it out to the LZ.

Half way back to Nui Dat the choppers hit the afternoon rain and the cooler air that came with it. It was a welcome relief from the still, damp heat of the rainforest.

The captured rifles, mainly the AK47's, were prized souvenirs to the soldiers and they had captured so many of them they were now selling them to rear echelon types. The majority of them would be traded for cartons of beer but Sean had traded one several months ago for a reel to reel tape recorder…and some beer.

He was unsure of what to do with the one he cradled on his lap. Looking at the poncho at his feet which held his former CO's body he felt guilty about claiming it as a souvenir. The reason for a family's suffering they were yet to feel was lying in his lap. He looked back at the body and then to the rifle. Without another thought he pulled the half empty mag from it and flicked the banana shaped item out over the side. Then, as they banked and he could see the Rach Hoa River below, he threw both the AK and the kid's Mauser out to be lost forever.

Closing his eyes, he forced himself to picture his fiancée.

I promise I'll make it home to you babe.

FOUR

They landed at Kangaroo Pad inside Nui Dat, the Australian military encampment, and unloaded in the pouring rain. Captain Davies met them and called for a debrief from the NCOs in a half an hour in the Intel hut after they had cleaned their weapons and themselves. Michaels' body was taken away to the morgue for cleaning and Lynch and Brownie were escorted across to the hospital for patching up.

After briefing Davies and his intelligence mob about their run in with the SAS, they were free to do what they wanted for the rest of the day as long as they stayed on base. Everyone was in a sombre mood after the fight, feeling down about the loss of another of their mates.

Michaels had been not just a good CO. He had been a good bloke.

Now he was dead at 26.

Post stand-to. No one was in a good mood. After returning from a patrol they were always supplied with a generous ration of beer. "Numb their minds" was the Army's way of controlling their stress. Most of the men were in their wood and corrugated iron huts playing cards and writing letters. The rain had made the atmosphere in the hut clammy. All shirts had been removed and this made life slightly more bearable. Radio Vung Tau played in the background. Johnny O'Keefe was singing *Sing, sing, sing*.

As the others played cards Sean was on his cot listening to a tape recording Anna had sent him the week before. He listened to each recording at least twenty times, eyes closed, and when he did, for those few minutes, he was back at home with her in Newcastle driving around in his 64 EH Holden, parking along the esplanade with burgers and cokes from one of Hunter Street's many milk bars, listening to Elvis or the Stones or Little Patty on the radio. They would eat and watch the surfers catch the last waves of the day before climbing into the back seat.

He held the player close to his ear, his eyes closed tight.

'Hi baby. Hope you're doing fine and are staying out of trouble. We all listened to your message last night down at the pub and had a bit of a party afterwards for you. I've got a little bit of a hangover but nothing too serious. James and that are here…say hi everybody!!' Sean smiled as he heard at least five or more people yell out his name, screaming and shouting and just being stupid.

'Alright! That's enough. In case you didn't hear that, that was everyone saying hello. Umm, James, Kimmy, Luke and Leanda, a couple of the regulars…I'm down the pub at the moment giving Kim a hand in the kitchen today. It's a beautiful Saturday morning and some of us are going to go over to the beach later to meet up with a few of the crew.'

'Here! Give it to me!' It was Sean's brother James. *'Hey Sean, don't listen to her. She's been in here all morning and hasn't lifted a finger to help. You're gunna have to hurry up and get back here so you can keep this wife of yours out of my pub. She's scaring away all my regulars, and they're all alcoholics so you know how scared they must be!!'*

'Piss off Jim! Don't listen to him, baby. I think he's still drunk. Melanie and Joseph called in last night to listen to you but they couldn't stay. She says to say hi and that she loves you and that. Hang on. Here's Luke.'

Luke Kennedy had been Sean's best mate since kindergarten. He lived in the same suburb and they practically grew up at each other's house. Luke was a refractory worker at the BHP steel mill working in the next workshop over from Sean's dad. He was a loyal friend and someone he was glad would back him up in any fight. Luckily he missed out by one number when the "Nasho's Lotto" was held but Luke felt guilty his mate was going and not him. They had lived their lives together, fought every fight together for almost two decades. Now Sean was involved in a fight without him and it had made Luke feel ashamed.

'G'day mate! How's things over your way. Yeah, that's great, shut up for a sec'.' He had always been the smart arse. *'I've just put down a deposit for an 'aicht tee Monaro. Vee-eight Chevy motor, four speed manual…same ones they raced at Bathurst. Me an' Thomo took one for a test drive last week… it'll eat your little baby six. The fucken power of this thing mate! Wait until you see the colour I chose! I'll pick you up from the airport in it when you come home. Yeah settle down! See ya mate!'*

'God. You boys and cars.' Back to Anna. *'Hang on. I'm just walking into the ladies for some privacy.'* He heard the door shut behind her.

'I miss you so much babe. I'm going crazy with loneliness. It's like I'm craving you all the time. Every time I see a bloke in an army uniform I think it's you. I just want you to be safe and come back to me. I try not to worry but some of the pictures they show on the news are…I don't like watching them but we always do just in case we see you. Dad saw a fella he knew from Gosford on there once so I pray that I could see you. Send some more pictures home and I'll get them developed here. From your last lot of photos you look like you've lost more weight. You look fit and sexy. Umm…Mum and dad wanted to hold a party for you at their place when you get back but we all think you'd rather have it here. There's a rock n' roll band from Maitland that comes down here a fair bit that are good. If you're keen we could see how much they'd cost. I'd better go now and finish up out in the kitchen. I love you, my husband-to-be. I miss you. You just make sure you stay away from those dirty women over there,' she added in a playful manner. *'Save it all for me for when you get home. We'll spend a month in bed if you want! Gotta go. Love you babe.'*

He turned off the tape and the image of her in the short summer skirt she would wear to the beach over her bikini came to him. She was the most beautiful girl he had ever met. He counted himself lucky she was his. Luke always seemed to end up with the hot birds and wondered if he hadn't met Anna first then Luke might have her.

Most of the girls in Newcastle had, or dyed, their hair blonde, but not Anna. She was naturally a brunette and proud of it. She had grown it down to her breasts although she said she would like to cut it short.

Just for a change, she would say, but Sean liked it long. He loved the way she would tie it back into a ponytail when they went for a ride on Thomo's Triumph and the way it would hang down over her face when she was on top of him.

He couldn't wait to be out of this place and back in her arms.

FIVE

This country would be so lovely if it wasn't for the humidity. And the war.

Dressed in a pale yellow shirt and a pair of stubbies and thongs, Sean sat back in the uncomfortable seat of the Huey and tried to enjoy the scenery as it passed far below them. As usual Joel flew with his eyes shut.

Both he and Joel had snagged 36 hours R&C leave – Rest and Convalescence – and had thrown on their civvies, diving into the first helicopter headed to Vung Tau. While the crewman of the bird still kept their fingers close to the triggers of the side mounted M60s, Sean felt calm in knowing that at the end of their twenty minute ride they would not have to deploy out into the jungle on another sphincter-clenching patrol. Instead they would catch a ride from the air base to down-town Vung Tau where they would drink themselves stupid.

Below them the Vietnamese went about their business; fishing, tending to rice crops and herding live stock that were constantly being spooked by aircraft just like theirs. Most of the peasant population tried to ignore the war around them. How they wished for an end to the "American war".

Looking behind them he saw another Huey coming up alongside 30 yards off to their left. He knew what cargo it carried. Painted on the nose and opened side doors was a large red cross on a white background indicating it as a flying ambulance; a dust-off bird. The pilot was talking, his attention focused on the Huey to his right as he conversed with the pilot of Sean's bird. Moving faster than themselves, the ambulance passed them but not before Sean looked at the two unfortunate soldiers that were laid out on stretchers in the back. One was prone and unmoving with his left boot missing. His foot was covered in blood. Above him worked two medics; one frantically trying to hook up a saline bag while another pumped away on his chest. The other injured soldier, a black kid, was propped up on his side, leaning on his elbow to keep an eye on his mate. Hearing the other bird beside them, the black soldier looked over at Sean as they raced by, the whites of his eyes staring out from the darkness of his face.

Sean could just imagine that kid's thoughts; wishing he were in their chopper headed to the nearest bar for a Budweiser or Lone Star or whatever he drank back home in the states...if he was old enough to. Sean held up his hand and nodded. He saw the young man smile and wave back before the Huey pulled away in front of them. It was the smallest of smiles breaking through the pain that showed on his face. Silently he wished the young negro all the best and wished he himself had not seen the wounded on his way to relax. It had put a dampener on the journey. He was glad he hadn't pointed them out to Joel. Why ruin his trip as well?

Set back two blocks from Bai Truoc, or Front Beach as the Westerners refer to it, the Ettamogah Pub was a favourite drinking hole for Australian and New Zealand servicemen. It was one of the many pubs, bars and clubs that had been established near the intersection of Duong Ba Cu and Duong Tran Hung Dao; otherwise known as The Flags district of Vung Tau. As usual the pub was packed with servicemen in civilian get-up and local girls in mini-skirts, platform shoes and over-the-top hair doo's. There were some American soldiers dressed still in their greens in the back at the last table but other than them it was all Anzac.

Joel grabbed a couple of seats at an emptying table while Sean retrieved the first of the many well earned drinks that would come their way. He returned with four beers, the first not touching the sides as they all but inhaled them.

Getting comfortable, Sean relaxed more with his second beer and looked around the room, looking for familiar faces to share a catch-up bevy with and the dark faces that had just returned from the jungles and mountains. These were the ones to avoid. Whether or not they intended, they always seemed to bring trouble with them. They were easy to spot. Their eyes looked beyond what was in front of them, staring through people, furniture and walls to whatever haunted memories plagued them. They would sit alone, hunched over their drink and rarely talked to anyone. Some talked to themselves.

Satisfied today's crowd was, so far, amicable, he lit up a fag and closed his eyes, savouring the taste of tobacco and beer on his tongue, the cool air of the fan on his head and the sounds of The Easybeats in his ears.

'Footy season starts next week back home,' he heard Joel state.

'Go the Dragons.' His eyes remained shut.

'You've still no idea do you?'

Here we go. One eye opened. 'About what?'

'Exactly.'

'Mate, Saint George has already got this year sewn up. Your Magpies haven't got a chance in hell of even making the semi's.'

Joel scoffed at that. 'You haven't seen this year's line-up…'

Sean leaned forward and started counting off on his fingers. 'Graeme Langlands, Billy Smith, Phil Hawthorne – a local boy. If just these three players limped out onto the field, pissed out of their minds, they could still beat your team. Eleven premierships in a row! No other team has ever done that. Eleven!'

'That's in the past.'

'One of those teams they beat, I do believe, was your Magpies.'

'It's a different team this year mate.'

'Eleven premiership wins.' Sean held up his beer in salute. 'Your last win was…what, seventeen, eighteen years ago?'

'1952.' Joel asserted with some pride.

'1952. Now *that's* in the past. Fuck; that was during the *last war*!' He leaned back again, smug, and laughed. 'Ever wondered why Wests sends over all those jumpers and footballs to our fellas over here. It's 'cause they're so desperate they'll try recruiting soldiers out in the field…even the wounded.'

'Oh God, you're full o' shit!'

'It wouldn't matter who they hired. Five bucks says the Magpie's not only fail to make the semi's *but*…are in the bottom half of the ladder when they roll around!'

A different voice above them cut in. 'Mate, I'd take that bet but I won't be around to pick up my winnings.'

Both Sean and Joel looked up at the man who had just joined in their conversation. Standing beside their table were two fellow Australians. One had his long dark hair slicked back and was clean shaven. The other let his longer hair fall as it wanted and carried an almost full beard. Only the Special Air Service Regiment let their lads get away with such a scruffy look.

'No one sitting here, fellas?' asked the taller one with the slicked hair.

It took a second for Sean to recognise the tall man beside him. He looked so different without a face full of mud and paint and war. 'Holy shit! How's it going? Glad to see that you both found your way out of the garden maze.' He stood and shook hands with Sergeant Andrew Wilton of the Australian SAS Regiment.

The professional soldier smiled as he held out his hand. 'Andrew Wilton. This is Lindsay Splatt.'

'Yeah, I remember. G'day Lindsay. I'm Sean Doherty and this is some piss head.'

Joel stood and introduced himself.

'Were you out there with this one the other day?' Lindsay asked as they sat down.

'Yeah,' Joel admitted. 'Interesting day wasn't it? So what happened to you lot?'

'Ah you know…more of the same.'

Typical SAS, Sean thought. *Always with the secrets.*

'So, I take it that you're the Magpie's fan, Joel?' Andrew asked as he sipped his can of beer.

'Black and white through and through.' Both Joel and Andrew raised their drinks.

'Not another one?' Sean groaned with exaggeration.

'Sean, I cop it all the time,' sympathised Lindsay. 'So I'll be glad to see the back of this cunt. He's outta here now on a transfer.'

'Let's not talk shop boys,' Andrew said. 'We've only got…nine hours to celebrate. We're here to drink!'

And drink they did.

As the afternoon wore on, a sea breeze picked up, bringing a much welcomed drop in temperature and humidity. Out of the group of four, Joel and Lindsay seemed to be drunker than the other two. When the Stones came on the juke box with *Jumpin' Jack Flash* both got up and danced around the best they could in their state with one of the local girls sandwiched in between them, giggling away in her own drunken haze.

Sean had lost track of both how many beers they had had and who's shout it was. Andrew had volunteered to get the next round and when he returned Sean had a question for him.

'Hey Wilto…You said earlier you were celebrating something. You going home?'

'Not home but definitely out of this shit hole though.'

'You lucky cunt. Cheers.' He clinked beers with him, took a mouthful and then added, 'But if not home then where?'

'England.' He smiled a drunk's smile.

'What the fuck's in England?'

'I'm transferring over to a British unit. Cross-training. What about yourself? Who you with again?'

'6RAR,' Sean said as he fished out a smoke and lit it.

'Infantry. I didn't go much on it myself when I was one. Pushed for this job as soon as I knew it was out there. You should too. It's the only way to be in the army without all the discipline and bullshit.' He stopped for a sip of beer. 'We decide what action we get involved in which is a lot more than you'll see as a foot slogger. It's fucking crazy.'

Sean was shaking his head before Andrew had finished. 'No mate. I'm a Nasho. Once my tour's up…' he whistled and pointed his thumb back over his shoulder to the door. '…I'm gone.'

He wasn't one hundred percent sure but he thought he saw a shimmer of change from within the SAS man opposite him. As he ashed his fag into the tray before him, Sean watched Andrew's eyes. For the briefest of instances they changed and Sean knew exactly what the cause was. It was because he had been conscripted for this war. Some, not all, but some full time servicemen resented the fact their government was sending over civilian soldiers to fight. They didn't believe civilians should be forced into war but Sean knew it was either this or gaol. And with one third of the Australian forces being made up of conscripts, he wasn't alone. He would never have registered as a consciences objector so here he was. Sometimes when he was in the middle of a night ambush lay-up in a torrential downpour with word Charlie was on his way towards them, he wondered how comfortable those prison beds were.

'So you'll be crying too when the Dragons keep your Wests out of the semi's then?' Sean asked, trying to get off the subject for fear of starting a pointless argument. He could see the sudden change in mood had abated in the other man's eyes.

'Wests?' A look of confusion appeared. 'Oh, I see. The Magpies. I thought you were talking about Collingwood not your Sydney Wests.'

'You're Victorian? We've got quite a few aerial ping pong blokes in our platoon…'

'Must be top blokes then,' Andrew interrupted with a grin.

'Nah,' he answered. 'Bunch o' girls the lot of them.' He laughed and hoped Andrew had a sense of humour.

Andrew smiled but didn't respond to the quip. Instead he began to sing. '*Good old Collingwood forever, they know how to play the game. Side by side they stick together, to uphold the Magpie's name…*" He began to thump a beat on the table but was interrupted by a crash behind them.

Sean heard the noise and looked around. The drunken dancing

trio had slipped up in some spilt beer and gone arse over tit, taking another serviceman with them. Cheers came from the group of men that filled the pub. Sprawled out on the floor, Joel was laughing. His back was soaking up the cause of the fall but he didn't seem to care. Lindsay helped the young Vietnamese girl to her feet, her frail gaunt arms wrapped around his waist.

From around the bar came the owner. He was a tiny man in a suit of white that was much too big for him. With his arms waving and native profanities pouring from his lips, he rushed over to the sight of the fall, clearly worried some of his shoddy furniture had been broken. Standing over the top of the laughing Joel, he directed down at him all of his undecipherable anger.

Before Sean had a chance to calm him down, Andrew jumped up and put an arm around the child-sized man. With a composed voice he spoke to him in his own language. Instantly the little bar owner relaxed. He nodded and then smiled. Andrew placed some money in his hands and patted the now grinning Vietnamese on the shoulder as he trotted off.

'You've just got to know how to talk to some people,' Andrew said as he helped Joel back on his feet.

The four men retook their seats with Lindsay patting his lap for the girl to sit down.

'The money?' Sean asked, impressed with the way he had handled the situation.

'A bottle of scotch.'

He returned to their previous conversation. 'So cross-training's like a transfer then?'

'Yeah. We've got a couple of Kiwis with us at the moment. We can transfer to anywhere in the Commonwealth as long as they've got another group of us lot to go to. Some of the Kiwi units have Fijian blokes with 'em. Tough fuckers them Fijians.'

The little bar owner returned with a bottle of Johnny Walker and four glasses. He smiled the whole time he was at their table. Sean was sure he would have stood there all day if it wasn't for Wilto gently pushing him away, repeating '*Cam On, Cam On*,' thank you, thank you, over and over again.

So with the scotch poured they all switched from beer to whisky and made the next hours a blur.

As night enveloped the town the night-life heated up. The afternoon downpour arrived right on time and forced everyone inside to drink, making the already packed bars almost impossible to negotiate. Music blared out of so many doorways and mixed with the sound of the rain. Even in the pub they now sat, Sean and Joel couldn't tell what song was playing so loud was the noise.

Andrew and Lindsay had left at around ten, not caring about the rain as they ventured out in a staggering fashion into the road, hoping to find a taxi or military transport that would take them over to the airbase on the north side of the town. The two 6RAR boys were so drunk they couldn't remember if they had wished them both good luck; Andrew with his transfer to England and Lindsay with…well, they couldn't remember what he was doing. Maybe he hadn't said.

Come morning they seemed to have drunk themselves sober so they headed out in search of a meal which they hoped would stay down.

Hours later after they had finally landed a ride back to the air base; Sean watched the dirty village roll by from the back of an American deuce-and-a-half. The roadside stunk with raw sewerage, making his increasing hangover feel worse than it was. A group of children tried to run after them with their hands out, wanting money, lollies or cigarettes and Sean watched as one GI threw out individual smokes, teasing them by aiming for the muddy puddles pocked in the road. The kids scrambled to grab those that didn't find the water, lighting them up with Zippo lighters probably stolen from dead GI's, maybe even the GI's this lot were replacing.

As they left the children behind, some as young as three, to smoke soiled cigarettes, Sean wished he could have left altogether like Wilto was doing that morning.

Fuck this place.

SIX

It had been three weeks since Michaels had been killed. Since then Sergeant Lynch had returned to full duties and had been keen to get back into the swing of things.

One of the platoon's men had also returned from R & R – Rest and Recuperation – during this time. Lcpl Grant Brooks looked fresher than he ever had after a week away from the war. Brooksy was a full time soldier. He was originally from the Newcastle suburb of Lambton and he and Sean often talked about things they had heard about their hometown from the letters and tapes they received. He was a good bloke and had signed up for a career in the army but a horrifying incident before leaving for R & R had changed him dramatically, putting a lot of doubt in his mind about the job he had once loved so much.

In the height of a severe contact in a small village within a rubber plantation he had killed a couple of children by mistake; children no older than six or seven. The children and their mother had jumped out of a make-shift foxhole from within the plantation and made a run for it when the contact was at its worse. Brooksy saw the movement out of the corner of his eye and bought his rifle around. Only when they fell did he realise his mistake. Harder still was the fact that the fight they were involved in was rolling on regardless of what he had done and his duties as a soldier came first despite whatever horrific emotions he might have been feeling.

Sean knew the screams of misery from that wounded mother for the loss of her children, screams that seemed to dwarf the sounds of warfare, the deafening crescendo of dozens of automatic weapons, would be permanently scarred in Brooksy's mind. Hopefully today's babysitting job would be a nice way for him to ease back into the war.

Yesterday the platoon had hitched a ride on the backs of a group of M113 Armoured Personnel Carriers to a section of jungle west of the abandoned village identified on their maps as Binh Ba 235. They had been ordered to check the area for VC and wait the arrival of engineers the following morning. They were coming in to clear a section of trees and heavy foliage and needed to be guarded by the infantry.

Sean was talking to Lynch and Brownie when they heard the arrival of the land clearing equipment on the track just east of them. Four large armour plated D8 Caterpillar bulldozers were carried like squat green Gods on the rear of their own semi trailer. Each fat metal beast wore heavy metal plating surrounding the cab like mutated versions of the Kelly Gang. Behind the operator's seat some cluey engineer had fitted viewing prisms taken from an APC. This gave them a protected view of the ground behind the big machine without exposing them to enemy fire. Across the green checker-plated panels on the side of the dozer cabs the names *Jughead*, *Brutus*, *Snoopy* and *Jester* were painted in white and yellow lettering.

Sean followed Lynch and Brownie up to the front of the column to meet the CO of the engineers. Lynch held his hand out to the shirtless man that had climbed down from the lead truck. He could tell by the way he carried himself he was the C.O.

'Sergeant Stephen Lynch, 4 Platoon,' he said gripping the hand of the tanned soldier.

'2nd Lieutenant Dave Doherty, Engineers,' he said, shaking Lynch's hand firmly. His voice sounded as though he had grown up drinking metho and gargling broken glass.

'Doherty?' exclaimed the sergeant. 'Christ, we've got a Doherty. Hey Spud!'

Sean had heard the surname and was already stepping forward to shake hands. 'Private Sean Doherty sir.'

'No shit! Where're ya from Sean?' a huge smile beaming across his face. He reminded Sean of the beach lifeguards back home.

'Newcastle.'

'Yeah? I'm from Wollongong. Where 'bouts in Newy?'

'Wickham. You been there sir?'

'Yeah. My brother and I used to go fishing off of Stockton beach years ago. He used to have a girl in… umm… Islington. So, Wickham eh?' he said and seemed to be lost in thought as he reminisced. Suddenly he snapped out of it. 'Where's your family from?'

Sean was a little thrown off by this question and went blank.

'In Ireland,' the Lieutenant prompted. 'Where abouts in Ireland are your folks from?'

'My Great Grandfather came out from Donegal when he was a baby, sir.'

'No shit! My old man's from Donegal. Came out when he was eleven with his family.' He nodded and added 'All the Doherty's I know come from Donegal so we must be related back home,' referring to Ireland not Australia. 'And none of this "Sir" bullshit either, Sean. The name's Dave.'

Sean smiled at that. *If only more officers were like Dave. Or Michaels.* 'Sure Dave. I guess you owe your new cousin a drink then,' he added, not knowing how far he was pushing it.

Dave laughed and slapped him on the shoulder. 'He's fucken Irish alright!'

Back to business, Lynch pointed out the perimeter they were guarding. The infantry lads were spaced out along the tree line on the far side of a grassy paddock with eyes looking outward into the surrounding vegetation. The Lieutenant nodded got on with the job of unloading the dozers from their trailers.

Time passed slowly as the dozers went about their role of knocking down all the trees, each churning up clouds of thick red dust in their working wake. A pair of them had a giant chain fixed between them and they would drive side by side with the chain strung out from one to the other, levelling ancient trees like tripping up giants. The other two dozers dragged and pushed trees away that had no doubt stood for many hundreds of years. At one stage *Brutus* shuddered, barked and came to a halt under a cloud of white smoke but it wasn't long before some support guys from RAEME – Royal Australian Electrical and Mechanical Engineers – had it running again.

Time dragged on but with all four dozers tearing away at the countryside they finally cleared the surveyed area. As the heavy beasts loaded back up onto their transports the platoon made its way back in. Joel waited back with Sean as they counted off the men before falling into place at the end of the stretched out line.

'A nice quiet morning,' Joel said to Sean as they stepped out into the knee-high grass of the field.

'I didn't think we'd see anything,' Sean remarked as he relaxed for the last leg of their journey; stepping in Joel's footprints then turning around to walk backwards for a few steps just to make sure all was clear behind them.

'Fuck I'm hungry,' Joel said as he walked in front. 'What day is it?'

'Umm…' Sean had to think for a second. 'Wednesday. Sausages an' gravy.'

'Sausages an' gravy.' He could almost taste them already. 'One meal they haven't learnt to fuck up yet. I'm getting pretty tired of empire sandwiches all the time.' Sean waved a few flies away from his face.

'Never knock the empire sanger mate. You just need more tomato sauce.'

The front of the patrol walked down a slight embankment and into a natural gully obscuring them from Sean's and Joel's view for a minute. Joel pulled out his fags and offering one back to Sean as they followed. They both crossed the small runoff of water that ran ankle deep through the gully and climbed up the slight rise to level out on the open field once again. The footprints of the rest of the group were clearly visible in the damp, flattened grass and they subconsciously walked in them purely from habit.

Resting his SLR on the mag pouches of his webbing, Sean dragged on the cigarette, looking to the engineers a few hundred yards ahead.

'You know what today is?' Joel asked.

'Yeah, it's fuckin' Wednesday!'

'No. Today is exactly 335 days in. We've got one month to go!'

Sean looked at him and smiled. 'You'd think I'd forget about that?' He blew out a cloud of smoke. 'Shit, one month to go.'

'You know there's times when I can't remember what home looks like.'

'From what I've heard it sounds like it's all changed already. They reckon the protests are getting bigger.'

'Fucken shits me, you know,' Joel snapped, his cigarette hanging from the corner of his mouth. 'People judging us for what they made us do. It just…it just pisses me off! I mean…it's my job to be here! So are they saying it's alright for me to be here but not you 'cause you're a Nasho? Double fucken standards. I still don't know who they're mad at. Stupid arseholes…' Joel's words just trailed off.

Sean took off his floppy bush hat and tucked it into the back of his belt. Sweat poured out of him and despite the heat he felt relaxed. The reminder of how long they had to go made him feel even better. High overhead a pair of jets raced by, the tearing, rolling noise drawing both their eyes skyward briefly for a second. He decided to keep the conversation on a high.

'So you and Katie planning on any more kids when you get home?'

'I was gunna ask you if you wanted to take 'em off me. Call it an early Christmas present.'

'I think I'll be right. Might even push for some myself when I get back.'

Joel smiled. 'God I miss 'em.'

'You know I was thinking... You remember that SAS bloke at Vung Tau? Wilto? Well he was saying he found a jewellers in Saigon that's got cheap jewellery. I mean fucken cheap. Comes in from Hong Kong...'

Joel laughed. 'You Uc Dai Loi, you cheap Charlie!'

'I could get a nice big wedding ring for Anna. Something that would put our jewellers to shame. Not stolen or nothin', 'cause you know I'm not the sort of bloke to benefit off of someone else's misfortune.'

Joel laughed again. 'No! You'd never do something like that, mate.

But do you want to be reminded of this shit hole every time you looked at that ring?'

'Yeah, you're probably right. I'd still be smelling rotten fish in ten years time every time she waved her hand.'

'I thought she was a clean girl?'

'Fuck off. You know what I mean.'

Joel sighed. 'Thirty and a wakie.'

'Piece of piss,' Sean grinned.

'Piece of piss,' Joel echoed his mate's comment.

Sean looked ahead to see the front of the patrol reach the waiting engineers. An early lunch would be good right about now, he thought to himself.

'All they have to do is keep giving us easy jobs like this one,' Joel continued. 'Nice and easy ones…'

Suddenly movement up ahead drew their attention. The engineers and the point man suddenly had scattered, diving for the ground. Sean and Joel both stopped dead, dropping to one knee, rifles into shoulders, searching.

'Where…?' is all Sean heard his mate say before the loud blast shook the air around them. A blinding flash followed by a column of expanding earth reaching into the skies erupted only thirty yards in front of them. Half ducking, half falling, they hit the ground as rounds cracked by their position. They kept their heads low, eyes focused on the ground before them as they tried to make themselves as small as possible.

Hearing first one then two M60's open up, Sean chanced a quick look to get a bearing on their attackers behind them. He couldn't believe they were almost right where they had just left the tree line.

Joel lifted and dropped his head with a quick jerk of his neck, eyeing the bastards straight away.

'How the fuck did we miss that!!' he yelled out over the crash of another mortar exploding off to their right.

Another mortar went off close to one of the dozers, dirt raining down on the large green machine. The front of the patrol had now turned around and was heading back to Sean and Joel. The engineers and mechanics had grabbed their weapons and were charging right along with them, most of them still shirtless. They split left and right to lessen the VC's chance of a group hit and to try and come in from the sides. However, it was a run through an open, flat plain. First they would need air support to shake up what remained of the tree line where at least a dozen Kalashnikovs had sparkled to life.

The earth seemed to buck underneath them as Sean and Joel both lay on their gut, aiming and firing towards the line. At this distance they would be hard pressed of a sure hit. They knew either air or artillery would be soon crashing into the trees and could do little but try and return fire and wait. The grass beside Sean hissed and cracked as a bullet raced by him, only a foot off the ground. He flinched and pulled his legs together, tucking his elbows in. He was scared. He felt helpless lying there on the hot ground, the grass itching him, his ears ringing with the concussion of another closer mortar.

Several more rounds passed even closer, this time punching into the ground by his feet. Crack, bang, crack, bang. They were hearing the bullets pass them before the gunshot itself. He had been certain the churned grass obscured him but now he felt naked. He was sure every gun in the shadows was aiming in on him. He was the closest to the enemy and he suddenly felt it all coming to an end.

Hearing a yelp beside him he turned and saw Joel trying to reload his Armalite but, fumbling with the fear that shadowed them both, he couldn't get his magazine pouch undone.

Braving a look behind them to the rest of his platoon he saw the occasional flash of gunfire but no discernible figures. The grass hid them well. Realising help was coming he fired off a few more rounds and decided they should crawl for the gully. They would at least be out of the line of gunfire. From there they could also traverse to either end of the field and then cut in around them. Sweat poured out of him and he wiped it from his eyes.

'Head for the gully!' he yelled at Joel who had finally gotten in his second mag. He nodded and they both crawled forward, the sharp bladed grass slicing his forearms deeply as he did.

A million thoughts poured into Sean's mind as he crossed what seemed to be the longest distance of his life: Images of Anna standing in his hallway with the sunlight behind her; his brother working on a bike he hadn't owned in years; Luke sitting in the passenger seat of his 64 EH laughing at a joke he now couldn't recall. Stupid things he hadn't thought of in years all fought for his attention as he tried to focus. His brain registered the change of slope and he knew they were almost there. His body was wet with sweat.

Finally his bloodied elbows hit wet earth and he could see the muddied water flowing steadily by. Then, lifting his head, he could only see the tops of the trees so he knew they were out of the gunners' sights.

'FUCK!!' Joel screamed with vexation as he cleared the rounds racing overhead. He crawled down and lay a few yards to Sean's left. They stopped to catch their breath.

In between the thunder of mortars and the chattering of persistent gunfire, Sean heard the welcomed sound of a jet approaching from the west. It tore directly overhead on a pass to identify the target, the noise of its two turbine engines shaking the earth less than eighty feet below it. Blocking their ears, Sean and Joel looked up and saw the USAF Phantom scream by so low they could see the two men in the cockpit. It banked around in a tight turn, climbed as it did so to give it clearance for the drop and lined up to come in on its first run. They both expected napalm and put their heads to the ground. It was the closest they had ever been to a strike and they were understandably a little bit apprehensive.

Travelling at over four hundred miles an hour, first one then two cigar shaped canisters were released from beneath the angular delta wings. Sean was waiting to hear the sound and feel the heat of detonation when a North Vietnamese mortar fell only two yards behind them.

Air weighed down on him with immense pressure then ripped the breath from his lungs.

Heat and cold seemed to take their turns in assaulting his body.

Noises faded in and out, vision came and went and he slipped in and out of consciousness.

At times he floated.

Then the pain came and he blacked out again.

SEVEN

Everything around him was quiet. He struggled to wake and open his eyes. Things came into focus.

The field was gone.

No jet could be heard.

Somewhere in the distance he could hear the faint murmur of a woman talking. He was aware he wasn't laying on his front, but instead on his back. It was dark and almost cool and he guessed it was night. As he rolled his head to the side, great shots of pain unexpectedly hammered his body and he vomited over the side of...a bed? The nausea combined with the pain and he tried not to move until it passed. He tried to force his body to roll back over and sit up but the pain was too great. The best he could manage was to lift his head slightly.

The hospital, he thought to himself. *I'm in Vampire, the 1ATF Field Hospital in Vung Tau.*

A horrifying thought popped into his head and he cautiously ran his hand down under the sheets to his groin. He was relieved everything was still there. He sighed with relief and looked around. The bed to his right was empty but someone slept in the one on his left. It was Brownie, his corporal.

'Hey,' Sean tried to say but it hurt his throat. He swallowed and coughed, his airway burning. 'Brownie,' he managed a little louder. 'Hey, Brownie.' No response. Footsteps approached from behind and he saw a nurse heading his way. She was tiny, almost frail looking with her red hair tucked up under her cap. She looked down the line of beds and saw it was Sean making all the noise.

'Sarah, can you call Doctor McNaughton?' she said to someone on the other side of the far door. 'Sean Doherty's woken up.'

She helped Sean lay back and smiled at him before checking the drip in his arm was still in and feeding him. He hadn't even noticed the tubing and it now concerned him he was on the other end of it.

'Is Brownie okay?' he asked as she took his pulse. Her touch was so soft, her skin felt unbelievably smooth. He saw her name tag said Sister Josephine. He almost smiled at the thought of a nun looking out for him.

Sister Josephine was always amazed that after staring death in the face, nearly all soldiers asked not about themselves but about their mates.

'He's fine. He's just asleep. As all normal people are at three in the morning,' she joked with him. 'I'd say the doctor will let him return to his unit tomorrow. I mean today.' She smiled the most beautiful smile he had ever seen and then he felt guilty for thinking of her as sexy.

'What...' he swallowed and his mouth made a dry, clicking sound. Before he could ask, she grabbed a glass of water off the table beside him and held it up to his lips. The water was crystal clear and cool. He wondered if he had ever tasted such pure water before. The water they took out with them into the jungle always tasted like crap after they added the anti-malaria tablets. 'Thank you. What happened? Where is everybody else?'

'Out of the men that came in, you and Shane there were the only ones that have had to stay in for observation. There were only three others with light wounds but they were not that serious.' She smiled that great smile at him again, 'The doctor thinks you'll be going home once you're fit to fly. You were extremely lucky. They pulled fourteen pieces of shrapnel out of you. When Doctor McNaughton gets here he'll explain your condition in more detail.'

Sean began to feel tired again and tried to stay awake. There were so many questions he had to ask but he soon found himself nodding off.

Opening his eyes he realised it was morning and a doctor approached with a different nurse. He looked around for Sister Josephine but she wasn't there. Neither was Brownie.

Doctor McNaughton was a tall, wiry man about forty years old. He wore bifocals and was clean shaven with blonde hair neatly combed back from a receding hair line. Sitting down on a chair beside Sean's bed, he looked at his chart.

'Good morning. I hope you slept well?'

Sean tried to sit up but winced in pain. Doctor McNaughton placed a hand on his chest.

'Don't get up on my account. You've been through to much already to go and open up my stitches by being polite.' He turned to the nurse, 'Sister, Corporal Brown that was discharged just now…see if you can catch him?'

She nodded and left them alone.

He reluctantly lay back down, the pain subsiding as he did so. 'What happened?'

'What do you remember?' he asked, paying close attention to Sean's movements, his reactions, his eye movements.

'We were babysitting an engineering crew. Umm…we were heading back in when we were ambushed. Joel and I managed to crawl to a ditch and…yeah; a jet was on its way in. Did it drop too close to us?'

Joel! His mind suddenly screamed out loud as he remembered he had been lying beside him. 'Is Joel okay? Have you let him out already?'

Doctor McNaughton thought for a few seconds then spoke. 'It's good to see your memory is still alright. I should tell you it was four days ago in which you were delivered to us. Until last night you hadn't opened your eyes since the flight in. You lost a lot of blood and we feared for a while there might have been some severe after-effects such as brain damage. Hmm…' He paused briefly before continuing. 'Unfortunately you and several of your colleges suffered serious wounds from mortar fire. Apparently one exploded only a few yards from you…'

'Where's Joel?' Sean almost snapped at him.

'I'm sorry to tell you this but Private Joel Copland died on the flight in with you. He had lost a terrible amount of blood and had extreme internal injuries…'

But Sean wasn't listening anymore. He closed his eyes with frustration.

'NO. Where is he?' he demanded.

'His body has been flown home to his family,' the doctor answered solemnly .

'NO!!' Sean almost screamed. 'NO! He's not dead! Where is he! He's here! JOEL! JOEL! He's got kids!! HE'S GOT FUCKING KIDS!!'

He moved to get out of bed but the pain hit him again. The doctor called for assistance and the nurse appeared with Brownie. He hurried over to Sean's side.

'Spud! Hey Spud! It's alright mate! Calm down. Calm down.'

Sean looked up at his corporal, not recognising him for a second. 'Who..?! Brownie. Get Joel in here. Prove to them he's still alive. JOEL!!' he screamed but Brownie just looked at him and shook his head.

Sean was breathing heavy and sweating.

I have to get Joel, he thought. *I have to get him in here to show these pricks they're wrong! Joel? Joel?*

He sank back onto his pillow, looking straight through them all. They weren't there anymore. None of them were. Just himself and… who?? Ghosts?

'Joel's dead, Spud. You were both hit by the same mortar. I'm sorry mate. You'll be going home once you're all better,' Brownie said quietly.

Sean couldn't hear him.

Tears came and he was unable to stop them. Eleven months of fear, horror, tension and grief all came flooding out.

EIGHT

His injuries had been life threatening. Mortar fragments had caused minor damage to his left kidney and a small piece of his liver had to be removed along with what seemed like hundreds of particles of his shirt, dirt and webbing. His liver would regenerate itself over time and he was warned of drinking alcohol and the damage it could cause to its regrowth. Blood loss was extreme; nearly three pints before they could get a chopper in for dust off. His stomach had been punctured but no internal poisoning had occurred. Time would tell if there was any brain damage from both the concussion and the loss of blood. Doctor McNaughton had almost given up on him but was amazed that Sean just didn't want to die. His heart stopped twice but started itself both times and it had never stopped for more than ten seconds. Some nerves in his left foot had been severed and until they got him on his feet, there was no way of knowing how these repairs had gone. To round out the major injuries he had a broken left knee cap, half of now left behind somewhere in a blood-soaked gully.

He would be scarred for life but nothing grotesque; mainly his back from shoulder blades to his left buttock, his left knee and his left calf and foot. Despite how close he had been to the explosion, he suffered no discernable hearing loss. The only thing the medical staff knew for certain was they would be sending him home.

Twelve days after the attack, the doctors deemed him fit for travel although he hadn't talked to any of the medical staff since hearing about

Joel. He even remained quiet and distant to Sister Josephine no matter how much she tried to cheer him up. He only talked to his mates when they had come in and ignored the doctor's advice by taking the odd sly beer (his brother ran a pub and he had Irish blood for fuck sake!) and durry that they slipped in for him. They were the only ones that understood how he felt. They had all gone through the same shit as him at one time or another and were as jealous as hell to hear he was going home.

Because when anyone goes home a party is thrown.

Macca and the unbreakable Brownie wheeled his chair out of the hospital to the gardens in the shade of some palm trees. Waiting here was Sergeant Lynch and Brooksy. These four were the only men of Sean's platoon that had been able to fly down and see him off. A cheer went up as Lynch cracked a beer and sprayed it all over. Despite the pain that still poked at his sides he was smiling and laughing as a tinnie was thrown his way.

'Drink up mate,' said the Sarge. 'You've got your clearance. This time next week you'll be drinking with your mates and chasin' women!'

'That's all he does over 'ere!!' Brownie said from behind Sean.

'…yeah, that's true. But he'll also be with his family.' The Sarge paused for a second before continuing on. 'He will be missed by us poor God-fearin' bastards. We were glad you were with us out there to watch our backs mate, even if you *are* a Nasho. I know that without your efforts out there, some of these cunts wouldn't be here today.'

'Hear, hear,' the small crowd called out in unison.

'Oh, fuck off. You're gunna make me cry!' Sean joked and wiped away a mock tear.

'Seriously mate. It's been good to fight along side ya, and Christ knows we're all gunna miss ya. I'm sorry not everyone could get down here but there is still a war going on you know. We'll see ya back in the real world, hey! Couple of weeks and we'll be home ourselves so make sure the beer's cold for when we get there.' He raised his beer. 'UP THE OLD RED ROOSTER!'

'AND MORE PISS FOR THE TROOPS!!' they all cried in unison.

After helping him out of the chair to stretch his legs, Macca gave Sean a list of everyone's name and address on it and promised that they would get together for a proper piss-up when they got home. Brooksy waited until the others had said their bit and then handed over a thick parcel the size of a carton of fags.

'If you've got room in your kit, do ya reckon you could deliver this for us? It's my daughter Molly's birfdee next Mondee and I got her one of those pretty Vietnamese dolls. Her mum collects dolls for 'er. She's too young to understand what I'm doin' over here…anyway I got her this. Her and her mum are living back in Newy with my parents until I get back. I know I should wait until I get home but she wouldn't have anything from me to open on the day…but only if it's not too much trouble mate.'

Sean had forgotten he was a father. *Christ*, he realised, *to have a baby daughter and to be responsible for killing a couple of children must be the biggest mind fuck of all time.*

He looked up at the fellow Novocastrian and saw not a murderer but a father that missed his daughter terribly. All he wanted was to be at his child's birthday party, watching her open presents and running around in the backyard with the neighbours' kids, eating too much cake and falling asleep on the lounge in her mothers lap… instead he would be out in a sweltering hot jungle, covered in perspiration and fear and praying she would never have to think of her own birthday as the day her father died.

'How old is she?' Sean asked quietly.

'She'll be four.'

Sean was moved by the amount of love Brooksy's voice projected when he spoke of her. He looked at the wrapped present in his hands. 'I'll have a bit of cake for you.'

'Cheers Spud. I'll grab ya another beer,' he said patting him on the shoulder and headed off to the esky.

Sean just sat there looking at the gift. A simple brown parcel that contained something a child would love forever.

Then he thought about Joel's wife Katie and his two boys standing over his coffin…

347 days in hell.

Not quite a year but it had seemed like ten life times.

NINE

The Qantas 707 came into Australian air space and everyone on board cheered as the captain announced the fact. Sean sipped his beer and looked out the window. Below he could see nothing but the vast blue expanse of the Timor Sea. Through the windows on the other side he could see the warm colours of the sun preparing to slip over the edge, pulling the night's darkness in its wake. Sean stretched his legs; glad the effects of the alcohol were numbing his pain.

'Almost there babe,' he said to himself as he looked at a picture of Anna.

The military had told his family he had been injured (but not the extent of his wounds) and he would be coming home to finish the remainder of his time here. After the shock of the news of him being hurt, everyone was overjoyed he was coming home for good.

He had heaps of plans for his small house on Fleming Street. Build a back room he could one day turn into a nursery, move the garden to make way for a longer driveway with a garage down the back. Fix the fireplace, redo the floors, a full paint job inside and out…It would be one of the best houses in Wickham.

Another cheer went up as the plane touched down in Sydney. As they taxied over to the hanger men clambered out of their seats and readied themselves for reunions each thought would never come. Sean grabbed the brown parcel for Brooksy's little girl, his bag and his slouch hat and gingerly followed the line of men eager to get off, the others giving him plenty of room after they had seen him limping. The closer he got to the door, the more he could hear the screams and calls of delight as loved ones spotted their husbands/fathers/brothers/sons. He could also smell…no, taste the air. It was so much sweeter than he remembered.

Saying thank you to the stewardess he stepped out into a cool Australian night.

It was almost eleven, the 707 being the last plane to land before the flight curfew. 'Bring 'em home in the dark', the politicians had ordered. The night told all the returning men that their country was embarrassed of them; they didn't want to see them. A real nice way to be welcomed home.

Gathered off the taxi way was a crowd of people and they mingled with the troops, hugging and crying. Standing on top of that flight of stairs, looking out to a sea of people eager to see them, Sean never felt so glad to be alive. Then he heard his name.

'SEAN!!'

The name bellowed out above all others. It was his brother James. He looked down and saw him waving like an optimistic mad man drowning. Sean grinned and waved back, pain shooting up his side but ignoring it. Nothing was going to ruin this moment for him as he followed the others down the stairs and across the tarmac. Anna burst from the crowd and ran to him, arms out to embrace him. They collided and he grabbed her tight, spinning around with her. She was crying and he had to hold himself from doing the same.

'I love you,' she said in his ear. 'I love you. Don't ever leave me again.'

All Sean could do was laugh. Happiness washed over him and he suddenly felt safe, a feeling he had not felt in a long time. 'Oh baby. I love you too.' They kissed and it felt familiar. It felt right.

He felt someone slap him on the back and turned to see his father, his brother James and his girl Kimmy, Melanie and her husband Joseph, and Luke and his girlfriend Leanda. They all took turns in hugging him and asking about his injuries but he told them not to worry, he would tell them all about it later. Right now he just wanted to get home.

True to his word, Luke was there to pick him up in his new car. It stood out like dog's balls in the parking lot, even under the dim lights of the car park. The Monaro was a gold colour and the chrome dazzled all around it. Sean threw his bag in the boot, carefully placing Brooksy's doll beside it and climbed into the back seat with Anna. The others had come down in Joseph's Fairlane and they were all soon on their way.

Before they hit the Pacific highway they pulled into a pub in the northern suburb of Gordon. It was half an hour to closing time and the pub was crowded. As Sean walked in wearing his dress uniform a few of the locals stared at him and mumbled to themselves as they found a table. James bought a round for everyone before their old man stood, clearing his throat.

'I'd just like to say a few words about how proud we all are of ya mate. You've done your job in this politician's war without argument. The country might have some worries with what you've done over there and that's nobodies business but your own. So fuck them all and welcome home son!' The small group cheered and drank to Sean.

Several of the people at the bar finished their drinks and headed for the door. As they passed the group one of them said not quietly enough, 'Baby killer.'

Before the bloke could take another step, Luke's fist shot up and out like a piston, hitting him squarely on his bearded jaw and sending him straight to the ground. The other two men who were halfway out the door stopped and turned to see their mate's head hit the wooden floor with a sickening thud. He was out cold. Before these two could react, Joseph, James and even Sean's father had all gotten to their feet ready for a punch up. Sean was a little shocked at all of this. Getting to his feet as well, he wasn't sure of what was going on as he hadn't heard the comment. The five Novocastrians stared viciously at the two scared locals.

The pub went quiet for a few seconds before the publican yelled, 'No fighting in here! Take it outside the lot of ya's!' Nobody moved.

The man on the ground began to come around.

'I think you owe my mate an apology,' Luke said to him as he sat up.

One of his mates helped him up and steadied him. He was furious. He took a step towards them but staggered, his mate grabbing him before he hurt himself anymore. He looked at Luke and saw the anger in his eyes. Luke was ready to swing again and the locals decided they stood no chance.

Taking in a deep breath he uttered quietly 'Sorry.'

Luke sneered. 'No mate. Not to me. To him.' He nodded to Sean.

Sean wasn't in the mood to fight. He hadn't been back in Australia an hour and was already the reason of a fight. He looked at the man whose lip had started to bleed, the blood running down to disappear into his shaggy beard.

Swallowing his pride the man turned to Sean. 'Sorry.'

Sean didn't acknowledge him.

'Good,' his dad said. 'Now fuck off.'

They watched as the three men left and then looked at the rest of the patrons. After a second the normal murmur of pub background noise returned and they all went back to their drinks.

'See the sort of shit you start" Luke said jokingly to Sean and threw back his beer, 'bringing all that anger back over here.' They all laughed and finished off their drinks as Sean told them the reason of his injuries.

'…The last thing I can remember is watching this Phantom come in on a napalm run to clear the trees. Next thing, I woke up in hospital...'

He took a sip of beer and looked down at the table, remembering his fallen mate. No one said anything. Reaching into his breast pocket he pulled out a photograph of him and Joel. It had been taken by Gazza only a month ago. In it they were holding up the skull of a water buffalo like a trophy, its horns five feet wide. Both were shirtless and smiling. Sean remembered the day well. One of the big beasts had been hit by an American truck so they had had a barbecue and invited some of the Aussies. One of the Marines had claimed the head as a souvenir and cleaned and boiled it, sticking the white skull with its massive horns on a post at the entrance to one of the American compounds. One day after more than a few beers, Joel, Sean and Gazza stolen it, took a few photos and then tied it to the front of one of the Australian APCs. As far as Sean knew, the skull was still leading their 3rd Cavalry Regiment into battle.

'How bad were you banged up?' Joseph asked.

Melanie took the photo and looked at it before passing it around the table.

'Umm, pretty bad they say. They had to take out part of my liver and sew up my stomach and left kidney…'

'Your liver?' Kimmy interrupted. 'Should you be drinking?'

The boys all burst out laughing and Sean continued. 'It'll regenerate itself over time. Most of the blood in me isn't mine. Lost half my left knee cap but that doesn't hurt too much. I've lost a little bit of feeling on the outside of my left foot. Damaged nerves. Nothing major. Just the size of a penny. It hurts a bit if I have to walk any long distances but it's not that bad. I guess my football days are over…'

'You were never that good anyway!' James smirked from behind his glass. Sean tried to slap him on the forehead but his brother just ducked it and laughed.

'So is that it?' Kimmy asked. 'Are you out of the Army now?'

'No, not yet. I'm on leave for two weeks and then I have to report back to base for a re-evaluation of my fitness.'

'They can't send you back can they?' Anna asked with understandable concern in her voice.

'No. I'm definitely out of Vietnam. They'll just see if I'm still fit for home duties to run out my time. At best they'll give me an honourable discharge and I won't have to finish my time. But that rarely happens. I've still got two arms and two legs so the bastards'll probably get me some crappy job for the few months I have left. However…I'd rather teach rifle drills to a bunch of recruits any day than go back over there!'

He skolled the last of his beer. 'Now, take me home.'

TEN

It was a strange feeling coming back to a town he had known so well but now finding it so different. Sure there were new buildings and new neighbours, but that wasn't it. Something felt different to him. He still felt that welcoming feeling but just not what he had expected. It was hard for him to explain. It just felt…weird. Maybe because it was dark… he didn't know. He hoped it would all feel right in the morning.

Luke turned into Railway Street and passed James' pub, the Lass O'Gowrie. He drove several blocks up and turned left into Fleming Street. Sitting on the new seats in comfort, Sean savoured the feelings of relief and joy as they pulled up to his house. His 1964 EH Holden was parked in the driveway, its white paintwork gleaming under the streetlights like a virginal pearl. The lawn had been mown and even the orange tree that had suffered due to his horticultural procrastination had been trimmed back and looked healthier than ever.

'Everybody chipped in and cleaned the place up for you,' Luke said as they climbed out of the coupe. 'Did a service on it yesterday as well,' he added, pointing at the car.

'Shit, Luke, you didn't have to do all this.'

Anna squeezed him tight as they walked up the path to the front verandah. 'Yes we did. We wanted to help out. You're back home with us now.'

Inside the house was just as clean. Every wall was clean, not a spec of dust on any shelf or ledge, even the carpet in the lounge room was clean. It looked as though it had been shampooed.

'How long did this all take?' he asked, completely flabbergasted.

'Only a couple of days,' Anna replied. 'Mum and dad even came over to help last night.'

'Shit.' He didn't know what else to say.

'I know,' Luke remarked. 'I couldn't believe Anna's parents could get their hands dirty but they did.'

'They did more work than you!' Anna shot back.

Luke looked back at her with a smile. 'Nobody ever works as hard as me.'

'I think it's time to go mate,' Sean said to Luke. 'You sound like you need some rest. All this talk about work must be wearing you out.'

'Still the sarcastic bastard I see. Righto. I'll see you two tomorrow… today,' he corrected, looking at his watch. He turned to go but stopped. Turning back he grabbed his mate and hugged him. 'It's fucken good to have you back Sean. I've missed you mate.'

Sean hugged him back, feeling his bruises flare with pain but paying them no heed. 'I've missed you too Luke.'

Anna tried not to cry as she watched her fiancée and his best mate embrace. She was just so happy everything was now going to work out.

In the dimly lit bedroom Anna looked at the scars that ran down his sweat covered back and traced them with her fingers. 'Is it still sore?'

Sean's head lay on a set of new bed sheets, a luxury he had not felt for a long time. 'My side still hurts a bit. It feels like someone's laid some massive rabbit punches into me.'

She traced one scar that ran from his lowest rib, over his hip and down to the centre of his bum cheek. 'I worried about you everyday you know.' Her voice was calm now she knew all danger was behind them. 'I'd sit and watch the news with dad…thinking about where you were… if you were okay… Some days it drove me mad. I even convinced myself at one stage you were not coming home.'

'What made you think that?' he asked quietly, knowing she had probably been through a hard time herself.

'I don't know...' she answered in a distant voice. 'I just woke up one morning and had a terrible feeling you were gone for good.'

Her fingernails lightly scratched up and down his back and he moaned softly with pleasure. He felt like he could close his eyes and drift into a blissful, beautiful, never-ending sleep. The bed was comfortable and her touch was like heaven. However... something still nagged at him.

Rolling over he looked at Anna lying on her side next to him. She reached across and felt the dog tags that still hung around his neck, a green bootlace holding them there. She traced her finger around the edges of both; one round, the other a stretched octagonal, the two metal discs tinkling lightly together as she did so. AUST 2790400 DOHERTY was marked on one side of each; his country, serial number and surname. On the other side was indicated O POS and RC; his blood type and religion of Roman Catholic.

'I remember when you first got these,' she said quietly, almost seductively. 'Very sexy. But I guess you can take them off now.'

'I've tried. It feels strange not having them on.'

Anna moved in closer and began kissing his chest.

A smile crossed his face as he watched her. He and his soldier mates had been to strip clubs whilst over there but he had never felt the need...correction; he had never followed through on any drunken urges to bed one of them. He knew Anna was at home waiting for him. Sure he would perve and flirt and play with the overly friendly, money hungry, child supporting whores and strippers of the Saigon nightclubs but he had never slept with one. Many of his mates had and it gave him a small feeling of pride to know he had not. To see her as she was now made him glad to be home. She was the first white girl he had seen naked in over 11 months.

She was beautiful.

She was his future.

A bead of sweat collected and rolled down her breast. It followed the contour of her cleavage, trailing across her other breast where it found the bed sheet and vanished into the fibres.

'Everyone is going to be at the pub today,' Anna said to him with a grin as she rolled over to her back with her long slender arms stretching high above her. 'We should get some sleep. It's going to be a long day.'

He touched her stomach lightly, drawing the tips of his fingers across her taught, tanned skin.

Can't we stay here all day? he didn't ask as he closed his eyes.

His sleep was troubled. The images that had invaded his dreams had left him feeling tired and unrested with broken sleep. But once he opened his eyes he forgot about the ugly images that clouded him.

The day was going to be unseasonably warm. Small clouds floated lazily overhead and a gentle wind blew taking the sting of the sun away. As much as he wanted to slip behind the wheel of his Holden, he thought it best to walk the few blocks to the pub. It gave him a chance to refresh his memory of his neighbourhood of Wickham and walk off the haunting images of Joel that had assaulted him all night.

The neighbourhood smelt the same. As they walked a pleasant salty sea breeze blew up the road from the wharves and the giant wool sheds, packed to the rafters with bales and their oily scent, took him back to his adolescence. It was all so ingrained in his consciousness.

A ship sounded its horn in the distance and he could picture a giant coal ship coming in gingerly, ballast pumps working overtime to keep her high off the estuaries' bed whilst tugs choreographed her every move.

In 1797 Lieutenant John Shortland had sailed into those same waters in a different type of ship altogether looking for a number of escaped convicts. The escapees had seized the *HMS Cumberland* as she had been making sail out of Sydney Cove 100 miles to the south. During his search for the criminals the young Lieutenant had noted the deep river mouth and had seen the value of it as a port. More importantly he noted the rich seams of coal, some which ran on or just under the surface. Several years later the river, which had been named the Hunter River after New South Wales' Governor John Hunter, was carrying coal ships as the new mining settlement began to export coal, as it does to this day. Originally known as a "Hellhole" due to the horrific and sweltering conditions in the mines, the settlement was the destination of the most dangerous of convicts, each forced to work naked. Years later it had taken its name from the English port of Newcastle and it grew as a town, eventually taking in free-settlers and freed convicts. Up until the 1930's it had boasted the largest soap manufacturer in the Southern Hemisphere. Today as a small city it carried a booming steel industry, high volumes of grain and wool export, a copper smelter and the exporting of the seemingly never-ending supply of high quality coal from it and the towns of the Hunter Valley to the northwest. It was a blue-collar city built on the backs of hard-working men and women, and that, despite his short stint in the green, was exactly how Sean saw himself; a proud blue-collar worker. It was also a history that gave great pride to its blue-collar working inhabitants, the Novocastrians.

Sean closed his eyes for the briefest moment and hoped that he could fall back into the blue-collar jobs that the town offered but as they were about to walk hand in hand through the pub doors, a niggling feeling overcame him once again. *Something isn't right.*

'YAAAAAAHHHHHHHH!!' A crowd of about twenty swarmed around him, the mates he had missed so much, as Anna pulled him through the doors. Everyone was cheering and slapping him on the back and the doubtful feeling buried itself. It was Friday and a lot of sickies were being taken. A schooner of beer was thrust into his hand and he was led to and fro to catch up with all. He was surprised to see some of the revellers who had turned up and wondered where others were. He knew returned servicemen were being ostracised but would his own friends shun him? Would those not here treat him as the men in the Sydney pub last night had?

One he thought strange turning up was a bloke called Simon Mansfield. A good looking bloke, as far as blokes go, he didn't knock around with Sean and his mates. He moved in a few years ago to a flat behind the wool sheds and Sean reasoned he had made the Lass his local rather than the Wickham Park Hotel while he was away. He seemed to know everyone here so Sean dismissed it and said G'day.

Anna's parents were there as was his own father and they got on fine together, something Sean and Anna had worried about. They were probably the two most different men in the pub but the unification of their progeny had bought down all social and class barriers. Sean smiled as he watched blue-collar and white-collar drink and laugh. His dad had always found it hard talking to management types but he was glad exceptions could be made.

So as he finally got a chance to breathe and sit down at a table with Anna, his brother James, Luke and Thomo, another of Sean's good mates from way back, he decided that worry in the back of his mind was just nerves about coming home early and the fear of how people would react to him so he let go of it completely. He was glad the pub in Sydney was no indication of his own local. He sipped his beer, looked at his girl and almost laughed with joy.

'What is it?' she asked.

He smiled. 'Now I'm home.'

For the next few hours Sean drank with his mates and enjoyed the return to his former life as best he could. He was trying not to think of those mates that were not here to welcome him home when his dad rested his hand on his shoulder and sat down next to him at the bar.

'Hey ya dad. How's it going?'

His dad looked at his youngest and smiled. Sean had become such a man over the last year and it gave him great pride to tell his colleagues his son was a returned serviceman just like his father and fuck those that thought less of him. 'Sean m'lad. What do ya want? My shout.'

'A beer'll be great.' One was already on its way.

'So,' his old man began, pausing for a second to cough behind his hand. 'Are you back into the groove of normal life yet?'

Sean took a sip of his beer, enjoying the moment with his father. 'I didn't think civvie street would be easy. A few things I'm still trying to get my head around but other than that…you've no idea how glad I am to be home.'

'Hey, I know exactly how it feels.'

Sean nodded in agreement but found it hard to picture his dad waking from nightmares covered in sweat thinking he was still fighting for his life.

'Anytime you want to talk about it son, I'll be here. OK?'

Sean felt embarrassed. His father had never talked about his time fighting the Japs. And this was the closest he had ever come to talking about it. All Sean could do in reply was nod like a little boy, awkward and uncomfortable. But to show his father that he understood what he was getting at, he reached over to the object by the beer taps.

'Here. I thought you might like this.' He pushed his army canteen along the bar and placed it in front of his father, the jagged bullet holes surprising his dad.

'Christ. Was this yours? What happened?' He picked it up, amazed at the damage, remembering back to his own time in New Guinea. He wondered if the Vietnamese fought as hard as the Japs had.

'I was wearing it on the small of my back when it got hit. Water poured out all over me. Thought it was blood. Scared the shit out of me.'

'I'll take this into work and show them.' His finger ran over the torn, sharp aluminium edge. 'You see, it is lucky to be Irish.' He began to nod. 'Bloody lucky.'

'That's what I had to tell you,' Sean suddenly remembered, glad for the change of topic. 'I met a bloke over there. He was a Doherty as well.'

'Yeah? Where was he from?'

'He was from Wollongong, but he said his old man came from Donegal also.'

'My grandfather came out from Donegal when he was six,' his father said with a proud grin. 'I'd like to get over there one day m'self.'

'Maybe when their fighting stops hey?'

Sean's father chuckled. 'Mate, they've been fighting for generations. The English have been bossing their way around for eight hundred years on that island. That war isn't going to end soon. Not in our lifetime.' He drained the last of his beer then, groaning, stood up. 'Right! I'm off home. Things to do. I'll catch you later son. See ya mate!' he called out to James.

He patted his little soldier boy on the shoulder. 'Good to have you home son.'

'Thanks dad. See ya later.'

His father collected the canteen then headed out into the warm autumn afternoon sun. Sean didn't know it would be the last time he would ever see him. He just sipped his beer and turned around to watch all his mates.

As the night wore on, he remembered in a few days it would be Monday. He would have to face Brooksy's little girl. He felt nervous and apprehensive without knowing why. He didn't have bad news for her. There was no way he was telling anyone over here about Brooksy's mistake, and besides, she would be happy to receive the doll. As he lost at pool to James he tried to remember if he had a photo of Grant. It would be nice, he thought, to give his wife a photo of him. She would appreciate a new photo to look at on those long nights alone filled with worry, terror and hope.

At closing time they all headed home. With his arm around Anna he walked down the quiet industrial road, silently fearing he wasn't drunk enough to keep Joel away.

ELEVEN

The noise that woke him was loud. Sitting bolt upright he concentrated on it but couldn't tell what it was. His hand shot out beside him, searching for his rifle, then remembered he wasn't in the jungle.

The carpeted floor felt dry, almost crunching underneath his bare feet as he walked naked to the hall. The light switch didn't work.

The noise was still there, sounding like it was coming from the kitchen. He felt helpless without a weapon. Thomo kept an old pistol, a Colt 1911 in his wardrobe that his uncle had sold him. Fear told Sean he had to get a gun. With a gun in the house he knew he would feel safer.

From the hall he could see the light in the kitchen was on and the noise had changed from a rustling and tinkling of metal to a frustrated grunting and cracking. Sean had nothing to defend himself with but his fists and, summoning up all his courage, turned the corner.

Every drawer and cupboard was open and thousands, if not millions, of knives, forks and spoons covered the shelves, benches, table and floor like a thick carpet of shimmering silver.

Standing there in his jungle greens with a pool of blood at his feet was Joel. He dug away at his open temple with a pair of pliers, the jaws sinking into the deep hole right up to the handle; a grinding, crunching sound filling the room as it forced its way through broken bone and nerve. He casually looked up at Sean with stone black eyes and said, 'Help us get this piece of shrapnel out, mate.'

This time he woke up. Sweat poured off of his body as he drew in a deep breath and tried to scream but he only gasped. Finally noise came from his throat and he bellowed like an injured animal. His fists were still clenched from his dream. Pain tore through his body as all his muscles tightened with the fear. He felt hands on his chest and jumped again, turning to see Anna beside him with a terrified look on her face. Her mouth was moving but he couldn't hear the words. Her face changed to a worried expression and her words finally pushed through past his terror.

'…wrong Sean. It's just a nightmare baby. It's okay. It's okay. Please baby…' She placed her head on his shoulder and he began to calm down.

His breathing slowed as he shakily got out of bed, opening the window to let in the breeze. 'Oh God…sorry, honey. Shit….' He let out a long breathe and leant against the window sill. The sweat on his body was cooling him down and the pain was subsiding. Outside the glow of streetlights muted the night sky an opaque yellow/grey. In the distance a horn sounded from one of the tug boats in the harbour. 'Just a dream,' he explained to her. 'It was Joel. He was in the kitchen. God it felt real.' He turned to see her sitting up still with a concerned look on her face. 'Don't worry. I'll be fine.'

Returning to bed she snuggled up against him with her head on his chest. After a few minutes he could feel her sleeping but he didn't want to. This nightmare had seemed so real to him, more detailed than any other dream he had ever had. To dream again like that was the last thing he wanted. The hangover he knew would come would be there in the morning waiting for him so he decided to just lay there until dawn and greet it.

He woke to the light pouring in through the open window and its harshness started his groggy headache. He rolled over to find Anna's side empty. She had gotten up much earlier and decided to stay up rather than go back to bed feeling like shit. The clock on the nightstand said 9:15 so he climbed out of bed, nursing his side as he walked sleepily out to the hall. The beginnings of his seediness were already planted but by now it felt like an old friend revisiting. The horrific visions of Joel hadn't returned and he had completely forgotten they had even been. As he turned the corner to the kitchen the image flashed back for a split second and he stopped dead. For an instant he saw him again, but quicker than blinking, it was gone. Coldness fell over him and he shivered as though he was standing naked in a winter storm. Goose bumps ran over him and his stomach turned.

'Good morning baby. I thought I'd let you sleep in.'

Looking up, he saw Anna standing in exactly the same spot as Joel had been. The shiver repeated. He opened his mouth to say good morning but instead turned and half ran to the toilet to be sick. His side hurt even more after vomiting, however he was determined to have a good day.

Luke turned up in his Monaro and Thomo rode over on his gleaming blue Triumph Trophy. They found Sean and Anna having a cup of tea after their breakfast on the small front verandah.

'Did you two share the same bed last night,' Sean greeted them as they walked up the short path wearily together. Thomo looked fine but Luke seemed half dead. 'Shit, you hold up well,' he said with dry sarcasm.

'Oh Christ,' Luke groaned, rubbing his eyes as he gently sat himself down on the cement steps. 'Did you see that bear last night at the pub?'

'What bear?' Anna asked, walking into it.

'The bear that followed me home and shat in my mouth,' he said with a smirk. 'Fucken spewed twice this morning.'

'Want a beer?' Sean laughed but knew how he felt.

'Get fucked,' he replied with no malice.

It was just like old times he thought and had to stop himself from smiling at the fact that he was calling them "old times" when he was so young.

'What are you up to today?' Thomo asked as he lit up his morning fag.

'The first thing I'm gunna do is take my car for a good run. I've missed it more than you two put together,' he said as he flogged one of Thomo's smokes. 'After that…I dunno. I'll have to get my bearings and see what's changed around here.'

Thomo glanced up and caught Anna looking at him. She turned away, sipping her tea, eyes smiling at Sean. An image two weeks old flashed up and Thomo thought about it, about what he thought he'd seen but decided to leave it. Looking at how great everything was going he wondered if it would be worth bringing up or even if it was what he thought. He *had* been drunk at the time. He drew in and blew out a long cloud, the hazy mental image dissipating with it in the morning breeze.

They cruised around for most of the day, going to all their old hangouts with the windows down and The Zombies, Len Barry and the Stone Poneys on the radio. After nearly half a tank of fuel they had visited places in Merewether and Warner's Bay, Bucky Brind's auto shop in Hamilton to catch up with him, shot the shit with Bucky's younger brother in his new Valiant Charger, and drove left, right, up and down over most of the town.

He had looked at the address Brooksy had given him so many times it had burned itself into his mind, but he drove through Lambton just so he knew how to get there. He didn't say anything to the others about it. Part of him didn't want to go to his little girl's birthday party, but something else in him wanted to stop right there and go in and just look at her. Tell her that her dad was doing just fine. Tell her he'll be home soon, home for her next party.

Don't worry. Everything will be fine. By the way, your dad tore apart a couple of children, gunned them down, little girls, just like...

Anna felt something was wrong. The car wasn't slowing as it reached the intersection. Luke and Thomo realised it a fraction later.

'SEAN!' Anna screamed but he didn't hear her.

The car raced through the crossroads missing a truck by a mere foot. Somewhere to their right they all heard, including Sean, another car lock up its brakes. This snapped him out of it and he jumped on the brakes himself, the Holden slewing to the road's edge, tyres squealing, just missing a parked car as they came to a stop.

They were all silent. Sean was the first to speak.

'Sorry. I didn't see the sign.'

He hadn't seen the road, the truck or his own car. In his mind he was looking at Brooksy holding a doll in one hand and a lifeless child in the other. The image he had never even seen in real life was still there but fading as he stared off down the road.

Anna placed her hands on his shoulders.

'Are you okay babe? You don't look too good.' For a second she thought he might vomit but he shook his head to clear it. The other car sped past blasting its horn.

'Sorry about that. I'm just tired.' He closed his eyes. 'Can you drive for us, mate?' he asked the two in the back seat, neither of them knowing which one he was talking to.

'Yeah,' Thomo answered, the worry in his voice showing through. 'You alright?'

Sean's head was pounding and his side burned with pain but he hid it.

'Just tired that's all. A big night last night. Not used to it,' he lied.

They swapped seats and drove on. Thomo tried to get the conversation going again but it just wasn't the same.

Now it was their turn to think something wasn't right.

The next two nights came and went with no real worries. Sean still had nightmares about Joel, but he chased these away each night with alcohol. He learned that if he went to bed drunk enough, the dreams were easier to forget. This change was noted by his friends and family who were unsure of how to react to this.

TWELVE

Monday.

Light filtered in through the curtains with the dull intensity of an overcast day. During the night it had rained, cleaning the city of its urban grime and filth, but they had both slept solidly, not hearing a thing.

Anna showered and got ready for work as Sean sat at the verandah table watching the clouds settle in around the town. It looked as though it may rain again before lunch.

The tea warmed him through, making his hangover just a little more bearable. Staring off into the distance he didn't hear Anna come out and he jumped when she stepped in front of him.

'Shit! Jeez you scared me there for a second.'

'Sorry babe. Are you ready?'

He drained his cuppa, locked the front door and drove her to her work in the city centre. He drove sedately, trying to navigate with a pounding headache. His u-turn in front of the Fred Ash building was sloppy and was commented on by several passing cars blasting their horns.

'Okay. See you baby. Oh, can you pick me up if it's raining?' she asked as she kissed him.

'Five o'clock?'

'Yes please,' she answered as she climbed out.

'Did you want me to pick you up for lunch,' he called out before she could shut the door.

'No. I've got a doctor's appointment at lunch. I'll see you this arvo!' she said shutting the car door and disappeared into the building.

Pulling out into the Hunter Street traffic, Sean thought about his old job, how it would be great to get back into it. He enjoyed the work and the people he worked with. To get some routine in his life would be good. He hoped it would sort out all the confusion he was in and return him completely to his former self.

Back at home he showered, shaved and dressed. He watched the clock crawl around to eleven then headed back out with the brown parcel. He was in Lambton in less than ten minutes but sat in his car a few houses up, watching Brooksy's home. Several cars were parked directly out front and he watched a neighbour and her two boys walk across the drying road, best clothes on, presents in hand.

He wasn't sure if a crowd was a good thing or not. He still felt funny about it even though he had promised Grant he would be there. Stepping out of the car, he breathed deeply with nerves. He had never seen these people before.

What will they think of me? he wondered. *Don't be fucking stupid*, a second voice told him. *They're family of a serving soldier and you're his mate. It'll be fine.*

Rain clouds threatened with even darker bellies but Sean didn't notice. His eyes were locked on the front door as he walked and they didn't leave it until he was knocking on the screen door. Down the hallway he could hear children laughing and playing games. He wanted to leave but heard himself telling Brooksy he'd be there for her. He straightened his back, cleared his throat and prepared to be greeted into the Brooks family home.

A woman stepped out of the noise filled room and headed up the hall towards him. She was a lot shorter than him with blonde bobbed hair and a good figure for a mother. She saw the parcel in his hands but was wary because she couldn't see a child accompanying him.

'Can I help you?' she asked, the uncertainty showing in her voice.

For a second Sean was lost for words, embarrassed he had forgotten her first name and just held out the gift to her. 'Mrs Brooks? Umm, it's for Molly.'

She smiled politely but still held back from opening the screen door.

'I'm Sean Doherty,' he said but saw she still had no idea who he was. He looked at the box and added, 'It's from Grant.'

He had hardly finished saying his name when the door flew open and she grabbed him tightly, tears welling in her eyes. She said something but it just bubbled out amid the laughing and crying. Finally he caught some words as she squeezed him tightly. 'Thank you. Thank you. Thank you.'

She composed herself, wiping away her tears and took his hand. 'Please come in.'

An elderly woman had come to the hall to see what all the noise was. 'Are you alright Mary?'

Mary! That was it, he thought.

'Sue. This is Sean!'

The words were lost on the old woman as she was rounded up by Mary and led back into the lounge room with Sean trailing behind, his hand in Mary's.

'Everyone!' Mary called out to the crowd. Sean entered the room and saw six other mothers and at least a dozen children. 'Everyone! This is Sean Doherty! One of Grant's friends from Vietnam!'

On hearing this, the curious faces of the women all changed to looks of almost recognition, as though they had known him for years. They all came over with questions about Grant and other soldiers he didn't even know coming at him from every angle. All the children just sat on the floor amongst their toys, looking up at this tall stranger that was causing a bizarre reaction from their mothers, wondering what was going on.

Sean was overwhelmed by the welcome and after they all quietened down to wait for answers, he turned to Mary and asked 'Which one's the birthday girl?'

Hearing this, one of the girls in a new green dress stood up saying 'It's my birthday today.'

Sean walked over to her and everyone watched in silence as he knelt down in front of her. She looked like Grant. He could feel the confidence, hope and love almost beaming out of her and he thought of the big difference between her personality and composure to that of her fathers.

'Is your name Molly?' he asked her politely.

'Yes, and today is my birthday and I'm four.' She held up four of her fingers to show him.

'Four. Yes, I know.'

'What's your name?'

'My name's Sean.'

'Do you work with my Daddy?'

'Yes I do! I was talking to him just last week. Do you know what? He gave me a present to give to you.'

Molly took the gift from him and courteously said 'Thank you Sean.'

All the mothers smiled, holding back tears as they watched her open the brown paper parcel.

'Look Mummy! It's a doll!' she exclaimed with excitement.

'Yes,' Mary said, kneeling down beside her. 'It's beautiful, isn't it?'

Sean recognised the vibrant colours. He could almost smell the markets. The reds, golds, greens and blues of the doll's ao-dais dress were as bright as the neon lights of Saigon's club district at night. Images and smells of the markets in Beria, Vung Tau and Saigon came to him as he pictured Brooksy haggling with the stall owner, smiling politely as he fought the price down.

Molly looked at the doll and then up at Sean. 'When's Daddy coming home?'

He was knocked back by her question, not expecting it at all.

'Umm…soon love…'

'Daddy will be home before you know it and then you can both play with your new doll together!' Mary hugged her daughter tightly.

'Ahh, here,' Sean remembered, pulling a photo from his shirt pocket. 'I've got a picture of Grant taken about a month ago.'

Molly and her mother looked at the picture. She instantly recognised him. Mary smiled as she gazed upon the most recent image of her husband. Both he and Sean were in their civvies, sitting on a bench in a bare army hut drinking beer. They were both laughing. If she didn't know any better she would swear there was no war going on around them.

'Thank you Sean,' she whispered under her tears and she leaned across and kissed him on the cheek.

Looking at her he could see how much they missed him. It was terrible the amount of anxiety and suffering they had gone through and for some reason he couldn't picture his family and friends feeling this way although he knew they had. It tore at his heart to see this. A girl, a four year old girl without her dad on her birthday. It was a fucked state of affairs.

Molly turned to show her friends the doll while Sean and Mary returned to the group of adults, a cup of tea and a hundred questions waiting for him.

THIRTEEN

Luke heard his name as he walked past the crane yard to the car park. It was 5pm and he planned to get home and relax after the big weekend. Looking up he saw Thomo sitting on his Trumpy.

'You go to work today?' Luke asked as he unlocked his car.

'Yeah, knocked off a bit early.'

'What'cha doin'?'

'Not much. Wanna get a beer?'

'Fuck off. I think I'm still drunk,' he half joked.

'Yeah,' Thomo confessed and nodded. 'I was a bit hung-over today as well. Long day.'

Luke reached in, knocked the gearstick into neutral and started the Monaro, letting it idle to warm up. Behind them Mr Doherty called out as he passed by several cars over.

'Hey Thomo! How's it going?'

'Mr Doherty.'

Luke turned towards his co-worker and mate's father. 'You want a lift home? It's gunna piss down.'

'Get some hair on your balls, son. It's only water.' He laughed as he marched off, walking home as he did every day.

Waiting until Sean's old man had moved on, Thomo spoke up.

'Look,' He turned serious for a minute, something he ever rarely did. 'I don't wanna sound like I'm spreadin' rumours or gossip or nothing…' He paused for a second, looking at the ground, trying to figure out what he was going to say. Luke waited quietly for him to continue. 'A few of weeks ago I saw Anna and Simon over at the Wickham Park Hotel. I was there with a couple of biker mates and we were there all night. They came in together and looked pretty cosy. They bought a bottle o' grog and left. We were on the far side of the bar and didn't see us. Now, I was pissed but they looked kinda touchy-feely with each other.'

'Fuck off! Simon *Mansfield*?' Luke queried, trying to dismiss it, but Thomo kept going.

'I asked her a few nights later when we were all at the Lass if she had been over at the Wicko but she just said no and walked away. I didn't mention *his* name. Ever since then she's been fucken weird to me.'

Luke listened to him, taking it all in and weighing it up.

She wouldn't cheat on Sean, he pondered. *Would she? Not with Simon.*

Thomo didn't say anything. He just let Luke sift through what he had told him.

'No,' Luke finally said, but he wasn't sure if he believed his own voice. 'No.'

Thomo though wouldn't lie about something this serious. However, he said he *was* drunk. Still...Simon had been hanging around a lot lately. Always turning up at the pub to sit by himself, sometimes joining in and playing pool, but mostly he just sat there on the far side of the bar. Watching them...

It finally hit him. *No, he wasn't...He was watching her.*

'Awww shit!' he suddenly exclaimed, seeing the whole picture now.

'What?'

'The night James got the call from his old man saying Sean was coming home. I went over to both Sean's house and her parents to tell her but she wasn't there. Remember? She turned up at the pub later on and I asked her where she had been. She said she'd been at home all night but with all the excitement about Sean coming home, I forgot. FUCK!!' He looked down in disgust, anger building in him.

Neither of them said anything for a minute. Around them Luke's co-workers drove out of the yard, heading home. The two mates looked at each other, trying to figure out if it was at all possible. Both felt sick at the thought of it being true.

The rain which had held off all day finally began to fall. The metallic drumming of rain drops on the roof of the Monaro broke them out of their thoughts.

'What do we do?' Thomo asked, not caring about getting wet.

Luke looked him square in the eye. 'We tell him.'

'What if we're wrong?'

Luke just looked at him and said nothing. Thunder rumbled in the distance.

Anna raced from the building to the car and jumped in, water flicking off her hair as she spun and shut the door.

'How was work today, honey?' Sean asked, all smiles as he kissed her hard on the lips. He felt almost rejuvenated after spending lunch with Mary and little Molly. She was such an optimistic kid with nothing but dreams and adventure in front of her. Her zest for life had rubbed off onto him. He wanted to live his life to the fullest now. He had survived a war and felt invincible. With Anna and his friends by his side he felt like the luckiest man alive.

'Looks like you've had a good day. What did you get up to?'

Sean brushed a rope of wet hair away from her cheek. 'I visited the family of a mate from my platoon. Had to drop off a present for his daughter.'

'Well aren't you just the little Santa Claus.' She said with a grin.

'Yes I am.' He pulled out into traffic. 'Are we still having diner with your parents tonight?'

'Change of plans. You and I are dining alone tonight. I'm going to cook you a beautiful meal and we'll stay at home. No visitors, no friends, just you and I…' She leant across and kissed him, 'together.'

He smiled contentedly. 'Good.'

They stopped off and bought groceries before heading back to the house. As Anna started to cook, she recommended Sean run out and get a bottle of wine to go with the fish. Although he wasn't a wine person he didn't argue. He was in too good a mood to let anything spoil it. Jumping into the car he raced around to see James. James enjoyed a good wine and picked out a nice white wine from the Upper Hunter to go with most fish. Sean grabbed two bottles.

Sean was heading for the door when Luke and Thomo walked in. They were both drenched from the rain and the expression each wore told him his good mood was about to say goodnight.

'Hey fellas,' he said wanting to say a quick hello and get back to Anna where everything was peachy.

'Sean,' Luke said standing in the doorway, blocking him. 'You got a sec?'

Sean smiled and conceded a nod, but his mates didn't return the smile. That niggling feeling of something being not quite right returned to him. 'What's wrong?'

She had been quartering the lemons when she heard him come in behind her.

'What are you doing here? You know you can't come here!' her voice a mixture of fear and surprise.

Stepping into the kitchen, Simon took her hand in his. 'I just saw him leave and I know he'll be back soon but I had to find out how you went at the doctors today.'

Anna looked down the hall checking no one else was around. Outside the rain was pelting down. With the noise of it on the roof she feared she wouldn't hear Sean's return.

'Nothing.' she said. 'It's all clear.'

A look of disappointment flashed across his face. He was secretly hoping she was pregnant so he could take her for his own. He loved her, had loved her for ages. He cursed Sean for coming home early to ruin it all. Had it been the full twelve months he and Anna would have moved away from here, out of this shitty industrial suburb of a dirty town to live with his brother at Coffs Harbour until they could find a place of their own. Get married. Raise their family. Be happy in love.

'So what do we do now?' he asked.

Anna pulled her hand from his. 'I think we should take a break for a while,' she said looking down at her feet. There was a time when she had fallen out of love with Sean and in love with Simon. Absence, she had convinced herself, doesn't make the heart grow fonder. Now he was home and things were different. She was pretty sure she wanted to be with Sean. It just annoyed her she had to make a decision now. She *had* been wanting more time to make up her mind. Guilt then washed over her like an eclipse. She had lied to Sean for too long. She had lied to him on the tapes she sent him, playing the part of the love-lost lonely girl waiting for her man to come home from war. Even on his return she had been unsure of how she felt.

'I hate all this lying,' she said to him. Part of her still wanted Simon. It was the excitement of the affair she enjoyed and she loved being with him. Simon was a better lover than Sean although she would never tell Simon that. To even think that made her blush with guilt.

'So do I,' he said trying to reassure her as he hugged her tightly. 'We can go away from here, like we talked about. Just quit our jobs and start again up the coast.'

She didn't answer him, just held him tight, feeling his heart beating fast.

Oh shit, she thought. *What have I gotten into? All this lying and deception and now…* 'I'm pregnant,' she heard herself say, surprised at how easily the words came out.

Simon moved back to look her in the eye.

'Really?' A smile was beginning to spread across his face.

'Yes,' she answered quietly with a nod.

'Oh God!' he exclaimed with excitement, hugging her even tighter. 'That's great. You and I, parents.'

Anna smiled but held back how she felt. She had never imagined she would announce her first baby by telling the father behind the back of her fiancée. It had all snowballed into something uncontrollable. Should she still go ahead with her plan to marry Sean and claim the child as his or leave with Simon and escape Newcastle?

'When our baby…'

Anna didn't hear the rest of Simon's sentence. Her attention was drawn to a movement. A shadow had crossed the hall and guilt was suddenly replaced with fear.

Simon felt her body stiffen and he looked down the hall to the front door.

Sean. He was standing there on the outside of the screen door, water dripping off him; fists clenched tightly waiting to take out his fury.

Simon froze.

Anna took a step back away from him, letting go of him.

Sean stared into them both, his anger holding back both words and actions. He then focused beyond Simon to his fiancée. He didn't give a fuck about Simon; he hardly knew him at all so what he had done didn't shock him. It was Anna that enraged him. All this time he had stayed loyal to her because he loved her. He had never cheated with another girl because of her, he had proposed to her because he loved her, respected her. He had trusted her. He had been going to set a date for the wedding tonight and talk about raising their own family. Now she was pregnant to this fuck, some slimy, sleazy snake that had waited until he had left the country to make his move. Shit, he was in *his house*!

'Sean…' Anna started but couldn't follow it up with anything worthy.

Simon was terrified. He didn't know what to do. He could make a run for it out the back and over the fence or he could stand his ground and show Sean *and* Anna he was willing to fight for her.

He didn't get the chance to decide. Sean turned without saying a word and headed back out into the rain.

The cheating couple stood quietly in the hall as Sean's sedan roared off down the narrow street, tyres spinning in the wet.

As the noise of it disappeared, Anna began to cry. It hit her suddenly and she ran to the bedroom, shutting the door behind her. Simon thought twice about going in and comforting her, opting instead to head home and wait for it all to blow over.

Sean, however, was far beyond from letting it blow over. He drove to Thomo's flat knowing he would still be at the pub with Luke, or hoping so at least.

He was calm despite the avalanche of bad news that had swallowed him up. The world outside his car seemed surreal. He took corners without realising he had done so. His body was driving but his mind was in a hundred different places at once…

He was meeting her for the first time at a football party one Saturday afternoon following a game, her brilliant smile like a beacon in the night.

He was kissing her breasts in the back seat of his car, this car, over by Nobby's Lighthouse; the first time they had ever had made love on the back seat.

The first time they had all gone out together with all of their mates…

The first time his old man had met her. He liked her. Said she had a good demeanour, someone he should be proud of.

Well, dad, you were wrong about that one.

He stopped outside of Thomo's flat. Shutting the engine off, he listened to the rain on the roof as he stared off into the wet afternoon.

The rain on the roof... It sounded like the rain on his bush hat as he lay in ambush for the nogs to emerge from the blackness of the jungle... It sounded like the drumming of an M60 as its tracer rounds punched holes into teenage boys,their own rifles barking wildly back at them as they fell with a splash to the wet jungle floor.

A crash of lightning bought him back to the pain at hand.

He checked no one was around and got out, climbing the stairs to the small one bedroom flat. The street was clear, the heavy rain keeping everyone indoors. It only took him a couple of seconds to find what he was after before heading back to his car.

FOURTEEN

Simon headed home through the rain, hands in pockets as he tried to keep dry by walking from tree to tree but he was soaked before he reached the first corner. Stopping under a peppercorn, he looked back at the house. Sean hadn't returned yet.

Probably down at his precious pub, he thought, *drinking as usual. Fucking baby killer, he doesn't deserve her. Now that she's pregnant there's nothing he can do. Anna and I will be together whether he likes it or not.*

Time will change it all.

Lightning crackled then exploded only a few blocks away startling him. He looked in the direction of it and saw the last of its bold, blue flash. He thought about going back to get her, pack her a bag and get out of this town. She could sleep at his place tonight and then head up the coast together in the morning. They could be there after lunch.

Better give her a day, he said to himself, *to calm down.*

He walked the next few blocks not caring about the rain anymore. Water fell in streams off the slanted roof of the woolshed warehouses, splashing onto the muddy ground beside the road. Crossing the road to avoid the mud he turned down his street.

It may have been the rain keeping his head down or the fact he was thinking about Anna that he didn't see the white car on the other side of the road but he did hear the car door shut. He instinctively looked up and fear stopped him dead in his tracks. Sean stood beside his car, no expression on his face, a black pistol in his right hand. He walked forward and raised the gun as Simon pulled his hands from his pockets, holding them up in a placatory fashion to shield himself.

Unblinking, Sean fired four rounds square into his chest. The impact of the .45 calibre bullets threw him back into a parked car. His body bounced off the car's door, the side window already shattered by the exiting bullets, and he dropped to the road, his head making a sickening wet thwack as it hit the ground. Sean hadn't broken his stride. He walked up to the lifeless mess and fired one more round into his head. Bone and brain skipped out along the road, spreading out in an arc like a watermelon dropped from a great height.

Sean looked up the road, staring off into the distance, his emotions boiling even more. He felt like a caged animal begging for freedom. Killing Simon hadn't given it to him. The town seemed to mock him. It was suddenly suffocating him. His vision became tunnelled and he feared he would pass out. Turning his eyes to the sky, the rain on his face seemed to wake him up, snap him out of his spell.

He breathed deeply. It was over.

He turned and walked to the car, climbing back into the Holden. No neighbours emerged to see what had happened. Maybe they had mistaken it for thunder. Either way he didn't care. Looking over at the crumpled body he felt no remorse. He wasn't sorry he had done it.

The cunt deserved worse than what he'd got.

But what now? What do I do?

Get away from here, his mind screamed at him.

His arm felt like lead as he reached up to start the car. It seemed to take forever to reach the keys. The motor finally kicked to life, purring away. He drove off, leaving Simon lying there, blood diluting out in a widening stream that collected at the gutter to be drawn down the drain and dumped into the Pacific.

He drove, just drove. He didn't know where he was going. After a couple of minutes he saw the flashing of headlights in his mirror. It was Luke's Monaro. He stopped the car, they all climbed out. Both of them saw the gun in Sean's hand.

'What the fuck have you done?' Luke demanded.

'Are you fucking mad?' Thomo said. 'Where's Simon?'

Sean held out the gun for Thomo to take. 'I'm going,' Sean said quietly and turned to walk to his car.

'Where are you going?'

'What's happened to Simon?' Luke yelled, grabbing him by the arm.

Sean stopped and turned, looking at his mates with a blank expression. He thought about what to say but only came out with a soft, 'I shot him.'

'Oh, God no.'

'Is he dead? Sean! Is he dead?'

A nod yes.

'Jesus.' Luke bowed his head trying to think. He thought of Anna and suddenly felt sick. Was she dead too?

'Where's Anna, Sean? Is she…have you hurt her?'

'She's at home,' he mumbled. 'She's pregnant.'

Luke was stunned. 'What..?'

'SHE'S FUCKING PREGNANT!!!' Sean roared, his anger now venting out onto his friends. 'TO HIM!' He pointed off into the distance. 'TO THAT FUCKING SNAKE OF A CUNT!! WELL, FUCK HIM!!'

Luke and Thomo were scared. They had never seen him like this. Waiting for Sean to calm down, they stood in silence as the rain continued. Off in the distance the sound of first one siren then two began to filter through the storm. They faded in and out but they were clearly heading towards their suburb. Luke looked at Sean. He seemed defeated, not caring anymore. He noticed his shoes and the blood spatter that had stained them.

'We'll get you outta here. If they catch you, you'll go to gaol. We can get you out of Newcastle.'

Sean looked up at them both and saw they were serious. They were going to stick with him through this.

'I can't let you get involved. It's not your fight.'

'Fuck that!' Thomo said sternly. 'You're our mate and we're not gunna just sit by and watch you go down for this. You know us better than that!'

'They'll find me eventually.'

'Not if you leave here for good,' Luke pointed out. He didn't want to lose his mate again but if that meant keeping him out of gaol then he would do whatever it took.

The police sirens were getting louder. They had to act now.

'Let's go Sean.' Luke said calmly, reassuringly.

Sean nodded his head in agreement. He climbed into the Monaro's back seat and as they drove off Sean watched his EH pass by as they sped down the street. He wondered if he would ever see his car again. He doubted it. Fishing into his wet pockets he grabbed his keys and handed them forward to Thomo. 'Here,' was all he said. Thomo simply nodded back.

They pulled up outside of Luke's and he ran inside. A minute later he came out with a sports bag and tossed it onto the rear seat. 'Clothes. And my savings.'

Driving towards the docks they were all silent with only the noise of the motor and the rain against the car. Sean was suddenly faced with the fact he might never see his friends again. 'I'm sorry for all this,' he said, his first words in ten minutes.

'Don't you worry about us mate,' Luke reassured him. 'We'll be right. It's yourself you have to take care of now. You might have to watch your back for a couple of months. The police will scale down the search after a while. But you can't come back here. Not for a long time, Sean. Probably not ever. There's talk of capital punishment coming back in. You have to keep going. Don't come back or you'll get caught.'

Sean closed his eyes, holding back tears.

'People only get caught when they come back. Don't be stupid.' Luke's voice cracked with emotion, himself trying to find the tiniest sliver of hope in the dark cloud that was swallowing them all.

'You can never be free here again.'

FIFTEEN

Four days later Simon's body was released by the coroner for burial at which Anna attended. The police meanwhile had been around to interview Luke and Thomo, questioning them about Sean's location and where he had acquired the gun but no one said anything. The Holden was towed away for inspection with Thomo never letting on he had the keys.

Everybody now knew about the love triangle and the baby. This was a shock to most people but all it did was make them realise why he had done it. Some of his friends agreed with his actions.

An Army representative came up from Sydney and talked to his father, trying to find out anything he could but to no avail. He was listed as AWOL and told he would be charged when he resurfaced.

Sean had only been home for less than a week and now that he was gone again, he seemed like a ghost. It was as though he had died over there and had never returned.

The pub went quiet as she walked in, eyes staring into her, hating her for what she had done. It had been the first time since that day that anyone had seen her and none welcomed her arrival.

Anna walked up to the bar and James, despite what he felt about her, thought she had balls for coming in here. He didn't think she would *ever* show her face in here again.

Someone over by the pool tables called out 'whore' but she ignored it, knowing it wasn't worth starting a fight.

'You're not welcome in here, Anna,' James stated in no uncertain terms. He didn't have to be nice to her anymore.

'I need to speak to Sean,' she said, summoning up her courage.

He almost laughed. 'You're fucken joking, right?'

'Please James, it's important!'

'He's not here you fucking bitch!' a female voice shouted at her. Anna jumped with fright and turned to see Melanie at the kitchen door with Kim, a knife gripped tightly in her hand. 'The police are looking for him and you think he's just going to hang around here, drinking and playing pool? You've done this to him! You've driven him away! It's you're fault! He was happy here! He was home again but you had to go and fuck someone else!!' She looked down and saw that Anna was still wearing her engagement ring.

'Get that fucking ring off!!'

Anna began to cry. 'I need to see him. I want him back. I still love him…'

'TAKE IT OFF NOW!!' Melanie bellowed and stepped forward, the knife now pointing at her.

Anna turned and ran from the pub, once a sanctuary to her. Her wailing faded off as she disappeared down the street with the ring clutched desperately in her fist.

PART TWO

"Men are at war with each other because each man is at war with himself."

Francis Meehan

SIXTEEN

The *Little Adele* dropped into the trough and everything she carried was weightless for a second until her toughened hull slammed into the dark surface of the Atlantic only to climb up the next wave and repeat the cycle. She was a tough vessel. Built a decade earlier by the Richard's Ironworks of Lowestoft, the side-trawler had been tested on tougher waters than this. Her blue steel riveted hull told the Atlantic waters every time she crashed down it would take a hell of a lot more than that to send her to the bottom.

On board, Daniel Carragher had nothing left to vomit. His gut was sore and his throat and nostrils burned as he held on tightly to the bulkhead; his knuckles white. The handsome 32 year old hated the ocean, something that went against the world's image of young, robust Irishmen who supposedly grew up on the high seas. He didn't even like fish all that much. He preferred lamb. It was what he had thrown up tonight.

Beside him was the boat captain, an old burly man with a short salt and pepper beard and a half rotten yellow knitted beanie that never left his head. He rode the waves like a veteran of the ocean, his knees bent slightly, his feet spread, his trunk mounted on a gyro. His legs acted like shock absorbers and, to Daniel, he looked like he could be punting along the Lagan on a warm spring day instead of keeping some form of control over a boat that, to all but the crew, seemed to be in the centre of a fight between the ocean and God himself.

Daniel felt like he himself was in a washing machine. He had fallen over that many times he had lost count. He was certain tomorrow (if they made it back) he would be sorer still with a bruised arse and legs.

Another crash against the water's surface caused him to bump his head. He held his curse, not wanting to look weak, hoping no one had seen it. Placing a hand up under his long dark fringe that was usually combed neatly, he felt the small lump that had formed almost instantly. At least it wasn't bleeding.

God, I hate the ocean, he thought again.

The normal eight man fishing crew had been boosted by three for the transfer; Daniel, Padraig and Kieran. All were experienced men in their fields. Unfortunately it didn't involve riding nuggetty fishing boats on the roughest sea in the world.

Padraig Molloy had been seasick before they had gone three miles and he now sat down stairs in the cramped mess, his eyes closed as he attempted to ride it out. At 43 years of age, the stocky dark haired pessimist had seen and lived the lives of 10 men with unbelievable hardships and amazing luck. This afternoon's ordeal would be just another adventure for him to tell his grandchildren one day, if he lived to have any.

Kieran Hough, the third member of their party, on the other hand was enjoying the roller coaster ride. Apart from crossing a narrow part of Lough Neagh once in a small tin dinghy, he had never been out on the water before. He stood behind the first mate and watched with interest and awe at their navigation and boating skills. He had mastered the sailor's stance and was having a good time. He was the youngest of the trio at 21 although he had been a member of their organisation since he was seventeen and was someone you could trust with your life. His brother, sister and he had been the tallest children in their school, a trait that ran in their family from their father's side.

The death of his brother two years ago was the reason for him being there tonight.

She crested another wave and fell yet again; Daniel's feet leaving the floor but he managed to hold on.

This is insane, he thought.

'Can we transfer in this weather?' he asked the boat captain in his singsong Belfast accent.

'This?!' he snapped back. 'This isn't weather! This is nuthin'! I'd take a load of Waterford Crystal on board with out crackin' a single piece in these seas. If you want'd rough seas you should'a set out with us a month ago. Fuckin' boat tipped ninety degrees over onto her port side. Slap down! Masts in the water! *Under* it! Now that was a wild ride!'

Daniel looked at the boat captain's face and could see he was having fun. He looked like the sort of man that could be happy if he never stepped on land again…as long as there was whiskey on board.

'There she is,' the first mate called out and pointed off towards the horizon, his arm in line with the pip on the radar's screen. Daniel strained his eyes to look for it but only saw white crests and black hollows. The sun had set not long ago and the blue light that preceded night had begun to close in around them.

'Yep, I see it,' the captain answered and turned the wheel slightly.

Daniel didn't notice the change in direction and still couldn't see their target. After a few minutes of more up and down he finally caught a glimpse of a light, then a shape. He pointed it out to Kieran who nodded and went below to get Padraig.

Slowly the silhouette of the *Brizo's Star* grew in front of them, turning to port to give them a lee against the waves. Daniel had thought the *Little Adele* was too small for these seas and as she approached the dry bulk container ship, she felt even smaller. His uneasiness increased as they slid in on her port side. Their 114 feet vessel paled against the leviathan that soared above them. Originally built by the Alabama Drydock Company in Mobile, Alabama and launched as the *James M. Kachur*, the renamed *Brizo's Star* was a leviathan of a Liberty Ship dry bulk freighter. At 387 feet in length and 56 feet wide the *Brizo's Star* looked to them as though it payed no heed to the black, obdurate seas around them.

Kieran and Padraig came up onto the bridge and watched as the captain kept pace with the behemoth at a steady six knots. All three were impressed by his skill as he held her line, constantly making small adjustments to the direction and the throttle, keeping the trawler a few yards off the steel hull that rose straight up like a dark red cliff out of the black water.

High above them, the crew access stairs lowered down, halting well above the trawler's deck. The small but powerful lights on the net masts of the *Little Adele* illuminated a figure in the twilight coming down the stairs. He waited on the last step and as the trawler rose in the swell, closing the gap to less than three feet, the heavily clothed figure jumped down onto the non-slip deck of the trawler below.

Daniel smiled. He was impressed at how easy he had made it seem. It was obvious it wasn't the first time the man had done it. A crewman met the newcomer, shaking his hand and then he led the giant of a man up the stairs to their own heated bridge.

At 6' 6", Chad McIntosh towered above all, even the lanky Kieran. His face looked like it had gone head on into a dozen cyclones and beat them all. He was bald with a shine to his head but he carried a great blonde beard at least eight inches in length. His moustache grew well over his top lip and unless he talked it was near impossible to point out where his mouth was.

'Afternoon Gentlemen. Cap'n.' The big man shook hands with all five men.

'How are you Chad? It's good to see you.' Padraig said shaking the Scotsman's hand.

'Yeah, it's good to be back 'round this side lads. If you know what I mean.'

Behind him out of the window they could see several men make their way down the ship's external stairs, each carrying two large duffel bags with three smuggled military rifles wrapped inside each bag.

One by one they would stand on the end of the relatively steady stairs and as the trawler reached the peak of its lurch upwards, they would pass down the bags to the waiting fishing crew. The crewmen would then in turn hurry off down into the hold to store them.

'Why not just crane them down to the deck instead of all this runnin' up 'n down?' Kieran queried.

'Too risky,' the captain answered. 'You need time to unhook the load. The waves are too unpredictable for that. The line could get caught in the rigging and I'll be fucked if we want that to happen.'

It was a slow and dangerous job and Daniel was glad he wasn't up there on those stairs, struggling down such a steep incline with those heavy bags.

'HOLD ON!' the captain yelled out suddenly. He felt a change in the vessel's motion through the wheel and he spread his legs even wider. As she dropped into another trough, she slewed sideways and collided with the larger red hull. Everyone bar the captain and Chad was tossed hard into the bulkhead.

On the trawler's deck, the crew fell. They had had no prior warning but were up in seconds, all unharmed and waiting to catch the next bundle.

'I think it's getting hairier,' the first mate said referring to the ferocity of the sea.

'We've got an extra passenger to come on board, if that's alright cap'n?' Chad said to him.

'An extra?' asked the captain, not taking his eyes off the actions outside.

Daniel looked at Kieran and Padraig. They didn't like the sound of this. The more people that knew where they were headed, the more chance of them getting caught.

Chad saw the expected look of unease flash across their faces all at once.

'It's fine. He saved my life on the way over. I wouldn't be here now if it wasn't for him, if you know what I mean.'

'You're kidding right, Chad?' Padraig asked. 'Who is he?'

Looking up at the stairs, they watched the crewmen throw down the last bag and begin the clamber back up. As they reached the top they disappeared only to have two more figures appear and climb back down.

Daniel watched the taller of the two throw down a small sports bag, shake hands with the other man and then jump. He landed squarely and picked up his bag. Just as he was standing back up the boat dropped again and his hand shot out to stabilise himself. He grabbed the nearest thing next to him which was one of the fishermen who laughed in a polite way, sharing a joke to make the newcomer feel more at ease.

'His name is Sean Doherty,' Chad stated as he watched Sean climb the stairs to the bridge.

'Doherty?' Kieran asked, turning to the Scotsman. 'Where's he from? Is he Irish?'

'No,' Chad smiled. 'He's Australian.'

The door opened and a cool Atlantic wind announced Sean's arrival. 'Thanks for the ride,' he directed to the boat captain who gave him an indifferent quick nod. Sean turned to the others. 'How's it goin'?'

Chad stepped over to introduce him. 'Sean, this's Kieran, Padraig an' Daniel.'

'How yeh goin' son?'

'Roight so, lad?'

Sean had even more trouble understanding these men than he had Chad. He had gotten used to Chad's accent but these were different all together. He shook hands with them all, watching the reaction of each.

'How was yer trip?' the tall one, Kieran asked him.

'Interesting.'

'We had a wee bit o' a party as we cross'd the equator, ifyehknow-whatahmean.' Chad explained to them. They all silently nodded.

'You gents may want tah go doonstares now,' the captain said as he watched the bulk container's stairs rise into position. He turned the wheel to port and the two vessels parted.

'Grab yer bahg 'n' follah me,' Daniel told Sean and they left the bridge out the rear door and down the hall.

Padraig waited until the two had left before turning on the Scot. 'What the fuck are you doing bringing him out here? You've bought an outsider into this without consulting with us about how it will affect our operation? Are you fucking mad? I can't believe you would be so stupid to even…!'

The big Scot's hand shot out and a pointed finger stopped an inch away from the Irishman's chin. 'Just you shut your mouth for a second because I'm only saying this once. That lad there is the reason that I'm still alive today. He bought his way on board wanting to work his way to Donegal of all fucking places. Our captain was fine with that. I bunked him in my room so I could keep an eye on him and make sure he didn't go snooping around once we picked up the guns in the Med. The pick up was to be at night so I knew he wouldn't see it. But I would have put a bullet in him myself and thrown him overboard had he come off a bit shifty.'

Padraig could see that Chad was serious.

The Glaswegian continued. 'Half way across the Indian Ocean we hit a storm. I was up on the deck with some crew trying to secure some broken derrick rigging when the boom whipped 'round in the wind. The cable caught me in the chest and I was going overboard. The last thing I saw before I went between the railing and the scuppers was this lad running, diving across the deck to grab my hand.' Chad's face had gone pale in the revisiting of his near death. 'I was hanging over the side with nothing holding me back from the bottom of the sea but this kid's grip.' He took a few seconds to gather his breath, wiping the spittle from the corners of his whiskered-covered mouth.

'That night over a few drinks, Sean told me his story. I trust him and we've become friends. I even asked him if he wanted to join our cause. Now, he declined but the night we picked the guns up from the Arabs, Sean helped which sped things up. But don't worry 'cause he has no interest in what we're doin'. He just wants to get on with his own life.

'So you take what I've just told you and go and see if you can get anything different out of him.' He paused briefly before adding, 'Because, friend or not, if I'm wrong and he turns out to be anything other than what I already believe, I *will* throw him over the side myself.'

SEVENTEEN

The *Little Adele* was travelling with the swell so the rocking wasn't as constant. With her Ruston Hornsby six cylinder turbo diesel engine pushing them for home at her top speed of 15 knots, the ride had become less harsh as she rode with the waves, although the angle of rise and fall were still the same. With the wind at their stern and the tide in their favour, they would reach the Dingle Peninsula in an hour.

In the small galley the three Irishmen and the Australian sat at an undersized table trying to keep themselves on their seats and their cups of tea off the floor. Padraig held onto the table tightly as he looked at the stranger. *How much did he know?* he wondered. *What had he learned off Chad? How far should our secrecy go?*

'So what brings yeh op dis way then?' Padraig asked, still angry for what Chad had done.

Sean paused for a second. He thought about lying but decided against it. Chad now knew his story and if he lied, all they had to do was ask him. From what Chad told him about these people, they had almost certainly done a lot worse than kill one man. Chad had let a bit slip during one of many drunken nights.

'Fuck. Where do I start?' He let out a sigh. 'Well, I can't go back to Australia. Not for a long time anyway. You see…I killed a bloke.'

He looked at the faces of the men around him but no one moved. There was no reaction at all. They just waited for him to continue.

'I'd just come home from Vietnam…'

This got a reaction.

'You're a soldier?'

Sean could hear the tension in Padraig's voice and he was suddenly aware of the black grip of a pistol tucked into the belt under his leather jacket. He saw the Irishman shoot a glance at Chad who remained silent.

Mental alarms went off amongst the three Irishmen. They'd stupidly allowed a soldier of the British Commonwealth onboard of their gun-running boat. Padraig turned to Chad with a look on his face that said this had gone far enough.

Sean jumped in with the explanation, 'I've gone A.W.O.L. I'm not a soldier anymore. You've got nothing to worry about with me. All I want to do is hitch a ride. Chad said it would be alright. Chad? Tell them.'

He looked at Chad, looking for a way out of the confrontation. On the table was a knife and if he was quick enough he may get to one of them, maybe even two. But this was their boat. There was no escape. Still… he couldn't help but gauge the chance he had with the knife.

Chad could see Padraig was close to shooting him, fixing a weight to his feet and dumping him overboard.

'I said ah'll vouch fer 'im, Padraig. Think about et. He's alone out here. He isn't even carryin' a weapon, ifyehknowwhatahmean.'

Padraig thought for a bit and then nodded for Sean to continue although he hadn't let his guard down.

'I was wounded in Vietnam. I came home early to find my fiancée having an affair…' Anger boiled up in him and for a moment he forgot about the men around him. 'She was pregnant to this bloke so…so I shot him.' He could almost hear the gun's discharge. 'I took off to catch a ride on a ship and met Chad.'

The three were mulling over his story, Padraig sitting there staring at him, reading his face and body language.

'Tell me about the storm on the way over,' Padraig ordered.

Sean looked up at his new Scottish friend and relayed the story just as Chad had told Padraig in the bridge. If anything Daniel and Kieran seemed impressed.

'An' what do yeh plan to do once yeh debark?' Padraig went on, ignoring Sean's heroics for the time being. 'Do yeh have any kin or friends over 'ere??'

'None that I know of.'

Padraig seemed to relax a bit, lighting up a smoke. 'Yew know where doze guns are goin' don't yeh?' he asked rhetorically.

The time for Sean to back out had long passed. That was a week ago when he had decided to go to Thomo's.

'Belfast.'

No one spoke.

The smell of Padraig's cigarette filled the small room but didn't mask the ever-present odour of fish nor tang of diesel fumes.

'Dat's roight Sean.' He flicked his ash into his half empty tea cup. 'So ah take it yeh know who we are then?'

'Yes.' Sean looked at each in turn. None of them had reacted. All, including Chad, were wearing their poker faces.

'Ah don't haf tuh tell yeh,' Padraig continued, 'that what yeh saw here stays here. We appreciate the help yeh gave Chad, but...' he leaned forward to emphasise his point, 'If we ever foind out dat you've told anyone, and ah mean th' fockin' milkman bahck'ome, ah'll focken' kill yeh myself.'

Sean's heart was picking up the pace. He was scared but at the same time he wanted to tell this prick to go and fuck himself. However he knew that would only get him to the bottom of the Atlantic pretty fast.

Padraig leaned back, putting his smoke out in the tea for added effect. 'Ah mean what ah say Sean. If ah sound like a bastard... then good. Yeh understand me?'

Sean looked at the other three men. None of them had blinked at the comment of killing him.

He looked back at Padraig. 'I understand.'

'Where abouts are yeh going to be stayin' t'noight?' Padraig asked.

'Umm...probably find a hotel for tonight and try to head to Donegal tomorrow. My great grandfather came from there. Unfortunately I don't know one end of Ireland from the other.'

Padraig slammed his hand down on the table like a judge bringing down his gavel. 'Roight!'Sean jumped with fright from pent up nerves. 'Dat's sorted!' the Irishman exclaimed and looked at his watch. 'Let's have a drink to celebrate!'

Kieran leaned over and grabbed a bottle of Bushmill's whiskey and some mismatched glasses from the small cupboard under the sink. He poured two fingers for each of them.

Holding his glass up, Padraig began speaking in a language Sean had never heard before. The other three then said something in unison before they threw their shots down.

Sean drank his as Daniel turned to him. '*Tio*cfaidh ár lá. It's Irish. It means "Our day will come". And *Sláinte* means "cheers".'

'Slainte,' Sean repeated.

'So you've got no plans then?'

'Only to find a place to stay tonight and then work out how to get to Donegal. Nothing other than that.'

Daniel smiled. 'We can get yeh tah Donnygaul if yeh loike. T'noight though we'll have a few drinks.'

EIGHTEEN

The lights of the fishing village of Dingle were a welcome sight to the landlubbers. Part of County Kerry, it was a small community of only 1400 on the Dingle Peninsula. The population mainly consisted of fishermen and farmers. It had begun life as port following the Norman Invasion in the Twelfth Century and at one stage had been one of the busiest ports in the country. Now it had reverted back to a simple fishing village that sometimes used its waters for a more dubious trade.

As they glided through the lightly rippled black waters of the cove, a dolphin surfed and played in the bow's wave like a faithful dog welcoming home its master.

The boat captain skilfully bought the *Little Adele* up to the jetty's edge where eight men stood waiting. Two of them caught the hawsers thrown to them to secure to the bollards at either end. The dolphin glided around in the foreground hoping for some fish to be thrown its way.

No sooner had she been made fast when they all began unloading her illegal cargo into four trucks. These would split up as they headed north, delivering their contents to secret weapon holds throughout the Republic and the North.

Several of the truck's drivers cast a suspicious eye at Sean as he came out onto the vessel's deck but they didn't say anything.

As the last of the bags were carried away, Sean shouldered his bag and followed Daniel up the ramp and onto solid ground. He smiled to himself as he stood on Irish soil, the first piece of dry land he had been on in almost two weeks. The smell of diesel oil and fish and salt had been replaced with a welcomed aroma of earth, grass, smoke and civilisation.

The noise of the departing trucks faded out and he could hear the sound of music in the distance.

'Come on then,' Daniel said, slapping Sean on the back as he walked towards the town centre.

They headed up from the harbour and came to a pub a few blocks up called Dick Mac's and Padraig led the way in. Warmth greeted them; both the heat from the fire and the welcome of the locals. A small cheer went up and a path cleared to the bar, each man receiving a pat on the back and handshakes galore.

These people congratulated Sean as well. One man shook his hand and said something in Irish. All Sean could do was smile and nod. Part of it felt like walking into the Lass O'Gowrie on his return from Vietnam; the cheers, the smiles, people genuinely happy to see him. Somehow, at that moment, this felt more like home than Newcastle ever had.

Without asking the other four, the barman had pulled three pints of stout and a pint of red, placing them up on the bar. He then turned to Sean. A garble of words came at him and before Sean had a chance to tell him he didn't understand. Chad raised both his hands and called for quiet.

The room hushed down, everyone looking at Chad and Sean.

'Ladies an' Gentlemen. Ah'd like to introduce yeh all to Sean,' he called out in English. 'He's Australian so 'e doesn't speak Munster or any form of Irish, ifyehknowwhatahmean, but he's a good mahn, he saved my life and he's here wiv me so aye hope you all treat him th' same as yuh would me!'

From the back of the room someone called out 'But we hate you, yah kilted git!'

Everyone, including the tall Scotsman burst into laughter.

'Well,' he yelled out over the noise, 'Yeh can all hate him right along side me then just as long as yeh treat us equally!' He put his arm around

Sean, laughing along with the crowd.

People shook hands with Sean again, this time speaking to him in English. A torrent of voices came from every direction; 'Where abouts in Ostrayl' yeh from?' 'What brings yeh ova tuh Dingle then?' 'Are yeh here tuh help th' boys out Seano?' 'Good on yeh Sean!'

Their distinct accents were almost as hard to understand as the Irish they previously spoke.

'Jayzus Christ!' Daniel said as he leaned over the crowd around Sean. 'Will yeh not let the marn have a fockin' drink! He's been at sea for days!'

From which the crowd replied, 'Oh, sorry Sean!' 'Oi'll get yeh a pint son,' 'No George, et's my round!' and 'Oh, fock off Danny!'

Sean turned back to the barman, a man with arms big enough he could carry kegs of beer two at a time. 'I'll just have a pint of the local'.'

'No worries lad. My names Seamus.' He shook hands with Sean.

'Good to meet you Seamus.'

He watched him pull a pint of Murphy's Stout and Sean was surprised to see the bubbles going down instead of up. Seamus let it rest before topping it up and placing it on the bar in front of him. 'There yeh go now.'

'That looks heavy,' Sean said with wary.

'Yuv ne'er had a proper stout before?'

'Our black beers look nothing like this.'

'You know me Nan used to say "Never trust a man that doesn't take a bottle' o' stout".'

'Well I wouldn't want to upset your Nan then.'

'Wait for her to settle then enjoy.'

He waited until the upside-down bubbles calmed then picked it up and looked at the juxtaposition of the off-white head and the black liquid. *Oh well*...Seamus watched closely as he took his first mouthful. Sean smiled back, 'Mmmm. Certainly has a taste about it.'

'Mother's milk. Guinness is good as well but I prefer this one,' Seamus added as he poured another.

Turning around, Sean had a good look at the inside of the smoke filled noisy bar. He blinked in astonishment. The pub, which was about thirty feet long by twelve feet across, was divided into two sections. The bar was located on the right side of the room. The left wall however was covered in rows and rows of shoes, leather sheets and cobbling equipment. It was as though a wall which had once separated a pub from a cobbler had been removed. One half for drinking and the other half for…cobbling.

Seamus noticed him looking up and down the opposite wall, trying to work it all out.

'Ah do boot repairs and leather work durin' the day and ah pull beers at noight.'

'What?'

'Our laws are a wee bit different tuh what yeh moight be used to bah'comb. We can have two shops in one here. Foxy's op on Main Street is half hardware. People can come in 'ere and get two things at the same toime; new boots and pissed!' He chuckled to himself as he pulled another beer for one of the regulars.

Sean shook his head in disbelief. 'It's the strangest thing I've ever seen, but…It makes sense.' He sipped his stout as he looked around once more. 'It makes sense.'

At either end of the bar were small snugs. It was the snug at the far end that Daniel directed him to. He looked at the other three men squeezed into the small booth. Padraig was sitting beside an elder man in his fifties and a young chap about his own age that looked too much like the old bloke that he had to be his son.

Padraig gave the introductions. 'Sean, dis is Tom O'Geary and his youngest son Michael.'

'Tom. Michael. Good to meet you both.'

'How's th' form, Sean?' Tom said with a wide smile.

'Padraig tells us dat you're lookin' to ge' tah the Forgott'n County,' young Michael stated as he sipped his pint of red.

'Forgotten County?'

'Aye, Donn'gaul.'

'That's right. My family came from there and I just suddenly had the urge to get up that way to see where I came from.' He hoped he didn't sound stupid.

'Och, so ya be a Herring Gutter then?'

All this local lingo was beginning to confuse Sean and the unsteady look on his face told them he was in the deep end here.

'Sure yah be a woolly one Sean,' The old man interrupted. 'Dinnae worry, you'll get a grip o' it. What be yer fam'ly name den?'

'Doherty.'

'Doherty? Ahh, *Dockerty*!' The old man used the Irish pronunciation of his name. 'Get away with yeh! I know many *Dockerty* fam'lies up that way. Should be a cinch to find some familiar blood, know wha' tah mean?'

'Well, oihm tehkin' me dah op there in th' mornin',' Michael cut in. 'I take him op once a month to visit me Arnty Celia, Pah's sister. I live in Belfast m'self but this one cries like a bairn if I don't come down here and play taxi man for him. You're welcome t' roide along with os if yuh loike.'

Sean couldn't believe this place. Known terrorists were kind to him, strangers were buying him drinks and now a ride to Donegal.

'Thanks. I'd appreciate it. Is it far away? Sorry but I don't know one end of Ireland from the other.'

Tom smiled at him. He liked Sean already because he was honest and up front. The one thing Tom O'Geary hated was dishonesty. 'It'll tehk os an over-nighter. We'll be stopping over at a friends place fur th' noight in Dunmore up in Galway. Although with Mick's drivin' we'll be at the fockin' norf pole a'fore lunch!' He leaned across the table, holding a hand up to shield his mouth as though he was telling a secret. 'Fockin' droives loike a madman he does! Can't slow him down!' He chuckled to himself and leaned back.

'I'll get Seamus tuh put yeh op for the noight,' Padraig said to Sean and waved the barman over. Seamus arrived with a bottle of Tullamore Dew 12 Year Old Special Reserve whiskey and enough glasses for them all.

'On the house Pad. For you an' your boys.'

'Ah ye dinea have tuh do that Seamus.'

'It's the least ah could do.'

'Ah slainte, Seamus. If yeh insist. You're a kind mahn!' he exclaimed as he graciously accepted the gift. 'Now, if et's no' too much trouble, would yeh have a spare room for the noight for young Sean here?'

Before Seamus had a chance to answer, Sean jumped in, 'Is there somewhere I could get some food. I'm starvin'!'

The big barman stuck his head outside of the snug, looking for somebody in the crowd. 'Ester! How far off is that food?'

A woman across the room carrying a tray of empty glasses replied something in Irish and gave Sean's group a wave and a big smile.

'Et's already on et's way lad. Now drink up. Today is a great day for Ireland!'

Through a drunken haze, Sean saw Joel sitting on the end of his bed. He wasn't frightened this time. Joel was smiling. He was clean shaven and dressed in a new set of greens.

'Do you like it here as well?' was all he said.

Sean didn't wake up. He just slept.

'I'll be here if you need me,' he said as he watched his friend at peace.

NINETEEN

The knock at his door bought him out of one of the deepest sleeps he had ever had.

'Sean, are yeh op yet?' It was Seamus.

'Yeah,' he replied groggily.

'Tom an' Michael should be here in half an hour. Ester's got some breakfast on for yeh.'

Sean's eyes opened and he felt the familiar head swim of a hangover.

'Sean?' Seamus called out again.

'Yeah, I'm up!' he sang out and got to his feet. He dressed and headed to the bathroom at the end of the hall to wash his face and relieve some of the poison still in him from last night. From the hall he could smell the sausages and eggs, bacon and hash browns, toast and coffee.

Downstairs he greeted Ester, Seamus' wife.

'Mornin' Sean. Did yeh sleep alroight?'

'Yes thanks. That bed was so comfortable. If I had a house to put it in, I'd buy it off you!' he joked with her.

Last night Ester had sung a few songs, much to the joy of the crowd. She had a beautiful voice that suited her romantic, enchanting face. Seamus' banjo playing had picked up the pace after his wife's sombre songs. The Lass O'Gowrie had never been so lively.

'Now Sean,' Ester began. 'Ah've got bacon and sausages and drisheen. The eggs…'

'Drisheen?'

'You probably know it as black pudding.'

'Black pudding?' he asked as he sat down at the big table.

'Aye, it's sheep's blood congealed in a stomach lining.' She smiled to herself as she watched him look from her down to the dark thick sausage and back up at her. 'Not many foreigners eat it but it's surprisingly good. Very salty so it's good for a hangover.'

'I'll see how I go,' he said with no real intention of eating clotted sheep's blood.

Voices outside in the bar headed his way and Tom and his son Michael came in as he was finishing off everything bar the blood meat.

'Eat op yer blood Sean!' old Tom said as he poured himself a cup of tea. 'Et's good for yeh!'

'No I'm full thanks Tom.'

'Typical tourist,' Michael joked.

Daniel, Kieran and Chad came down to say goodbye before they left. They had stayed upstairs as well but were hanging around town for a few more days to sort out some business. Daniel would be heading back to Belfast with Kieran and Padraig on Monday. Chad was catching a lift up the coast with another fishing crew, then another boat onto Scotland. They wished Sean luck in whatever it was he was doing, saying if they were ever in Donegal they would find him for a drink. Sean knew it was an empty promise but agreed anyway as Chad near crushed him with a hug to say thank you, once again, for saving his life.

The three of them headed off in Michael's blue Vauxhall, east along the Dingle Peninsula, heading inland. The countryside hypnotised Sean with its lush beauty. Clichéd rolling hills were criss-crossed with stone fences that ran for miles. The sun rose up above the morning's mist and the true richness of the environment burst with colours of deep greens, ripe reds and rainbow flowers in the front yards of centuries old stone farm houses. Farmers herded longhaired sheep down the narrow roads, their collies keeping them bunched together just like the farmers and their faithful blue heelers back in Australia. At the farm on his left he saw a tractor towing a trailer full of peat away from a shallow quarry with two men digging with long, odd looking shovels. Everything seemed familiar yet so different.

As they crested a hill Sean suddenly asked if they could stop. Pulling up after the bend at Scrallaghbeg, Sean climbed out and walked forward beyond the front of the car. He looked out towards the diminishing mist which veiled Tralee Bay below them to the north. Gliding across its rippled surface, just like toy boats in a pond, were numerous fishing craft of all sizes, some returning from an early haul while some were departing for a second run. To his right the Slieve Mish Mountains rose out of the waters edge, shallow at first before climbing up to dominate the peninsula. In the distance he could see Tralee, the town made famous by the 19th century song *'The Rose of Tralee'*.

He stood there for a minute as he took in the beauty of the land of his forefathers. It was like a living painting that he could touch and be part of. The ghostly fog on the water below was beginning to disappear with a light breeze that crept up the hill. With it came the salt smell he loved so much. He could also smell the heavy rich aroma of burning turf from the houses below down at the water's edge. Although he had never known such a scent it made him feel like he was home. The sights and smells of this place, this island, made his heart rise in his chest and he felt like sitting there and doing nothing but watch the boats come and go and the land change colour as the sun passed across the sky. Content. He had never been so content before in his life. And if he had been alone he probably would have allowed himself to cry, just a little, with happiness.

Footsteps crunched the gravel behind him. Tom, understanding of what Sean was doing, waited for a minute before he spoke.

'It's beautiful yes? The reason why so many that have gone sing of returning. This is just the start of it Sean. Wait until we reach your Donegal. It truly is beautiful.'

Sean nodded and breathed in deep. With his eyes closed he breathed in deep once more, savouring the first images of his new home. An infinite number of futures scrolled through his mind and he was free to pick anyone of them. *My life restarts here.*

Tom was right about Michael's driving. He drove flat out down to Tralee and on up through Limerick, Enis and Gort. His father would tell him countless times to slow down and he would oblige, but after a few miles, the speed would start to climb again. Sean didn't mind the speed. What he didn't like was the stone fences which lined the roads and allowed no room for error. One slip up and they would be pin balling it down the road, bouncing from one fence to the other, hopefully not into on-coming traffic. But Michael drove the car well, almost like someone who did it for a living.

They chatted about this and that and generally enjoyed the ride and each others company. Most of the questions came from Tom who told him a friend of his had moved to Perth, Western Australia a few years back. He wanted to know everything about the country from their similarities and differences to the price of beer in their pubs.

The three of them had been driving for almost four hours when they decided to stop for lunch at a small fish and chip shop on the outskirts of Galway. While it wasn't more than an hour to their stop for the night, all three agreed it would be better to arrive with full stomachs and not eat their hosts out of everything.

It was here bad luck would fall upon them. It was only through the most impossible coincidence, the type of coincidence that changes a life forever, that a man in a white Rover happened to glance across the car park at the three entering the shop as he was climbing into his own car with enough fish and chips to feed eight men. The driver of the Rover recognised Michael. His training kicked in and he noted the registration of the car and drove to the nearest phone booth and called in what he saw.

The man in the Rover had gone unnoticed to the three and they continued on inside for a filling meal and leaving ten minutes later contented. Only when Michael pulled up at an intersection twenty minutes after that between the villages of Cummer and Tuam, did he realise something was wrong.

Tom and Sean had no idea what was happening as Michael floored it through the stop sign. Two white vans seemed to appear from nowhere, closing down on them faster than Michael could react. A second later they were hit from behind by the first van. The small Vauxhall sedan punched across the road and directly into a stone fence, the front of the car flattening itself across it. Hot water sprayed out of the burst radiator like a severed artery as the passengers inside were thrown around like dolls. The second white van then came in from the right and nosed itself up against the driver's door. As they screeched to a halt their side doors slid open and three men from each poured out. All were wearing balaclavas.

The noise of the impact echoed around the small valley and the men in the vans knew they had to act fast. Before Sean had even had a chance to open his eyes, the back door was thrown open and a figure grabbed him by the arm and dragged him out onto the road. A fist hit him in the cheek, opening him up. Sean stumbled from the blow but swung back twice as hard. As the first masked assailant came at him Sean's fist landed perfectly across his nose. He heard the bone and cartilage snap under the impact. The man fell backwards over the feet of another and as Sean was aiming for a kick to the man's head a blow to his own temple sent a flash of white pain through his entire body. He, too, hit the road, landing heavily on his side. Hands grabbed him from all directions, some frisking him down for weapons, the rest holding him down. As he was dragged across the bitumen he looked across and saw that Michael was either dead or unconscious. He was being thrown unceremoniously into the back of one of the vans. He also saw two of them carrying Eastern European versions of the AK47.

Fear hit him like ice water, flashes of Vietcong strobed through his mind. Then he thought Police or Army. However, the balaclavas and assault rifles gave him little hope of leniency that comes with authorities.

Tom and Sean were bundled into the other van and as the sliding door shut behind them they were handcuffed with their arms behind their backs and a black hood pulled down tight over their heads. A kick to the stomach dropped both to their knees and then they were off.

Taking the corners fast, Sean and Tom slid from side to side on the bare metal floor. Without being able to see the walls of the van and with his hands tied behind his back the next sharp turn threw Sean into the wall, his head banging into the wheel arch. He let out a grunt of pain.

'Shut th' fock op yeh Fenian cohnt!' a voice yelled at him from the veiled darkness.

'But he's not…' was all Tom could say before Sean heard a thud of another kick landing on old Tom.

'Let him go yah bastards!' Sean screamed out. 'He's an old man for fuck sake!!'

With his outburst over, he braced himself for the kicking he knew would come. Nothing happened.

Standing above the bound men, the kidnappers were more than a little confused. Sean's accent had thrown them and they all looked at each other. Who was this third man, they wondered. For a second they thought he was English.

Sean didn't relax and kept his muscles tense in anticipation of a flogging.

After ten minutes the vans braked suddenly and turned hard. They came to a stop and the doors flew open.

TWENTY

Tom and Sean were pulled from the van and half marched, half dragged into a building. It was cold and their footsteps echoed. From the sound Sean could tell that it was a large building like a warehouse or barn. The floor was concrete and dirty, gritty underfoot.

He tried to shake the hood off but received another hit, this time to his nose. The unexpected pain made him stumble and the men either side of him had to carry him the rest off the way. It felt as though his nose had been splattered across his face, the metallic taste of thick blood trickled down his throat. Each time he coughed his nose would explode with a sharp pain which added to his headache.

Another door opened. He was led in, felt his wallet being taken from his back pocket and then pushed to the ground, his knees landing heavily on the hard surface. Pain cannoned up through his legs as his broken knee cap took the brunt of the fall. He fell to his side to relieve some of the pain. As he fought back a scream, final thoughts flashed through his mind.

This is it. I'm dead. Shot through the back of the head for no reason in God knows where.

Then the door shut behind him with a crash and they were gone.

He was alone.

Listening for a while, he made sure he was the only one in the room then shook the hood off of his head. Blood from his nose smeared up across his face in a long red streak. The first thing he did was spit out a mouthful of blood then he looked at his new surroundings. There was nothing else in the room. The floor was bare and the walls were high with a small window at the top for some illumination. It was too high and too small to climb through.

The floor was filthy and the edges were covered in years of accumulated dust. He guessed it at 15 feet by 20 feet and the door behind him was heavy timber. The centre had been used recently. Footprints and splashes of black dried blood told of the violence the room had recently seen. He wasn't sure if he imagined the metallic smell of the coagulated mess.

He got to his feet and tried to move his hands to take the painful pressure off his wrist bones but every movement just made them feel tighter.

At least my wrists are taking my mind off my nose, he joked to himself.

He leant against the wall in the far corner. They would be back soon. He knew they would only come to torture him and then put a bullet in his brain. *Just tell them you're Australian*, he thought. *They've got your wallet. You've got no fight with them. You're just a tourist here. Tell them you are an Australian!* He began to feel a little better about the situation. *You might still live through this.*

BOOM!!! The gunshot seemed to shake the entire building. It had come from another room. Then he heard a voice call out.

'Michael?' It was Tom. 'Michael?!!' His voice cried out with terror and fury. 'YOU BASTARDS!! YOU FOCKING BASTARDS!! OH GOD NO Michael!!'

Sean shut his eyes trying to block out the nightmare. The fear of the jungle came back to him. Death was paces away, on the other side of the wall and it would come for him soon enough and there wasn't a thing he could do about it. There was nothing he could do.

He was going to die.

He sat still for a minute thinking.

Fuck them. If I'm going to be killed like a diseased dog then I'm going to take one of them with me. A newfound strength poured into him. Adrenalin and endorphins numbed his pain. Glucose, produced by his liver, fed his body the energy it would need to fight. He dropped to the floor and forced his cuffed hands around underneath him, passing his feet through. The cuffs pinched and tore at his skin but he ignored it as the blood helped to lubricate the tight metal. With his hands back around in front he stood and prepared to fight to the end.

In his mind he tried to picture the last few moments of his life.

As the first one would step in, Sean would come from behind the door, bringing his clenched fists down on the gunman's arm as hard as he could, hopefully breaking his wrist and causing him to drop whatever weapon he was carrying. The gun would clatter around on the ground and he would then bring both fists up into his throat. A two-fisted aimed blow would crush his larynx, causing a slow, suffocating and painful death.

If he could only get to the weapon before the next gunmen rushed in he thought he might stand a chance to fight his way out. Realistically though, he didn't think he'd get that far.

Fuck, though, he'd give it a go.

Standing by the door he could hear the murmuring of Tom in the other room. He thought about telling him to pull it together but it wouldn't make a shit of difference. His son had just been killed and they would certainly be next. But he had to say something.

'DON'T GIVE THE CUNTS THE SATISFACTION TOM!!' he bellowed as loud as he could, the adrenalin now surging through him. 'MICHAEL WOULDN'T WANT YOU TO GIVE UP!!'

Most of what he said was for his own benefit, trying to get himself ready, get himself pumped up. He was ready to fight. His fists were trembling in anticipation.

'COME ON YOU FUCKERS!!' he screamed. 'LET'S FINISH THIS NOW!!'

He heard a door open and shut. Footsteps passed his room and continued on. After a minute of silence his natural stimulants began to fade and the shakes spread to his entire body. Then he felt ill. He slid down the wall and spat out more blood. He coughed and heaved but he couldn't throw up so he lay on his side as his breathing returned to normal. The drilling feeling of his headache returned and began to bore away at his brain. Thirst hit him. He bit his tongue so as to fill his mouth with saliva but little came and what he swallowed tasted of blood which made him feel ill again. He sat up, leaning against the wall and he closed his eyes thinking of what to do next. For twenty minutes he didn't move.

He had no idea.

He was fucked.

As if sensing his weakness, the door to his room opened. He hadn't heard their approach and had lost his chance to get the upper hand. Or at least get a few good shots in. The first man through the door was aiming a pistol at Sean's head and he moved to the side as another gunman came in carrying one of the Romanian AK rip offs. It was levelled at Sean's chest. The smell of cordite, that unmistakable smell of modern gunpowder entered the room with them as it lingered on their clothes.

'Get up,' the rifle man said.

Sean looked up at the eyes behind the black woollen balaclava. He wasn't going to be ordered around by these murderers just to make it easier for them to kill him.

'Get fucked!' he snapped back.

Both gunmen blinked. They hadn't been expecting that. Sean allowed himself a little victory but he knew he would pay for it. The pistol bearer took a step closer to him. Instead of the expected gunshot, the man saw the bootlace around his neck that held his dog tags. He reached down and yanked them out, the bootlace cutting Sean's neck before it snapped. The man looked at them, rolled them over in his hands.

'Where are yeh from?'

Shit! Sean suddenly thought he might still be able to get out of this alive.

'Australia,' he said quickly.

A third man came into the room. This one wasn't dressed in jeans and a leather or army jacket like the others. This one wore a royal blue three-piece suit with smart black leather shoes to complete the image.

Clearly in charge, he still wore a black balaclava, his brown eyes almost hiding in the shadow of his brow.

'An Australian? Hmm. What were you doing with these other two men?' He spoke with an English accent that conveyed an educated upbringing and a life in the upper levels of society.

'They picked me up. I was hitching a ride up to Donegal.'

'Are you acquaintances with these other two men?'

'No.'

He had no sooner said the word when the pistol man bought down the ugly black weapon on Sean's forehead. He grunted with pain and dropped away from him, holding his hands over the bruised spot. The sharp pain made him feel like vomiting again.

'Stop lying Sean.'

Through the ringing sound in his head he realised they knew his name. He remembered his driver's license. At least it proved he was Australian.

'And those?' The suit motioned to the man with the pistol who was dangling the dog tags before him.

'I was a soldier.'

'But you're not anymore?'

'I quit.'

'You quit?'

'I wanted to travel but not to where the army wanted to send me.'

'Going to end up in Vietnam were you?'

Sean nodded.

'Doesn't matter. The American's are going to loose that war anyway but we're digressing. Did you come in from Cork? Waterford? Wexford, Sean? Or somewhere in Kerry?'

'I told you. I'm Australian! You've got my wallet. Those other…'

'Sean, I said stop lying. You've got no Irish punt on you, no passport. I reason you have only been in this country for a day or two. Plus you're travelling light. Why?'

He was talking to Sean the way a teacher does to a student who has been caught out in the midst of a prank.

'Cork,' he finally answered. He had no idea where half these places were so he just named the first one he could remember. 'I came across on a ferry from England. I landed a few days ago. I lost my passport somewhere in Cork. Pickpocket I think. I was hitch-hiking north when they picked me up.' He watched them closely, hoping to Christ they would buy his bullshit.

The suit looked aggravated. The pistol man shook his head. It wasn't looking good.

For a second he was reminded of a Vietnamese rebel they had captured after a battle which had seen the biggest losses to their regiment. He could see some of his mates interrogating the man, punching and kicking him as they asked him questions in a language he didn't understand. That man had sat balled up on the jungle floor trying to protect himself, not knowing if he was about to die (he didn't).

Now he was in that man's place.

'Do you expect us to believe that Sean? Firstly, no ferry that runs out of England lands in Cork. Cork ferries only leave from Swansea, Le Havre, Roscoff and Cherbourg. That's in Wales and France Sean. *Et si vous née en France, alors je suis un sale Irlandais.*' He shook his head with a smile knowing he was the only one in the room educated enough to understand his derogatory joke. 'Unless... you didn't come over on the Titanic did you Sean? It stopped in Cork, did you know that? No, you wouldn't. Secondly, men like that don't go around picking up hitch-hikers.' He said this like it had left a foul taste on his tongue.

Sean gave his best innocent look. 'Men like what?'

The suit smiled. 'The Provos, Sean. The Irish Republican Army. The only reason they would pull over would be to kill someone. But you are not dead.'

'So this makes you the Salvation fucken Army', Sean couldn't help himself.

The suit laughed at that.

'The Salvation Army? Ha, ha, ha! You hear that boys? That's good Sean! You're fucking funny!'

Sean didn't like the way he swore. It sounded unnatural. It didn't sound like he had ever sworn before.

The suit turned and said something out of earshot to someone outside. Footsteps faded away and the suit then turned back to Sean.

'So,' he said in a way that told everyone he was concluding their little talk, 'Can you help us out Sean by telling the truth? Think of Tom. Maybe you can still save him? Michael unfortunately would have died from the injuries sustained from his accident so we lessened his pain. It was for the better wouldn't you say so Sean? It doesn't have to be the same way for you or Tom.' He leaned forward like the School Principal Sean thought he could be outside of this torture room. 'Well Sean? Can you help me today by telling me where you had come from and your destination ?'

Sean looked at the floor, spitting out some blood. He then looked the principal in the eye.

'I don't know anything other than what I have told you so you can go and FUCK YOURSELF YOU TOFFEE-ARSED CUNT!!' He'd had enough. He wouldn't play ball with these pricks. They wouldn't get anything out of him except a mouthful of lip.

The Principal, as Sean now thought of him, walked over and bent down closer to him so his face was less than a foot away. Sean could smell food; a recent meal and wine on his breath. His suit had a few crumbs on the vest.

Good, he thought. *This wanker had to hurry his lunch down because of me. That'll make two little victories today.* He smirked in celebration.

The Principal looked into Sean's eyes. 'This isn't your fight mate. You'd best fuck off home.'

With that said, two more men came in; one carrying a length of four by two timber, the other had a claw hammer. The sight of the hammer made him reel with fear. He knew pain was coming. More pain. They came at him quickly and as Sean kicked out at one, the pistol man hit him in the face again. He slumped sideways to the floor, stars of white dancing across his vision. Then another punch. He blacked out for a second but then felt them un-cuff his hands. Forcing him over onto his back, they placed the centre of the two metre long piece of timber under his neck, the ends out left and right.

The realisation of what they were doing finally hit him too late. 'GET OFF ME!! YOU FUCKERS!! GET THE FUCK…' he screamed but another punch to his already broken nose shut him up.

The man with the claw hammer pulled several long roofing nails out of his pocket, each six inches long with a large flat disc at its head. They were designed to stop sheets of tin or other building materials sliding over the end of them. Here they would serve the same purpose but a more evil one. The pistol man held Sean's right arm flat against the wood beam and forced his fist open, his palm up. Sean groggily swore and spat. He tried to kick but someone was sitting on his knees. The hammer man held the nail's point on the centre of Sean's palm, raised the hammer and with one swift stroke drove the nail through the soft tissue and into the wood. Sean bellowed in pain as the muscles and nerves in the centre of his hand were speared. With each hit, white-hot pain shot up his arm as the nail buried past raw nerve endings. Only when the flat head of the nail pressed onto the bloody surface of his palm did the hammer man stop and move to the left hand. The pain doubled as he was secured to the beam, the hammer man missing the nail once, smashing into the ball of his thumb, instantly turning it black as blood formed under the surface. He screamed with every breath. The pain in his side had never seemed as bad as the pain he was suffering now. If he hadn't been in agony he would have heard them laughing at him, telling him to 'Go home yeh focken' t'ief, back to your convict fam'ly.'

The pistol man got sick of his screaming and bought the 9mm weapon down one final time onto his temple.

Unconsciousness saved him from feeling the worst of the beating.

TWENTY ONE

Rebecca Donahue had just turned off the N17 onto the small one lane road on her fortnightly visit to her parents outside the village of Belclare. They still lived in the same old farmhouse she herself had grown up in.

She had moved to Limerick after completing her degree in medicine at the University of Dublin and now worked in the Paediatrics Department of St John's Hospital in Limerick. Last year she had treated herself to a second-hand but show-room immaculate red '66 Alfa Romeo Spider 1600 Duetto and she was zipping along the narrow road when something in the gully by the road caught her eye. A second look as she sped by gave her goose bumps as she recognised the shapes as three human bodies lying side by side in the grass. Two were facing down either side of the third that was on his back, arms spread in a Jesus Christ pose. She hit the brakes, clouds of white smoke pouring from the tyres as she came to a stop. Reversing up, she could see blood covering each of them. Rebecca knew it was a professional hit before she opened her door. They were only a few yards off the road and she guessed they had only been recently dumped there. They stood out too much to be ignored or missed, even by the most fatigued driver. Turning her lights on to warn other drivers, she got out and hurried over to them. Her revulsion at such an act got worse when she realised the central "Jesus Christ" body was actually crucified, nailed to a length of timber.

As she knelt down to check for a pulse, Sean's eyes opened. She screamed with fright and almost fell over backwards. Gathering herself, her professionalism kicked in and she began checking him over.

Sean's mind was all over the place, half asleep, half aware, but all in pain. His hands felt like they were on fire, like he was gripping two hot coals. His face was swollen with great pressure.

'Please…' he mumbled through split lips and a minced face. 'I need help.'

'It's alroight,' Rebecca said to him, her voice full of reassurance. 'Ah'm a doctor.'

Behind her she heard the noise of a motor approaching. She turned and saw a truck full of sheep pull up.

'Are yeh alroight luv?' the driver called over to her. 'Oh Jaysuz!' he exclaimed upon seeing the bodies around her.

'Get to a phone! Call for an ambulance! GO!!' Rebecca ordered him and he took off up the road towards the nearest house.

Sean could feel the nails rubbing against the bones in his hands. Every minor movement he made transmitted more agony along his arms. Even breathing caused the slightest movement that translated to pain.

The woman that had been looking down at him had disappeared and all he could see was the cloud-patched sky. It was late afternoon and the sunset was painting them with borders of pink and orange. He lay as still as he could and watched them float by.

Rebecca ran back to her car and took the first aid kit out of the boot. She hurried back to him, placing the box by his shoulder and checked the pulses of the other two men either side of him. They were both dead. The younger one had a bullet hole in his temple. The older one looked to have been beaten to death. Being so old it would not have taken much for him to suffer a cardiac arrest or a fatal organ shut down.

She didn't bother rolling them over in case they had been booby trapped with mines or grenades as had been done in the past and she felt nervous just kneeling beside them.

Sean slipped back into unconsciousness again and when he came to, he was surrounded by police, paramedics and men in big green padded jackets and pants. It was the bomb squad. They were talking to the police, nodding in agreement about something.

The woman appeared above him again. Beside her knelt a couple of paramedics.

'Here 'e comes. He's awake now.'

'Just hold still mate,' the red headed medic said to him as he hooked up a drip line into his right arm. 'We'll have yeh out o' here in a sec'.'

'What are they doing?' he asked them in a groggy, slow voice.

'The Army. They just had tuh check yeh ov'r before we could move yeh. It's nothing to worry about mate.'

'Sean,' he said quietly, pain washing up and down his body.

'What's that?' Rebecca asked, leaning closer.

'My name's Sean.'

She smiled down at him. 'Hello Sean. I'm Rebecca.'

'How's it goin' Rebecca,' he whispered as his strength began to fade again.

'Ah was doin' foine until ah ran into you. Ruined mah weekend now, yeh know.' She let out a small chuckle.

'Sorry about that,' he grinned through busted lips and closed his eyes again.

He didn't see them load Tom and Michael into body bags.

But he didn't have to. He knew they were gone.

The third floor of the University College Hospital gave Sean a good view of Galway. From his bed by the window he could see down to the River Comb, the city centre beyond it with the docks and the Bay of Galway to the south. There wasn't a cloud in the sky and a light nor' westerly chilled the town. He could see a few rugged up locals beneath him in the streets fighting off the cooler-than-normal summer wind. The hospital however was warm and comfortable.

It was his third day in there. His first had comprised of minor surgery to both hands. His nose had been reset and the cuts and bruises on his face and wrists had begun to heal. He looked down at the bandages around the centre of his hands, the image of the nails still clear in his mind. The pain of the ordeal was still there in his memory. The wound would heal and the bruising would go but he would have the scars of a violent *stigmata* for the rest of his life.

When he had come out of the recovery ward, the police of the Republic of Ireland, the Garda Sionchana, were there to question him. They asked if he had any identification but he told them it had been stolen, passport and everything, by the masked men allowing him to give them a false surname. He said he had been hitching up north and was picked up by the two men in the blue sedan.

Sean hoped his poor acting paid off when he seemed shocked to the question of his links to any known paramilitary members. They asked how long he had been in the country, how he got there, what he was doing there and more questions that Sean lied in answer. He gave a few valid answers about his attackers but nothing they couldn't have found out themselves. Thanking him for his time, the two men left, saying they would be back before his release.

Sean knew they would eventually find out he was here illegally and he would be arrested and deported back to Sydney under Police or even Military escort by the Australian embassy in Dublin. He wondered if the embassy would have details of Australians on the run. He wasn't sure but decided to play it like they knew everything about him. It surprised him an embassy pen-pusher hadn't been in contact with him, even to see if he needed any assistance. Surely they had to be on their way.

To be on the safe side, the Garda had left an officer on the wing just outside of his room. 'Purely tuh make sure no one comes back teh cause yeh any more harm' they had told him but he knew it was to make sure he didn't do a runner.

He had to get out of there. He thought about knocking the copper out but he didn't have the strength in his hands to use them properly yet.

His clothes had been taken away for examination so he only had the gown he was wearing and some hospital slippers. The bag with his spare clothes and all his cash was gone.

Rebecca had called in on the second day to check up on him. She was on her way back home to Limerick from her parents. The night of his arrival at the hospital, she had stood in during surgery to make sure he was going to be alright. After an interesting conversation with the head surgeon about the possible origins of the scars covering Sean's back and legs, she had travelled to her parents, not getting there until after midnight. Sean had told her not to fuss about it but thanked her sincerely for all she had done for him. He thought about asking her for some clothes so he could later escape but he didn't want to involve her more than he had to. She was too kind a person to drag down into his troubles. When she left for home, she gave the nurse on duty her business card to give to Sean on his release, knowing he would be too proud to take it from her personally.

The events of that terrible day had made it into most of the national papers. One photo showed the scene where he was found and some medical personnel involved in his rescue standing over three obscured figures. None of them had found out his name but most had discovered he was Australian. The embassy would definitely be on its way now.

One of the papers that ran it as a front page headline was *An Phoblacht*, the republican newspaper that was backed by the Sinn Féin, the pro-republic political party. It had been set up back in February by two former IRA veterans Hugh McAteer and Jimmy Steele

'2 MURDERED, 1 CRUCIFIED' was the bold headline.

Sean hadn't seen this particular paper but someone he knew had.

The nurse on duty walked in, drawing his attention away from the picturesque city. She was a dumpy little woman with a cute face and a personality that could make anyone smile. Violet was her name.

'How are yeh feeling Sean?' she chirped as she entered. Always happy was Violet.

'Good thanks,' he answered, trying unsuccessfully to emulate her joy for life. 'My hands are a lot better now.'

'That's good then dear. You've had another dozen calls today from the media trying to get yeh to do an interview. Are yeh sure yeh don't want to? Some of them are offering money for only five minutes of yer time.'

'I'm just not up to it yet,' he lied. The last thing he wanted was his name and photo all over the world's press.

'Don't worry dear. Nothing gets past old Violet!' She smiled to herself before continuing. 'Speaking of which, there are a couple o' gentlemen out in reception at the moment who would like tuh visit with yeh. Say they know yeh. The Garda won't let them in until yeh agree. Do you know a Daniel and Padraig from Donegal?'

Sean's eyes lit up. He was getting out of here.

'Yes. They're friends of mine.'

'Roight so then. I'll tell the officer you'd like to see them.'

She left and a few moments later, after signing false names and addresses on the Garda's visiting sheet, Daniel and Padraig were escorted in, Violet leading the way.

'Eh scrapper!' Padraig almost yelled as he came in.

'Please sir,' Violet corrected him without losing her loving glow, 'There are other patients on this floor that need rest.'

'Oops, sorry love,' he said with a laugh. 'It's just good to see him that's all.'

Smiling, she left them to talk.

The Sean they had seen a few days earlier in Dingle wasn't in that bed. The man they were looking at had changed. Apart from the grotesque bruises and swelling on his face and the bandages around his forehead and hands, they could tell something else in him had changed. He seemed stronger.

They didn't have to come back for him but they had to see how much he had told the Garda. It was worth the risk.

'Fockers,' Padraig uttered as he looked at his wounds. 'Put yeh on a cross?! That's fockin rough!'

'You don't know how glad I am to see you two,' Sean smiled as he sat up. Up until them walking in, he thought he was screwed, bound for home and gaol. 'Is Kieran here as well?'

'He's headed on back to Belfast.'

'Did you see it in the papers?'

'I'm sure I picked up one paper and they were mentioning you in the feckin' shippin' news!' Daniel laughed as he sat down on a chair beside him. 'It's everywhere.'

'I'm sorry I couldn't help Michael and Tom,' Sean said with regret, bringing the mood down some. 'They killed Michael minutes after taking us.' He sighed as he heard Tom still screaming out his son's name.

'Fock. Tom and Michael…' Padraig just shook his head. 'Their funerals are tomorrow, back in Dingle.'

'Cunts 'll pay for this,' Daniel uttered with assurance.

Padraig looked at Sean's medical chart at the end of his bed. 'Has anyone from your embassy been in yet?'

'No, but the cops want to see me again first thing in the morning.'

'Do yeh need a hand?'

'I need some clothes…'

'Done.'

'…and some money…'

'Yep.'

'Padraig…I can't go to gaol.'

'You saying you want out of here?'

Sean just nodded.

The elder Irishman nodded as he mulled over things in his mind. He stood there quietly for a bit as he looked at Sean's wounds. *He was a strong lad, that's for sure. If only…no. Too early.* He let the thought go and turned to Daniel. 'He's gonna need some place to rest for a while.'

'That's fine,' was all Daniel replied.

'Okay.' Padraig smiled down at him. 'We'll be back t'noight before visitin' hours are over. Don't go falling asleep on us now.'

'I'll be waiting.'

They got up and left, leaving Sean in a much better mood than he had been before they had provided a way out.

Just shy of nine they arrived. This time another man was with them. He was dressed poorly, smelt a little unpleasant and wore a heavy black beard in good need of a trim. He, Padraig and Daniel were escorted by the new matron on duty up to the new Gardee who himself had just taken over for the night shift. She left them and returned to her office.

Daniel watched as Padraig approached the young man in blue, pulling him aside and talking softly, up close to his ear. The officer looked at the man in the dishevelled clothing and nodded, aware of who they were and why they were here. Just as the Royal Ulster Constabulary in the north had sympathisers for the loyalists, the Garda in the republic sometimes unknowingly employed republican sympathisers who would leak information or carry out favours for the IRA. Padraig shook the man's hand and they slipped into Sean's room.

The young constable made sure the door closed behind them and sat back down, silently praying they would not be found out. He could hear movement in the room. The bed groaned as weight shifted around on it.

Hurry up lads, he thought to himself.

'It's a good night to be indoors isn't it constable,' the voice said from behind him down the hall.

He turned to see a nurse coming towards him, the cute brunette with her tight fitting uniform, a clip board nestled under her arm. *Christ. Keep walking love.*

She stopped beside him.

'Better in here getting paid to read the paper than out there chasing drunken teenagers around,' he replied with a smile.

'Right-so, that wind coming in off the sea has picked up.' She looked up at the door to Sean's room. 'These will have to be his last visitors tonight. That young man needs some rest.'

'Don't worry about a thing love. I've already told them to make it quick.'

He saw her smile and wondered if the smile was hinting at something else. She had been past twice before already. *Of all the times to be getting flirty*, he thought, *it had to be now*.

So use it then.

'I was wondering if you might be able to round me up a cup of tea. I'm not allowed to leave my post you see…'

'Cream and sugar?' she interrupted.

'That'd be grand. Make it as sweet as you.' He returned her smile and watched her head down the hall.

This might not be a bad night after all, he said to himself.

The door behind him opened. The three men emerged.

'Have a good one officer,' one of them called back as they headed for the exit.

'Night then,' he replied as he watched them walk to the stairs. As they disappeared around the corner, the biased representative of law in Ireland stood up and looked through the door to see the patient settling in for the night. All was fine so he went back to his paper all the while thinking about the dark haired nurse.

As they reached the car park, Sean made sure his bandaged hands were deep in the pockets of the bum's coat. He felt dirty just thinking about it. The smell of sweat and tobacco were almost overpowering.

The lighting was poor here so no one would realise that the three men that had entered the hospital were not the same men leaving. They crossed to the light grey Opel parked in the shadows. Daniel opened the rear passenger door for Sean and they were soon speeding along the darkened streets out of town and away from the hospital and the homeless man who was getting a good night sleep in a comfortable bed.

Sean told them all he knew off his attackers.

'Did they say who they were?' Daniel asked as he overtook a semi, accelerating hard to get around him.

'No. The bloke in the suit had an English accent.'

'Probably UVF,' Padraig said. 'Strange for them to be down this far. I might see if our lads down here know of anything happening. Strange.'

Dan settled back in around the truck. 'Who's our Galway commander?'

'Neville White.'

'UVF?' Sean inquired.

'Ulster Volunteer Force. Loyalists who support the Monarchy and all its bullshit. Re-formed a few years back. Not nice people to go getting in trouble with Sean. Especially if yer a Cath'lic.'

'Shit, I've never heard of this other group. On the news back home it's all IRA.'

'That's because yeh live in the British Commonwealth. All yer news in biased towards the focken Queen. You never hear of the hard times those conts put us through, all the torture and kidnappings of innocents. Women and children included.'

'There's a few loyalist groups,' Daniel explained. 'UVF is the main one. They have their breakaway variations just the same as we have ours. It's almost a year since the IRA split into two; the Provisional IRA an' the Official IRA. We try not to step on each other's toes but sometimes it happens. These are crazy times right now Sean. Marxist socialism, communism, republicans, loyalists, unionists, traditionalists and atheists. That's just in Belfast.'

They drove northeast, through Athlone, Cavan, stopping at Kilconny, a small town only a few miles from the border. A safe house on the south side of town was ready for them.

They drove past once to make sure everything was clear. Once the signal was given from inside the house they drove around the back to a dirt alley that led by the rear garden shed. They parked and walked inside. It was close to two in the morning but they were just as cautious as they would have been if it were midday.

The fireplace had been stoked and two giants, hard boys that had seen plenty of fighting and plenty of prison cells as well, welcomed them.

Padraig introduced Sean. 'This is Neil and Liam. They're good lads. Boys, this is Sean.'

'How's it goin' Sean?' Liam asked, 'We read about yeh in the papers. Are yeh alroight?'

'A bit sore but I'll be fine, thanks.'

'Here,' Neil ushered him towards the big arm chair by the fire but within reach of the main table. 'Have a seat. Are yeh hungry? Can I get yeh a drink?'

Sean thought it quietly amusing that these gorillas of men were nursing him like two worried mothers. 'Anything with alcohol in it,' he grinned.

'Aww,' Daniel joked as he sat down beside him. 'There's nothin' wrong wit' yeh at all!' He laughed as he moved one of the ageing but well used Tommy guns off the table to make room for his own glass. 'Christ I'm hungry. What food have yeh got here?'

'Tomorrow we'll get across the border and head home,' Padraig announced. He turned to Sean, 'Dan'll put you op fer a while until yer back on yer feet.'

Sean looked over at Daniel who just smiled and nodded back at him.

'Thanks mate. I appreciate this. I appreciate everything you lads have done for me. With the amount of bad luck I'm having lately…'

'It's no problem for me, Sean. It's mah sister Melissa you'll have to impress if yeh want a peaceful recovery.'

'You live with your sister?'

'Aye. Last year Craig was killed and the Prods came and forced her out of her home. Craig was my brother-in-law. It's me and Melissa but the real boss o' the house is Max. Mel's son. He's four. So for feck sake don't get on the wrong side of him!'

TWENTY TWO

The cows rested quietly beside the hedge under an ageing oak. They had ambled down from the hills twenty minutes ago and as luck would have it, stopped only ten yards in front of the men hidden in the shadows. The only thing in their favour was the lack of cow bells around the fat beasts. The hidden soldiers were surprised their own presence had gone unnoticed; not by those inside but by the overfed cattle. For over five hours now they had been watching the small stone building using newly issued night vision goggles. It only gave them a forty-degree view that was grainy with its blotched green and black image but it was a view that would otherwise be completely invisible to the naked eye. Using only the light provided by the stars overhead, the goggles strapped to their heads had revealed three people had crossed the short lawn and entered the farmhouse only an hour before. No one had come or gone since then. The lamps inside had gone out twenty minutes ago leaving the low flickering light of the fire dancing over the inside of the kitchen window.

For one soldier this was a new type of warfare. He was amongst the best in the world and had proven himself countless times on the battlefield. But here it was a new arena. And he was determined to be the best here as well.

In his earpiece he heard three clicks: their signal for one minute. Lowering a black gloved hand to a small hand piece, he clicked the receiver twice: Affirmative.

He heard two responding clicks, two more and then another pair; Go time. Turning his head slightly to the side, he nodded to his mate beside him. A double tap to his arm came back. They were ready. His gun lay beside him, a shortened version of the M16 known as a CAR 15 or XM177 but referred to by soldiers as the Colt Commando and used primarily by Special Forces. It was now cold and wet with the dew that lay over the ridge line. Grasping it, he and the team got to their knees, squatting, not taking their eyes off the building. The cows were yet to move.

He concentrated on his breathing, running through his pre-planned actions.

Move cleanly, deliberately and quickly and clear your sector.

Drop anything remotely hostile but watch your background for friendlies.

Subdue all others.

Double click. Go.

It had been a long day for the young Irishman. He had been up since seven that morning and the warmth of the fire soothed his tired muscles. He craved a hot bath, to sit up to his shoulders in cleansing soapy water and smoke his pipe, a cup of tea, pale with too much milk on a stool by his side, a radio playing softly in the background. But here he was out in the country side in a building older than his Nan's Nan, sitting in an uncomfortable chair in filthy clothes which smelt of dry sweat, smoking a cigarette given to him before the others had retired for the night just to keep watch in case someone came snooping around. His only atonement was the fire. He stared into and beyond the crackling coals and flames; his thoughts taking him home to his family.

Without realising it, he was dozing, his head bobbing as he tried to stay awake. He didn't hear the highland cattle startle and trot away as they were spooked outside.

The door to his left burst open and something exploded half a second later on the ground to his right with a tremendous concussive force, temporarily blinding him, his head ringing, his senses useless. The pressure wave of the explosion had punched him hard in the chest and he was disorientated and unable to react. From the same door a harsh white light cut through the darkness, sweeping its way across the room. A second light came from the doorway at the far end of the room and swept the opposite way. He caught an image, a silhouette of a figure in black. He forced himself to reach for the assault rifle that leant against the small table beside him. His hand reached the ugly black weapon which had been warmed by the fire just as the first beam zeroed in on him. He died sitting in that uncomfortable chair, his hand spattered in blood as it convulsed and knocked the rifle to the floor.

The familiar smell of burnt cordite filled the room, the smoke of it reflecting the high-intensity torch beam under the barrel of his gun.

'Clear!' the soldier called as he saw the life vanish from his target.

Behind him the other five equally disguised figures entered the small bedrooms off the hall. As soon as the doors crashed inward he heard screams of 'Hands up! Don't fucken move!!' but their warnings were ignored. More gunfire exploded in the confined space, shaking the air around them. After a few seconds the calls came back; 'Clear!'

His heart was still racing, his mind charged with adrenalin as he stepped around the dead boy in the chair. The rifle on the ground had its safety off but there was no way the lad could have gotten the drop on the home invaders. No one ever did. It was what they trained for. They were the best soldiers on the planet and few could rival them in the application of their trade. They were the British Special Air Service.

'Two prisoners in the first bedroom,' one of them called out.

'One dead, second bedroom,' a second confirmed.

All six men of the 22nd Regiment SAS, each dressed in black with their faces covered by a balaclava converged on the lounge room.

The prisoners, two men aged in their thirties, still dressed in their daily attire were dragged out by their feet on their bellies to the lounge room, their hands cuffed behind their backs. Neither spoke but the looks of rage on their faces told the story as they looked up at their dead comrade, his chest and throat a bloody red pulp. His eyes were still open, his face still contorted in surprise.

The soldier returning from the second bedroom turned to the man who had killed the boy. 'Call base, tell 'em to prepare for prisoners,' he said in his gruff South London/Cockney accent. 'We'll start an immediate sweep for the weapons and booby traps.' He pointed behind him, 'Tell 'em the one in the bedroom was Glenn Brown.'

Nodding, the soldier that had fired the first shots of the night took the transmitter in his hand and walked outside to the crisp air of the eastern Scottish Highlands to ensure a clear transmission. He could see the faint, yellow lights of Stonehaven almost twelve miles away on the east coast.

'Red base, Blue team.' From the bushes he saw the movement of the remainder of the SAS team that had chosen the short straw and covered their entry. They were kicking themselves they didn't get to breach and clear.

'*Go Blue*,' the reply was almost instant.

'Two, repeat two targets down with two, repeat two prisoners.' He turned and walked back to the open door, looking down on the captured men, the whites of his eyes like a pair of cold beacons burning through his black balaclava. The looks coming back at him were a mixture of rage, fear and confusion. It was his accent that caused them to be nonplussed.

'*Roger, Blue team. ID on deceased?*'

'Deceased; one Brown, Glenn and one Hall, Christopher. In custody; one O'Connell, William and one O'Connell, Eamonn.'

'*Roger Blue team. Second squad inbound with local authorities. Prisoners to be handed over once they arrive. Hand over once search complete and RTB.*'

'Understood. Blue team out.'

The prisoners had reason to be taken aback at this man's voice. His accent was Australian. On active duty exchange from the southern country of Britain's Commonwealth was Sergeant Andrew Wilton.

TWENTY THREE

Sean dreamt about the jungle. Joel was on point and crouched down on the green leafy floor, his boots swimming in a sea of…clover? Yes, it was clover. Not leaf litter or red dirt or shrubs or fallen branches covering the floor, but clover.

Come closer, Spud.

Joel was motioning to him, leaning against a tall giant, probably hundreds of years old. He peered around the base of the tree, surveying the land ahead. He motioned for him again.

Come closer.

Cautiously he crept forward, his eyes scanning the ground for traps and tunnels. All he saw, however, was a never-ending carpet of soft, lush clover, the endless green broken up here and there by tree trunks, their roots smothered by the small tri-heart shaped trifolium.

The canopy seemed excessively high here; at least 300 feet up. Sunlight pierced through in small, brilliant beams, illuminating the leafy ground, turning it a dazzling green.

He looked for Joel.

Come closer.

The more he moved forward, the further Joel seemed to be.

Come closer.

I'm trying.

Come closer.

I am.

Listen.

What?

Get down.

Why?

Joel motioned upwards with nothing more than a movement of his eyes.

Get down.

Sean could hear it now, moving fast through the air, tearing the sky in two with a deep roar.

Get down.

It was the sound of incoming artillery.

Get down.

It was homing in on him like a screaming locomotive.

Get down.

He dropped to the ground; the cool, dewy clover softly kissing his face.

Here it comes.

Sean didn't know if he had rolled off the lounge before or after the explosion. He lifted his head from the rug and wondered if the rolling, echoing noise was outside in the city of Belfast or a remnant of his dream. As he sat up a light flooded over him.

'Are you alright?' Daniel asked as he crossed the lounge room to the window wearing only his underwear.

'What was that?'

'Bomb. A big one.'

Sean hurried over and looked out into a neighbourhood waking up. Squares of light flickered on up and down the opposite tenement building, a mirror image of their own.

'See the smoke?' Daniel pointed out a dirty column that rose diagonally with the sea breeze less than a mile away, the black column lighter than the artificially lit night sky. The base of it shimmered orange, picking up the flames of its source.

'Gotta be the RUC building on Springfield Road.'

Sirens drifted up to them, the buildings in the distance reflecting their strobing lights. A quick crackle of gunfire sounded and died. No reply came back. Sean was still looking down on the suburb of Ballymurphy – the Murph – below and to the north from the third storey window of Daniel's flat when he heard someone behind him.

'Where is it?'

He turned to see Melissa, Daniel's sister, headed towards them, a robe pulled around her.

'RUC building on Springfield I think,' Dan repeated to his sister, his gaze never leaving the scene.

'Christ, it was loud,' she said as she stepped up beside Sean.

She was slightly shorter than he. Her long brown hair framed a naturally attractive face, a face that could be hard to overlook in a crowd. When he met her only several hours earlier he hadn't noticed, but now, under the hugging gown, he noticed a figure that showed no signs of motherhood.

Max must keep her active, he thought.

An image of a pregnant Anna popped into his mind and he subconsciously blinked hard trying to erase the picture, a shiver of cold stabbing over his body.

Suddenly he realised that in the excitement of the situation he had forgotten he too was wearing only jocks. He ducked over to the lounge and pulled on the jeans Daniel had lent him. Cursing under his breath with pain, his bandaged hands fumbled with the top button. As he reached for his shirt someone knocked rapidly on the front door.

'Are you awake Danny?' a voice called out from the balcony that ran the full length of the building.

'For fuck sake!' Daniel asserted as he opened it to a skinny balding man in his thirties. 'Keep it down! Max is still asleep.'

He nodded his apologies. 'Sorry Mel.' He turned to Daniel. 'We're needed. Best get a move on.'

'Come in. I'll be two seconds.'

The skinny man slipped into the apartment as Daniel ducked off down the hall.

At first he hadn't seen him sitting there, doing up the buttons of a shirt but now skinny stopped and looked warily at Sean. Mel saw the worried reaction and stepped in.

'Donnie, this is Sean *Dockerty*,' she said, again using the Irish pronunciation of his surname. 'Sean, Don Blackmore.'

Donnie held his hand out. 'How's about you Sean?'

'Fine thanks mate,' Sean stood to greet him but Donnie baulked at the bandages.

'Ahh, so you're *that* Sean!' He nodded again. 'How they comin' along?'

'Getting' there.'

Daniel returned zipping up his jacket. 'I think Max is awake.'

'Nice one boys,' Mel said sarcastically but made no move to check up on him hoping he would re-settle.

'Sorry, Mel.' Donnie looked over his shoulder out the door. The thumping of an approaching helicopter caught his attention and he stepped out onto the balcony, eyeing the sky. It passed wide of them before continuing on to the bomb site. He stepped back inside.

Daniel kissed his sister on the cheek. 'Back soon.' He gave Sean's arm a pat as he hurried past, following Donnie out into the early morning.

Sean felt like a fifth wheel just standing there, not being able to help, sleeping on their lounge, getting in their way. He saw more people hurry past the window, men dressed in dark colours, one carrying a vintage sub-machine gun of some description. In the distance the familiar crackle of a Kalashnikov re-announced itself.

He turned to Mel who was putting the kettle on. She placed two miss-matched and chipped mugs on the counter and turned to face her new guest.

'Welcome to Belfast.'

TWENTY FOUR

The lounge on which Sean slept was surprisingly comfortable; its ability to be used as a bed had been vouched for by Daniel who said he had used it on several drunken occasions when his own bedroom had seemed too far away. He rolled over onto his side and pulled the blanket up under his chin. He opened his eyes. Looking back at him was another set of eyes that belonged to four year old Max, his face only a foot away from his own.

Sean blinked as he focused on the boy. He was sitting on a small chair he had dragged up to the lounge's edge. Max seemed to be studying the new face in his house. He sat there in silence, not moving, just observing. He showed no fear. This was, after all, *his* house.

Sean yawned.

Max looked back at him and with the honesty that only a child could get away with said, 'Your breath stinks.'

'You must be Max,' he laughed. 'Well I apologise Max and I promise I will clean my teeth the second I get out of bed.'

'Its no' a bed. It's my lounge.' Max leaned forward slightly and almost whispered, 'An' you talk funny.'

Sean growled and made a scary face and laughed as Max screamed and ran off down the hall back to his own room.

'So that's how you get your kicks then. Scarin' wee bairns.' It was Daniel's voice behind him.

Sitting up he saw his new friend smoking by the kitchen window, the yellowing wallpaper testament to his habit. He slumped back in a battered red armchair. He looked as though he hadn't slept.

'Hey.'

'Sleep alright?'

'Yeah. You okay? I didn't hear you come back.'

Daniel sighed.

'Yeah, I'm fine.' The last of his cigarette fizzled out as it dropped into one of the chipped teacups. He turned his head to look out into the bright morning. It was meant to be a nice summer's day but he was hating it already.

Sean could see he was in no mood for pleasant banter. After dressing and folding up the blankets, he put the kettle on and sat at the kitchen table. Finally he asked, 'What happened?'

Daniel ran his fingers through his hair, his red eyes still gazing out to the city below.

'The Brits arrested dozens of innocent civilians last night. One of them had been shot in the stomach, just an old man. They wouldn't even stop the fucken bleedin'. Just threw him into the truck and drove 'em all away. It's been a bad week. Just found out the SAS killed two more of ours yesterday in Scotland; one of our active service units. Funerals should be next week. Depends on when the bastards will release the bodies.' He rubbed his eyes and groaned. 'Can you watch Max for a few hours? I need a bath, take a nap. I'm fucked.'

'Sure.'

'Thanks.' He got up and rolled his head from side to side, his neck cracking loudly. 'Melissa just ducked out to get some milk. I'll take you out to find some clothes then around to meet the lads. Make yourself at home.' He shuffled up the hall leaving Sean alone in a strange house looking after a stranger's kid in a strange war torn country.

Yet Sean felt although things weren't at their best, it was a new start for him.

Melanie Doherty turned to her father; the look of fear and shock on her face opposed that of his, which was one of confusion.

'How bad is this? He's not that old!' Melanie objected. 'Why is this happening now?'

Part of her wished she hadn't nagged her father into going to the doctor after hearing him fighting for breath after a short stroll to the pub the other day. She had literally dragged him into the doctor's office and being stronger willed than him, she got her way.

The doctor leaned back in his padded chair and placed his glasses on the desk. He looked the older man directly in his eyes as he continued with the bad news.

'Whatever is causing this has led to a massive reduction in your lung's capacity. It may feel as though this has just occurred but I believe your lungs have been deteriorating for a while.' He sighed and picked up his glasses again, scanning the paperwork before him. 'So before yesterday you say you had no chest constriction, no short breath…'

'None.' The father of three breathed in and wondered if he was now imagining the short raspy intake or if it was getting worse. 'I walk every day to work. Always take the same path. Yesterday though… I just couldn't get over the hill.'

'What if he stops smoking?' Melanie queried. 'Would it become better, you know, repair itself?'

The doctor pursed his lips. 'Quitting could slow the rate of damage and maybe, and I mean maybe, it would get gradually better. But…' he shook his head. 'The lungs don't have regenerative capabilities. It may not even be the smoking. It could be something toxic you may have inhaled; a chemical at your workplace, fumes of some sort..?'

Melanie looked back at her father, her hand squeezing his to let him know he wasn't alone in this. 'Is there anything dangerous at work? Paint? Chemicals?'

'Not that I know of. None of the other blokes at work are sick.'

'You work at the steel works right?' The doctor looked up from his notes.

Mr Doherty nodded. 'Relining the furnaces.'

'The products you use, they produce a lot of airborne particles, don't they?'

'Yeah. All the time. Why?'

'Do you use any respiratory protection like masks?'

'No.'

The doctor sat quietly for a while, his eyes staring through the wall beside him as he thought. Finally he turned back to them.

'We will have to look into running some tests. I have seen this before though. Do you use asbestos anywhere at all at work?' Mr Doherty nodded. 'Asbestos,' the doctor continued, 'is a mineral and its affects on the respiratory system *are* being found out to be harmful. The tiny fibres become airborne and if inhaled they can cause scarring of the lung. The scars go on to form tumours, restricting the ability of the lungs quite dramatically. It's like breathing in minuscule pieces of barbed wire.'

Mr Doherty nodded again. He knew the material they used contained it but none of them knew it was that dangerous. In his mind he saw the big clouds of dust they would work in day after day.

The doctor sighed. 'At first I thought it might have had something to do with your years in the army but everything is pointing towards your current job. It's called Asbestosis. A form of Pneumoconiosis. If the person smokes it does increase the risk of lung cancer. We're going to need to get some chest X-rays taken.'

Melanie and her father looked at each other, not believing what they were hearing.

TWENTY FIVE

Would this city bury itself? Sean wondered this as he and Daniel walked past the largest Catholic cemetery in Belfast. The city – which took its name from *Béal Feirste* meaning "mouth of the sandbars" where the River Farset met the mouth of the sea – had been awake most of the night. It was as tired as he. Riots filled the streets almost every night, gunshots would be exchanged between Catholic and Protestant mobs with British soldiers and the Royal Ulster Constabulary seeming to just sit back and bare witness with no intention of stopping it.

Daniel had explained to him about the Orange Parades and how every year on July 12th the Orange Order marched through the streets of Belfast to celebrate Protestant King William's victory over the Catholic King James at the Battle of the Boyne in 1690. The marches of thousands of men in bowler hats, thrusting closed umbrellas and walking canes and wearing orange sashes could last for months. Most of the time they insisted on marching past or even through the suburbs and ghettos of their adversaries. This inevitably bought sectarian violence and retaliatory attacks making the summers in Belfast the most dangerously explosive months.

Less than a mile from where they now walked the riots of last night had broken through the barricades and almost seven hundred young, angry Protestants, fuelled up by a prior Orange march, had begun a two hour running battle with the locals along Crumlin Road in the suburb of Ardoyne. The fear of dozens of Catholic families being forcibly evicted to watch their homes and all but what they were wearing burnt to the ground had caused the IRA to act in defence. Three loyalist gunmen were killed and over a dozen were wounded as the IRA defended the area and repelled the crowd back north, doing the job of the police.

It was now near five in the afternoon and the city seemed quiet but tense. Smoke still climbed into the air from fires not too far away and Sean already knew tonight would be no different. Traffic hummed in the distance, kids played in the grassed boundaries of the cemetery kicking soccer balls and teasing each other. From a window here or a balcony there came the sounds of a radio playing a new Credence Clearwater Revival song on the radio.

No sirens, no helicopters, no gunshots, no bombs, no screaming, no dying.

Give it time, Sean thought. *The sun's still up.*

They chatted as they walked and Sean was told of how the IRA came about.

The group known throughout the western world over as a terrorist organisation descended from the Irish Volunteers, a dedicated and patriotic group established in 1913 that staged the failed but now famous Easter Rising in April three years later. The Irish Volunteers were recognised by the Dáil Eireann – the revolutionary parliament of the self-declared Irish Republic – as the legitimate army of its land thus becoming known as the Irish Republican Army. Because the Dáil's manifesto refused to recognise the British Parliament at Westminster, the IRA then waged a guerilla campaign against British rule in Ireland during the 1919-21 Irish War of Independence which ended with the signing of the Anglo-Irish treaty. This treaty divided the country, gave the southern twenty six counties to the republic and allowed the British to keep rule over the six counties to the north. Naturally many within the IRA were opposed to any division of its homeland so a split also occurred within it's ranks. Some backed the pro-treaty Free State National Army led by Michael Collins. The anti-treaty IRA now had to fight a civil war with its former comrades over the next eleven months. The IRA eventually lost.

They did not, however, die out. Its members laid low with the intention of one day overthrowing the British rule in the north and reunifying their northern brothers with the Irish Republic to the south.

A second campaign against the British north was tried during World War II but, again, failed. The third attempt was codenamed Operation Harvest and became known as the Border Campaign. From December 1956 to February 1962 the IRA from the south (the IRA in Belfast was inactive at the time) launched attacks at British and unionist targets with the goal of wearing the two governments down, causing the Crown to withdraw. But in the end it turned out to be a military failure for the republicans yet again. The number of men now in the IRA dropped dramatically. However they justified it as having kept the IRA in the hearts and minds of its people and provided a chance for priceless training.

Then in December 1969 the IRA faced yet another split within its ranks. Arguments broke out between its commanders about its ability to defend nationalist areas of Belfast and Derry from loyalist attacks. Even more controversial was its Army Council's decisions to now recognise the parliaments of Northern Ireland and Britain. From the division, the traditional republicans formed the Provisional IRA. They had the majority of the backing from its supporters; nine out of thirteen IRA units in Belfast sided with the Provisionals. The remainder formed the smaller Official IRA.

Following the violence of August 1969, the Provisional IRA began to arm and train to protect nationalist areas from further attack and began planning for an "all-out offensive action against the British occupation".

Sean also learnt of the grossly discriminating councils and government that forced Catholic families to live in poverty conditions, families of six or more being forced to live in single bedroom apartments while single Protestants were given brand new flats with multiple bedrooms. There was of course a political reason for this. The Representation of the People Bill introduced in 1946 only allowed ratepayers to vote in elections. There could be ten Catholics living in a house but only the one ratepayer was permitted to vote, a good way to keep the elections in the controlling hands of the Protestants. He was also shocked to discover the vast majority of the unemployed were Catholic, their jobs being given to their neighbours to the north even if they were not as qualified. Basically to be Catholic in Northern Ireland was to be a second-class citizen living in poverty.

They also talked about their own families and the differences of their childhoods. Daniel explained Donnie's roll in the IRA as being second in charge of several of the weapons stores in Ballymurphy and Lower Falls, someone to see when rifles and ammunition were needed.

Sean talked about his tryouts for the local representative side for Rugby League while Daniel explained how his dreams of one day playing for one of the big football team like Glasgow Celtics, St Patrick's Athletic of Dublin or even Manchester United had been taken away from him when he was just sixteen.

Sean noticed Daniel had stopped and was watching some young lads in the park kicking a soccer ball. Dan watched intently as one of the boys made a dash up the fence, passing the ball high into the crowd gathered in near the goals. The ball fell to three boys, but only one of them was quick enough to head the ball sharply to the keeper's right, barely missing his fingers as he dove for it. Daniel smiled as the boys jumped around in celebration.

If only…he thought to himself. He turned back to Sean. 'It's strange how things turn out in the end. Your life is never what you imagined it to be.'

They continued on their way, talking as they went. They held little back from each other, a trust having developed over the last few days. In a way it was a relief to talk about their own hard times; like talking to a councillor or a therapist and having some of their burden lifted off of them. A therapist however could never fully understand. Only a fellow soldier could. By the time they reached the small pub just off Falls Road they considered each other more than just acquaintances; they were well on their way to becoming close friends.

Turning up an access lane they approached Collins' Bar from the rear. The two men guarding the pub's rear doors had been notified of their arrival by spotters that were placed all over the suburb. The spotters in this area of the neighbourhood were just kids of at most thirteen years of age. One of the guards was dressed heavily for summer in a German Army jacket, a Tommy gun cradled in his arms. The other man looked like a hippie but had an old Lee Enfield .303 rifle slung over his shoulder. Both smiled a welcome as Daniel led Sean up the stairs.

'*Danny, maith thú a fheiceáil?*' the Tommy gun man asked in Irish.

'*Buachaillí go raibh maith agat Fine. Cén chaoi a bhfuil díbh féin?.*' Daniel replied and shook hands with them both then he introduced Sean in English. They shook his hand and ushered them both through the heavy doors.

The room was thick with smoke and the light that came in from the southern widows produced opaque beams of washed-out blue. On the far side of the bar the acrid smoke from a pipe curled its way up through the light like a charmed cobra. On seeing their entrance the barman began pulling two pints of Guinness.

The chatter of the pub was one of only a few sounds that relaxed Sean; a noise he had grown up with. For a second he could imagine James working behind the bar, Luke and Thomo pissed and laughing, sitting at the bar waiting for him.

Daniel led Sean to the bar. They were met by Donnie starting his second pint.

'Afternoon lads. You get some sleep Dan?'

'Aye. You been 'ere long?'

'No. Billy's just left. He's off to mass. Says 'e wants to meet you Sean.'

They grabbed their beers and headed for a table near the window.

'Who's Billy?' Sean asked.

'Billy McKee. He's the Belfast Brigade's OC. One of the big boys. Up there with Twomey and Cahill and Adams. Stick around long enough an' you'll meet 'em all.'

'Sorry we missed him. How was he?' Daniel queried.

'These riots have got him all jumpy. It's like he's full of fecken coffee.

Tommy O'Donnell, he's another staffy,' Donnie added for Sean's sake, 'he's sayin' that tonight's goin' to be worse. Word is the marchers are headin' towards Short Strand.'

'They're goin' to need help if it does.'

'What's Short Strand?' Sean cut in, feeling a little lost again.

'It's a Catholic area to the east, just over the Lagan. It's surrounded by a Proddie neighbourhood. If they get cut off the whole place could be burnt to the ground.'

'Nothin' planned as yet?'

Donnie sipped his Guinness then shook his head.

'Billy says to sit tight, but be ready.'

After a few pints and introducing Sean to some of the locals, the three ate dinner and watched the last of the news which showed images of last nights riots.

When Sean went to the toilet, Donnie leaned over to Daniel. 'If something happens tonight, do you want him with us?'

Daniel looked down the hall. 'I don't think we could stop him. I know I've only known him for a short while but that beating he got in Galway seemed to spark him up.'

'Can we trust him? Remember what happened in Derry?' This last question was more of a statement.

'He's no tout. He's the real thing.'

'Why is he doing this? This isn't his war.'

'The last bloke that said that to him nailed him to a fucking board. I wouldn't go saying that to him.'

'Well he certainly has balls.'

The TV glowed on into the night but none of them were watching it. The crowd had died leaving only half a dozen patrons including themselves. Donnie paced about nervously waiting for a phone call or a runner or something. All this tension and stress were killing him.

A phone rang behind the bar and the publican said a few words before handing the piece to Donnie. 'Hello?'

Both Daniel and Sean waited silently, each trying to hear the conversation. All Donnie did was nod back.

Daniel turned to Sean. 'Grab your jacket if you want to help.'

The battered Vauxhall tore along the back roads, weaving its way east through a city that seemed to be burning all around them. Rioting had spread almost the entire length of the city and the fires lay as beacons to the riots destructive path. For several blocks they raced alongside the tall impenetrable wall, the peace line that kept the areas segregated. The Brits called it the "interface". Some locals called it the second Berlin Wall.

They had already collected several guns from a weapons hold on Divis Drive in Lower Falls and were now heading towards the river. It was almost ten o'clock at night and they chose streets that were not overly crowded. The RUC and the British army were stretched thin across the city, being stopped and searched was not likely to happen. As long as they were not stupid and avoided the known checkpoints they should be all right.

The phone call had come from one of the 3rd Brigade soldiers in Short Strand. The Orange march had headed on past the isolated ghetto, stirring up an angry, vengeful crowd of hundreds in its wake, every one of them intent on making Short Strand part of their loyalist neighbourhood by forcing out the republican Catholics dead or alive. The target the mob was aiming for was the Catholic Church of St Matthew's. As far as anyone knew, the Army was again sitting on their hands letting it all happen and the police were as useful as a plough upstairs.

They crossed the River Lagan into East Belfast. This was an older part of the city, older than the Murph or Lower Falls. It was an area that was predominately loyalist paramilitary bar the tiny Catholic neighbourhood. Donnie pulled into an alley that ran along the south side of Bridge End, their path ahead blocked by burning double decker buses which had been hijacked by youths and parked across the road in the last half hour. Here they stopped, gathered the rifles and ran down darkened alleys towards the back fences of a group of houses. Donnie led them through a gate and up towards the back door of a three storey tenement. His knock was answered by a man in his forties. He led them swiftly through the crowded house and out the front. As Sean crossed the living room he was aware of the large group of people here and wondered if they had been evicted themselves.

Once outside on Strand Close they could hear it, the distant, muffled roar of a crowd. The riot was not far.

Adrenalin began to pump through him. The rush of carrying a loaded weapon into combat gave him some purpose again. He had direction again. Not since Vietnam had he felt like this, like he was living, not just existing.

They passed side streets that were empty and dark due to the lack of working street lamps. They passed shop fronts which wore hardboard wooden panels over or in place of glass. The road veered right and they arrived at the intersection of Saint Matthew's Court and Seaforde Street. Turning left they headed up the dead end road to the school and the home of St Matthew's Church.

A man ahead called out to them. 'Donnie. You come wi' me. You two cut through here. Come in on the far side of the church.' With that he turned and ran off down the road with Donnie towards the church.

'Let's go.' Daniel said and they headed for the lane that ran along the rear of the primary school beside the ancient building.

The sexton's house was fully ablaze and Sean hoped no one was trapped inside. As he ran he worked the bolt on the old German Mauser K98k, loading one of its five 8mm rounds into the breach, leaving the safety off the weary twenty six year old rifle. His pockets quietly rattled with the two cardboard boxes of extra ammunition, forty rounds in total. Daniel had four extra fifteen-round magazines for his M1 carbine. Both of them were furious the M16s which Chad had bought over were yet to be distributed amongst the northerners.

A flash of light from up ahead painted the houses a dirty orange; a petrol bomb thrown from within the loyalist's ranks. An echoing crack bounced off the weathered walls of the church, the gunman hidden somewhere in the shadows making them intuitively duck as they came up behind the parochial house. Another petrol bomb landed on the road ahead of them lighting up the area briefly. Sean could smell the burning fuel. It was a dirty odour that gave him shivers.

Napalm. Vietnam.

Remember the children that had been trapped in that burning village? Their screams? And the smell?

Fuck up, he told himself and forced his concentration back to the war at hand.

He also smelt the familiar burnt cordite, the gunpowder smell he loved so much.

Daniel crept up to the corner of the building and peered around. The crowd was only sixty yards away; their attention was elsewhere, probably the church and its defiant defenders. Sean knelt beside him and looked around the corner, the rifle butt tucked snugly into his shoulder. He watched the dozen or so at the head of the mob hurling stones down the road. Glass shattered somewhere.

Then they both saw them. Three gunmen were making their way around the edge of the crowd, coming in their direction. The three were yet to see Daniel and Sean.

The pair both bought up their rifles and took aim. Sean's heart was beating fast. He tried to control the rush that was fogging his thoughts. He focused on the man approaching them, estimating him being only eighty yards off. Sean heard Daniel flick off his safety but before he could fire they both saw the lead man shudder and fall half a second after the sound of a distant gunshot rang out. The two behind the lead man ran for cover beside a wall. The fallen man was still moving and calling out to his comrades.

Without hesitating, Daniel changed his aim to the men by the wall. He breathed out and squeezed the trigger.

Sean flinched at the cracking sound of the old American rifle and saw the shot go high, knocking brick dust from only inches above the man's head. Daniel squeezed the trigger a second time but the rifle jammed. He worked the bolt, ejecting the dud and chambering a new round as the two men across the way searched for the sniper.

Sean looked down along his rifle just as the two spied them. They were raising their own rifles towards him, dropping to their knees.

Everything was now in slow motion but with extreme clarity.

How did I get back here again? The thought came to him from nowhere as he tried to concentrate, but his mind wouldn't keep quiet. *Is this where I belong?* Sean bought the two open sights of the rifle into alignment. He focused on the front sight, then saw it blur as his focus shifted to the first man beyond it, aiming for the invisible line that ran between his shoulders, a centre-mass shot.

Just angry targets.

He squeezed the trigger. The rifle bucked hard, almost as hard as his SLR had in Vietnam.

Yes.

Yes I do belong here.

These people are now my family.

He kept his aim on the target as he followed through on the shot, the sights falling to the same spot as the recoil died. The man had fallen but he wasn't dead. He writhed around on the ground at the feet of his mate, screaming in pain. Sean reloaded as Daniel fired several quick shots, one of which punched a hole in the kneeling man's jacket but missing his body.

Sean saw Daniel's target hadn't reacted to the shot and knew he had missed. He now aimed on the same man. The front sight levelled on his chest, the man's own face looking down his own rifle sights back at them. The loyalist fired first. Both Sean and Daniel heard the bullet crack as it passed between them. Sean returned the favour but rushed missed. As he reloaded he heard several detonations beside him, chips of stone and cement hitting them both. Instinctively they both ducked. More rounds peppered their location.

'Get back!' he screamed at Daniel and they both retreated around the corner. The fire kept coming in on them. They ran back further, taking cover behind a tree, the gunshots chasing them all the way.

'He's up above us somewhere!' Daniel pointed out.

Sean gave a quick look around the tree towards a row of houses across Newtonards Road. In answer he saw the flashing of a burst of fire from an automatic weapon. Some rounds passed wide, some bore deep into the tree.

'Fuck! Submachine gun in one of the windows! We're fucked if we stay here!'

'I'll cover you. You run for the wall over there,' Daniel instructed.

'Fuck that! You run and I'll cover. I'm a better shot!'

From the far side of the church they could hear gunshots, both single and automatic.

'Go!' Sean ordered and as Daniel ran around the left of the tree, Sean bought his rifle around the right of it. He was expecting to see the muzzle flash chasing Daniel but the sniper had guessed what they were planning. Sean had to duck back in behind the tree as a volley of rounds hammered the ground around him.

Daniel made it to the safety of the wall and checked above and behind him for any more snipers. He was clear. Glancing across to the tree, he saw Sean looking back at him. Sean pointed to him and then the sniper. Daniel nodded. Sean was going to make a run for it. Daniel took in a few deep breaths and then stepped out around the corner, rifle up, finger already squeezing down on the trigger.

As Daniel stepped back out into the open, Sean burst forth from his hide with all the energy his legs could muster. He had only gone two yards when he heard the sniper fire. Keeping his head down, he pushed on towards the wall, weaving his way through the headstones. Bullets punched the ground around him. Halfway to the wall he heard Daniel fire only once. The chatter of the sub-machine gun stopped. Sean reached the wall as Daniel came back around the corner.

'Better shot, huh?' Daniel mocked.

'Beginner's luck.'

From here they could see the rear doors of the church. On its steps several men took cover from gunfire directed from further down the road behind some wooden pews they had dragged outside. Chips of stone and wood exploded around them as they fought back. One of the men sat up and aimed a Tommy gun towards the crowd and fired two short bursts. As he did his companions took the initiative and bought up their own weapons and fired off a volley of shots. The Protestant crowd fell back, screams coming from within their ranks.

The man with the Tommy gun saw Daniel and nodded recognition. Daniel nodded back.

Sean crept forward to look around the corner of the wall. The men they had shot earlier had crawled back or had been dragged back by their mates. The crowd had retreated to a safer distance but from here he could still pick them off if a target presented itself. As he looked down the road at the mob, two young men stepped out from a doorway only twenty yards away and hurled a Molotov each. The flaming missiles curled high, spinning as they passed high above Sean then down to fall towards the rear of the church. The two men then bolted for the safety of the crowd. Sean let them run, not wanting to shoot unarmed people in the back. This didn't stop one of the defenders from firing off several rounds toward the fleeing youths. They didn't fall or stagger and made it safely to the mass of people.

The first petrol bomb fell short of the steps, its volatile contents exploding harmlessly over the footpath with a brittle crump. The second had travelled further and broke against one of the stained glass windows. Some of the fuel splashed inside of the church and Sean could hear the shouts of people inside as they rushed to quell the fire before it took hold.

Daniel and Sean held their position for the next hour. The gunfire from the loyalists increased, sometimes directed at them but mostly to the men immediately in front of the church. The crowd had fallen back further but it still probed at their defences.

The gunmen came in waves. Volley after volley they hammered at them. The defenders were seriously outnumbered but were holding on. They couldn't let them burn the church down. It was a symbol of Catholic defiance. If the church fell, the ghetto would follow.

'I thought the Army would have turned up by now,' Daniel remarked as he kept an eye over the street.

'What are they waiting for?'

'Probably for us all to kill each other first. I can guarantee you if it was us attackin' a Proddie area then we'd have been facing the Brits a hell o' a lot sooner and it wouldn't take long for them to overrun us.'

'They're letting this happen aren't they?' Sean realised.

'It's like they've planned it,' Daniel said as he aimed towards some movement in a side alley. *Show yourself you bastard,* he thought to himself.

A shot boomed from deep in the shadows, the round aimed at the church. Daniel fired off four rounds at the muzzle flash. He heard someone yell something and every gun now seemed aimed at them. Like a fast beat on a tight drum, more than six guns now fired at the shielded corner. Cement popped all around them like tiny volcanoes as Daniel dropped his head to the ground to shield it. Several rounds ricocheted with high pitched screams, the torn pieces of bullet jacket ringing off into the night sky.

Sean dropped his rifle and grabbed Daniel by his belt. He reefed hard and pulled him back behind the wall as the shots kept coming in.

'FOCKEN 'ELL!!' Daniel yelled as his head cleared the danger. He had never seen such gunfire before. All he and most of the other Provisionals had ever encountered were exchanges of no more than a magazine full within two minutes. This was now a full blown battle. The sounds of gunfire seemed almost constant, their flashes and tracer rounds lighting up the street like fireworks. Not since the Civil War had the streets of an Irish city seen such gunfire.

Gunshots rang out from the church as they hit back at the hidden machine gunner.

'Danny!' a voice called out to them from the first floor of the primary school. 'Danny! Are yeh alright? Are yeh hit?'

Sean looked Daniel over but couldn't see any blood.

'I'm fine!' he yelled back.

'Behind ye Danny!' the voice from the school warned.

Sean spun around and saw several shadows moving along the wall to their rear. Before Daniel knew it, Sean had snatched the M1 out of his hands and swung it around. He opened up as the first man came around the corner. This man was met by six .30 calibre rounds, two hitting him in the forearm causing him to spin and drop his own rifle, his arm shattered. The other four rounds exploded around the next man, missing him but scaring him senseless as brick and mortar flew in every direction. They retreated back around the corner.

As Daniel got to his knees Sean tossed him the carbine. 'Reload!' he barked as he took the Mauser up again and turned back to the corner to see a rifle appear. It was aimed blindly by the man on the far side and he instantly began firing.

Sean fired back, more brick exploding, and he saw the weapon jerk back around the corner into the dark.

The guns behind them died only momentarily and in this respite they heard someone again calling from the school. 'Pull back, Danny!'

Sean knew they themselves had no view of the area. The men in the church and school where now their eyes and if they said to pull back then Sean had no option but to take their advice.

'Are you ready?' he asked Daniel.

Daniel slapped in a new magazine, his last, and worked the bolt. 'You first.'

Sean turned back to the corner where their last attack had come from. No movement there. He forced out a breath as he looked around for somewhere to fight back from. The majority of the mob had left once the gunfire became too intense, returning up Newtonards Road. All that remained were the gunmen. Nothing but gunmen. He noticed a recess in the wall of one of the houses on the opposite side of the small cemetery. 30 yards give or take. Sean's best time for the 100 yard dash was 12 seconds flat. 30 yards at full sprint would have him there in a shade over 4 seconds...if he were barefoot, crouched for the start and not carrying a rifle. He guessed an extra second to rise up and another for the extra weight he was carrying. At best 6 seconds. A lot of time exposed. But no choice.

'Follow me.'

Jumping to his feet, Sean ran harder than he ever had before. He heard the attention his actions had attracted. Stooping over even further he pushed on through the barrage that was aimed in on him. He thought he could feel each individual bullet as it passed him, some close, some even closer. His long strides guided him through the old monuments and tombstones, his feet trying to pick their way across the rubble-strewn surface. If he tripped now he was as good as dead. If he stopped for cover behind a headstone he would be trapped. He had to push on.

Daniel waited until Sean had put some distance between them. He waited until he made it to the small footpath on the far side then he took off, running the first few feet crablike, skipping sideways, carbine raised and aimed at the first muzzle flash he saw as he came out around the corner into the open. Six quick shots and then he turned and ran like hell was on his heels.

Every gun in and around the church and school gave them covering fire, trying to hold off their attackers for even a few precious seconds so their boys could make it to safety.

Lifting his head as he made it to the footpath, Sean saw the shadow of the corner wall at the same time his foot came down on a piece of broken brick. He knew he was going down the second his foot rolled over on itself. Before he lost balance he pushed hard and launched himself across the footpath. His momentum carried him through the air further than he hoped and he crashed into the shadowed corner, falling heavily into the wall, his Mauser clattering beside him. He winced in pain, the wind knocked out of him. His left knee stabbed with pain as it landed on the hard ground. Sucking in air as he grabbed his rifle, he was relieved to be out of the line of fire.

Daniel came into view and Sean noted how close some of the rounds aimed towards him came. Several pocked away at the headstones only inches from his head but he ran on, driven by the determination to survive. Crossing the open area a lot more gracefully than he had, Daniel came to a stop standing over the Australian. He held out his hand and lifted him to his feet.

'You say you used to play rugby? That was barely thirty yards.'

Sean smiled. 'I don't remember the Maitland footy team ever shooting at us.'

From their new position they were safe from any probing attacks but they still had to brave their enemies' gunfire if they wanted to snipe back.

The sounds of gunfire died down over the next two hours. Soon it would be light. Daniel looked at his watch. The battle for Short Strand had gone on for almost five hours and the IRA and the local Citizen's Defence Committee had fired over 800 rounds. To their east a bright opal blue line declared daylight was coming.

'How you boys doin' down there?' someone called from the side door of the church. Both noticed no gunfire met the man in the doorway.

'Doing just fine Phil,' Daniel called back. 'How's things in there?'

In a brave, defiant act, the moustached man took several steps out into the open; no shots were heard. With carbine in hand, and finger still resting near the trigger, he began walking towards them. His eyes remained on the once distant targets, checking for signs of danger.

The loyalist attackers had withdrawn. Shouting could still be heard in the distance, the calls being drowned out by the sound of approaching ambulances.

'Henry McIlhone's dead. I don't know if you knew him. He was one of the local defenders,' he said as the younger two stepped towards him out into the open.

'Oh, Fuck,' Daniel replied, his sorrow and anger, despite his fatigue, showed through.

'On the other side of the church,' Phil stated. 'Shot through the throat. Billy's been hit as well. Fuckers shot 'im in the back.'

'Is he gonna be alright?'

'Don't know. Brits are only letting the Ambulances in now.' The man looked down at Sean's jacket. He nodded towards it. 'Someone's looking over you boyo. Christ, they were close.'

Sean looked down and saw four holes in the fabric on his side. They were only small, just by his lower ribs. He pulled the jacket open and saw his shirt underneath also was damaged. The bullets had come within a quarter of an inch from hitting him.

'They couldn't have gotten any closer,' Sean remarked as he fingered the hole, feeling his sides for injury but finding nothing.

Phil held out his hand. 'You must be Sean. Heard a lot abou'cha. I'm Phil. Glad you could help us out tonight.'

'It's no trouble. Glad to help.'

'No trouble hey? I saw you pull this one 'ere back from the Reaper,' he smiled and nodded to Daniel. 'He owes you more than a drink.'

'He's got to do a whole lot more than that to get a free drink outta me! C'mon,' Dan said as the residents began to leave the safety of their homes to clean up and thank the defenders.

'Let's get these guns out of 'ere before the Army finally decides to do it's job and turn up.' He turned and led them back towards the still standing Catholic Church, Short Strand's symbol of defiance.

Later that day in a back room of Collins' Bar, Sean stood before one of the Ballymurphy Senior members of the Provisional Irish Republican Army and, with Daniel, Padraig and a slightly wounded Donnie present (a bullet had grazed across the knuckles on the back of his right hand) he took the oath in front of the tricolour of the Irish flag, pledged allegiance to the Irish Republic of 1916 and became one of them.

He was now a member of the Provisional Irish Republican Army.

TWENTY SIX

The two bodies were redressed in civilian clothing picked up from a charity store, the clothing they had been shot in now locked away in an evidence room at the Edinburgh Police Headquarters. The bullet fragments had been removed from their chests; three rounds from young Chris, four from Glenn.

For the last three days the morgue had been busy with people from the police, the Army and suits up from London coming in and out all the time, looking at the bodies, taking finger prints, hair samples…it didn't seem to end.

The authorities had been furious when their information proved to be wrong. The entire operation had been planned from what they had believed to be concrete evidence that over one hundred weapons were coming in to Scotland from the European mainland. This was to have been a one-only shipment thus giving them one chance to seize the cargo; weapons ranging from pistols to heavy machine guns and explosives, and trace its point of origin. A West German detective working in conjunction with Scotland Yard had contacted them to say he had a man working from within the ranks of Germany's criminal underworld. He had confirmed the cargo had left its German warehouse three days ago on the 19th and should arrive on the 21st with all the weapons bound for Northern Ireland. The search conducted after the raid had found nothing. And The British Government wasn't happy.

Every night there was a riot and every day there was a funeral. Most were small family funerals attended by one hundred or so depending on whether they could get to the funeral with so many roadblocks and check points in place; not just the Army and Police but UVF check points as well.

Today however would be different. Today they buried their two volunteers, unmercifully gunned down by the British as they slept. Or so the rumour went.

The army and the RUC were on high alert. Catholics would leave the service with anger and revenge in their eyes. The Protestants would be out to stir up as much trouble as they could to upset their grieving neighbours. If the roles were reversed the story would be the same.

Sean, Daniel, Melissa and Max all travelled to the church together, meeting people on the street all heading in the same direction. Polite hellos were said as the mass of people grew.

To his right Sean saw a man making his way through the crowd, crossing the street, heading in their direction. He was shorter than the two of them and much older. His hairline was receding and a dark moustache had been groomed perfectly for today. As he approached Daniel he held out his hand.

'Good to see you Danny,' he said to him, his English accent surprising Sean. He then shook Sean's hand.

'Thank you Sean, for your help the other day. I'll talk to you both later.' He then turned and merged back into the mass of people.

As Sean watched the man walk away, shaking hands with others as he met them, he had no idea he had just become a face and a new identity in a large file filled with known terrorists and aggressive republicans.

Several blocks away sitting far back from the window in a darkened room of a four-storey building, a member of the British Army's Military Reconnaissance Force snapped off two more close-up frames of the unknown man that had just shaken hands with the IRA top dog visiting up from Dublin. The 35mm Canon camera with its oversized R800mm f5.6 super-telephoto lens clicked again.

'He's a new one,' the camera operator said to his companion by his side, his eye never leaving the viewing window, his left thumb and forefinger constantly playing with the focus and depth. 'I think the other young bloke I've seen before but not this one.'

The second man steadied his military binoculars. To him there was something about this young man that didn't quite fit the profile that went with a Provo volunteer. In the back of his mind all he kept thinking was how he fitted in by looking different.

But how do you write that down on a report?

'Looks a bit different to the others don't you think?' He cast the observation to his colleague to feel out his opinion.

His mate sneered as he looked out into the distance. 'Maybe he's had a bath this year.'

'Who was that?' Sean asked Daniel.

'That's Sean MacStiofain. He's the Chief of Staff up from Dublin. Our boss.' A proud smile crossed Daniel's face. 'Seems the big man knows us from Short Strand.'

The Australian looked back at the man ahead. He could see the weight of a country on his shoulders but it was a weight he carried with pride. People took audience with this man like some would a president or prime minister. Everyone he met as they walked along seemed to swell with pride when meeting him. Although it was a hard day on everyone, he was there to show his support, to tell the families they would not suffer alone. Being out in the open like this was a brave move for him. He knew the Brits would love to pick him up but couldn't for the repercussions of such an act, especially today. It would inflame a riot like nobody had ever witnessed if they tried something stupid like that. MacStiofain would know he couldn't be touched. He could walk right up to and through a military check point and they wouldn't dare look him in the eyes.

In comparison Sean realised he had just met their version of Ho Chi Min, a man trying to fight the invaders with the support and backing of the majority of the people.

'He's English?'

Daniel nodded. 'He even served in the RAF. Used to be John Stephenson. Goes by his Gaelic name now.'

At the church the crowd numbered in its thousands. Inside was the family of both men, their seats held for them by other volunteers. Those that had managed to squeeze into the building had standing room only. Sean and the others waited out on the street with, what seemed like, half of Belfast. They could hear the people inside, the droning of communal prayers, the strong voice of the priest that carried out into the street.

Outside the crowd waited, no one talking, a suburb in silence. Sean looked around at the people that had gathered. He noticed some men that had been at the Short Strand battle. One of them caught his eye and the man nodded at him.

Sean nodded back, a feeling of pride and acceptance warming him. Then from deep within the church came the sounds of a lone bagpipe, the skirl of sharp notes of *Flowers of the Forest.* It was a tune Sean had heard before. The same tune played every Anzac Day dawn service across the cities and towns of Australia, a lament for the fallen. He had last heard it during the Anzac Day service in Nui Dat back in April. The bass sounds filtered out through the open doors and windows announcing to the mass of people that their last journey was beginning. All eyes looked to the door of the church. The piper emerged from the darkness dressed in a kilt bearing the green and gold tartan of Ireland. The crowd parted, opening up a lane that would wind its path to the cemetery. The piper came down the stairs, leading the way. Behind came the first coffin containing Chris Hall. Six men carried it out; Chris' two brothers at the front of it, his best friend in the centre left, a cousin centre right and two Provisional comrades at the rear. His coffin, a polished deep red casket, was draped in a tri-colour. A wreath, black beret and black gloves were sitting on top. As they emerged from the darkness of the church, Sean heard faint crying from the dead boy's mother who was buried in her husband's shoulder, his arm around her. Other family members followed. The casket carrying Chris Hall stopped on the street at the base of the stairs. It waited for its comrade. Two friends and four Provos carried Glenn Brown's body from the church in a pine casket dressed in the same fashion. He had no brothers, only sisters that followed close behind his parents, both walking staunchly behind their fallen son. Quietly they came down the stairs to the street. With both boys now side by side the slow procession to the Milltown Cemetery began. As they passed, Sean, Daniel, Melissa and Max fell in behind with the rest, listening to the tune that called through the streets and lanes that were coloured with the forbidden green, white and orange of the Republic.

He had never met the two they now followed but Sean felt loss and anger. It was a feeling he had every time they had sent home one of their own from Vietnam. It was like a cold steel ball in his gut that could only be removed through action, through revenge. He was beginning to become angrier when he felt someone take hold of his hand. He looked down and saw Max looking up at him with a worried expression on his face. Sean smiled down at him, his anger gone. Max smiled back, one hand in his, the other in his mother's. Sean wondered how many funerals little Max would attend in his life. He had already gone to his own father's only a year ago and there was the funeral of Henry McIlhone, the man killed in Short Strand, tomorrow. Despite the hardship the little man steamed on full of hope and smiles.

They were far away from the caskets as they were readied to be lowered into the ground but Sean didn't mind. He was quite happy not to see this part of the ceremony. It signified the end of it all. No going back from here. It was a stupid thing to think but he couldn't help it. Not seeing them disappear six foot down still kept them alive in his head. That was how he felt with Joel. He had not seen him dying, die or dead. No coffin, no funeral, just the word of his army mates. Again, stupid but…he was still with him.

The crowd had been expecting it but not him. From within the mass of people came four men, all converging on the caskets. Each man wore black trousers and jacket with a black beret, black sunglasses and a black cloth pulled up to mask their face. Carried down by the side of each man was a Kalashnikov. They lined up side by side and a command was given. The barrels rose in unison, pointing up at 45 degrees. Sean saw the children had been to too many of these as most of them covered their ears in expectation.

'Fire.'

The shots shattered the silence, the noise rolling around cemetery, bouncing off buildings in the distance and echoing back. Sean saw more than a few people flinch, despite knowing it was coming.

'Fire.'

Sean noted Max, now in his mother's arms, was watching the riflemen thirty yards away. He wasn't smiling or scared. He was simply observing what was happening. Sean wondered if the gunshots had bought back memories of his father's funeral. *Had he received a gun salute as well? Was this taking Max back there?*

'Fire.'

As the noise of the last shots dissipated, the gunmen each reversed their rifles for a minute of silence before melting back into the crowd, each man going a different way. Sean saw the people directly in front of him move and allow one of the gunmen through. The tall man passed right by Sean, pausing for a second with surprise at the presence of the Australian. He nodded ever so slightly and disappeared behind him into the crowd, the faint smell of burnt cordite trailing behind. Sean looked across to Daniel, his expression asking *Who was that?*

Daniel leaned closer to him and said quietly 'Kieran.'

It had been the first time since saying goodbye to him in Dingle, Co Kerry that he had seen Kieran Hough and he was glad to see he was still well. Sean wondered if Kieran knew he too was now a Provo.

TWENTY SEVEN

The last keg was dropped down the chute to the basement. James caught it and skilfully, with the practice of swinging hundreds of the heavy containers, turned and rolled the silver barrel on its rim to its place without even looking. The soft, metallic sound of it settling to a stop echoed up through the door to the street. Above him Ziggy, the driver of the delivery truck, finished loading the empties and appeared in silhouette, a clipboard in his hand. James caught it as it fell to him.

'How's business been goin' James?'

'Yeah, not bad Zig.'

'You have been putting in more hours than normal.'

'Just trying to keep busy.' Which was true. An active body leads to an active mind and an active mind doesn't think about what he could have done to save his brother. It was even harder on a day like today.

'I know what you mean, mate,' said Ziggy as he wiped his face. 'If I'm not working twenty five hours a day my wife's all over me. It's terrifying! Always wanting a kiss here, a cuddle there. Give her five minutes and she tries to have sex with me.' The driver shuddered. 'I'll show you a picture of her one day. If I can find one of her. She's so ugly the chemist won't let me develop film there in case there's a photo of her on the roll. Says he can't handle another heart attack.'

James was waiting for him to laugh at the joke but as he handed up the signed forms he could see he was serious. Or at least half serious.

He took the clipboard and tipped his hat. 'Catch ya next delivery James.'

'See you Zig.'

James turned and began sorting out the kegs into their respective brands, placing them in lines ready for tapping when needed. He enjoyed working down in the cellar. It was a place where he could think and be by himself. The music from the radio upstairs was filtering its way down through the floor and he hummed away while he worked. As he completed taking the spirit inventory a shadow appeared across the door to the street above.

'At least you're not singing.'

He looked up into the bright winter's day and recognised the sexy figure of the woman above, the low winter sun dangerously outlining her curves through a near see-through skirt. 'You love it when I sing,' He chuckled softly. 'Best thing you'll ever hear. How's it going Leanda?'

'What are you doing down there? The birthday boy should be up here having a drink with us.'

'Isn't it a bit early for that?'

'How about a cup of tea then? The boys are already inside.'

'Sure. Shut that door for us. I'll see you up there in a minute.'

As the cellar's illumination was reduced to its four dull light bulbs, James sat down on the nearest keg. Sighing, he rubbed his eyes wondering what his brother was doing.

'Sean.' He lifted his head, looking up to the ceiling, up to the music. 'You better have a drink for me today, you bastard.'

Friday, August 14.

James' birthday.

Sean hadn't forgotten. He'd wished him a happy birthday as soon as he had been woken up by Max.

'Say "Happy birthday James",' he had said to Max, who now always seemed to be there when he woke up. He liked the "funny talking man on the lounge".

'Happy birthday James. Who's James?' he had replied.

'My brother back in Australia.'

'How old is he?'

'He's twenty seven today.'

'Wow. That's old. That's like nearly a hundred.'

However that was this morning back in Belfast. It was now two in the afternoon. Padraig had picked him and Daniel up and driven them across the border into the Republic and up into the Iron Mountains in County Leitrim.

Kieran had been meant to join them but he had been wounded during a shootout with British troops the previous month during the Lower Falls curfew. The Brits had sealed off the Catholic suburb to search for the weapons used in the Short Strand battle. Over three thousand troops swarmed in, firing more than sixteen hundred canisters of chlorobenzylidene malononitrile – CS gas –, a harsh form of tear gas, into the streets and warren-like lane ways. The British stated anyone who stepped out onto the footpath during the three day weekend curfew, man, woman or child, would be shot without question. This was of course ignored by the paramilitary wing that had split from the Provos, the Official IRA, and these three days were met with major running battles, of which the Brits fired almost 1500 rounds. Kieran had taken a round to his thigh. He managed to flee but would be off his feet for a while.

While Sean remembered today for the good times with James, the Irish remembered today for darker reasons. It was a year to the day that the British Army had been deployed into both Derry and Belfast on Operation Banner. Fearing the Irish Government was going to send its own troops across the border into Derry in retaliation to the Catholic slums being burnt out by the RUC and loyalist mobs during the Battle of the Bogside, the British Government ordered in its own troops to step in between the two warring parties. Some Catholics welcomed the intervention but it did not take long for the British soldiers to side with their fellow unionists. All of which led Sean to be sitting at a large wooden table with an old friend.

It was all so familiar to Sean. Frighteningly so. The feel, the smell, the weight. The old friend was part of him now. Nothing could ever take that away from him. It had been hammered into him. Even if Sean wanted to forget, he couldn't. He pictured himself fifty years from now as an old man, unable to walk, unable to remember how to get to the shops, probably unable to control his bladder but still able to perform this task like it was yesterday.

7.8 pounds, 3 foot 3 inches long with a 20 round magazine. The original was built in 1965 from Eugene Stoner's design for Armalite, a division of Fairchild Engine and Airplane Corporation and built by Colt Firearms in Hartford, Connecticut. The model he held in his hands was the 1967 M16A1; instantly recognisable by the forward flash suppressor instead of the original three pronged barrelled 1965 version. Its 5.56mm copper-jacketed projectiles would leave the right-twist rifled barrel at a muzzle velocity of 3200 feet per second. Faster than the 2700 fps SLR round but not as hard hitting. He smiled for the briefest moment as the stats came back to him. Numbers in school had never been his strong point but things tended to stick when a regimental sergeant major drummed them into your memory. The facts came forward as easily as if he were recalling his own name.

The weapon that Chad had smuggled from the Mediterranean to Ireland had already had its serial number removed. It was now one of 120 new rifles without an identity. He looked at the weapon as he ran his scarred hand forward over the barrel's length. The hard, black plastic was room temperature. His fingers rose and fell as they traced the stock's ribbed contours to the cold metalled forward sight. In the jungles it had almost sweated with the heat. He turned the weapon over and looked at it, oblivious to the numerous eyes watching him, waiting to learn what he knew. It excited him again, to be of use, to be needed. It comforted him. Just as the weapon comforted him.

Metal and plastic. And lead. Don't forget the lead.

All too familiar. All too easy.

His hands moved quickly. The plastic handgrips twisted and fell away, magazine snapped away from the body, the take-down pin pushed in and the upper receiver and barrel hinged, falling forward. The charging handle, the bolt assembly, the firing pin retaining pin, the firing pin itself, bolt cam pin, buffer and spring, all withdrawn and separated. Within seconds the assault rifle was laid out in front of him on the table in its many pieces.

'Fock'n 'ell,' one of the men beside him exclaimed. 'It looks like you've done that before.'

'Once or twice,' he replied, looking up at the twenty or so men surrounding the table, allowing himself a grin. It wasn't just the M16 that he knew in detail inside and out; the M60, the Owen sub-machine gun, the AK47, a wide selection of pistols and his favoured and most trusted weapon the L1A1 SLR; the same rifle used by the British in Northern Ireland.

'Now...this is the American made M16A1. This little beauty is what the yanks and some of the Australian forces in Vietnam are using at the moment.' He smiled to himself as he recalled Joel favouring the Armalite over the heavier SLR. They had argued their opposing points for months but never reached common ground. It had not made a difference in the end. Bullets don't stop incoming mortars.

'Accurate but not much chop out beyond five hundred feet due to the small calibre.' He reached out and picked up two live rounds of varying sizes off the table. He stood both upright in front of him. 'This smaller round belongs to the M16, the larger to the SLR being used by the Poms. Big things fly further than small things so simple physics states that they are going to be able to hit you from farther away. At least six-hundred yards or more effective range for this,' he held up the SLR round, 'and five-hundred, *at best*, for the M16. The one advantage that this weapon has over the Brit's SLR is that she can fire on automatic. But the thing you have to stress to your lads is to not blaze away on full auto. If you want you can empty a full magazine in under three seconds but I'll guarantee you that three quarters of those rounds will be punching holes in clouds. And the time you'll need those rounds most, you'll be changing a mag and not much use to your mates. Only use single shots or short squirts on auto.'

'Do they have any major problems like jamming or such?'

Sean turned to look at the man speaking. He was a young man probably only a few years older than he with a thin moustache and hair down to his shoulders that framed a serious face of someone who should have been a lot older. Apart from their appearances and varying ages it reminded him of basic training back in Australia, with him now playing the roll of the drill sergeant with all the answers.

'They are infinitely more reliable than the first M16 produced but they still have to be kept clean. The breach and operations have a low interference tolerance so they have to be clean and lubed.' He picked up the butt of the rifle. 'The cleaning gear is kept here in the stock. Rod, patches and oil.' He withdrew the kit from under the shoulder plate. 'The best way to learn all this is to do it. So if everyone can grab a rifle I'll take you through it. It's so easy your kids could do it.'

'My kids *do* do it!' one of them commented, bringing laughter from the group.

Quietly smoking in the back corner of the barn, Daniel and Padraig smiled. It was the end of the first of three days they would be spending up in the hills. They had to get these Area Commanders, county reps and their assistants of both the Northern and Southern Command up to scratch with the Armalites so they could, in turn, train their own men. Everything was going better than expected. There had been only some slight hassles with Sean taking the "class" although both Dan and Padraig now knew enough about the M16 they could have done it themselves. Padraig decided Sean had taught them both so well the previous week that he might as well teach the others. He readily accepted the responsibility.

Padraig blew out a long string of smoke that slowly pulled away, caught in a cool summer breeze that intruded through the open barn door. 'Does he still talk about going to Donegal?'

'Not any more. He's happy to stay and fight.' Daniel watched the other provos thoughtfully begin stripping their rifles.

'With all the riots goin' on, anyone and everyone is gettin' out. He mustn't be allergic to flying lead.'

'Everyone's allergic to it if it's flying fast enough in your direction.'

Several of the area representatives burst into laughter and Daniel and Padraig looked up to see Sean smiling as he tried to finish off his story or joke, the stocky O'Hagan from Derry slapping him on the shoulder and grinning like a clown. Padraig watched them quip back and forth, including Sean in on the jokes and only rarely speaking Irish around him.

'I've talked to Billy McKee about him. He wants to take my idea to MacStiofain. He thinks Sean should be included.'

'You what?' Daniel had not contested the idea to bring Sean into the Provos in a training capacity, but he wasn't too sure on Padraig's new idea. 'When did this happen?'

'I saw him after Jimmy Steele's funeral.' Three days earlier they had buried another of their comrades. Jimmy Steele, the former IRA veteran and reviver of the republican newspaper *An Phoblacht,* had died of natural causes a week ago. Over ten thousand had turned out for his funeral including Daniel, Sean and himself.

'You haven't even talked to him about it yet. He's only helping us out here because none of us know as much about the gun as he does!'

'It's a fecken rifle, Dan. Point it and pull the trigger! *We* could have showed this lot how to strip it. These lads are experienced servicemen. Give them two minutes with one and they could have taught themselves. He wanted to do this. Think about it! He's already told us by doing this. His wounds have been healed for ages. He could have walked to Donegal on his feckin' hands by now. Look at him. He likes it here. He's taken the oath. He wants to help. Think of the advantage he could have.

'Sooner or later a British soldier will be killed over here and when that happens they are going to come at us with everything they can get their hands on. We have to be ready for that. We have to use the resources that are available. That includes Sean.'

Although he felt responsible for him, Daniel couldn't argue with the facts. The past seven weeks, Sean had been trying to learn everything he could about the "Troubles" as they were being called. He had been introduced to some of the GHQ Staff; namely the heads of Operations and Security. It was the meeting with Alistair Beehan that had proved the most interesting. He was the Training officer for the Northern Command and was interested in obtaining any information about Sean's training and his time in the Army, from new defensive manoeuvres to guerrilla techniques used against them in South Vietnam. He was the instigator for him being here today.

Daniel picked up one of the M16s. 'What if he wants out at a later date?' he questioned, his eyes not looking up from the Armalite. 'He's seen an awful lot that the majority of our lads would never be allowed to see.'

'I think it's too late for that now judging by how he's applied himself out here.' Padraig looked down the barn to the Australian. He was still talking and laughing with some of the hardest men ever to be gathered in the same room together. 'It's a volunteer army Danny, you know that. Anyone of us can leave at anytime we want. No point in making a man fight for something he doesn't have his heart in. But something's driving him Danny. He's got more determination than some of the lads who've known nothing but war. No, he's here for the long haul. Otherwise he'd be long gone.'

Daniel wondered what Padraig meant by that last sentence; gone by his own choice or... *Gone.*

Sean was impressed by how serious these men were taking it all in. Not once had he needed to raise his voice to get them to be quiet or stop fucking around or to have them repeat a job they had failed at beforehand. They listened better than he himself had during basic. They were picking things up quicker than his platoon had.

But what other choice do they have?

He was standing at the end of the line at the base of the hill, looking down the row of men, watching them as they fired off single shots at the targets, squares of cardboard fifty yards away. They were familiarising themselves with the characteristics of the rifle; the recoil, the weight, the accuracy. They were hitting the targets in no more than five inch groups from the standing position; the least effective firing stance. Once they had finished the single shot drills they moved onto firing short bursts on automatic from a kneeling position. Once they accustomed themselves to the lightweight, almost inconsequential recoil, they were all keeping tight groups on short multiple bursts.

Suddenly Sean screamed out, 'GUN JAM!! LAST ROUND!! RELOAD!!'

Instantly they all stopped firing, pressed the magazine release button, the magazine falling to the ground. Grabbing a fresh mag, they fitted it, all of them working back the receiver ejecting the chambered "dud" round before hitting the forward assist to ensure no miss-fire. They were back firing in less than three seconds without once taking their aim away from the target.

Sean smiled. Professional soldiers they weren't; these were far more driven. They had the ultimate goal.

So why would I want to be anywhere else, he concluded.

By night on the first day they could strip and reassemble the rifle in the dark. They had all progressed faster than any of them had anticipated so Sean had talked to Padraig and put the idea to him of running them through some army skills such as camouflage, reconnaissance, ambush scenarios and flanking attacks. Some of this would be standard stuff to the Brits but other areas were new; techniques that had been developed in Vietnam. One tactic they adopted successfully was making sure soldiers operated in pairs. Even when they were in greater numbers they could split up and cover each other if needed. They could also then "pepper pot", a technique he had used countless times. This method of advancing or retreating under fire allowed two soldiers to provide covering fire as a second pair moved forward, or backward, also firing as they ran. This leapfrogging had proved successful against the Vietnamese. Whether Sean thought they would translate to the Irish environment he wasn't sure, but the commanders told him war translates anywhere. Thick jungle became intersecting hedgerows, rice paddies became waterlogged fields, and the busy and deceptive streets of Saigon were now the dirty, riot filled lanes of Belfast and Derry. Rivers were still rivers, hills were still hills.

And more importantly, bullets were still bullets.

TWENTY EIGHT

It had been exactly what he had needed.

With his birthday now just a dull headache and patchy memories of fun, James had gotten up early to clean before Kim awoke, letting her sleep in.

As he cleaned up he found a five dollar note under the pool table and placed it in the till. The money he found he kept aside to pay for "free" drinks he gave his old man. He knew there was no point in robbing himself.

The party had gone on long into the night. James thought people were starting to get back to being normal, or whatever used to pass for normal around here. Thomo had spent most of the night dancing with whichever girl happened to pass him, grabbing them and pulling them in for a quick waltz, a twist or shimmy.

Luke on the other hand had drunk everyone under the table, laughing and cheering all night long, singing along with the music that blared from the corner, dancing with Leanda, Kim and Melanie when they weren't being dragged into the whirlpool that was Thomo. Luke didn't want the night to stop. He moved from person to person, buying them drinks and chatting, getting everyone in the party mood.

Before James' dad had left, Luke had spent a good hour talking to him, bringing up the old times like when he and Sean used to get chased out of Milosh the Greek's yard during the summers as they tried to nick the grapes the old wog would use to make his illegal grappa or when they met Ian Walsh, the Aussie and Saint George Dragon's captain down on Merewether beach back in '65.

James collected the glasses and replaced the empty spirit bottles before he could finally not stand the growling of his stomach. He cooked enough bacon, tomato, eggs and mushrooms for both himself and Kim and was loading it up onto a tray when she came down the stairs, her tiny nightie struggling to hide what it should.

'I was going to surprise you with breakfast in bed.'

'The smell woke me up. What time is it?'

'It's only eight.' He carried the tray over to the nearest table.

They ate and talked about the previous night, comparing stories and piecing a great night of drinking together like a blurred jigsaw puzzle.

A knock at the door startled them both but James guessed who it was.

'Piss of Les!' he shouted, knowing his most loyal and drunken regular was getting the morning shakes and most likely looking for the dog's hair. 'You've got hours till I open!'

'James. It's Melanie.'

Kim, being closest to the door opened it, letting in the fresh looking eldest of the Doherty clan.

'What's happening sis?' James said with a mouthful of mushroom. 'You want some breakfast?'

She shook her head and sat down next to them. 'How do you both feel?' *This is going to be hard.*

Her younger brother grinned at her. 'Not as bad as I thought I would.'

'I think I will have something,' she said, looking to Kim. She wasn't hungry but needed to speak to James alone. As Kim left them, Melanie exchanged small talk with James but she knew she was just putting it off. She had to tell him now. Searching for courage, she finally bought the words out.

'Did you talk to dad last night?' she asked as she stared down at his plate.

'Not for long. He was a little pissed. I couldn't understand half of the shit he was going on with.'

'He's sick James.' *Too blunt.*

At first the words didn't register, but the look on her face made him rethink what she had said. She wasn't joking or lying. 'What do you mean sick? How sick?' For some reason cancer popped into his head.

'I went with him to the doctors the other week. His lungs are shutting down.'

'Oh fuck!' A shiver ran over his body. Suddenly he didn't feel like eating anymore.

'They got a second lot of tests results back the other day.' Tears began to well in her eyes.

'Fuck no!' James stood and turned away from her. He walked over to the window, his mind racing. 'FUCK!!'

Kim appeared at the kitchen door but didn't approach them. She was scared and didn't know what to do.

Melanie tried to control her emotions. Her mouth trembled as she continued. 'We couldn't tell you on your birthday. He asked me to tell you later.' She walked over and stood behind him.

'James…' She paused but he knew what was coming next. 'Dad's dying.'

James leant against the window frame, his hands clenched onto the sill. Rage burned through him. He felt like he was going mad.

'James…please…' His sister reached out and placed a hand on his back.

He couldn't hold it back any longer. It came out of nowhere. Before he knew it he had picked up a stool and driven it through the window, glass exploding out over the footpath. The shock of his reaction bought forth all the tears Melanie had pent up. She dropped to the ground as her legs went weak, sitting on the floor, her first sign of weakness ever. James turned and screamed at her.

'WHEN IS THIS FUCKING WORLD GOING TO GIVE US A BREAK!!!?' He kicked another stool over and watched it skip across the floor, crashing into the bar.

As the stool rolled to a stop all he could hear was his heartbeat and his sister's crying. Somewhere behind him Kim was sobbing too. Burying his face in his hands he too began to cry. He dropped to the floor next to Melanie and they both wept in fear for their father and in anger at the world for all the shit it had dished out to them in their lives.

Daniel loaded his bag into the boot of Padraig's car, the last bag to go in. Everyone was packing for the return to their home towns. All had gone better than expected. They were now all technically proficient with the M16 and the many techniques Sean had taught them had adapted well. Daniel was also surprised by how well the lads got on with Sean. He had expected some hesitation to say the least but there had been none. Turning around he saw Sean shaking hands with the County representatives, realising Sean had bonded with most of them. He watched Terry O'Hagan approach Sean to say goodbye and he felt a slight pinch of jealousy, which he knew was stupid. He shut the boot and headed over to them.

As he walked past one of the cars his eye was caught by something in the open boot of a green Opel. He stopped. Sitting in the dark corner, surrounded by almost a dozen Armalites, was a tattered old football. He stared at the well used but forgotten ball. It looked like it had been a long time since anyone had kicked it, its white majority now a yellowy-brown, the black hexagonal patches, scuffed and browning. A smear of oil or grease ran across from one brown patch to another. In contrast, the rifles were gathered together on a blanket, almost lovingly. Each of them dazzled him with their cleanliness, their parts oiled and cared for. It seemed his life could be summed up by the contents of the Opel's boot space. The trade had been easy for him. There had been no question about it. He could have tried out and even made it to the professional league, escaping the horrors and persecution his country was going through, even payed for his family to move when he could afford it. But that was only one family though. What about his friends? What about his neighbours?

What about his country?

As he stared at the football he recalled the day he willingly sat his football boots in the corner of his wardrobe, shutting the door on them and his dreams. As the years went by he convinced himself that's all it had been; a dream.

Still…he couldn't look away from the ball. He saw his hand reach out and pick it up, not realising he had done so. His hands remembered the feel of it. He desperately wanted to kick it and recalled when he and Padraig's nephew had once tried to kick a ball all the way up to the top of Black Mountain which stood behind his home. Gripping it he realised it was under-inflated. Not entirely flat but not worth kicking either. The smell of leather cast him back to innocent memories like a small, round time machine to his childhood. He remembered family members being told that the GAA didn't want their young playing the English game. Football, cricket and hockey were the three games trying to be outlawed by the Gaelic Athletic Association so he had been guided towards Gaelic Football and had excelled in that game as well. But English football just came naturally to him. And although he would never publicly announce his childhood heroes to his Irish comrades, he dreamed of playing alongside the great players of Liverpool, Manchester United, Newcastle and Dublin Athletic. Growing up in a predominately Unionist city, English football was played by children everywhere; children that were unaware of the sectarianism undercurrent that parents answered to when allowing their kids to play in the streets...the same sectarianism that had led him down this path he himself had chosen.

'Christ, I forgot that ball was even in there.'

Daniel turned, lowering the ball in embarrassment. It was Neville White, the Area Commander of Co. Galway.

'My lad's,' the elder man explained. '…before they locked him up.'

'Sorry Nev. I was just…' but he trailed off, unsure of what he was sorry about.

Nev placed a small sports bag on the back seat and returned to Daniel at the back of the car. Smiling, he nodded towards the boot. 'I think there's a bike pump in there somewhere.'

TWENTY NINE

'Motorbike approaching. One of ours,' the static filled voice stated over the two-way radio by Padraig's side.

Padraig turned away from the scrappy football match that was taking place in the sunny paddock in front of the old house. Sean had surprised him by showing them up in the second half when the game had changed to Gaelic football unexpectedly and he could use his rugby skills. His soccer skills in the first half left a lot to be desired.

Padraig walked to the dirt track on the other side of the barn where the bike would arrive. Nev White followed, withdrawing a semi-auto pistol from his belt and checking it was loaded.

'Full time!' the Fermanagh representative Cormac O'Keefe shouted to the teams. 'The Six Counties win without breaking a sweat!'

Gathering their jumpers the county representatives all headed to the house for a drink, most lighting up a smoke before returning to the loading of the vehicles. As Sean emerged from the house gulping down a glassful of water he turned to watch an old black BMW motorbike speeding up the track behind the barn, emerging on the other side to stop by Padraig and Nev. Sean noted the Galway man had tucked his ugly black pistol back into his belt. He also realised with much astonishment that the rider of the vintage machine was a woman.

'Who's she?' he asked Daniel.

They both watched her dismount, removing her helmet to let an avalanche of silken hair, as black as a crow's eyes at night, crash down around the shoulders of her weathered leather jacket which she removed next. From a distance they both recognised her beauty and confidence. Her virtuous face was contradicted by an aura that seemed to whisper "don't fuck with me".

'Bernadette Devlin just found some competition,' Daniel finally answered. '*This* is my new girlfriend,'

Despite her hands aching and her backside being sore from such a long ride up from Galway, Megan O'Brien stood proudly before her comrades, not showing any signs of weakness. She had volunteered to travel to the hidden training camp high in the Iron Mountains of Leitrim knowing she could get there quicker than any motor vehicle on her beloved Beemer. With the increasing army and Police presence, phone lines could not be trusted and they weren't stupid enough to even consider radio contact. If the Brits ever found out the location of the dozens of training camps in either country then the setback to their struggle would be disastrous. So now, after a long and painful ride, she shook hands with Neville, her Galway Area Commander.

'Megan, this is Padraig Molloy from Belfast,' the barrel-chested man said, nodding to the man beside him.

Padraig received her warm hand. 'Megan. What brings you up here?' "It had better be important" was implied in the tone, his manner abrupt as it always was when he met someone new.

'You.' Her blue eyes stared directly into his, not backing down an inch. 'You put in a request for information on the deaths of two of our boys and the torture of a third. Well, I have something.' She let out the hint of a smile.

Not that he had forgotten about what happened to Tom, Michael and Sean; he was taken aback at her directness at him. He hoped his surprise didn't show. 'Really?'

She led them to the nearest car carrying a worn leather courier's bag. She opened it and first pulled out a 9mm Walther PPK semi-auto pistol, placing it on the bonnet. Digging deeper she found what she was after.

Spreading several 6x8 colour photos out so all could see, she began to explain. 'This was Angus Brentwood,' she said, indicating the first photo. 'A UVF Assistant Quartermaster from Belfast. Some children found him in a bramble patch several days ago. He had been tortured, his feet and hands smashed to a pulp, various other wounds that go along with a beating. A bullet to the side of the head was the end of him.'

Neither Padraig nor Nev showed any visible reaction at the sight of the dead man. They both just quietly took it in and waited for her to continue.

'The Garda believe he had been there for at least a month by the amount of body decay and bloating.'

'Garda? He was found in the Republic?' Padraig asked.

'Just north of Gaillimh,' she explained, using the Gaelic pronunciation for Galway town. 'On the edge of Lough Corrib.'

'What was he doing down our way?' Nev inquired.

'From what we've found out, it seems he was on the run from his fellow loyalists. Six months ago, when in Dublin, he fell in love with a Galway girl who was finishing her studies there. She however was a Catholic. So in true Montague/Capulet fashion he decided his loyalties now lie with her and they were both on their way to America to start afresh. He'd sold information to the north's constabulary concerning weapon hides and was going to use the money to run. Before they could leave the country someone found out and caught up with him as he was heading to the girl's parent's house to pick her up.'

Padraig could see where this was going.

'It is our assumption,' Megan continued, 'and that's all it is; that our three men were recognised by the hit squad that had just carried out Brentwood's murder. For Michael O'Geary to be recognised means the men responsible had to be from Belfast. There's a possibility they thought we were there watching them but I doubt it. Our lads were only passing through, travelling north, so it was just the wrong place at the wrong time.'

The two men nodded as they processed the information. Nev pointed to the next photo.

'The vans were stolen?'

'From an industrial area in Muineachan. Both torched just south of the border.'

'And him?' he asked next, looking at the next slightly out-of-focus shot of a man dressed in expensive-looking light summer clothes. In the picture he stood beside a tree at the side of a house. The smile on his face told them he had no idea his photo was being taken. He looked tall compared to the other two men beside him, one dressed similarly to the central figure, the other in a suit.

'Merc Southcombe. An English businessman with possible ties to the UVF but definitely a heavy sponsor of the Apprentice Boys in Belfast and Derry. He made his money through agricultural supplies and is in Dublin as we speak in talks with our own Deputy Trade Minister.'

Padraig picked up the photo and eyed it closer. 'I hope you can tell us what ties this all together.'

'On the day of the attack on our three,' she continued, 'he was seen dining at a pricey restaurant in Gaillimh. He was interrupted and driven away by a man in a white Rover. It would have gone unnoticed but he seems to be a generous tipper, leaving the waiter no less than a ten pound tip.

'The tie between him and Brentwood is a little frail but Belfast believes Southcombe is also behind procuring funds for weapons. Prior to his change of heart, Brentwood had visited England on two separate occasions for meetings with a Dutch arms dealers. So he knew a lot of sensitive information. I know there are a few too many maybes but the secrets Brentwood would have sold would have been priceless. If one of ours did the same we act the same way.'

Padraig placed the photo back down beside Megan's Walther. 'He must have taken the defection of Brentwood personally. Maybe he knew him, had dealings with him. It may come down to the simple fact he wanted to talk to Brentwood before he killed him.' Padraig nodded as he thought of a plan of action. 'I'll talk to the boss when I get back home. How long is he in the country for?'

'Talks for two more days at least. After that…who knows?'

'Two days.' Padraig closed his eyes and the other two could almost see his mind working overtime. 'With your permission,' he said to Neville, 'I would like Megan to go to Dublin.'

Nev simply nodded.

Padraig turned to Megan. 'Roger McGuinness is our Dublin representative here at the moment. Work out with him a plan to lift Southcombe. Take him alive. I want to know who else was involved in the O'Geary's murder. Use our Dublin unit. They're experienced men. I know some of them personally.' Turning to look at the farmhouse, he observed the contingent of men preparing to depart.

'One more thing. The man they tortured…he's going with you.'

They watched the trio converse and look at various photographs, not realising the topic concerned them. The sun was at its peak and they relaxed quietly against Padraig's car, enjoying the sunshine, the music from the car's radio and a cigarette. Both watched the young woman talk but they were too far away to hear her. She seemed to hold her ground with Padraig who could be quite domineering.

'How're your injuries holding up?' Daniel asked, not diverting his attention away from the woman.

'Fine,' Sean answered, not stopping to think about the question too much. His left knee did ache faintly but not enough to complain about. 'What do you think they're talking about?'

'Don't know. They *have* looked over this way a couple o' times.' After a minute or so he added, 'She seems to know Nev. Maybe she's from Galway. Republic plates on the bike.'

They watched Padraig pick up a photo. He nodded and turned to look at Daniel and Sean. He motioned for them to come over.

'I'll guess were about to find out,' Sean said as he flicked his cigarette away and began to follow Daniel across to them.

'I think you just want to find out her name.'

'*You* haven't stopped staring at her since she got here.'

'Can you blame me? A few days in the mountains with a couple o' dozen men for company and you don't want to meet her? I don't think you were conscripted into your army. I think you wanted to be around all those tanned lifeguards from those beaches of yours. Maybe you *don't* want to know her name?'

'You just want to know her name so you can scream it out the next time you have a wank.'

'Aye. I do!' Daniel tried to hold back his grin as they came up to them.

'Danny Carragher, Sean *Dockerty*,' Padraig gave a quick introduction. 'This is Megan O'Brien.'

Up close she was even more beautiful. Her sharp blue eyes stood out like two liquid jewels against her flawless buttermilk skin. High cheek bones, a perfect mouth with a sly celtic grin. And both lads were turned on by the sexual confidence she exuded in the company of men. She was stunning. The two lads shook her hand, Megan gripping tightly to imply she was a soldier just like them, not just some messenger girl.

'Sean was the one tortured that day,' Padraig explained.

Megan's bright blue eyes showed surprise for the briefest instant. 'I'm glad you're still with us Sean.'

'So am I but I don't think Daniel is,' he nodded towards his friend, 'He's lost half his wardrobe to me'.

She smiled and he saw her eyes betray her again, baulking at his strong accent. In all her chasing around of information to find the murderers, she had always assumed the three men kidnapped were Irish, completely forgetting one was Australian.

Padraig continued. 'Megan is a member of Cumann na mBan, our woman's volunteer council. She thinks we may have found the man who tortured you.'

They all saw Sean's face change. It seemed to drop, his colour draining before returning. Now his own eyes showed them his emotions. They screamed revenge and rage.

He turned from Padraig to Megan and simply said 'Yeah? Fucken where?!'

Sean stood beside Roger's car, his bag already in the boot. He was lost in thought, looking off to the mountain range across the valley but not seeing it. Over by the other cars Daniel was talking to Padraig trying to convince him to let him go with Sean and Roger – and Megan of course. But Sean wasn't paying attention to the argument. He was thinking about the School Principal; the man in the suit.

He could still hear his voice. He knew he would be able to identify the bastard in an instant and wouldn't hesitate to kill him. That was the problem though. Padraig had said he wanted information from him, that he wasn't to be killed until they had drained him of all he knew. He was to be tortured if necessary.

If this man turned out to be who they hoped then his days were at an end. He would not see the end of the week. His body would be dumped in any of a number of places; the river, a peat bog, maybe just a deserted lane way, thrown out of a moving van. The police in London, or where ever he lived, would inform his wife and children, if he had any, and they would mourn and cry and scream while Sean would savour his revenge. He knew he would not feel guilt. He hadn't when he had killed Simon.

'Resurrected from the dead.'

The voice startled him. He hadn't noticed Megan walk up beside him.

'Just like Jesus. I hear you even have the marks of our Lord.'

'Yeah.' He held out his hands, palms up. It still felt weird looking at such a holy image knowing it was evil that put them there. His year in Vietnam had convinced him there was no God and it puzzled him how people saw some kind of reliance in the marks that had caused him pain. 'Don't go thinking I'm any kind of saviour. They're just scars. I seem to collect the fucken things. At times I can still feel the nails inside them.'

Megan took his hands in hers as she studied them. He watched her as she turned them over and feel the smooth circles on the back off each hand, her hands warm and soft against his rough, scratched mitts.

'Do you want to kill him,' she said bluntly, the words surprising him.

She looked up from his hands, letting them go, and stared into his eyes. This time they did not betray her. They held his gaze. They told him nothing other than she was serious.

'Yes,' he answered. He tried to hold her gaze but looked away, back down to his hands.

'What did he say to you? Before he did this?'

'He told me to go home. That it wasn't my fight.'

'And where's home, Sean?'

He knew what she was doing. She should have been a shrink.

'It's here now,' he answered.

'Then our fight is your fight.'

THIRTY

Sean knew Dublin would be different to Belfast. In no way did they look as though they were on the same island, both built by similar people. The Belfast he had witnessed was a city of bleak buildings covered in graffiti that praised one paramilitary group and mocked another, pocked with bullet holes and scarred by fires and violence, surrounded by barricades, barbed wire, police and soldiers. The air in Belfast was thick with fear and hatred. It was a struggle to survive each day, to struggle to see the night only to have to fight through to dawn.

Dublin could not have been more of the opposite if it tried. What had once started life as a Viking settlement had prospered into a city where the streets were filled with the colour of markets, the busyness of people shopping, expanding trade all around and it's people living as they should. Restaurants lined the River Liffey and music of small ceili bands filtered out of so many pubs into the streets of an afternoon and played long into the night. The people put up no walls, literal or psychological. Everyone he had met in the day he had been there seemed pleasant and accommodating, but still keeping in mind the troubles going on less than a hundred miles away. Not that the northerners had been discourteous or rude. Far from it. They too had been good to him. Up there however they had to keep their guard up, always having to be wary of the face they didn't recognise. At least in the Republic they seemed a bit more laid back while still not forgetting their brothers and sisters across the border, be they Protestant or Catholic.

They had arrived last night after dark, dropping Roger's car and Megan's motorbike off at a safe house in Moore Lane in the city centre. It was a small two bedroom apartment with a lock-up garage behind the building. From here Roger took Sean, Daniel and Megan out for dinner, eating in a pub called Conway's, one of Dublin's oldest pubs and, as Roger explained to them, a favourite drinking hole for some of the leaders of the 1916 Easter Uprising. Some of them had been arrested there during the fighting.

They settled into a booth at the far end of the bar, away from the musicians as Megan ran through the information she had collated.

'Southcombe is staying at the Clarence Hotel, penthouse suite.'

'We have a man working there.' Roger explained. 'There's hardly a place in town we can't get into.'

'Call your man and have him watch this bastard every second he's there. Daniel and I will check it out in the morning. We'll see if it's possible to lift him outside, check out what sort of muscle he has watching his back.'

Roger shook his head as he sipped his pint. 'It's a busy area, Megan. I'd go for a pick up in transit. Even on the way to the airport.'

'That's leaving it a bit late isn't it?' Sean asked. 'We'd only have one chance at this and if we fuck it up he could leave the country.'

'We have the advantage here,' Roger said. 'He's on our turf. I know he leaves the day after tomorrow but we can do this.'

'What if we could lift him sooner?' Daniel chipped in.

'We'll know about that tomorrow,' Megan said. To Roger she added, 'We'll need some drivers that know every lane of the city.'

'My men are the best around. They could drive this city blindfolded.'

'My second cousin's blinder than a welder's dog,' Daniel said with a smile. 'Maybe you could get him a job down here.'

'What did he do?' Sean asked. 'See you naked and poke his eyes out?'

'He wishes he had his eyesight to see my beautiful body,' he said, winking at Megan

She let out a laugh. 'Christ, would you listen to this shite!'

'I've seen him in his undies,' Sean said to her. 'I wished I was blind.'

'How are we going to get Sean to ID him?' Roger asked, getting them back on track. 'He can't be seen by him and Sean never saw his face.' Behind them the small crowd applauded the ceili band as it finished off a jig.

Megan looked at Sean and smiled. 'That's as easy as picking up the phone.'

The sun rose colourfully above *Black Pool*; the Irish translation of Dubh Linn. The city had been active for many hours with delivery services and garbage men moving about before the sun crested the horizon. Learning that Merc Southcombe was an early riser, the two three man teams were up early and in position for his departure.

Morning traffic was picking up, blending them into the early rush. Sean and Roger sat in a stolen blue Opel on Ormond Quay, across the river from the hotel. Their driver was a young 23 year old Dubliner called Coen Devlin, a member of Dublin's IRA Southern Command. He had grown up in The Liberties suburb, not far from St James' gate, the Guinness Brewery, and was taught to drive by his older brother using the best teaching tools they had; stolen cars.

There was much debate between the Dublin volunteers as to who was the better driver but it seemed too close a contest to call. Coen was the more agile driver, being able to control the car through wet corners and alleys like a veteran rally driver through the icy forests of Finland.

His brother Ethan, older by two and a half years, while not as quick at the wheel, knew the streets of Dublin better than any man Roger knew, better than most of the cab drivers which had spent their lives on the cobbled stone and paved streets. He seemed to know which streets became congested in the afternoon commute and which were favoured by the heavier traffic such as cargo trucks and armoured money transporters. It was these small but important details that could be the difference between seconds and minutes in a job.

So between them the Devlin brothers had the city covered from west of Phoenix Park to the docks, from Milltown in the south to Saint

Margaret's Road in the north and they could cover it faster than any other driver in the country.

Ethan's car, which was a brown Leyland and of course wasn't his, sat fifty yards east of the hotel on Wellington Quay with Daniel in the front and Megan in the back. The two men smoked as they waited.

'So Daniel, how did you and Sean meet?' Megan asked, breaking the silence.

Daniel kept his eyes on the hotel ahead, flicking ash out the window as he spoke. 'On a fishing trawler in the Atlantic.' He remembered watching him jump down to the deck of the *Little Adele*.

'What was an Australian doing on a trawler in the middle of the Atlantic?' Her tone was playful. She was a morning person.

'Fishing,' he replied matter-of-factly.

She looked into the side mirror at him, seeing him smile. 'Smart arse.'

'Here we go,' Ethan said and started the motor.

They watched a young man in a porter's uniform walk out of the hotel's lobby. He stopped near the road's edge ran his fingers through his hair.

'That's it,' Daniel stated and got out of the car, walking back down the road away from the hotel so he could get a clear view over the five foot wall that separated the road from the river. Across the river he could see the blue Opel parked beside the phone booth. He signalled and watched Roger and Sean exit the car, Roger entering the booth with Sean waiting just outside.

In the booth Roger dropped in a coin and dialled the number to the front desk of the Clarence. It was picked up on the third ring. Roger motioned for Sean to come closer.

'Good morning, the Clarence Hotel. This is Cathal speaking. How may I help you?'

'Good morning to yourself Cathal. This is Sean Michaels here,' he made sure to use names that, if Southcombe repeated it, Sean would recognise from that day. 'I was wondering if I could be put through to

Mr Merc Southcombe's room please.'

'You're in luck Mr Michaels. He's right here in the lobby.'

I know, Roger thought.

They heard some talking and the hand over of the phone. Sean leaned in closer to the earpiece.

'Yes? How can I help you?'

Roger looked directly at Sean as he waited for confirmation. Sean shut his eyes as he tried to concentrate, blocking out the noises of the awakening city around them. He was back in that room in Galway…

…pain all over his body…

…the pistol man standing over him as he lay on the blood-stained floor, his back propped up against the filthy wall…

…an assault rifle aimed at his chest just waiting to bark death at him…

…the "School Principal" in front of him, balaclava covering his face but nothing could disguise his voice.

'My name is Sean Michaels, Mr Southcombe. I'm from the Dublin office of the London Times and I was hoping we could arrange a time for an interview concerning your talks with the Deputy Trade Minister.'

'I'm sorry Sean, but I've a full agenda while I'm here in Dublin and I fly out tomorrow morning. You've caught me at a bad time.'

'Oh well. Can't be helped,' Roger played along.

'Tell you what. Call your counterparts in London and have them call my office. I will be glad to talk to them when I return home. Good day Mr Michaels.'

The phone went dead. Roger hung up the receiver and looked at Sean. He could tell by the look on the Australian's face they had their man.

'That's him.'

Daniel watched them leave the booth. Roger gave them the signal and they returned to the car. He stubbed his cigarette out before he got back into the car, and looked back at Megan.

'It's him.'

'Let's go.' She tapped Ethan on the shoulder and they pulled out into traffic.

They timed it perfectly. Southcombe's car had been bought around to the front of the hotel and he and his protection of four were walking out of the front doors as the young republicans drove past, slowing down just enough to see what sort of protection he had with him. They would later talk to their man in the lobby, the porter, to compare details but they had to see for themselves what they were up against.

Southcombe climbed into the rear of his silver Jaguar, the door being held open for him by one of his minders whom then got in beside the driver while the other three men entered a black Ford Cortina that had pulled up in front of the Jag.

'Four men watching his back, all definitely armed. I saw at least two pistols get in the black car. Have to assume the drivers are armed as well,' Daniel scanned the faces but didn't recognise any of them.

'The plates on both cars are Dublin,' Ethan pointed out.

They parked around the corner and watched through their mirrors as the two car convoy came into view. Both turned north onto Capel St and crossed the river. Once they had reached the other side Ethan spun the car around and began to follow.

Coen had his car facing away from the bridge, playing it safe. Like his brother, he waited until they had passed him and then bought the car around in a quick u-turn. Stopping at the intersection, he gave way to the brown Leyland and pulled in behind. There were three other cars between them and the Jag. Relaxing, both brothers settled into their job and blended into the morning traffic.

'Once he gets to where he's going,' Roger told them, 'I want to run the road most likely taken back to the Clarence.'

Up ahead the black Ford turned right onto Abbey St Lower. Some of the normal traffic followed, as did they. A left onto O'Connell St Lower and they wove their way around finally taking a right into a busy Dorset St.

'He's not taking any direct path,' Coen told them. 'Either his driver's lost or he knows how to stay ahead of any fore-planning from people like us.'

'I was hoping they wouldn't do this.' Roger shook his head.

'We can't plan a lift around this,' Sean said as he watched the Cortina lead the Jag into another side street, all the time staring into the back of the head that sat in the rear of the Jag.

Ahead of them Ethan slowed and let them and several other cars pass him, making sure that he wasn't in the Jag's mirrors too often. Coen watched him pull back into traffic four cars and a double-decker bus behind.

'We'll see where he's going first.' Roger settled back and waited for the ride to end.

After a further five minutes they finally passed the Jag and its escort as they pulled up at their destination.

'Just a normal house. No idea who lives there.' Roger didn't look sideways as they turned right at the next corner. Both cars stopped and Daniel and Megan left Ethan to watch the house as the rest of them returned to the safe house in Moore Lane in Coen's car.

Looking over a map of the city, the five of them bounced ideas off of each other as they tried to decide on the best course of action.

The house the Jag had stopped at was only two blocks from Croke Park, Dublin's biggest sporting stadium.

'I doubt he's a hurling man,' Daniel remarked.

'So we take him as he comes out.' Sean looked up at them but Roger shook his head.

'We don't know how long he's going to be in there. If someone sees two cars parked across the road loaded with armed men then we're done.'

'I'm not saying we park across the road from him…'

'Okay, what about the hotel? As he enters or leaves…' Megan offered.

'We've already got a man inside,' Coen pointed out. 'Why not use him and hit from inside? Early morning wake up call.'

'No. It's key access only to get the lift up to the penthouse and I'm sure he'd have his men on the door.'

'We've more men than him!' Daniel exclaimed.

For a second Roger didn't say anything. He played a few scenarios out in his head but finally shook it off. 'No. He needs to be taken alive. It's too confined in there to be sure he isn't killed. And he could retreat to his room and await the Gardaí to show.'

Sean was beginning to get frustrated. 'What do you suggest?'

'I'd prefer to grab him in transit but his driver changes routes too often. That only leaves us a small window in which to grab him between here,' he pointed to the map, 'and the airport. There's too much risk if we tried it at the airport itself so we only have this small stretch of road.'

Looking at the area on the map, Sean could see it would be too difficult to take him on possibly the busiest road in Ireland.

'Unless something comes up today,' Roger continued, 'I don't think we could take him without one of us getting hurt or him getting killed. It's too unpredictable. I'm sorry Sean.'

Sean heard the words but it took a few seconds for them to sink in. He just looked at them all in disbelief, shocked they were going to let this opportunity slip by.

'Fucken pissweak!' He picked up his jacket and headed for the door.

'Sean!' Daniel called out to him. 'Sean!'

The door slammed shut and they could hear his footsteps as he hurried down the steps.

'I'll talk to him,' Daniel said and went after him.

Megan walked to the window and opened the curtain. After a few seconds Sean came out onto the street, marching off in anger. Daniel ran after him but made no attempt to stop him. He just fell in beside him and they continued down the road.

They walked in silence to nowhere in particular. Daniel understood Sean's anger at their inability to act. He, too, wanted to lift this bastard. Even if they obtained no information from him (but he doubted that) it would be a sizeable blow to the loyalist movement and, because of his stature and position in the upper class, to British society itself.

'You hungry?' he asked Sean after they had gone several blocks, zigzagging their way towards the river.

Sean fished out a packet of smokes and stopped to light two of them, handing one to Dan.

'Fucken starvin'.'

The Irishman looked up and down the street. He had only been to Dublin once before but he knew where he was. 'Come on then.'

He led them to a pub called Keating's, only a few blocks north of the Liffey. An early morning Guinness filled them up as they sat at the window waiting for their breakfast to arrive.

'So we just head back to Belfast then?' Sean asked, the creamy head from his stout sticking to his upper lip.

'It's like a holiday down here, isn't it?' Dan flicked ash off his cigarette.

'Is there a way we could get him once he's back in England? Do we have men over there?' He persisted but Daniel just waved it off.

'Let it go Sean. He'll get his. Just not today.'

Sean just shook his head and stared out into the passing traffic. They ate their breakfast in silence, listening to the radio that softly played behind the bar, Bobbie Gentry declaring that she'd never fall in love again.

As Sean returned from the bar with two more pints, Daniel bought up a new subject.

'What do you think of Megan?'

Despite his frustration at the morning's events, Sean couldn't help but laugh. 'I fucken knew you fancied her! That's why you're in Dublin. Not to watch my back but to bed her!'

Dan just smiled and shrugged his shoulders guiltily. 'What can I say?'

'That you're a horny, dirty bastard walking around town with one loaded gun in your jacket and one in your pants.'

'You…'

'And,' Sean interrupted, 'your loyalties leave a lot to be desired!'

Daniel began laughing. 'What the fuck are you talking about?'

'You're meant to be helping me but instead of thinking about what to do with *that* gun,' he pointed to Dan's jacket, 'you're working for that thing in your pants.'

'You're jealous, aren't you?'

'Of you?'

'You're not attracted to her?'

'She's a stunner, I'll agree, but I don't think she would take too kindly if I…if either of us tried to hit her up.'

Dan laughed. 'So it has crossed your mind then?'

Sean grinned. 'Of course it has.'

Holding his pint out in front of him, Dan toasted Megan. 'To the most beautiful soldier I've ever seen. May she never fall to the enemy or old age.'

'I thought you were talking about me there for a second.'

'Not even if I were queer. *Sláinte*.'

'You can taste the difference, can't yeh?'

Sean sipped at the glass, working the liquid around in his mouth then gulped it down. 'It's a lot smoother.' He could already feel it warming his gut. 'Yeah, it's nicer than Scotch.'

'So why,' Dan asked rhetorically, 'is Scotch more popular around the world?'

Sean didn't respond. He just let him talk.

'Because of the fucken Brits. Irish whiskey used to be the most popular drink in America until they crushed sales with monstrous taxes and tariffs. We couldn't trade to other countries because they were putting pressure on us. Our whiskey sales don't line their pockets. Flooded the world with Scottish whisky and almost drove us out of business. What we could sell they taxed like it was going out of style. It was a trade embargo.'

It was after midday and they were slowly getting drunk. They had nothing else to do today and the weather was becoming overcast.

'I first got drunk on Irish whiskey,' Dan stated as he looked at the gold liquid in his glass. 'My da' and one of my uncles sat me down when I was sixteen and opened one of his old bottles and we drank together for the first time. It wasn't long after I had joined Fianna na hEireann. That's the junior wing of the IRA. Now that I had given up football... I was so sick the next day.'

'Mine was beer,' Sean declared. 'Our country's fuelled by the stuff.' He took a drag and thought back. 'It was my brother's end of year football party. Me and Luke and Thomo sat at the far end hiding pitchers under the table. Everyone knew we were drinking but they thought as long as they could keep an eye on us it would do no harm. Probably did it to teach us a lesson. That first hangover...you never expect it to be like that. I remember thinking I wanted to die just to be rid of that deathly feeling.'

'I remember,' Dan began as he drew back on his cigarette, bringing up a new topic, 'when I saw my first dead person.' He leaned back into his chair and ran his fingers through his hair, brushing it back out of his eyes. 'A couple of mates and I were coming home from training. One of 'em was Padraig's nephew.' His face changed ever so slightly as his hand moved up, down, left right forming the sign of the cross. He didn't have to explain the reason of this action and continued on with his story. 'We had heard all this ruckus up ahead on the other side of the park near the tree line and when we got there we saw four men running away. Lying just off the edge of the path was this bloke. His head and face had been smashed in; blood ran like a fucken river through the grass. I can still see him there. I don't know what he did or if they caught the ones who did it...' He looked at Sean, his attention not wavering. 'I couldn't sleep for days after.'

'My first dead body was in Vietnam.' Sean picked up his glass and drained it before continuing. 'We were only two weeks in and on our first patrol. We were virgins at this and were pissing our pants with fear. After a day of walking through the thickest scrub I've ever seen we had a contact. Our scout had seen something up ahead and it turned out to be a mortar crew returning from lobbing some at...shit, I can't remember. They were lobbing bombs at someone! Anyway, all hell breaks loose and we hit the dirt. I fired off two mags without seeing a thing, which is stupid, I know! But if it keeps their heads down then I don't care.

'After the shooting stopped we move forward to check things out. I remember one of our lads going through this dead nog's pockets but when he put his hands in this guy's jacket, it was filled with blood. He'd been near cut in two by an SLR but his shirt had held him together. His eyes were still open too, just looking up at the trees like he could see something we couldn't. Not like in the movies.'

After many pints, several nips of whiskey and an hour of talk that seemed to revolve around girls or war, they saw Coen outside, walking up the street toward the pub.

'Hey, there's Coen.' Sean jumped up and went to the door. 'Coen!' he yelled out over the traffic, waving at the young Irishman. Coen saw him and crossed the road.

'Three pints thanks Liam,' Sean said to the publican as he headed back to the table. He grabbed a third seat and dragged it over as Coen came in.

'Been looking for you two for ages,' he said as he took his jacket off.

'What's happening back at the fort?' Dan asked as he offered him a smoke.

'No thanks. Well nothing's happening. Roger's gone somewhere, Megan went somewhere else and I went to get Ethan and tell him it's been called off. You two eaten?'

'There's shin soup if you're hungry,' Liam said as he bought over their pints.

'Shin soup it is.'

'Where is your brother?' Sean queried.

'He's still watching the house. He knows we're not doing anything about it but he always does this. Claims it as practice; following cars around trying to pre-empt where they're going. So what have you two been doing other than drinking?'

'Just talking and watching the world go by,' the elder Irishman explained.

'Really? I'd like to hear about Vietnam. If it's okay?' Coen looked at Sean who seemed to stare through him at the mention of the word.

'Maybe later,' he answered.

Daniel saw Sean hold back and stepped in. 'No war stories Coen until you've had a few drinks,' he held up his own pint glass. 'So drink up lad!'

It didn't take Coen long to get a glow happening; three pints and a shot of whiskey to be exact. Once he started talking he couldn't stop. He kept the others in stitches as he told them stories of his experiences growing up in the slums of Dublin and dirty jokes his mother had taught him.

Finally he bought up the Vietnam topic again. 'What's it like over there, Sean? In the jungle and all that? Is it as bad as what you see on TV?'

The smile that had been on his face faded. He sat his Guinness down, his head bowing with it. He stared at the half emptied glass.

'It's worse. A thousand times worse 'cause TV can't hurt you.' He paused for a while, the others waiting patiently. 'My best friend was killed there. His name was Joel. We...we were hit by the same mortar round. He was killed and I wasn't. He took the brunt of the blast. At times I feel as guilty as hell. If he hadn't have been next to me then I would be the one dead and he would be with his family.'

Coen listened with respect as Sean told him of his last week over there. He didn't interrupt. He tried to picture it; this man who was the same age as him but seemed to be more mature than all of them put together.

'The last time I saw him was as we lay in this gully, watching a Phantom come in above us. Phantoms don't have guns so it had to drop a bomb on 'em. It banked and lined them up and that was it. Everything went black and he was dead.'

No one said a thing. Sean took a gulp of stout, Daniel as well. Coen didn't know what to say.

After a minute of watching the traffic go by, Daniel looked at Sean and asked, 'So that wanker back home in Australia wasn't your first I take it?'

The younger Devlin brother looked at Dan, shocked by the question after what he had just heard from Sean, not believing the brusqueness of the query. He looked over at Sean but didn't see the anger or revulsion he had expected. For a second Sean didn't react. Then he smiled. Well... not smiled but grinned. And not in a perverse way. More in the way of when someone recalls a memory long suppressed, the image finally surfacing to be re-read, but still with some guilt.

'It was an hour before sunrise. We had an ambush set up and as the jungle was turning that cold blue colour it did each morning, we saw movement coming along this track. There was about a dozen of them heading home. We had a full platoon so we had them outnumbered. They didn't suspect a thing and came right in to us, heading straight for me. I remember hearing them just talking, chatting away, no cares in the world.' He looked up at Coen. 'You know what a Claymore is?'

'A Scottish sword?' Coen answered with a sly grin.

'It's a perimeter explosive about the size of a thick book and curved in an arc, full of C4 and hundreds of ball bearings. Just sends a wall of 'em out. We had several claymores surrounding our lay up, 360 degrees. We let the VC come right in...' Sean stopped and took a sip, the others anxious for him to continue. 'I hit the clacker when they were about ten yards from us. There was a...huge, blinding flash. I dropped the clacker, picked up my SLR and began searching for a target. There were only a few left standing. It just cut through them. Then the M60's opened up. Fucken gunfire everywhere. Rounds passing within inches of your head.' He snapped his fingers several times beside his ear. 'They crack as they pass. That's when you know they're close.' He sipped his stout, his mouth dry. 'A few of them survived and ran out of there as we moved forward. The first bodies I came to were the ones that had walked towards me. There were six of them. It was like every one of those ball bearings had zeroed in on them...like they'd turned inside out.'

He stopped for a second, just staring out to the traffic but not seeing it. Instead he could see the bodies again. Six pulpy masses of flesh torn asunder...the smell of cordite being overpowered by the stench of their spilled innards.

'I'd killed six men with nothing more than the closing of a circuit. It was like cheating. Shooting someone is totally different. Somehow more…I don't know. More personal I guess.'

Dan watched his new friend. He waited for his mind to return from the jungles, from the terrors he had seen. After a minute he still had not moved. 'You all right?'

Sean blinked hard and looked up at him. 'I never thought it possible to be so scared.' He pushed some memories back deep into his mind, wishing they would go away forever. He would never tell them he had once literally shit himself the first time he had been shot at from less than five yards away, the rifle barking at him that night being the first thing louder than his breathing he had heard in over twelve hours. He doubted anyone other than a fellow Vietnam serviceman would understand. 'I don't think I'll ever be that scared again.' He paused before adding reluctantly, 'I've seen shit no one should see.'

Silence again.

Dan just smiled back, readjusted himself in his seat and took a gulp.

'What about yourself?' Sean asked, eager to get the topic on someone else.

'Me? Not unless I killed someone the other night in Short Strand. Nah. Seen people get shot. Only wounded, not killed. I don't think I killed that joker last month…may have winged him but I don't know.' He flicked ash into the tray and finished off his drink. Outside it was beginning to rain.

Coen watched the two of them, neither of them looking at each other nor him. He then looked over and caught Liam's attention. He held up three fingers and his own glass. Liam the publican nodded. When the three whiskeys arrived, Coen picked his up and held it to his lips. He took a small sip. 'I shot my neighbours cat with a pellet gun when I was fourteen. The thing ran up and down the street wailing like mad and I was grounded for a month.' He threw the rest of the whiskey down and shuddered as it burned his throat.

Sean and Daniel both turned to look at Coen. The Dubliner began to grin.

The other two looked back at each other and burst into laughter, tears rolling down their faces as they doubled up in hysterics.

'A cat…!!' Sean tried to say something but couldn't get it out over the laughter.

'We'd better…' Dan began, his own laughter drowning his words. 'We'd better watch ourselves!! He's a car thief …and…and a cat killer!!'

'I never killed the cat,' Coen corrected. 'It's still alive, the old fuck. It didn't die.' He laughed along with them, glad he had lifted the mood of their little corner. He watched them try to drink their whiskeys as they fought to gain control of themselves.

Sean finally got his down and slammed the empty glass down on the table. He reached over and gave Coen a slap to his shoulder, the giggles finally dying off. As he looked at the young republican it finally hit him.

'That's it,' he said quietly to himself. His face turned serious, the road ahead now so clear.

Dan saw the look on Sean's face, his mind now back on the job. 'What?'

'It's so fucken simple!' Sean looked back at Coen. 'All we ever needed was you and your brother's skills!'

He couldn't wipe the excitement from his face as he told them how they would have Southcombe before the city sat down to its breakfast tomorrow morning.

But they had to work fast. They had to find Roger and his Dublin Brigade.

THIRTY ONE

It had rained all night and still was at 6:30 the next morning. Sean looked up at the heavy clouds from the open window and breathed in the smell of summer rain. He realised in every country he had been to over the past year, even on the *Brizo's Star* in the middle of the Indian Ocean, there was a certain smell of rain and it always seemed to be the same. It would never change. It was constant and reassuring, metallic and cool.

The sheeted rain he now watched coming in from the Irish Sea was nothing compared to the monsoonal rains of Asia other than the smell. Over there it was a burden and a hindrance. Rivers could appear at any time, turning a gully or valley into a new roaring tributary as it would pour for weeks, delaying military operations.

Here, this morning, the rain was their ally. It was playing a major part in their operation. Without it Southcombe would be touching down in Heathrow by 10:25am.

Sean resisted the urge to smoke as he waited in their Moore Lane residence. He had a slight headache from yesterdays drinking and didn't want to aggravate it any more. Roger and Megan were waiting on the lounge, ready to leave once they got the call to carry out their end of the plan. Whilst Roger's task was simple, his timing was imperative. Megan's however was more dangerous as she would be on the ground when the lift took place. She was to only go into action if things got out of hand. She was their back-up, their ace in the hole.

When they had explained the plan to them last night, both lads had seen the twinkle in Roger's eye when he knew it would work. However two things had to happen; Coen and Ethan had to get the exact cars they needed and the rain needed to keep up. It had been hard to judge which of the two their Achilles' heel was. So far the rain looked to be on the side of the republicans. The autos however were in the hands of the two best car thieves in Dublin.

Sean checked his watch. He hoped the boys would not be late. Then the phone rang. Daniel answered it, praying for good news. The other three watched him, waiting for a sign that it was on.

'C'mon,' Sean uttered to himself.

Daniel placed the phone back on its hook and nodded. 'They'll be here in five minutes.'

They were all off their seats and moving. Their gear had been packed for the past hour; weapons loaded, their steps gone over until each persons role could be recited by all. Roger's car and Megan's motorbike had been picked up during the night and taken to a separate safe house in Kilmainham. They locked the door behind them and descended the stairs. Sean and Daniel waited in the doorway and watched Roger climb up into the cab of a Guinness delivery truck, the driver beside him being one of the Dublin brigade. Another car pulled in behind it, a light blue Rover. This was Megan's get away if she needed it. She got in and both vehicles pulled out and were replaced by Ethan and Coen in their new cars.

Sean looked at the cars, their gleaming painted panels shimmering with the rain. He could taste the victory he would soon have. Ethan nodded to them from inside the black Ford Cortina. A common car but not a common paint colour, this dark blue sedan had been resprayed over night, heat lamps used to cure the paint to a stage where they could give it a quick buff, all the flaws now hidden by the beading water.

Coen sat behind the wheel of a 1969 XJ12 Jaguar saloon. It was identical to the car being used by Southcombe whilst in Dublin, the licence plate replaced with a false one to match. The hardest car to find, it had been acquired only an hour ago from the Dublin Hospital doctor's car park.

Daniel made for the Jag but was stopped by Sean. They had already agreed Daniel would ride with Coen and Sean with his brother but he now felt he had to take Southcombe.

'I need to do this one,' he said to Dan.

'Are you sure?'

Sean nodded.

Daniel patted him on the back and they ran to the cars, Daniel climbing in the rear of the Cortina, Sean in beside Coen in the front of the Jag. Both cars turned out into the sparse morning traffic.

Merc Southcombe awoke at 6am precisely; his morning wake up call had been confirmed the night before. He showered and shaved and dressed in his dark grey suit pants and white shirt, his black tie embroidered with his family crest. His hand-tailored Nesbit and Sons of London single breasted four button jacket still hung in its place in the wardrobe until he was ready to leave.

At 6:20 his tea arrived with the morning's copy of the *Financial Times*, the *Daily Mirror* and *The Times*. A splash of cream and one sugar, he settled into his morning routine of covering all three papers front to back whilst eating a light breakfast of toast and jam. At 7:17 he put on his jacket and checked himself in the mirror. Pleased with what he saw, he picked up his brief case and crossed the floor of the penthouse suite to the front door and opened it. A waiting UVF man in the hall said 'Good morning sir' and entered to pick up Southcombe's suitcase. The other UVF men were in the hall by the elevator waiting for him. They knew of his schedule for the day and had been up early in preparation of his leaving.

Whilst they were a loyal group of bodyguards, they couldn't wait to see him finally get on the plane for London. The pride that had swelled in them on notification of their job of protecting one of their sponsors had dissipated with his almost military routine and dictatorial attitude. Everything had to be planned down to the last minute, to the last second. It was beginning to drive them crazy. They only had a few hours to go. The cars would pick them up at 7:20 and drive him to his breakfast engagement (hence the light meal of toast) and from there to Dublin Airport for his flight at 9:30, gate 6, British Airways, first class, goodbye.

In the car park in the building directly behind the Clarence Hotel, Southcombe's two drivers started their cars. The V12 Jaguar engine rumbled to life, finally settling into a purr as it warmed up. To its left the Cortina pulled out of its parking space and headed for the exit, the Jag close behind it.

For them to pull up directly in front of the hotel they had to circle the block. As they turned the second last corner they found the road blocked by a reversing Guinness truck which was having trouble lining up a delivery access lane to the hotel. The driver of the Cortina climbed out into the sheeting rain and ran up to the cab of the truck, pounding on the driver's door, his leather jacket pulled up around his neck.

The truck driver wound down his window. 'Just give us a second mate and I'll be out of your way.'

'Well fucking hurry up! I'm running late!'

'No need for attitude my friend! It's this rain. Can't see a thing.' The trucker smiled at this, knowing it would only make him angrier.

'If you can't see what you're doing then fuck off and let us through!'

The passenger of the truck leaned across to look at the drenched man down on the street. 'How about having a bit of patience boyo? We're only doing our job. Either fuck up or back up and go around.'

The Cortina driver turned and looked down beyond the Jag and saw two more cars had turned into the same street, blocking them.

'Just hurry up!' the Cortina driver shouted and ran back up the street to the warmth of the car. 'Southcombe's going to be pissed off,' he said to himself. He knew any excuse he gave would be stomped on when he finally picked him up.

Roger and the truck driver watched the man climb back into the black Ford. He then looked to his left down to the river and saw another black Ford Cortina and a silver Jag coast along through the rain on Wellington Quay before disappearing out of view.

Without the rain they could never have pulled in off. As Ethan bought the Ford in to the curb he saw the front door of the hotel open. As he stopped the car he saw five men exiting, each trying to keep their heads pulled into their jackets. One carried an umbrella not for himself but for the man in the suit.

In the back seat behind him Daniel kept his head low, a Browning 9mm loaded and cocked in his right hand, his left on the door handle.

'They're crossing the footpath to the Jag,' Ethan said as he watched them in the side mirror. 'They haven't noticed anything yet.'

Daniel didn't say a word.

Megan was two doors down heading towards the hotel keeping close to the buildings which would give her a thirty yard buffer from the minders when they reached the cars. In her left hand she carried a large black umbrella. Her right hand was deep in her coat pocket, her fingers wrapped around her loaded Walther, a silencer threaded onto the barrel, the safety catch on, her thumb waiting to flick it over. She walked with a quick step. Just another Dubliner on her way to work trying to keep out of the rain.

Dressed in her dark green skirt and coat with light green stockings, she watched the five men leave the hotel. She noted her blue Rover two hundred yards away heading along Wellington Quay, coming towards her.

Neither Daniel nor Sean were visible in the cars that waited.

The rain was getting heavier.

'Here he comes.' Coen informed Sean who was crouched down in the foot-well of the front seat of the Jag.

Sean heard the rear door open and felt the car move as Southcombe sat down on the leather seat. The rear door shut.

They only had seconds.

As the minder closed the umbrella and stepped forward to open the front door and climb in beside Coen, Sean sat up, facing the rear, the Browning Hi-Power semi-automatic thrust out towards Southcombe.

The minder tried to open the door but it was locked. As he looked down to get the driver's attention he saw a third person in the car aiming a gun at his boss. For a second his mind went blank. It felt like he was imagining it. The man he was to be guarding now had a gun aimed at his head. Finally his brain got the message through to the rest of his body and he reacted. He dropped the umbrella, went for his own gun and began to yell a warning at the same time. Then something hit him and his world ended in darkness.

The other three minders had broken off from Southcombe as he was being secured in the Jag. They were hurrying to the Cortina and the first of them was reaching the car when he thought he heard something. He alone turned and saw the Jag beginning to pull away.

He was wondering what the driver was doing when he then turned and saw Southcombe's number one minder still on the footpath. He was buckling over and falling, his gun clattering into the pools of water at his feet.

Realising what was going on, he reacted quicker than his companion had. His gun was out in an instant and was drawing up to the Jag, his eye acquiring his target in the front seat.

Megan understood there was a chance they would pull this off without firing a shot, but she was ready for the opposite. The deaths of these men, if she did kill them today, would not haunt her. She had killed before today and, God willing, she would continue the fight tomorrow.

She kept an eye on the man by the Jaguar as he tried to open the front door. Coen had begun to pull away from the curb and the minder was going for his gun.

No going back.

She let the umbrella fall from her left hand, the semi-automatic pistol free of her pocket, her left hand coming across cradling her right. The Jag minder had his gun just clear of his belt when she aimed at his broad back. The Walther coughed twice, both 9mm hollow point rounds hitting only an inch apart and disintegrating as they tore through his left lung and heart. He was dead before the ejected shells of her Walther, and his body, hit the ground.

With her hair now drenched and plastered to her head she took two steps forward and retargeted to the gunmen by the black car. One of them was beginning to move. Going for his gun, following the Jag. The sights of her Walther now seemed to control her movements. He filled her sights and she fired two more rounds then changed target to the next man closest to her. He was yet to note what was happening but it didn't matter. She fired twice, two marks appearing on his back as he fell. She moved back to the first gunmen who had spun from the impacts and now faced her as he fell back against the car. She fired another round, this time at his head.

The third gunman broke away from the other falling two, making room between him and them. He had seen Megan take the last shot at his fellow minder and had his gun out as he ran for cover behind the iron pole of a street light. His gun fired three shots wildly, stone exploding and glass shattering from the front of the hotel, the sound booming across the river like thunder.

Megan changed magazines despite there being one more round remaining. As she slipped in the mag she saw the third man aiming. Dropping to one knee she re-aimed the Walther. She heard him fire once. The shot went high, the round cracking as it passed her too close. In the background, beyond the men, the few people that were out in the rain were now screaming and running for cover. More gunshots from over by the car but not from the minders. Daniel had his window down and was firing constant covering rounds as the Cortina pulled away. The man behind the streetlight tried to duck but caught one of the many 9mm rounds first in his back then in the side of the head. Blood exploded out along with half of his face, his right ear now hanging down to his shoulder by a thin strip of skin. As his lifeless body fell, Megan put two more rounds into him and was up and running. She fired one more round into the heads of each of the bodies that lie at the curb as she passed them, then moved to the light blue Rover pulling up in the space that had been vacated by the Cortina. She climbed into the back seat and the car sped off into the continuing rain.

Southcombe's eyes met Sean's and he immediately knew who he was. His face dropped in shock, enough to tell Sean he had his man. Hearing his voice on the phone Sean had only been 75% sure he was the man that had him nailed to a board, had poor old Tom put down like an ageing dog and killed his son Michael without blinking. But the look in his eyes as he stared back over the pistol into Sean's eyes was all the proof he needed.

The car began to pull away.

Sean's peripheral vision caught the shooting of the first minder. They then flashed by the Ford, two more men going down and a third racing for cover. *That girl can shoot*, he thought as they roared off up the road. He heard gunfire being exchanged, a second gun answering back. They turned the corner fast, the heavy Jag sliding across the two lanes as Coen used the car's weight to line up for the next corner.

Sean tossed Southcombe some handcuffs. 'Right wrist only.'

The Englishman complied.

'Turn around. Hands behind your back.'

Sean reached over, the gun always trained on him and with his free hand he secured the second clasp making sure both were unmercifully tight.

After five blocks Coen settled back down into a casual drive, blending in with what traffic there was. Their ally the rain hid from the outside world the actions taking place in the interior of the Jag.

Southcombe hadn't said a word. He kept his eyes locked onto Sean's; a film of sweat on his upper lip betrayed his fear. Despite this, Sean noticed he still looked like a rich, powerful man. He looked like the kind of man that could hold his own with some of the wealthiest and possibly smartest people in Britain. He was built in the way the greedy are, his face telling of a success none of them would ever know. The thickening jowls a result of sickeningly expensive plates in restaurants; of Russian caviar and Napoleon Brandy, venison from Scotland personally prepared for him by his chef in one of his many extravagant dwellings. To Sean the rich always seemed to be fat.

'You know your mistake don't you?'

Southcombe just stared back, his face struggling to hide both the rage and trepidation that boiled away within.

'You know and it's now killing you inside.' Sean goaded. 'One tiny mistake and look where it's gotten you.' He couldn't help but smile. 'Remember what you last said to me?'

Southcombe remained quiet.

'You told me it wasn't my fight. That I'd best fuck off home. Well you made it my fight and now, this is my home.'

THIRTY TWO

The garage door to the awaiting house in Kilmainham was open when they turned in to the drive. A man at the entrance was ready to shut the door the instant the Jag was inside. He then pulled Southcombe out and with a gun at the back of his head, forced him in through an internal door into the house. No effort was made to blindfold him. He would be telling no one of what he had seen. This fact was not lost on Southcombe. He knew he was in serious trouble.

'On your knees,' Sean said to him when they were in the lounge room.

Before he had a chance to kneel, the man who had dragged him from the car kicked the back of his knees, pushing his head forward. He fell hard onto the carpet, toppling over further and landing on his chest, his face smacking the floor, his brow taking the impact. The gunman placed his boot on his neck, holding him down, the pistol aimed at the top of his head.

Coen crossed to the window and looked through the crack in the curtains, careful not to move them and attract attention. He looked up and down the street. Nothing out of the ordinary. They hadn't been followed. On the drive over half of his time had been spent checking his mirrors, trying to spot a car that took his seemingly random but planned route; looking for that one car that appeared too casual or twice in different areas, but there had been nothing. He sat on the arm of the tattered lounge so he could keep one eye on the wet street and the other on Southcombe.

The back door opened and a fourth man, another of Roger's, whispered something to the man standing on the Englishman. He nodded, the other man leaving the way he had come.

'We're ready to leave once they get here,' he said to Sean.

The Australian motioned for him to get off Southcombe. He stepped off and turned him over. Specks of dirt and carpet had stuck to his expensive suit. A large bruise had appeared at his receding black hairline courtesy of the meeting with the floor.

Sean leant down and pulled a wallet from the inside pocket of Southcombe's jacket. It was hand-stitched leather with gold initials embossed on a magnesium alloy insert on the lower right corner. He flipped through it. Four hundred and thirty six English pounds in one sleeve, two hundred and seventy five Irish punt in another. He unfolded the driver's licence from the next sleeve and read the details: Merc Stirling Southcombe. Fifty two years of age. A London address that meant nothing to him but had to be a rich suburb. He handed the money and the licence to the gunman beside him. A photo of a woman. Had to be his wife. She was a stick insect thin creature with an even thinner smile…

'What do you plan to…' Southcombe had only said so much when Sean moved like an unleashed spring, his fist driving down into Southcombe's face, the impact breaking his nose and sending blood shooting out of his nostrils down across his chin.

Sean held up a finger to his lips to quieten his moaning. 'Shut up,' he calmly said to him. He tossed the wallet to the gunman who went through it himself before replacing all the items, including the money. Next, Sean went through the trouser pockets. Some change and a small key on a gold key ring. He held it up, showing the gunman. He nodded, understanding what it was and disappeared out to the garage returning a few seconds later with the leather briefcase, placing it on the kitchen table. Sean tossed him the key and he began shuffling through the papers within. Sean then knelt down next to the Englishman's head.

'You wouldn't be stupid enough to still have *my* wallet, would you?'

Southcombe knew it was a rhetorical question so didn't answer.

Sean cast a glance up at the man going through the brief case. He shook his head. Sean didn't explain to Southcombe it had contained the only picture of his mother he owned. So often had he looked at the picture that, if he had any artistic ability, he could have drawn a perfect copy of it, so much had he studied it. He removed the thought of his mother from his mind and looked down at the Englishman. Weeks ago the roles had been reversed. Weeks ago he had been on the ground in that room with this prick standing over him, death lurking outside the room, begging for a chance to come in and claim the Australian, begging for the nod from Southcombe.

It hadn't come.

He remembered Rebecca, the doctor that had found him. She had saved only him. Tom dead on one side, Michael dead on the other… He knew his new companions would not be as sympathetic to Southcombe as he and his loyalists had been to him.

He lowered the Browning pistol to the bridge of his cracked and bleeding nose. Southcombe's eyes looked in fear from the black barrel up into Sean's eyes and back again. It was so tempting but he knew he had to deliver him. It would all be for nothing to just kill him now. Instead, he tapped the barrel hard on his broken nose. Southcombe moaned in pain and pulled his head away. Sean watched him squirm as he held the gun above his nose again. The fat businessman's eyes were full of tears as he held back the pain.

'They're here,' Coen said from the window.

Sean smiled menacingly down at his captive before whispering, 'You started it.'

The gunman closed the briefcase and dragged Southcombe to his feet. Roger and Megan came in through the front as Coen and the other gunman led him to the back door of the house. They all crossed the small backyard through the rain and passed through a gate into the yard directly behind and into a second house. Two more gunmen were here waiting.

Roger held out his hand to Sean. 'Good luck.'

'You're not coming?'

'Things to tie up here. You'll be fine. It's only an hour or so to the border. The Farmer will take care of you.'

Sean was sorry to be leaving Roger. He was a good man, well disciplined and liked; a true leader, something that had stood out up at the training camp in the mountains. 'I hope to get to work with you again someday.'

'Don't worry. This war's gone on for nearly eight hundred years. There'll be plenty of time for another drink.' Roger turned and shook hands with Megan. 'Take care of this lot,' he said with a wink. She smiled back. Then he turned and left through the front door, his car waiting for him.

Southcombe was dragged into the garage through the internal door and into the rear of a transit van, the three gunmen with him, Coen climbing in behind the wheel. Beside the van was Megan's BMW. She opened the garage door then kick started her beloved bike. Sean waited by the door, ready to slide it shut. Megan stopped beside him, pulling on her helmet.

'I'll see you at the border,' she said to him and roared off up the road past the Kilmainham Gaol.

The van emerged and he shut the garage door before climbing in beside Coen. Not until they had picked up Daniel with Dublin now far behind them did Sean light up a cigarette to calm his nerves.

THIRTY THREE

Seven miles northwest of Dundalk, in the north of County Louth, their escort vehicle turned off the N63 onto a short dirt road. It led them through a gate and over a shallow hill to a farm house. It was a large complex with a decent sized farm house, one dominating barn, several smaller sheds and a larger shed for machinery repairs with two silos that stood to the height of the barn roof. Cattle yards and loading ramps sat fifty yards from the house along with two six thousand litre fuel containers. Sean saw at least five dogs standing under the awning of the house barking their arrival to whoever was inside. Farming equipment lay scattered around the grounds in various states of decay, some next to brand new pieces. It was typical of the farms he remembered from Australia. Rubbish here and there, a new car beside a rusting old one. Mangy dogs barked from the front door of an ancient house with a recent extension.

The van drove inside the dry barn and they all got out, the three Dublin gunmen pushing Southcombe in front of them to an opened horizontal cellar door. Here they were met by three other men, IRA men from South Armagh, just across the border to the north. They disappeared into the darkness below ground, dragging Southcombe with them, shutting the door behind. Roger's men from Dublin then got in the van and signalled Coen to do the same.

He shook his head. 'I'll stay.'

'You sure?' one of them asked.

'I'll be fine. Tell Ethan I'll be back tomorrow.'

'You be careful up here,' they said eyeing the house with suspicion. They backed the van from the barn, turned around and left.

The escort vehicle that had met them in Drogheda to lead the to the farm had pulled up outside the barn in the rain. From it two men had exited and approached Sean, Daniel and Coen.

'Come with us,' the shorter one said and led them back through the main barn doors. Before they ran through the rain to the large farmhouse, Sean saw Megan's BMW parked up to the side of the barn under a crude form of roofing beside two tractors.

The dogs relented their barking when they recognised the two escort men running across the muddy yard; some wagging their tails as the men reached the dry verandah. The door opened to them and they all entered, taking their boots and jackets off in the hall landing.

Sean was surprised at the interior of the house. Whilst the outside told of a dwelling that had stood fast against many seasons of rain, snow and gales, the first room took him back to Dublin with the fine carpet, rich and bold like a hotel's smoking lounge; unsoiled and spotless, the wood work of exposed trusses above in the cathedral ceilings, artwork that looked original, intricate wallpaper which bought the large room together. Several coats and caps hung on coat racks made from deer antler. One of the jackets was a woman's leather motorcycle jacket.

They were led through to the next room. This resembled an upper class pub with large winged chairs and leather lounges around the perimeter except for one wall on which traversed eight book shelves, each bearing a mixture of Irish language texts and poetry by authors such as O'Rathaille and O'Suilleabhain, studies on ancient history from all cultures, masterpieces from Homer, Hemingway and the obligatory Joyce, Beckett, Yates and Shaw. A coffee table made from dark oak and topped with glass sat in the centre. On it were an ashtray, a pipe stand, a newspaper and a glass of whiskey. At the far end of the room was a small bar loaded with every type of spirit available. There were even two beer pump handles rising up out of the deeply polished wooden surface, one black and the other red. Watching over the room like frozen sentry from high up on the wall were two giant Red deer heads with massive antlers that reached out for the ornate ceiling.

The men that had led the way stood to the side and ushered Sean, Daniel and Coen to the faux pub. On the other side of the bar stood a giant of a man in a Roche Emmets Gaelic Football jersey. He had a thinning, short beard of light, almost greying hair and an even thinner head of hair. A pair of gold-rimmed glasses sat on a nose that had to have been broken at least twice. Behind the glasses rested hard blue eyes, eyes which could stare down a marble statue. At 6' 4", Patrick "The Farmer" O'Fearain was one of the most feared and powerful men in the South Armagh/Louth area.

Born in the north in 1909 he had joined the IRA at the age of twenty-one at a time when they were seriously undermanned, without direction, leadership and support. He had worked his way up the ladder, gaining respect and fear after killing two men, one a Protestant, the other a Catholic, in a pub one night during a fight. Both men had attempted to rape a local woman who happened to be the cousin of his mother. While the family and town applauded him for his loyalty, the ferocity of the attack bought him the same respect some New York neighbourhoods give their Mafia protectors. He was now a name known throughout the IRA and the surrounding counties.

Patrick O'Fearain made his money through smuggling, everything from fuel to grain and livestock. Even butter moved back and forth by the truck load such was the difference caused by British tariffs. His ability to evade the law came down to a simple mistake made by none other than the British and Irish governments. When the border was set out in the 1920 Government Act of Ireland, it cut off the six counties of the north from the Republic. Landholders and farmers soon found out that their neighbours that had once simply been in another county or even just on the other side of a hedge or road were now in a different country, some even having their own property cut in two. This was the case with the O'Fearain family. Except luckily for them the border ran right through the centre of their house, the main barn and the machinery shed. The rooms in which they slept were in a different country to the rooms in which they ate. Smuggling was as simple as carrying a contraband item from one end of the main hallway to the other. When the prices of certain items were dearer in the north, they just took it from the south and sold it for a profit across the border. When the market changed and the north was cheaper, the items sold the other way. In a short amount of time he and his family had become one of the wealthiest in the two counties.

When O'Fearain's father died five years earlier, he took the reigns and put his monies and energy into the war. The South Armagh Brigade of the Provisional Irish Republican Army didn't answer to Belfast or Dublin. The Farmer called the shots and had the support of a loyal community. The number of volunteers had swelled since the beginning of the Troubles more so in South Armagh than any other county (per capita) and it largely had to do with the way in which The Farmer's men recruited and the way they treated the people of the area. The Irish language was pushed as the dominant spoken word as were Irish sports like Gaelic football and hurling. People became proud they were living the way the Irish had intended with their own people governing them, protecting them, respecting them and supporting them.

The British Forces had a lot of trouble gaining entry to certain areas, always being hassled by the locals, even children and old women became involved. If they weren't hassled they were ignored. People acted as though the Brits didn't exist. They would simply step around a soldier and carry on with their day as if they were invisible. For an army to survive in hostile areas it needs information and trust from the indigenous people. Trying to gain this from the Catholics and pro-republicans of South Armagh was like trying to open a safe blindfolded and without the combination.

Although a British soldier was yet to be killed in the Troubles, most believed it would happen soon in South Armagh and under the leadership of Patrick "The Farmer" O'Fearain.

The big man smiled, looking at each of his new guests in turn. He shook their hands across the bar, smiling.

'*Fáilte fir, fáilte roimh chách. Is é mo ainm Patrick. Cad ba mhaith leat le hól? Tá a fhios agam go bhfuil mé tart!*' Welcome men, welcome. My name is Patrick. What would you like to drink? I know I'm thirsty!

Daniel stepped forward. '*Áthas orm bualadh leat. Tá mé Daniel. Beidh mé ag titim de uisce beatha, go raibh maith agat.*' Pleased to meet you. I'm Daniel. I'll have a drop of whiskey, thank you.

The Farmer looked at the others.

'*Tá mé Coen. Ceann de na leaids Bhaile Átha Cliath. Agus má tá tú roinnt, Ba bhreá liom beoir,*' Coen replied, introducing himself and asking for a glass of beer.

The farmer nodded and looked at Sean. Daniel was just about to inform The Farmer he didn't speak Irish that well when Sean spoke up with confidence, a whiskey being his choice.

'*Tá mé Seán. Agus bheadh titim de uisce beatha go hiontach, go raibh maith agat.*'

The Farmer smiled and opened a bottle of Tullamore Dew. As he poured he said to Sean without looking up, 'You've begun to learn Irish.'

'*Tá, beagán.*' Yes, a little.

'That's good Sean. I'm impressed.'

Sean could see Daniel was as well. Over the last couple of months he had picked up certain words and phrases in the bars and meetings with other Provos. It was mainly simple stuff but he was getting a hold on it.

The Farmer handed the drinks across the bar and came out from behind it into the room, his frame seeming to grow more as he approached them. Pointing to the chairs he invited them to sit. Behind them, the two escort men left the room, closing the door behind them.

'So,' the giant man said as he settled back into his chair, 'a Dubliner, a Belfast lad and an Australian walk into my bar… Finish off the joke.'

The three young men looked at each other, lost for words. What was he playing at?

Finally Sean leaned forward, grinning, 'The Australian says "Drinks are on the Irish".'

'Hah!' The Farmer smiled. *This Aussie's got some balls.* 'I didn't get rich buying the rounds, boyo.'

Sean didn't back down and stared him in the eyes. 'I didn't say it was you.' He motioned to Daniel sitting beside him.

The Farmer looked at Daniel and laughed out loud. 'You'll have to watch yourself around this one.'

'You don't say,' Daniel replied and looked at the smiling foreigner beside him.

'You know,' The Farmer continued, 'I heard about what you did in Dublin this morning. All over the telly and radio. The Brits are going crazy. The IRA has already claimed responsibility for the kidnapping.' He took the newspaper from the coffee table and turned it over so they could all see the headlines.

"2 MURDERED, 1 CRUCIFIED". It was the copy of *An Phoblacht*, the republican newspaper reporting the day of Sean's first run in with Merc Southcombe.

'That's the second time you've made the news.'

Sean dragged the paper across and looked at it. It was the first time he had seen any report on what had happened to him that day. The photo on the front was of the paddock where he was found with emergency crews standing over three obscured figures. It took him back yet again, the pain in his hands coming back to him.

'You almost hold a grudge like an Irishman, you know that?' The Farmer studied Sean's reaction as he skimmed the paper.

When he had finished he simply pushed the paper back to where he had taken it and sipped his whiskey. He saw The Farmer looking at his hands.

'Can I see them?'

Sean placed his glass on the table and held them out, palms up. Leaning closer, The Farmer took Sean's hands in his, his face lowering to look at the detail of the scars.

'My God. Just like Christ.' He let go and sat back. 'I'm not a religious man but you should be careful of who you show those to. You might start a new following. Jesus of Arimathea, Sean of Australia. Pretty close.'

'That was Joseph of Arimathea,' Coen corrected, 'Jesus was from Nazareth.' He suddenly wished he had kept his mouth shut, worried he would receive a few harsh words for correcting a man such as The Farmer.

O'Fearain just waved his hand, dismissing the minor detail. 'Who gives a fuck? Like I said, I'm not religious.'

'We're glad you could accommodate us on such a short notice,' Daniel said, trying to get things back on track.

'No problem son. So what do you plan to do with this man? Have you heard from Belfast?'

'Not yet. I'd like to get a message to them today if possible to see which way they want to go with this.'

'Not from here but one of the lads can take you to a house a few miles away and make the call. I haven't used my phone for nearly six years now. First the cops and now the Brits have tapped into it. They haven't heard boo outta me in a long time. The missus still uses it to talk to her friends and she knows what to say and what not to. Good lady my wife. No man can survive this world without the right woman by his side. Remember that boys.'

The man certainly liked to talk. Probably because he couldn't use the phone. The three just smiled.

O'Fearain looked Coen up and down. 'Christ. How old are you son? I probably shouldn't have given you that beer!'

'Me? I'm twenty three!'

'Twenty three? Shut the fuck up!' He leant forward to get a better look, adjusting his glasses. 'You don't even shave yet. Did you two check his driver's licence before you let him behind the wheel? Christ, you don't look anymore than fifteen.'

'I *am* twenty three sir. I'm basically the same age as Sean. And I'm glad I don't have to shave; saves me time in the morning.'

The Farmer nodded. 'Time for what? Sneaking away before the ladies wake up? Or before their husbands get home?' He laughed again. 'Right so, right so. Back when I was in my late twenties I had this huge beard down to here. As thick as a bramble bush it was. That was when I was playing football. I had to shave it off because it was just too much of a temptation for the lads on the other side to give it a tug when we scrapped. Oh don't worry. I let them know when they'd pulled on it one too many times.' He gave a few quick jabs, left, left, right, right, and chuckled to himself.

Behind him the door opened and a woman in her late fifties entered. The three younger men stood as she came in but she waved for them to sit back down.

'Our other guests have arrived, love,' The Farmer said as his wife sat down beside him. 'Lads, this is my wife Clare.'

They all greeted her, watching as she looked from one to the other, just as her husband had. Whilst they had the façade of a lovely old couple none of them let the fact be forgotten they were running one of the toughest group of fighters right out of this very house. They'd been told on their way up the Farmer had killed before and they all wondered how dirty Clare got her hands.

'I thought you lot would all be over in the barn,' she said as she turned and kissed her husband warmly on the cheek.

'How'd Megan go? Is she all cleaned up?' he asked her.

'Aye. The poor girl needed a tub. She was freezing, the poor thing. The coldest summer rain we've had in a while. I gave her some of Cherie's clothes.' She smiled and turned back to the three, eyeing them over, measuring them up, deciding who was who.

'You're Sean. You're the Australian. You must be Daniel. Belfast Brigade. Which makes you Coen. My Lord! How old are you dear?'

The Farmer gave a laugh, the rest just smiled.

'I'm twenty three Mrs O'Fearain' Coen said with a grin.

'Twenty three?' She said no more, just looked at the three of them and then smiled back.

Sean noted she made no correction of being called Mrs O'Fearain. Most elderly people he knew liked to be called by their first name, especially the women. It made them feel younger. Clare O'Fearain however seemed to like the power and respect that came with being married to the man by her side. She was a tough one.

The door to the rear of the house opened and Megan came through drying her hair with a towel. She wore a pair of jeans and a slate grey blouse that had belonged to the O'Fearain's youngest daughter Cherie before she had moved out long ago. With wet hair Megan looked even more amazing. Thin wet ropes of black hair clung to her face just either side of those eyes that just seemed to pull people in. She smiled as she looked at the three on the lounge.

'Finally made it I see.'

In no way did she resemble the girl who, only a few hours earlier, had coldly gunned down four men without a hesitation. Sitting down on the single seat next to the bar, her legs tucked up under her, she looked more like the flirty sister of a school mate, the kind boys try to sneak a perv at. And for the first time since leaving Anna, Sean felt attracted to another woman.

Aware he was still looking at her he turned back to Mrs O'Fearain. The elderly woman gave a sly smile at Sean. He had been caught. Suddenly he felt embarrassed which he thought was stupid. He was a grown man that had just taken part in a kidnapping and multiple murders and now he felt like he was back in high school. Thankfully no one else had seen him blush as the elderly Irishwoman got their attention. She got to her feet and headed to the door.

'I hope you boys are hungry. We're having a big tea today. Come dear,' she said to Megan. 'You can help me in the kitchen. Patrick, put a top on if you're going outside.'

Together her and Megan left.

The Farmer downed the rest of his whiskey and stood, taking the newspaper and tucking it into his jersey. 'Right then lads. Let's go out to the barn and see what we have. Kane will take you down to the Hurney place, Dan. They'll let you use the phone, but don't spend too long on it or Lawrence will be telling me what for the next time I see him at the pub. Sean, could you grab that thermos of tea off the bar and those mugs. The boys will like a cup. That cellar can get mighty cool when it rains.'

THIRTY FOUR

The rain had not let up. It teemed down from the northwest now; the wind that carried it was cold, blowing down from the Arctic, across Iceland and the north of the country all the way to France.

Outside on the small verandah, The Farmer handed Sean and Coen an umbrella each. He himself was now rugged up tightly in a thick woollen jumper and wore an ageing tweed flat cap.

'Alright girls!' he said to his excited dogs, each of them wagging their tails as they sat at his feet. 'Whose turn is it today? No Sarge, you went last. It's Missy's turn today. Come on Missy. You other girls stay here.'

Sean and Coen were amazed that Missy, a red cattle dog that was just a ball of muscle, understood what was being said to it. It alone stood and waited by her master's side. All the other dogs simply kept sitting, wagging their tails, subservient and loyal.

The Farmer opened his umbrella and led the two of them across the muddy yard to the barn. They sat their umbrellas on the bales of hay beside the cellar door as it was opened from the inside. Light shone up from the hole in the ground giving a false impression it was warm and safe inside.

'After you lads,' the big man said, motioning for them to enter. Coen went in first, his feet finding the stairs that took him below the ground. Sean followed behind. The Farmer gave a command to Missy and she ran down before he shut the door behind him.

The stairs took them down to a room thirty feet long and twenty wide. The walls were thick stone, once a hold for arms and a hideout for rebels, it was built during the Easter Uprising of 1916 and used again during the following civil war. The floor was the same flat stone, worn smooth by years of use and now dirty and muddy with footprints.

Waiting by the base of the stairs were The Farmer's gunmen. Two sat on wooden stools beside an old wooden table, the third standing at the far end over the prisoner. On the table were Southcombe's briefcase, his expensive clothes and shoes and an AK47. A single light hung in the centre of the room, its harsh white light unnecessarily adding to the foreboding atmosphere.

Southcombe had been stripped naked. His hands were still cuffed behind his back. A thick chain six feet long had been fixed with a padlock to the smaller chain linking the cuffs. The other end was secured to the wall. The Englishman sat curled up against the stone wall in a ball trying to protect himself from what he feared and knew would come.

Sean took in the room, realising its use was not dissimilar from the room he had been taken to in Galway. Dry blood, both Southcombe's and previous prisoners, spotted the floor at the end of the room. The aroma of the fresh bails above them filled the air. He noted a metal eyebolt above the battered man to which the chain could be fixed so as to hang victims by their wrists or however the torturers saw fit. In reality he doubted anybody forced down here would ever resurface.

One of The Farmer's men stood allowing his boss to sit. He took the thermos from Sean and poured a cup for himself, the others shaking their heads as he held it up.

The Farmer groaned slightly as he rested but it was purely for show. He was still a fit man, only giving up his beloved Gaelic football a year before his father had died. He groaned to let others think they had the strength over him, that he was weaker then they, but it was just a mind game he played and now he did it purely by habit.

Missy sat by his side, her small eyes not looking away once from Southcombe. Even she knew he was defeated.

The Farmer began. 'You know the young man on my right.' It was a statement, not a question.

Southcombe's eyes moved over to Sean's for an instant then returned to look at the old man. Other than this he did not move.

Sean took a step forward to get a better view of the Englishman's face. The bruise on his forehead had turned purple and looked like a giant pimple. The blood under his broken nose had stopped running and was now black and cracked.

'No,' Southcombe replied.

The Irishman nodded. With the flick of his hand he signalled for Southcombe to be strung up. The South Armagh men moved in, undoing the chain from the wall and passing it through the eyebolt in the heavy timber beam above. Pulling it tight they forced Southcombe to his feet with his arms still behind his back. His hands were lifted to a point where he had to stand on the balls of his feet to take some of the weight off his shoulders as he hunched forward in an unnatural bow. He looked straight down at the floor, unable to lift his head to properly see them or the dog without causing himself more agony. It was a painful position to be in, a position one of the South Armagh men had been put in by the Royal Ulster Constabulary only last year. The chain was padlocked in place.

Sean stepped forward again, taking his time before speaking. 'Do you remember where I said I was going?' Sean's words came almost without emotion, like he was talking to himself in private. 'Donegal,' Sean answered for him. 'I was looking for family…for distant relatives. My dad's family emigrated from Ireland. I don't know what I was expecting to find…just looking for anyone with the same last name and go from there. Get some work on a farm; work my way 'round till I found a relative. Learn the language.

'You see, I can't go home. You don't need to know why. But I was going to disappear up there. Cause no harm. Try and sort things out. I'd had enough of the world and its shit. I was tired; tired of getting fucked over. Every time I get a plan in my head, something seems to get in my way. A war, a girl, even myself. I should have become a local at the only pub in some quiet town, trying to get the attention of a farmer's or fisherman's daughter, a girl not afraid to do some hard work alongside me. I would have never heard of you and you definitely would not have heard of me.'

He looked down at him, Southcombe not daring to look back.

'If you hadn't have gotten in my way, you wouldn't be hanging here now.'

Southcombe, in his first act of defiance since arriving at the farm glanced up at Sean.

'Tis in vain for soldiers to complain.'

From the back of the room The Farmer scoffed quietly. 'Jesus Christ, a Brit in my barn quoting Tone.'

Sean, not understanding the quote from Wolf Tone, ignored the comment and leaned ever so slightly towards him and whispered.

'Tom and Michael should still be alive.'

'We are not the ones,' The Farmer spoke up from the far end, signalling Sean to step back, 'that should be worrying you at this point. You see we, as humans, know when to show restraint, when to demonstrate empathy to another's pain. A dog however...' He patted Missy on the head, her wet fur coarse on his callused hands. '...a dog is still only a *semi-tamed* wild animal. It has no guilt or remorse after it attacks its prey. They can revert back to their wild origins in an instant. They live to hunt and to kill. Even if it is for fun. Just like man. A dog can kill a sheep without the need to eat it. There is something in the dog's ancestry that gives it a blood lust. Unless you get one of those fluffy white poofter lap dogs that piss themselves at the slightest noise. My dogs, unfortunately for you, are not like this. My dogs enjoy the taste of blood. This one...has tasted it before.' He paused for a minute to let the Englishman look at the dog and wonder what role the animal would take in his torture.

'So, Mr Merc Southcombe, I will ask you once more...do you know the man here on my right?'

They saw Southcombe turn his head slightly, his eyes not looking to Sean but the dog salivating by its master's side. The dog looked straight back at him, smelling the fear that filled the room.

He nodded. 'Yes.' His voice was quiet and full of fear.

'How do you know him?'

Southcombe looked down at the floor, his neck muscles straining, burning with pain.

When he hadn't answered after ten seconds, The Farmer gave Missy's collar a shake.

Sean and Coen almost jumped with fright at the noise that came from her. Her bark was terrifyingly loud in there. It was raspy and crackled, not like a dog at all but more like some demented monster gargoyle with a horrifying scream gurgling past a throat full of blood. Sean had to look down at the animal just to make sure it was the same happy dog that had followed them over from the house.

'Please…' Southcombe begged, the first time he had shown any weakness.

'Please what?' The Farmer tilted his head to get a better view of his face. 'Please sir, may I have some more? Well she is hungry. At that angle she would go straight for your throat if you were lucky. Maybe she might go for your face. What do you think? Lips and nose. Nice fat cheeks. She may just eat off your face and leave you disfigured.'

The snarling of the dog continued.

'No…' he began to blubber. 'Please don't…'

'Just answer the question then. How do you know him?'

Tears ran down the Englishman's face. His body shook as his muscles strained to keep him upright. If he fell his shoulders would tear at the sockets, dislocating both arms.

The Farmer leaned over further, looking at him hanging there. 'You're lucky you have such a fat gut and so small a dick. I can't even see it from here so maybe Missy here won't see it and tear it off. The scrotum comes apart so easily.'

Southcombe's crying got louder.

The Farmer let out a sigh like he had lost his patience.

'If you won't talk to me then you can talk to her. Missy.' His command was stern.

Sean watched the dog rise to its feet.

'No…please don't do this…no…I'm sorry…please…'

Missy took a step forward; her head low like she was stalking, her feet lifting deliberately, each one coming down silently on the stone floor.

'How do you know this man?'

'I don't know!' Southcombe was beginning to panic. He tried to move away from the advance of the dog but cried out in pain as his arm twisted.

Missy took another slow step closer.

'How do you know this man?'

Sean's own heart raced with the tension that filled the room. Coen had begun to sweat.

Another step closer. Her snarling was constant. Her white teeth were bared.

Southcombe lost control of his bladder and bowels, the contents running down his legs and splashing onto the floor. The Farmer ignored it and pushed for an answer. 'How do you know this man?'

Missy was only six feet from him now, her slow advance designed to bring a prisoner to the brink of panic.

'Galway!' he suddenly cried.

Sean felt the joy flood over him. The prick had broken. They had won, he had lost.

But still the dog moved forward.

'What happened in Galway?' the Farmer demanded, his voice more hurried.

Southcombe could now smell the dog, its odour mixing in with his piss and shit.

'The people I was with kidnapped him! I wanted no part of it!'

The Farmer looked at Sean. He could see the comment had pissed off the young foreigner. The Farmer got his attention and held up his hand. *Give it time.* Sean nodded. He knew O'Fearain was doing what he did best. If he couldn't get information out of him then no one could.

'Missy knows you're lying. She can smell it. Or is it the blood that is now thumping through your veins, so close to the surface she can hear the pulse.'

One step closer. Her foul breath reaching his bloodied nostrils.

The Farmer pulled the newspaper out from under his top. Despite his age and the less than perfect light, he could still read the small print without the need for his glasses, another prop he used to fool others with. ' *"Two murdered, one crucified. Two republican men were found murdered yesterday in a paddock off the N17 just south of Tuam in what appears to be a blatant sectarian attack. One had been shot through the head, the second killed during what appears to be a severe beating and both dumped beside a third that had been savagely beaten also before being nailed to a piece of wood through his hands. The grim discovery was made by Doctor Rebecca Donahue of Galway and the chance encounter on the quiet road may have saved the life of the third man yet to be identified."* You had this man here nailed to a piece of wood? And you call us Barbarians? Do you think you're some kind of Roman Emperor?'

Southcombe shook his head, the sobbing getting quicker as the dog came to within three feet.

'Show him your hands.'

Sean held up his hands, the smooth skin of his scars clearly discernible.

'Look at them. Look at them!'

Southcombe's blurred eyes lifted away from the dog and focused on the scars then looked back to the animal creeping towards him.

'You were in charge of this weren't you?'

Missy was only a foot away, her hair standing up along her spine, saliva pouring from her mouth marking a trail back to her master.

'You ordered the deaths of Tom O'Geary and his son Michael!' The tone of his voice was growing.

Southcombe's eyes were shut, his face pulled as far away from the dog as possible.

'You were responsible for the men who, under your command, nailed this man here to a piece of wood!' He was almost bellowing now.

Coen turned his head away, not able to bear it any more.

'YOU WERE IN CHARGE!!'

Southcombe wailed like a mad man. He was in hell.

'YOU ORDERED THEIR DEATHS!!'

Missy's nose touched his neck, her demonic snarl now sounding like The Devil itself.

'SHE *WILL* EAT YOU!! MISSY, HOLD!'

Missy opened her jaws and clamped down on the side of his neck; her lower teeth pushing up against his windpipe, the top teeth breaking the skin. She tasted his blood and wanted more but held him firmly, just waiting for the command in which she would bite as hard as she could, clamping down like a vice before she began her violent head shaking which would tear out a piece of his neck the size of an apple.

'SAY IT!!'

Southcombe wailed.

'SAY IT!!'

'YES!!' He finally broke. 'YES!! IT WAS ME!! It was me!' Snot and tears ran down his face, his crying forcing his words out in a quick stutter.

The Farmer turned to Sean and grinned slightly.

Sean's own heart was racing flat out now. Part of him felt vaguely ill but they had broken him. He knew Southcombe was the one responsible for what had happened and there had been no reason to do this other than to let him know they had him, that he was dead for what he had done. That and the fact The Farmer hated the English. Some of the men he knew in the Australian Army had the same sort of hatred for the Vietnamese.

'Missy. Back girl.' The cattle dog released his throat and trotted back to her master's side, her tail wagging as he patted her on the head. He then signalled for his men to let him down as he turned to Sean.

'You should see to Coen.'

Turning around, Sean saw Coen had left the room. He had been so captivated by what was happening he never heard the door.

Coen was standing by the open door of the barn sucking in as much fresh air as he could. Sean saw he had been sick; a long string of saliva hung from his chin.

'You okay?'

He just nodded, his eyes closed, face up to the sky, raindrops hitting his pale skin.

'He talked,' Sean said as he pulled out a packet of cigarettes.

"Wouldn't you?' came the sarcastic reply.

'Yeah I reckon I would. Smoke?'

Coen spat and nodded. Sean lit two and handed one to him.

'Thanks.' He took a long drag, the taste of tobacco a nice change to the mix of bile and beer. 'He would have confessed to whatever you asked of him.' The exhaled smoke was torn from his mouth by the wind. 'So did the dog eat him?'

They both moved back out of the weather into the shelter of the barn's doorway.

'Nah,' Sean laughed. 'I'd hate to see what happens if Belfast says he's too much baggage.'

'I thought you wanted him dead?'

'I do, but if a dog is going to eat his guts while he's still alive I'm not sure I want to be there.'

They stood in silence for a while, watching the rain come in across the hill opposite. After a few minutes they heard then saw a car approaching. Daniel was returning.

'Got a spare one?' he asked as he climbed out of the car.

Sean passed him one, waiting for him to light up before asking, 'What's the plan?'

'We're to head back in the morning. Back to Belfast. Southcombe doesn't leave here alive. He's to stay with O'Fearain for him to interrogate until he can talk no more then they're to kill him. The boys back home want people to know what he was involved in. Discredit him and his family. Apparently his friends are big players in their government.'

Daniel looked at Sean waiting for a reaction.

The Australian simply shrugged his shoulders.

'Cunt's own fault.'

THIRTY FIVE

The news the Belfast heavies were giving him Southcombe had come as a surprise to Patrick O'Fearain. He had been sure he was going to be asked to assist in the transportation of the Englishman up north but not this. This seemed more like a gift. All he had to do was question him some more (he was going to anyway) and give all the information obtained to them.

However allowing him to do what he wished with this high-class, well known, up-standing English businessman made him suspicious. They would only be doing this as a favour, something they could hold over his head for a later date when they needed something from him.

He could live with that. Besides, he could always refuse the favour.

Fuck Belfast, he thought to himself as he led Missy and the others back to the house. *I've already done them a favour by taking these four into my home, hiding them when Belfast couldn't organise shite.*

He turned and looked at the three young men beside him.

How the fuck does an Australian end up in the Provos? he wondered. *It looks like he's been at this game for a lot longer than a few months. He's confident with himself, carries himself with direction and strength but at the same time he looks like he's lost. Sometimes it looks as though he's been born into this fight and other times like he's holding back some terrible past; ghosts of where he had come from.*

They left Missy with her sisters and headed into the warmth of the house and the comfort of the bar and its contents. Coen turned down the offer of a whiskey but Sean and Daniel were more than happy to have free drinks shouted for them for the rest of the night.

At the dinner table Sean noticed the flirting he thought he had seen from Megan earlier on when they had arrived at the farm had not continued. He had to admit to himself he was a little disappointed. As they ate, drank and talked amongst themselves, she seemed to ignore him. Most of her attention was directed at The Farmer and his wife, the old man doing most of the talking, but being politely corrected now and then by his spouse. The couple loved having the company of a young woman in the home again since their daughters had left for good.

After dinner they all returned to the bar; The Farmer pouring Baileys for all except his wife who took a port.

When Megan sat beside Daniel on the two seater lounge, Sean felt another kick of jealousy. It was stupid; he knew but still couldn't help the way he felt. He had only known her for a couple of days but the more he listened to her and watched her ignore him, the more he felt for her. The more Baileys and whiskey he drank, the more he knew he had to get some sleep just to get her out of his head.

'I hate to bring an end to tonight because you both have been such gracious hosts, but I need to get some sleep. Sorry,' he said as he looked at Megan, the last comment coming out with a hint of sarcasm.

'Are you sure lad?' The Farmer seemed genuinely upset he was loosing one so early. 'I was going to check on our guest in the hole in a few minutes.'

'No thanks. It's been a long week and I have a lot of shut eye to catch up on if it's fine.'

'Still can't handle his drink,' Daniel quipped, smiling at Megan beside him.

'I'm not an alcoholic like you,' Sean replied but the smile on his friend's face just got bigger.

'I'm not an alcoholic. Alcoholics go to meetings.'

The Farmer stood. 'Don't you listen to him Dan. We all need at least one vice in life.' He grinned as he got up and led Sean to the door.

'Good night all.' Sean said from the doorway. 'Thanks again Mrs O'Fearain for dinner. It was beautiful.'

'Don't forget Megan dear. She did the sauce and greens.'

He turned to Megan and realised his urge to leave the room had grown. He didn't want to get drunk and do something stupid like try and pick her up.

'Thank you Megan. You're a killer with a whisk.' He instantly regretted saying something so stupid. Before she could reply he had left the room and was following The Farmer down the long hall.

Towards the end of the hall the elder man stopped by a framed picture hanging on the wall on his right. He looked lovingly at the picture before explaining what it was.

'It's my da'. During the Civil War.'

Sean leaned in to look at the old black and white photo. In it was a man in his mid thirties posing in civilian clothes and a long coat with a .303 rifle held casually in his arms. He had the same face as The Farmer but a different build. He wasn't as tall as his son had become.

'My da never liked pictures of himself hanging up in the house. Wanted pictures of the family up but none of himself. Said it was a bit conceited. I had to wait until he died before I could put it up. Found this one in with my ma's things after she passed on. I thought of putting it up in the bar but Clare said it would be better here. Do you know why?'

Sean looked at the surroundings. They were more than halfway down the hall. Several other paintings and photographs hung on the walls around them but away from this one, giving it room, drawing in his attention from the rich wallpaper.

He shook his head. 'No.'

'The border runs right through this house, did I tell you that before?' The Farmer dragged a finger down the centre of the photo, right in the middle of his father. 'Right down the middle of this picture. At the moment I'm standing in the north, you're in the Republic. Armagh and Louth.'

Sean nodded, recalling his first border crossing. He and his party had simply walked across someone's private property, crossing the invisible border somewhere in the middle of a ploughed paddock.

'He always wanted a unified Ireland,' the Farmer continued, 'so da's right in the middle of the two, holding them together, trying to bring them back to one.'

He looked at his father for a few more seconds, nodded silently at the picture and then led Sean to the next door on his left. He opened the door and turned on the light. It was a large room with a desk in one corner, a wardrobe in the other and a double-sized bed in the centre of a great rug. A window in the far wall with its heavy curtains pulled back rippled from the rain outside.

'You can stay in here tonight. It was my eldest son's room. He's in Crossmaglen now. Still fighting the fight though. The bed's not as big as the others but it's a lot more comfortable. Plus you won't be woken up by the other two when they decide to bed down. I think Daniel's up for a long one.'

'I don't think anything could wake me up tonight,' he said, the thought of more nightmares was always present when he was going to bed but The Farmer didn't need to hear about that. 'Thanks again for putting up with us and for what you had to do today.'

'Think nothing of it Sean. All in a days work for a South Armagh Volunteer.' He turned and headed for the door. 'See you for breakfast lad,' he said and closed the door behind him.

Sean sat on the bed and rubbed his eyes. He was tired. The whiskey had done its job and he was happy to let it shut his brain down for the night.

He stripped off, turned off the light and climbed into bed; the 9mm Browning placed under his pillow. The last thought he had before sleep took hold was of Daniel. He was wondering if his attempts to flirt with Megan would pay off.

Sean seemed to wake up a split second before the explosion of noise shook the house. A brilliant flash of light illuminated the room with several strobing pulses. The thunder had pulled him from a deep sleep and for a few seconds he was disoriented, thinking he had fallen asleep while on watch in the jungle. After he realised where he was he turned on his bedside lamp and looked at his watch; 02:12, still time for another four or more hours. He knew what time farmers woke up and wondered if this one was any different. Maybe he would be up in two.

He turned off the lamp and lay there watching the flashes of lightning on the next hill, the sound reaching him within three seconds. Every time he closed his eyes another crash of thunder pulled him back from his sleep. After a while it became frustrating so he lay there and listened to the storm as it moved further away.

Some twenty minutes later all he could hear was the noise of rain against the house and the odd distant rolling of thunder. He began to drift off once again.

Something else woke him up this time. Someone else was in the room. Adrenalin surged. He was now fully awake. His hand silently slipped under his pillow and was grasping the handle of the Browning when he made out the silhouette of the person coming towards him, the sound of clothing falling to the floor.

The blanket pulled down and he felt Megan's body slide in next to his. Her naked skin was warm as she pushed up against him, her hands pushing his shoulders down, pinning him as she manoeuvred on top of him, straddling him. He could feel himself growing under her as her face lowered to his. Her lips hovered above his for what seemed like an age, teasing him, building the tension. He lifted his head and she pulled back slightly only to come down and meet him with a kiss that washed away all his fears. Her tongue ran across his, feeling his mouth. He sucked on her tongue and she gave a light moan. She tasted like Baileys.

His hands reached up and grasped her waist, pulling her down onto him, grinding themselves together. Her breasts flattened out on his chest, her nipples hard as she moved in closer, kissing his neck…his ear…his shoulder… The emotions surged through his body like a drug. He had never felt this way with Anna. At least he couldn't remember feeling like this. If he had, he had long forgotten about it. He pulled her tighter, his arms wrapping around her slender hips, loving the feeling of her smooth skin against his.

Megan reached down and took a hold of him. He was hard. She guided him in and sat up, leaning back to take him in all the way. Outside lightning flashed in the distance, the glare painting her a silvery blue giving Sean the first view of her naked body.

She rose and fell as the light repeated outside, her jet black hair spilling forward covering her face. Sean cupped her breasts and squeezed them gently. As Megan pushed forward into his hands she flicked her head back and he could see her smiling, her eyes shut in ecstasy. Her gyrations were deliberate and controlled, taking her time. They rocked together in rhythm for several minutes, their bodies becoming sweaty as they both prolonged the act.

She leaned forward and kissed him forcefully and rolled to the side pulling him over with her. Sean was now on top, her legs wrapped around his back, locking him inside her, forcing him into her deeper. Grabbing a handful of hair he pulled her head back and kissed her neck and throat, her ears and chin. He felt her shudder with pleasure.

Lightning flashed again, the blue light revealing each was looking into their lover's eyes for the instant they were illuminated. He fell into her eyes. In that moment he knew all that mattered was them and the hours they would spend together until dawn. The Troubles of Northern Ireland didn't matter; Vietnam and its impossible war didn't matter. Nothing did. All that mattered at that time was the two of them. He continued staring into the darkness at the memory of her eyes long after the lightning had abated.

Sean flipped her over. She knelt before him, her forearms flat on the bed. Her muffled cries of bliss telling him she was nearer now, fighting to hold it back. He pulled her in towards him, her smooth cheeks slapping into his pelvis. His hands ran up along her sides feeling her clammy skin from her thighs to her arms then around to her breasts, his fingers dancing across her taut nipples, down along her belly to her clit. She shuddered again. She was almost ready. Her face buried into his pillow as she howled with gratification and bucked back into him. Sean pushed harder. Megan bucked in response. She suddenly pulled away from him and dropped onto her back. Her arms pulled him down to her and she kissed him again, moaning into his mouth as he pumped faster. His fingers wrapped around her hair, her legs around his back again, her pelvis thrusting hard against him. Sean felt her fingers digging into his back. Her orgasm had started. He heard short, sharp gasps from her as he thrust and held, thrust and held, thrust and held. His body wasn't registering the pain on his back as he came with her. He kept her head in close to his, their faces together in the darkness. He kept his rhythm up, surprised to hear himself groaning with rapture as they both bucked and shuddered until they were spent.

Finally they stopped.

Sean rolled to the side but held on to her, pulling her onto her right side. They remained locked together for almost five minutes as they caught their breath. Her legs relaxed and stretched out to press up against his, her toes curled over lightly tickling the tops of his feet.

'I couldn't sleep,' she said at last, her first words since slipping in more than twenty minutes ago.

Sean laughed quietly.

'I'm glad. I just hope Mrs O'Fearain is asleep. Wouldn't want her sleepwalking her way in here.'

'Maybe she's gone in to wake Coen.'

They both got the giggles as the last flash of lightning lit the distant valley with its ghostly blue.

'I'm heading back to Galway in the morning. Once the rain stops.'

Sean's head lay on her flat stomach, his whiskers scratching her soft skin, her fingers gently running through his shaggy hair.

'Do you have a man back home?' His voice showed no jealousy.

'What sort of girl do you think I am?' It was said in a playful manner.

'You want me to judge you after what just happened? I'm not sure you'll like the verdict I reach. And I've known girls who stray when their man is not in the immediate vicinity.'

Despite the cutting words and his history, Sean had a smile in his voice and Megan could hear it.

'And they've strayed with you have they?'

'You don't go into everyone's room like this?'

'Not all of them. Just the cute ones.'

'Ah! So I'm cute.'

'I have been drinking remember?'

'So have I.'

'I have no man back home. I'm an independent girl. I'll no' be tied to a stove. I like my freedom.'

Sean smiled and returned to watch the weather though the window wishing time could stop for eternity and lock them in this moment.

'Tell me of your family back home.'

It was the first thing she had said in over ten minutes, each of them content to listen to the rain as they kissed each others body softly.

'A dad, one brother, one sister.' He could see them perfectly in his mind's eye.

'Tell me about them.' Her voice vibrated through her body, his ear again now flat against her belly.

'Dad's been alone since Mum died when I was young. I never wanted him to remarry but now I know that was just the selfish thoughts of an immature kid. He served in the Second World War, volunteered just like half the country did. He ended up fighting in New Guinea against the Japanese. Doesn't talk about it much…

'I always thought if I turned out to be half the man my dad's become then I've done something right.' He could see his old man sitting beside him at James' pub, a smile wide across his face as he studied the busted water bottle he had given him, his "free" beer in front of him, happy to be surrounded by his offspring. Only then did Sean realise that was all his dad needed to be happy; his family. He had his son back from the war in one piece (sort of) and his family all around him. That's all he himself would want after having a tough life. *And I had to go and fuck it all up!*

It was the first time that Sean had accepted responsibility for where he was now. He exorcised the thought from his mind and bought forward James. 'I've an older brother James. He runs a pub back home. Top bloke. You'd like him. You couldn't ask for a better brother. Or sister. Melanie's the eldest. She ran the house once Mum died.' Suddenly he wanted to talk about anything else. He wanted to listen to her breathing.

Rain flowed down the window pane distorting the view of the heavy clouds outside. Sean could hear the water dripping onto something metallic and hollow outside, the drumming constant and soothing like the ticking of a grandfather clock or the beating of a mother's heart.

'Are there many women in the *Cumann…?*'

'*Cumann na mBan*. Why? Are you plannin' to fuck all of 'em you randy bastard?'

'Depends on how many there are.'

'Well they're all terribly ugly with breath like fat hogs and skin like an eels.'

'They let you join?' The sarcasm in his voice was laid on thick.

'Only to trick young men from far-off lands into helping us. I'm Aglaope of the islands Sirenum scopuli and you, my love-struck Argonaut, cannot help it but wreck yourself at my feet.'

Sean rolled over and looked at the dark silhouette of her face. He could just make out her eyes. 'I have no idea what you are saying.'

'Do you know of the Sirens of Greek mythology?'

'Does that mean you're going to sing for me?'

Her hand came up to feel the coarseness of his cheek. Her fingers were warm. 'I only sing when I'm drunk and I don't get *that* drunk anymore.'

'You were drunk enough to come in here. No, wait. I think I just insulted myself.' His head lay back down on the pillow. 'Anyway. It's just as well. You've probably got a terrible singing voice.'

In an instant Megan had rolled over on top of him, pinning him down with surprising strength, her face close to his and the warmth of her naked body beginning to arouse him again.

'There's nothing wrong with my voice. Maybe I should go and ask Daniel what he thinks of it?'

Sean wrapped his arms around her, his hands sliding down to the smooth curves of her backside. 'Let Dan sleep.' His fingers gripped her soft flesh, pulling her up onto him. 'He's had a big day.'

THIRTY SIX

The rain had stopped without him realising. Both of them had drifted off to sleep with the heavy down quilt pulled up over them holding in their body heat. The clouds that had bought the rain had thinned to let a blue moonlight into the room.

Sean woke and quietly picked up his watch and read the luminous hands. It was close to five. Slipping out of bed, he dressed and quietly left Megan to her dreams. He walked down the hall, through the dinning room and the bar to the front room. Opening the front door he saw The Farmer slipping on his boots.

'You're up early Sean.'

'Couldn't sleep.'

The Farmer nodded. 'I'm going to relieve the others. Let them get some food and a kip.'

'Have they been at it all night?'

'Aye. We'll see how much he talks today.'

Sean grabbed his jacket from the antler rack and stepped outside. 'I might join you.'

The dogs trotted along beside them, circling in and out of their feet as they crossed the water-logged ground. The farmer looked off to his left. 'It's going to be a nice day today.' A thin line of blue showed on the horizon. 'Maybe even a little warm.'

As they neared the barn both of them became aware of noise from within. They could hear screams and yelling. The boys were definitely still at work. Sean followed The Farmer down into the cellar, the dogs obeying his command to stay topside. The muffled yelling now became clearer.

'…of them! Don't expect us to believe that shite! Two more and we can stop!'

Sean saw the two Provos were up close to Southcombe. One of them was sitting on the chair, the other standing over the bound man. Southcombe had been re-shackled since yesterday afternoon. The chain ran, once again, up through the eyebolt in the ceiling. However this time the end of it had been attached to his ankles. It must have taken a lot of effort to get his entire body up off the floor. At first Sean didn't think he was still alive; he hadn't reacted to the door opening and the two of them entering, but another hit from the object in one of the Provo's hand made him stir. The man on the chair got up to greet them both.

'We've got heaps of information from him. Plus six names,' he looked in Sean's direction, 'men that tortured you that day. He swears he can't remember the names of any more. He says they were only hired at the last moment.' He lit up a cigarette and flicked the match back at Southcombe, the small red hot missile sticking to his bloodied skin and hissing out. 'We racked our brains asking him everything we could come up with about his activities in the north, people he met, who his friends are, family friends, UVF contacts, weapon numbers and locations, meetings he attended and where. Doubt he's got anything left in him.'

Sean bummed a smoke and looked down at what had become of Southcombe. He felt his stomach turn at the sight of such a thorough beating but the thought of the O'Geary's demise and his own torture quelled his revulsion.

Southcombe's feet had turned white with the lack of blood flow past the chains. Blood flowed up his legs from dozens of lacerations. His genitals had not escaped the interrogation either; dried blood covered his scrotum where something sharp had sliced deep into the shaft of his penis. Every part of his body was bruised or covered in blood. Some of the skin not covered in blood showed small circular burns from cigarettes. His face looked nothing like it had when they had left him the previous evening. His heavy brow was split in three places, both eyes were blackened, his left nearly closed with the swelling. All four men could hear him struggling to breath through his mouth, his nose clearly broken and filled with blood. Sean guessed there had to be at least a pint of blood over the floor beneath him. His hands rested limply in the slicked mess and several of his fingers were now at grotesque angles.

With the rain and the lightning that had crashed around them all night it must have seemed like he had visited hell and was going to be there for a long time yet. It had been some night. For both of them.

One of them handed The Farmer two sheets of paper. The first page contained the list of six names and two addresses of Sean's attackers. The second page contained information that would be hastily consumed by PIRA seniors in Belfast concerning UVF activities and names. Sean saw the knuckles of the man who handed over these pages were red; his right hand slightly swollen.

The Farmer skimmed the two pages to see if anything rang a bell. None of it did. It didn't worry him. This was big town stuff. All he cared about was what was happening in his part of the world, in his two counties. *Let Belfast and Dublin fight their fights*, he reflected. None of them up there were fighting for South Armagh so why should he concern himself with city troubles. He tucked the paper into his pocket and patted the man on the shoulder.

'Good work Finbar, Pat. Get on over to the house and clean yourselves up. The wife'll have some breakfast on by now. Then get some sleep. I'll talk to you both after supper.'

The man flexed his hand, trying to work some of the stiffness and swelling out of it.

Sean nodded towards his hand. 'Try and get that hand into some ice.'

The torturer looked down at it. 'I hope it's not broken.'

'You'd know if it was.'

The men both left but not before they handed Sean the weapon they had been using. Looking down at it he saw it had once been a hurling stick. The flat paddled end had been wrapped in rusted barbed wire. Now covered in blood, hair and pieces of skin, it was a terrible looking instrument. The symbolic representation of something that had once been used for fun within their culture now covered in the blood of an Englishman was not lost on him. The handle was well worn from a lot of use and he wondered for which purpose had it been used for more; sport or torture. Back in Belfast he had heard someone use the term "reap what you sow". This hurling stick summed it all up.

Turning his attention to Southcombe on the far wall, he could see his eyes looking away from them; glad to have a brief reprieve from the pain he had been receiving.

Sean turned to The Farmer. 'Can I see that list?'

The Farmer handed it over and watched Sean read down the list. He walked towards Southcombe, the stick swinging casually by his side, cigarette hanging from his mouth.

Bloodied eyes turned and watched him drag the chair up close to him and sit, the stick resting across his lap. Sean read through the list of names again, taking his time, dragging it out, making the bastard sweat. His eyes would look at a name, then down at Southcombe, then back to the page for the next name. The Farmer leant against the wall and watched with interest, keen to see what Sean would do.

After a few minutes Sean calmly began.

'Every now and again in life…' His pause was purely for effect. '… we cross paths with someone that we shouldn't. Someone that can fuck you up.'

The Farmer smiled. Sean continued.

'Who was the man that was on my left? He was carrying a 9mm pistol.' A cloud of smoke exhaled from the corner of his mouth.

Southcombe blinked at the question, his eyes drunk with exhaustion. 'Please…let me…down.' It was no more than a whisper.

'He was wearing an old black leather jacket.'

'I…please…I don't…I don't know.' He sounded like a whimpering child.

'He would have been on your right as you came in through the door.'

Southcombe closed his eyes. Sean watched him, waiting for him to reply. After twenty seconds he reached out with his foot and pushed him.

'Wake up. The man with the pistol; what is his name? He was the one whose nose I broke.'

Southcombe blinked hard several times. 'Uh…Raeford. Brian Raeford.' Southcombe didn't care he was sending his men to their graves. All he wanted was for these men to stop the pain.

'Is he from Belfast?' His voice was still calm.

'I think so.'

'You don't know? You're not certain?'

'No.'

'Okay.' More smoke filled the air. 'What about the man who had the hammer and nails? Do you remember him?' He leaned closer to him.

'I think…it was…Michael Avery…Michael Avery...'

'You think?'

'It was Michael Avery.'

'Is *he* from Belfast?'

Southcombe shook his head slightly.

'He's not from Belfast?'

'No...Lisburn.'

'Lisburn?'

He nodded.

'How do you know *he* was from Lisburn but not know if *Brian* was from Belfast?'

'I…I remember him talking…about football…Lisburn fan.'

'Did you trust him?'

Another nod.

'You trusted Brian Raeford?'

A nod yes.

'If you trusted these men then why don't you know the names of the other two?' Sean's voice became slightly stronger.

'I didn't know them. Noel got them. He…he had worked…them before.'

Sean leapt from the chair and knelt in close to him, the chair clattering as it skipped across the hard floor. The broad, barbed wire covered face of the hurling stick hovered above Southcombe's head with Sean's own face so close to his he could see the Englishman's eyes widen in fear. Sean spat out his cigarette into the pool of blood beneath him.

'The beating you've had from those other men,' his voice boiled out with a growled hatred, 'is nothing compared to what *I'm* gunna do to you if you don't start talking. They're only following orders from him, but *I* don't have to answer to anyone. *I* was the one you tortured that day. You killed two unarmed men and I won't blink at the sight of this club slashing away at your stomach until you drown in your own guts and shit. SO ANSWER THE FUCKING QUESTION!!!' He jumped to his feet and lifted the stick high above his head. His face was red with rage, his eyes wide, staring back down at Southcombe.

'I don't know!' he managed to say amongst the stuttering.

'BULLSHIT!!'

Sean swung.

Southcombe closed his eyes as the sharp, bloodied end came speeding down towards his stomach. The broad side of the stick hit squarely across his sternum. The barbs dug deep into his skin, some of them chipping into his ribs. It slapped hard, bouncing away from his flabby skin, pulling some skin away with it. Southcombe screamed with agony as Sean lifted the weapon high again. Fresh blood began to run from the thirty-odd new puncture marks. He tried to bring his arms up to protect himself but he had no energy left from the all-night torture he had experienced.

'WHO ARE THEY?!!'

'Please…I don't know their…' He was crying now.

'I'M GUNNA GUT YOU LIKE A FUCKING FISH IF YOU DON'T TELL ME!!!' He turned the stick in his hand, preparing to slice with the jagged edge on the next swing.

'I'm…telling…the…truth…!!'

Sean swung again. This time the forward edge grazed across his belly, tearing out a fleshy trench four inches long just beside his navel. It took a while for the blood to start flowing from the yellow fat and torn white meat. He let out another bellow then went quiet, his eyes shutting as he passed out from the pain.

Sean wasn't finished. 'WAKE UP YOU CUNT!!' He swung again, stepping in as it came down. He misjudged and drove the edge of the head into his ribs. Along with the snapping sound of two ribs was the breaking of the hurling stick diagonally along its length.

Furious for letting himself get carried away, he threw the shattered handle at the unconscious Englishman and fell against the wall, sliding down to rest on the cold floor. He closed his eyes as he caught his breath, feeling his heart rate racing. Despite the relative coolness of the room he was covered in sweat and could smell the whiskey leaving his pores to mix in his nose with the metallic reek of blood.

His heart rate began to fall. His thinking became clearer. To his right he heard a noise and had forgotten The Farmer had watched the whole thing without interrupting him. He looked up at the old man and saw a grin on his weathered face.

'You know, I don't think he knew the names of the other two men.'

'I know.' He took in a few more calming breaths. 'I just wanted to be sure.'

The Farmer walked past him over to Southcombe. Bending forward, with two fingers he felt for a pulse. It was there but weak. 'Bastard's still alive. Don't know for how much longer though. I wasn't expecting him to have made it through the night. Those Hurney lads like their job more than most people like sex.'

Sean didn't see The Farmer shoot a quick glance in his direction.

'How much more use is he to you?'

'Not much. I'd say he's all talked out.' The old man opened one of Southcombe's eyelids and watched for a reaction of his pupil. 'Time to be rid of him.' He straightened and walked over to Sean, his hand held out to help him to his feet.

With all the noise he had been making down in the cellar he had not heard the throaty rumble of the BMW motorbike kick to life and begin its long trip back home to Galway.

THIRTY SEVEN

After breakfast, Sean, Daniel and the dogs walked around the front yard, the two of them smoking, chatting and dodging puddles, the dogs following them, playing at their feet; the younger ones nipping at each other while the older ones tried to ignore them.

'You know it's only because you're a foreigner,' Daniel said, his voice showing no jealousy.

'You know you're jealous,' he parried. 'But who walks into someone's room in the middle of the night like that?'

'You giving out?'

'Not at all.'

'I told her my room was on the right. Must have gotten lost. That's the only explanation.'

Sean laughed along with him. 'So much for the luck of the Irish.'

'That saying is *meant* to be sarcastic. Us Irish get no luck.'

'You were probably up against the door listening.'

'I don't want to hear you sobbing like a baby when you can't get it up.' He took another drag on his cigarette. 'It doesn't look like you made much of an impression. She fucks off without a goodbye kiss? You're not going to start crying now are you?'

'Fuck off.'

But he felt disappointed. While he had done nothing to stop her advances last night, earlier he thought he had taken advantage of her in some way. He hadn't quite flirted with her but the signals were there to be interpreted and now he felt used. All this time and he thought he was in control.

Wrong again, Sean. Thanks for coming.

They heard the front door open. Coen and Mrs O'Fearain emerged, the Dubliner heading over to them.

'Mrs O'Fearain is taking me into town. They've organised a ride to Dublin for me.' The young volunteer still looked a bit shaken up from yesterday evening's events.

Sean held out his hand. 'Thank you for all you've done.'

'When are you heading back to Belfast?'

'Later on today.' He nodded towards the barn. 'Once we finish up here.'

Coen just nodded. He showed no emotions, just a nod that said nothing more than what it should.

Sean had a feeling that, although Coen was a member of the Dublin Brigade of the PIRA and had vowed to fight all enemies of the Republic of Ireland, there seemed to be a flicker of doubt in the young man's eyes over how they had gone about exacting what was, when all the bullshit was swept aside, Sean's revenge.

It was the first time Coen had seen anyone tortured up close. He was fresh to their armed struggle and may have joined out of some romantic or heroic vision or maybe even jealousy at his older brother's involvement, but now he had seen what happens in the deep end. This was the dirty part of war. Sean wondered if what little Coen had seen was enough to make him leave the Provisionals. He was glad Coen hadn't been with him a couple of hours ago in the cellar.

'We'll look you up next time we're down your way.'

'That'd be grand.' They all shook hands again. 'Be careful up there now.' His voice was genuine. He sounded worried for the health of both of them.

Daniel winked at him. 'Nothing can touch us. Well, not me anyway. A lot seems to happen to this joker but I'll be fine.'

The car pulled away down the path. They watched it as it disappeared over the small hill behind the wild hedges that lined the road.

The time had come to kill Merc Southcombe.

They had decided not to dress him in his clothes but to leave him stripped; a final humiliation. The location in which they would dump the body had been decided upon. It was close to one of the main roads but far enough away from the O'Fearain's farm and across the border in the north. A call would be made to the local church after they had dumped the body ensuring they were well clear.

When Sean and Daniel entered the barn's basement they saw Kane unchaining Southcombe's body from the wall, letting it fall to the cold floor with a wet thud, like a fresh side of ham falling from the shelf of a larder.

Slipping in and out of consciousness, Southcombe's mind was having trouble registering the events taking place. He was unaware of someone standing over him, a pistol cradled unmenacingly in his left hand.

At the foot of the stairs The Farmer waited for Sean and Daniel as they each walked over to stand either side of him. The nerves that should have been racing through Sean were not there. His mouth was not dry with apprehension; his skin was not sweating with anxiety at what was about to happen.

He had seen what was coming for weeks.

All The Farmer did was nod his head once. Kane worked the slide of the pistol, a Spanish semi-auto .22. The dry metallic sound echoed in the silent room. No fanfare. No speeches.

He raised the pistol, aimed at the side of Merc Southcombe's head and pulled the trigger twice so fast the soft crack of both detonations blurred the echo into one. Southcombe's head jumped up off the flat stoned floor as the energy of the impacts shook his head, the hollow-point bullets breaking up as they passed through his skull, the fragments shredding through his brain. There were no exit wounds. A small thick fountain of dark blood pulsed out, gradually decreasing in height and rate as his heart stopped receiving signals from his brain. Kane flicked the safety back on and pocketed the weapon before walking back to where The Farmer, Sean and Daniel stood.

The Farmer held out his hand and, as Sean took it, the South Armagh leader looked deep into the Australian's eyes for…anything.

There was nothing.

Without a word Sean and Daniel turned and climbed the stairs of Patrick O'Fearain's torture cell one last time leaving the reason for Sean becoming a gunman in the IRA to be dumped naked on the side of a South Armagh road.

Neither looked back.

PART THREE

"The bow is bent, the arrow flies,
The wingéd shaft of fate."

Ira Aldridge

THIRTY EIGHT

'Hey Wilto!'

Sergeant Andrew Wilton placed his book aside and looked up from his bed, recognising the Welsh accent that beckoned him. Standing in the doorway to his barracks bedroom was a fellow Special Air Service Sergeant.

'The Boss wants to see you in his office.'

'Cheers .'

Dressed in his civvies, the tall Australian SAS man swung his legs over the side of his bed into his thongs. He brushed from his eyes the long hair SAS men were allowed to wear due to the nature of undercover roles and headed down the hallway, across the assembly area of the Stirling Lines barracks to the offices by the parade ground. Once more he brushed his shaggy hair off his face before knocking twice on the open door.

'Boss.'

'Come in Andrew.'The major's voice commanded with its deep bass tones. 'Have a seat.'

He sat down on the other side of the simple wooden desk of Major Russell Purvis. The men referred not just to the major as "Boss", all officers within the SAS receive the same title.

Closing the folder he had been reading, the blonde haired and moustached Major Purvis picked up a piece of paper, scanning over it before beginning.

'You're back early from leave. How was Paris? Been a while since I've been there.'

Andrew surveyed his CO. A man with definite Viking ancestry, Purvis was close to completing his allowable two years offered to officers joining the Regiment and keen to leave his mark.

'Fine Boss. Got a bit boring after a while.'

'The worst thing about Paris is there's too many French. However I was thinking of going over once the weather warms up though. Take the wife on a dirty weekend away.'

Andrew grinned but didn't answer. He'd heard the major's wife was not the type of woman anyone would dream of taking anywhere for a dirty weekend.

'This is just a chat to make sure things are going fine with you. Must be different from what you've experienced in Vietnam.'

'Not as many bugs here and it's a bit cooler,' Andrew said with dry humour as he thought back to the two years in Asia; one year as a regular soldier before he had been lucky enough to have earned his sandy beret and one year spent with 3 Squadron Aust. SASR. When the opportunity came to join up with the Hereford-based SAS in cross-training he jumped at the chance and hadn't regretted doing so. He had learnt so much more since arriving in England eight months ago, but also loved being able to show these Pommy boys how the real soldiers in the colonies do it.

'So everything holding up alright here? No plans to live off grounds yet?'

'No point. I don't have a family over here and I can save more money that way. I'm doing all right just where I am.'

Major Purvis nodded knowing it had nothing to do with money. No one did this job for the money, or lack of it. A lot of the lads liked to live close to where the jump-off point was rather than in the town of Hereford. They could use every opportunity to get more training in the live fire rooms or the many other places where they could drive, run or abseil into situations which they could push their mind and body to the edge of peak performance.

Plus it was a hell of a lot of fun.

Since the move to cross-train, Andrew had been on only two "jobs" for A Company of the 22nd Special Air Service; both being raids on locations within Britain's borders trying to cease terrorist operations being carried out by the IRA, the last resulting in two kills, his first since leaving South Vietnam. It wasn't as though he was ostentatious enough to keep a tally of the number of men he had killed, for he knew several soldiers that prided themselves by their body count and boasted about it whenever the chance to brag arose. Rather, it was just that he knew the number of men whom had lost their life to him because they had been filed in reports throughout his career. The young Irish lad in Scotland had unfortunately, due to his own life choices, had become his thirteenth. It was hard for him to feel anything but neutrality when he thought back to the men he had killed. It was a job. He had no hatred for them because they were doing what they believed to be their job. Their goals were just different to his. He thought it resembled two opposing teams in a contact sport that drove on despite the hits they received during the match. And if every country suddenly found *one* God and thought the same happy thoughts, he would be out of a job.

The Major continued. 'Well you've certainly fitted in here. All your CO's have nothing but praise for your leadership skills.'

'Thanks Boss.'

'You've still got two more days leave. Might not be able to scrounge up more time off for a while, the way things are heating up. Our lads down in Oman are getting stuck into it. You should get out and have some fun while you can.'

Andrew shook his head. 'All the fun's to be had here.'

'Okay.' He switched from trying to be persuasive back to business in the blink of an eye. 'So on Tuesday you'll report to Captain Fordham, 0730, for a debriefing on further developments on Irish republican activities this side of the water.'

'Have they re-established their units here?'

'I'm sure things will head that way again. The news of the Cabinet Minister's friend, that Merc Southcombe fellow, has caused a stir on both sides. Went to Eton with him, he did. Terrible news. This will strengthen the Provo's numbers I'm sure. And in turn we will come to be called to work again. We'll know more by next week. Don't worry though. There'll be plenty more Paddies lining up to die.'

Back in his quarters Andrew tried to get back to his book but his mind kept wandering, thinking back to that last raid in Scotland. He wasn't thinking about the young boy he had killed as he burst into the living room; he never reflected on those he had killed. They had paid a price for the choices they had made. He couldn't help that. What he was thinking about was how the raid on the farmhouse could have gone better. Were there things that could be improved? Did they leave something out of their actions, something that could be used against them in further operations?

No British soldier had been killed since the Troubles began. However with the recent explosive escalation in sectarian violence he wondered how long it would be until the Queen lost one of her valiant sons to an Irish bullet. All he knew was if he ended up over there then he didn't want to be the first.

He played the scenario out in his head over and over again until he was sure nothing could have been changed. Still unsatisfied with his diagnosis, he changed into a set of greens, grabbed three of his fellow on-base comrades, headed over to the armament room, booked out some stun grenades, a sub-machine gun and a Browning 9mm semi-auto pistol each (all with live ammo) and put in a few hours in the Killing House training rooms.

Sean MacStiofain, the Dublin based 42 year old Chief of Staff of the Provisional IRA sat in the large winged chair in the sparsely decorated living room of the Dundalk dwelling, several miles south of the border. The owners of the house had been notified only an hour before that their residence would be used for talks of the utmost secrecy. The Army Council had the use of literally hundreds of houses, flats, shops and pubs in both countries, all volunteered by the occupants to be used whenever it was necessary to help continue the fight. Some houses were used to hide weapons and ammunition, some were staging points for operations, some even used for interrogation. The owners of this particular house felt privileged MacStiofain and his comrades would use their place for further planning. They, of course, could not be present and waited upstairs with two armed escorts listening to the radio on high volume.

MacStiofain was a stern man, a fact that made others in his company uneasy. Some volunteers didn't even like to drink with him, his dourness too gloomy for them. Today was no exception.

To MacStiofain's right sat Ruairi O'Bradaigh; a short stature schoolteacher from County Roscommon and a fellow IRA Council Member. Beside O'Bradaigh sat newly appointed council member Billy McKee; the Belfast OC wounded at the Battle of Short Strand and the Provisional's Belfast Commander. The wounds still gave the slender man grief but he had promised to be at the meeting, making the journey south from Belfast early this morning.

On MacStiofain's left sat the balding Joe Cahill, his retreating hair hidden under a plaid cap. Yet another leader with a full history, back in 1942 he had been saved from the gallows by a stay of execution for the murder of a police officer.

To Cahill's immediate left sat one of their youngest and most headstrong leaders, Gerry Adams. A bold up-and-coming political Sinn Féin thinker from the Murph, he was more at home in the planning room and on debating floors than on the "front line". When McKee had decided to attend the meeting, MacStiofain chose not to ask Adams to be there due to the bad blood between the young leader and Billy McKee. But Adams had heard of the meet and insisted. The Chief of Staff just hoped they could get through this without it breaking out into another screaming match as had happened last time.

On the other side of the room a nervous Padraig Molloy waited on the brains of their operation. He knew the reputations of each of these men and was trying his hardest to show them he too was a thinker as well as a soldier. McKee had agreed with the idea Padraig had bought him last month and said he would vouch for him and the Australian when the time came. For Padraig this was the chance to move up the ladder if all went well.

'It's a good idea Padraig.' MacStiofain continued in his native English accent. 'We should have utilised the resources we have long before this. I for one should have realised the benefits. But to use this new lad so soon…Don't you think this is too big a risk?'

'The boy has taken the oath just like we all did.' Padraig tried to choose his words carefully. 'He was one of the few that fought for St Matthew's. Billy was there. None of us were. He knows what this lad has done for us.'

MacStiofain glanced across at McKee who simply nodded back. He would only step in if Padraig needed it and he seemed to be doing fine so far.

MacStiofain continued. 'I met Sean and Daniel at the funeral for the Hall and Brown lads the other month. Personally thanked them for what they did and I totally agree they are both supreme examples of the type of soldier we need. He…*they* have also gone on to bring down one of the UVF's top financiers. The information obtained by them has been of great use to us.'

Out of the corner of his eye he again saw Billy nod his head ever so slightly at this last comment; himself planning the raids on the houses of five of the six men involved with the O'Geary's murder and Sean's torture. Two were killed during their abduction, two more caught and forced to talk (only one of them keeping staunch and silent until his inevitable death) whilst the fifth and sixth were yet to be found. Number five was thought to have fled the country; the assumption was he was now living in England, his family leaving their house deserted once news of Southcombe's murder had become public. The sixth was somewhere in Belfast but deep in loyalist territory.

'You have to remember,' Padraig persisted, 'that this lad thinks well on his feet. He thinks like a soldier, knows how the Brits do their thing. That matters on the street. I believe he can carry this out.

'Our American supporters,' he continued, 'have yet to realise the type of war we are trying to fight by continuing to supply us with pre-world war two rifles. Now I understand that Gerry is trying to organise more Armalites, this time directly from America but if we are to continue fighting the most modern army in the world then we need equipment *now* which will match the Brits. Just five days ago three boys from our 2nd Belfast unit took on and forced back a British Army patrol in Ardoyne and again two days later in New Lodge…'

'Yes, I know that…'

'…because we are using new tactics and weapons. They still think we're going to come at them with rocks, a couple of old bolt actions and a jar of Shell…'

'…and Flannery's been told of this…'

'…and the other day made them shit in their pants.' He stabbed his finger on the arm of his chair to emphasise the point. 'The Brit's morale has jumped on the last ferry home to Liverpool. If we want to carry on this armed struggle all the way to victory then we need to re-think the way we are going about it and that includes using people that have extraordinary skills on the streets *and* people they would *never* suspect.' Padraig took in a deep breath and hoped he hadn't been too potent with his opinion.

'Nobody,' the Chief of Staff began, trying to calm things down, 'in this room agrees with you more than me about restructuring the way we fight. To send this boy across the water though…I don't know. He's only been with us for a short while. You know I wasn't too pleased with the decision to have him train our lads in the use of the rifles your Scotsman bought over. A lot of our own men don't know where some of our training camps are based for a reason.' He held up a hand to pre-empt any debate. 'I know he's taken the oath and done some terrific work for us in relation to training with the new rifles, but…' He stopped mid-sentence, unsure, and looked across at Billy McKee. 'Bill. What do you think?'

McKee took a moment before speaking, collecting his thoughts and thinking about how best to push forward Padraig's plan.

'From what I'm hearing from our boys, he's a quick thinking lad. He's taken on the Northern Vietnamese and survived. He has taught our lads quite a bit about how his army and the Vietnamese fought. It was his plan when Southcombe was taken and it came off without any problems.

'Now I'm not saying our boys don't have the wits he possesses but here's how I see it: One; he's a well-rounded, capable soldier whom was professionally trained and can think on his feet when it counts. Two; he's not an Irishman so the chances of people linking him to us are almost impossible and who would ever believe an Australian *is* one of us. It fits in with the plan perfectly. Three; he's a hell of a shot. He beat Terry O'Hagan in a shoot off during their training and we've all heard from our boys, and Terry, how good a shot Terry is.' They all chuckled at that. 'Four; he won't be doing this alone. We'll still have our own people in place.

'When it comes down to it, what we are after are the best people for the job. I don't care what their accent is as long as they know what they're fighting for. You of all people should know this Sean.'

Having an Englishman as the head of the Army Council was something that had taken a lot of people a long time to get used to. Sean MacStiofain (and the rest of the council) knew he wasn't the only Brit in the IRA. They had Welshmen, Scots and former British soldiers within their ranks. There were even a couple of Protestants in some of the rural Brigades. Hell, Wolfe Tone, the man who was revered as the founding father of Irish Republicanism over 200 years ago, had been a Protestant from Dublin.

MacStiofain turned to his right. 'Ruairi?'

Ruairi O'Bradaigh unfolded his arms and readjusted his heavy rimmed glasses, the light reflecting off of a rising phoenix button worn on the lapel of his jacket, the symbol of Provos. He was yet to meet this Australian but had heard good things about him. As far as he was concerned, if his soldiers had accepted him into their brotherhood and he was willing to fight for a united Ireland then it was fine with him.

'It sounds like he knows how to handle himself. I'm fine with it.'

'Joe? Gerry?'

The silver-haired Joe spoke up first.

'It's your call Sean but I'm not so sure. I think we could put him to better use here until he becomes a bit more experienced, more familiar with what we are trying to achieve. If he's still inclined to aim for this type of job later on and if the need is still there, which I'm sure it will be, then maybe. I'm sorry Padraig but that's the way I feel about it.'

Padraig nodded, letting him know he showed no animosity towards Joe's opinion.

'You, Gerry?' MacStiofain asked, knowing if an argument was to happen tonight then it was about to begin.

Gerry knew what this Australian had done in Dublin had had a major impact in London. More people whom were working for a loyalist state were out of the way because of him. More importantly, their own volunteers were now better armed and trained because of what this soldier had bought them. The torture of Sean Doherty had been added to a list of persecution exactly eight hundred years old this year and Adams wished him every opportunity to fulfil his own needs of reprisal…as long as they fitted in with his overall plans.

'The lads got my vote. I think he can do it.' He nodded at Billy and sat back, folding his arms and saying no more. He knew he had surprised them all.

Thank the Lord for that, MacStiofain thought to himself as he deliberated the problem. What it came down to was this young Australian had only been with them since June. It just seemed like too short a period to go from joining their ranks to becoming part of an Active Service Unit, especially the type of ASU they were planning here. The soldiers that were chosen for these units were the best they had. They had proved themselves capable time and time again, carrying out operations that ranged from simple stake-outs and information gathering to more heavy handed jobs like bank robberies, gun trafficking, kidnapping and execution.

Something in his gut made MacStiofain baulk at this. He stroked his closely cropped moustache as he mulled over all he had learnt of this

Australian named Sean Doherty. *Would this lad be capable of carrying out whatever orders they would pass down to him, no matter how he might feel about them?*

If they had a chance to take out the British Prime Minister would he be part of it? Or an assault on a member of the Royal family in the form of a suicide attack? Because that's what one of their operations could end in. They ran a higher risk than the volunteers based in Ireland. Yes, there was support and safe houses but not to the extent their home-based volunteers had. They were basically spies, working alone in the enemy's territory. They were the IRA's version of the commando; small armed groups which were almost completely self-sufficient. They were some of the best that they had. They had to be. Nobody would come running with backup when they would need it most.

He looked up at Padraig. With the loss of their last ASU in Scotland, a team had to be assembled. There was still a large consignment of weapons and ammunition to be retrieved, if the German hadn't already sold them. Things had to go forward.

'I understand he can speak Gaelic now.'

Padraig knew he had succeeded. His Australian friend would be going across the water. 'Young Daniel's been teaching him. He's picking it up pretty quickly.'

'Quicker than I had by the sound of it.' MacStiofain had taken it upon himself, once he had joined the IRA, to learn the true Irish language as soon as he could and encouraged all Irish men, women and children to learn what had been forcibly taken away from them.

'Alright. He never gave his full name to the Garda in Galway so he has a clean record. I don't want him being picked up by the constabulary because the lad we sent over was recognised from a Wanted poster. As far as this side of things go…see if we can get someone he's worked with already and has some time under his belt.'

Gerry Adams looked concerned. 'How many people are we planning to put in? We don't want to overcrowd it?'

MacStiofain shook his head. 'He's not to be part of the ASU but our link with the team. Mostly he'll only work from this side.'

'My choice would be Daniel Carragher. He was with him in Dublin and Short Strand,' Padraig offered. 'That'd be my first choice.'

'Danny's done work away from home before hasn't he?'

Padraig nodded. 'Couple of times. Once across the water and the weapons drop in Kerry.'

'Clean record?'

Padraig nodded again. Of course there was no way of knowing what the Brits had on him but Danny had never been arrested or targeted before.

MacStiofain let out a sigh. It was time to get on the road. There were still things he had to take care of at home and he had missed dinner for the second time this week. His stomach rumbled just to let him know it was still there.

'Fine. We can trust him to do his best. How soon could this be organised?'

Padraig could see MacStiofain was getting tired.

'We have to establish a new network over there. New houses, cars, new papers can be sourced in Brussels', *seeing they have better forgers than in Dublin*, he didn't say. 'A month at the most. Once everything's ready they could be in the next day.'

MacStiofain leaned forward ever so slightly, wanting the Belfast man to be clear on what he was to say next.

'Security is priority on this one, Pad. Be sure your people have somewhere to fall back to if it goes tits up. We can't afford any bad publicity if it becomes known. Opinion is swinging our way and it must continue to do so.'

Padraig nodded. 'I'll take full responsibility if it fails, but it won't Sean. Nothing will go wrong. Not this time.'

For almost a minute the Chief of Staff said nothing. They could all see his mind working over as he played it all out in his head. A chess player working out moves six turns ahead had nothing on him. Finally he stood and the others stood with him. With his hand out he approached Padraig.

'See to it. Our guns first, then set them up for long term operations.

Thanks for coming down. And sorry about keeping you waiting before. We'll talk to you soon.'

Joe stepped forward with a smile and shook his hand, his big hands gripping firmly.

'Prove me wrong Padraig.' There was sincerity in his tone. He had voiced his opinion and a fair decision had been reached.

Padraig said his goodbyes before knocking on the door that led to the hall. An armed guard on the other side opened it. As he walked back to his car through the cool easterly wind that was forcing all of Dundalk's residents indoors, he allowed himself a smirk of accomplishment.

All the way back to Belfast he couldn't stop smiling. He knew he would go far.

THIRTY NINE

Mr Doherty sat in front of the television watching more depressing footage of Australian troops after an ugly confrontation with the Viet Cong. A fire support base had been attacked and the news crew deliberately showed close-ups of the dead natives being bulldozed into hastily dug trenches beyond the wire.

Sean's Regiment had returned months ago, but that would not have made any difference. He would have come home to a pregnant fiancé. She may have broken it off with him in a "Dear John" letter before he had left Asia. Who knew if he would still have done what he did…if he had survived his remaining time in Vietnam that was.

Who knew…?

He wondered where he was. The police were still looking for him, visiting the Lass O'Gowrie every now and then, talking to James, Melanie and his friends but he knew they wouldn't give him up. He himself had never asked where he had gone because he didn't want to know.

Well that wasn't true. He desperately wanted to know where his son was but knew knowing couldn't help him.

Outside a strong southerly blew cold air off the ocean forcing everyone indoors near bar heaters and fireplaces. He owned three bar heaters and two were in the lounge room to keep his illness at bay, a blanket draped over his legs for some extra insulation. A chest cold had attacked him four days ago and was yet to let go. The third bar heater was in the bedroom set on high. He just couldn't handle the cold anymore. Beside his armchair sat his ashtray made of heavy blue squared glass, now clean and unused. He should have put it away or even have thrown it out but hadn't. One day he would.

Maybe tomorrow.

He had begged Melanie to go and buy him a bottle of scotch, claiming it would warm him up but she hadn't caved in.

What's the point, he said to himself. *If I'm going to die what's one drink going to do.*

He hadn't been to the pub in two weeks. James had visited him a few days ago when Melanie was at work, the two of them taking turns to look in on him to make sure he was doing fine, and they had shared a few beers on the back verandah, trying to soak up as much spring sunshine as possible. Neither of them had mentioned Sean during the two hours they had spent together, instead talking about anything but.

'Are you alright Mr Doherty?'

He hadn't heard Luke enter the room and was aware the look on his face probably could have been misconstrued as one of pain.

'Yeah. Just a bit cold.'

Luke had volunteered a few hours tonight to help him out and keep him company. James was swamped at work and, with the cold snap that had come north, Melanie had caught herself a cold.

'Are you hungry yet? You've got to keep your strength up to get over this bug.'

'No I'm fine,' he replied, embarrassed someone who wasn't family was tending to him like he was a geriatric.

'Well I'm starving. I've got some cutlets there if you'd like. I'll cook up all of them and what you don't eat I can save for later. And…I think I might be able to sneak in a bottle of stout for you as long as you eat something and don't tell Melanie.'

Mr Doherty looked up at his work colleague and his son's best friend. He smiled at him. Although he wasn't hungry he would eat something just to keep him happy. 'Steamed vegies?'

Luke nodded with a grin. 'How do you want your potatoes done?'

'Mashed, but let's have that beer first.'

It had been a week since the death of Janis Joplin and the radio stations were still going through all the Joplin songs they could find, giving all her fans the music they needed to come to terms with her great life cut short. Sean however was not a fan. He climbed out of the chair he had positioned by the window, switched the frequency to get her warbling voice out of his head and poured himself another whiskey.

A month ago when Hendrix had partied too hard on barbiturates and vomit, Sean listened to the radios of the neighbourhood echo through streets and backyards with groovy licks and far-out riffs in a musical eulogy for a real musician. However the station he found bought out President Nixon's distinctive voice babbling on about another 40,000 more US troops home before Christmas. The radio went dead.

'Hey!' Daniel called from the bathroom. 'I was listening to that!'

'Bullshit! No one likes that crap.'

'Don't tell me what I like and what I don't,' the Irishman countered. 'Not in my fucken home!'

'Refill?'

'Aye.' An empty glass appeared at the doorway behind him. He took it and topped it up, handing it back to the still-waiting hand. He then returned to the chair, settling back down as he sipped at his drink.

Daniel entered the living room dressed in a cheap but clean suit. His Friday night special, as he called it. Their plan for the night was to have a couple of jars here with Donnie before heading out for a drink. The last three nights had seen them acting as armed sentry at the northern junctions which faced the Protestant suburbs and they were looking forward to trying to relax for the night.

Since arriving back in Belfast months ago Sean and Daniel had become well known amongst the republican crowd, especially Sean due to his nationality and previous military history. He now knew more people in Ireland than he did Australians back home. Many Provos and their families had opened their doors to him despite the high levels of poverty and he was on a first name basis with most of the Brigade leaders and several members of the Army council. The later had been partially due to Padraig whom had done nothing but sing his praises to everyone he met. Sean naturally tried to play this commendation down. He just told people he was there to help out in something he now believed strongly in and while he may be Australian, his blood now felt as equally Irish as the next man.

Sean's grasp on the Irish language had also increased as he talked to the various characters of this troubled city. Many of the elderly community simply refused to speak English, as did a few of the youth. Some of the volunteers had come up from the Republic and Sean had to concentrate twice as hard when he discovered although native Irish was spoken in both the north and the southern twenty-six counties, the Republic had many greatly different words and pronunciations for the same thing, especially down south in Munster. He was in fact learning two Irish languages and found out some of it would also translate over to Scot's Gaelic if he ever met any hardcore Scotsmen.

Daniel dragged a tattered seat over from the table and joined his friend as they relaxed after a long day of doing nothing other than picking up Daniel's repaired second hand television that now sat proudly back in its corner. They knew it would be a struggle to carry the heavy thing the two blocks from Mr Cleary's apartment where the out-of-work electrician had repaired it so they had borrowed Donnie's car under the proviso they shout him a few drinks for the use of his Vauxhall. After the awkward and back-breaking job of dragging it up four flights of stairs to his third storey flat, Daniel had waisted no time cracking the lid off of a bottle of Jameson.

'Been a while since this one's been on the tear,' a voice announced from the doorway. It was Donnie, striding through with an old familiar face behind him.

'Jesus Christ!' Daniel exclaimed as he turned to see the two in the doorway. 'Kieran, you can walk! It's a fucken miracle!'

Both Daniel and Sean near jumped out of their chairs to greet the young rebel, himself in a suit, albeit poorly tailored for such a large frame.

He gave Sean a tight handshake. 'How you doin' Sean? Made yourself at home I see. Thought you'd be a herring gutter now for sure.'

Sean grinned up at the tall volunteer. 'I try to leave but this one won't have a bar of it. How's the leg?'

'Drinks first then the bullshit!' Donnie called as he headed for the small kitchen. 'What are youse drinking?'

'There's a bottle on the counter.' Sean said as he ushered the limping Kieran to a seat before sitting down to his own whiskey.

'Where's Melissa?' Kieran asked.

'Don't you worry about where my sister is.' Daniel sat down next to him. 'It's hard enough trying to keep this one away from her,' he said, nodding towards Sean. 'Come on then, shoot those down and let's get going.'

'Anyway Sean,' Kieran continued, ignoring Daniel. 'What's this I hear about you pulling one down in South Armagh?'

'How the fuck did you hear about that?' he asked over the laughter of the others.

'You would have been proud of him Kieran,' Daniel informed him. 'This one was a looker *and* a volunteer.'

'So I heard.'

'It was all a misunderstanding,' Daniel continued. 'She'd been giving *me* the eye for the few days beforehand and on the night in question she'd had a few to drink and simply walked into the wrong bedroom.'

'That'd have to be it,' Kieran said as he winked in Sean's direction. 'No self respecting Irish girl would ever lower her high morals by laying down with an Australian! British convicts the lot o' them!'

Sean squinted in mock pain. 'Oh. My sides! They're splitting! You cunts are just too funny.'

Donnie turned on the TV, the familiar opening tune to *Coronation Street* playing out through the speaker, a fuzzy picture focusing in, filling the black and white tube. He spoke over his shoulder to Daniel. 'I think your TV is still busted.'

'It's *meant* to be black and white' Daniel commented, knowing what Donnie was thinking. 'If I had enough money to buy a coloured

TV, do you think I would be taking it to Cleary's to get it fixed? It'd end up coming *back* black and white.'

'That's what I'm saying. I think he did send it back black and white!'

'It *is* a fucken black and white television!' Daniel roared at him.

'Because you sent it to Cleary's.'

They all laughed.

Daniel stepped over to him and shut the image off. 'Stop wasting my electricity. You've already drained the colour out of it. Hurry up and drain that glass so we can head out.'

Screwing up his face in mock disgust, Donnie looked at the others in the room. 'What a prick of a host! Lend him my car to pick up his now-busted colour telly and this is the thanks I get!'

Daniel turned to Sean. 'You got your gun on you?' Sean nodded and patted the waist band of his pants with a big smile. 'Shoot this wanker for me then, would you?'

Laughing as the whiskey began to relax them, they gathered jackets and headed out into the cold. At the end of the street they passed a group of women and kids painting the exterior walls white. It had been an idea from the wives of the prisoners: rid the streets and alleys of shadows for the Brits to hide in by giving their boys silhouettes to shoot at. At night they would paint the walls and corners of the buildings and alleyways white, long bands eight feet high. In the days following the army would paint them dark again. The wives would return and the cycle would continue. The nocturnal work force shouted out a cheery hello and the group of lads continued on. Five minutes down the road they came to one of the many shebeens, illegal drinking halls that had sprung up over West Belfast over the last year. They entered through a gate, down the thin alley beside an auto repair shop to a disused storage room which had become a speak-easy for "operators" and gunmen of the IRA.

The warmly heated room was large enough to seat fifty comfortably. There were only twenty or so at the moment, a mix of men and women dressed up for a night of it, already seated amongst the mismatched furniture that sat scattered around in front of the makeshift bar, itself made from two large tables at the end of the room. Music came from an unseen radio somewhere behind the bar, from amid the crates of stolen beer and spirit bottles and beer kegs.

As they entered the small crowd cheered at the sight of Kieran's tall frame coming through the door, the men getting up to shake hands with him and consoled him on being shot. He wasted no time in dropping his strides to proudly show off the large ugly scar on the side of his thigh.

Drinks were bought and the group headed for a spot in the corner of the room, taking two ratty lounges that should have been at the tip. They toasted their drinks and threw them down before settling in with a pint each.

'Hey Donnie!'

Don looked over at the group by the bar. 'How's it goin' Martin?'

The young man nodded and raised his glass. 'A lot better now I'm in here!'

'It's certainly been busy the last few nights.'

'Listen. Jim Bryson called in earlier looking for you.'

The room suddenly seemed to quieten at the mention of this name. Sean looked over at Daniel, his face as still as stone as he watched Donnie.

'Jim?' Donnie posed. 'What the hell does Jim want with me?'

Sean was unsure if Donnie feared this man the same way everyone else seemed to. Just the sound of his name appeared to stop all mid-drink.

'Don't know mate. Said he was going to call back in later if you were hanging around. You too Kieran.'

Kieran didn't even nod; he just sat there looking back with a worried expression on his face, his brow furrowed as he tried to think if he had done anything wrong recently that would warrant a visit from him.

'Cheers Marty.' Donnie returned his attention back to his drinking circle. He looked at the expressions on everyone's face and saw the apprehension on all but Sean's face.

'They certainly know how to kill the mood,' Kieran said over the top of his glass.

'What the fuck does Jim Bryson want with you?' Daniel asked.

'Did you not just hear me ask that of Marty?' Donnie replied angrily.

'Well you know him better than any of us. Sometimes I think you have this whole other circle of friends that are all complete fucken nutters just like yourself!'

'You're the fucken nutter.'

'This Jim Bryson,' Sean asked, 'he's a Provo?'

Donnie nodded yes. 'Probably one of the most feared men in Belfast. Good thing you're on his side. Even so, I'd stay dog wide of him.'

'Even then it doesn't matter,' Daniel interrupted. 'Bloke's a fucken psychopath. Going to get himself killed one of these days and I don't want to go down with him.'

Donnie lit up a fag and held out the packet, both Sean and Daniel taking one.

'You see, Jim prefers to work alone. Sometimes he gets around with "Toddler" or Paddy but most of the time he's on his own. People find him a bit…'

'Terrifying,' Kieran jumped in.

'He's not that bad!'

'There is no one,' Daniel stated, 'colder on the streets of Belfast tonight than Jim Bryson.' He turned to Sean. 'And I mean in here.' He tapped his chest. 'He's one of Gerry Adam's goons. The man walks the streets alone in the dead of night with more weapons than a normal man could carry on the off chance he might run into a loyalist mob or even a Brit patrol.'

'He's got no fear,' Donnie tried to justify.

'He's got no brains! I'm not sure I want to be here when he turns up. I don't trust the fool and neither do half the men in here.'

Donnie tried to wave the issue away. 'Sit down, we just got here. We're meant to be having a good time.'

'No one can have a good time knowing at any minute Jim Bryson is going to walk in through that door. Especially if he's coming in here for a drink, or is already drunk! It's probably safer being a Proddie. At least they don't have to mingle with him.'

'Keep your fucking voice down boy!' Donnie looked around at the other patrons, worried about the scene Daniel was making. 'Christ, you're carrying on like a mad woman.'

Daniel noticed some were looking in his direction, trying to work out what was happening over in their corner. 'Fine.' He sat back down next to Sean. 'Don't expect me to hang around if he turns up here in one of his moods. I've still got some whiskey at home and I'll gladly drink it alone if I have to.'

After an hour the rain began to fall outside and the place had filled with locals getting out of the wet and into a warming nip or a soothing pint. The radio had been replaced with a banjo player; a red faced, white bearded, fat gnome look-alike with stumpy arthritic fingers that had retained their awkward shape after decades of plucking.

Sean's small group had grown to include four more gunmen and the girlfriends of two of them. Everybody now had quite a shine going. They weren't pissed yet, but the night was only half over.

For the first half hour after threatening to walk out, Daniel kept looking to the two doors at either end, expecting to see Jim Bryson but he soon forgot about him.

A tin whistle and a bodhran joined in on the next song, the sound filling the small room, drowning out most conversation. Again Sean thought back to the Lass O'Gowrie, wondering what his brother and friends were doing right at that moment.

Just as he picked up his round of drinks the music stopped. All talking stopped, all movement stopped. The hairs on the back of his neck stood up as he sensed something was wrong. He turned and saw every single person in the room was looking towards the rear door. The people nearest the door took a step back. Then Sean could see him.

He knew who it was without even asking.

It was Jim Bryson.

The description he had heard before was nothing like what he saw. Sean had been expecting a tough hulking man but instead he saw a young lad roughly his own age if not younger. Still, he was a sight to behold. Standing there in the open door way with rain falling behind him, Jim Bryson looked more than mean. The baggy woollen jumper he wore was soaked through, making him look like a fisherman gone barmy. Carrying his monstrous Lewis machine gun, "Big Louie", cemented the image further. With one wet hand resting on the cylindrical magazine which sat atop the ancient weapon like a big flat cake tin and the other scratching his stubbled water-beaded cheek, Jim's eyes scanned the room. They seemed to pass over Sean without noticing him, but Bryson, his reflexes and senses tuned to spot irregularities and differences, had taken in the new unfamiliar face before finally settling on Donnie. He took a step forward and half the room took one step back, allowing a corridor for him to walk down.

Donnie turned to greet the feared man, his hand out. They shook hands after Bryson had relieved himself from the weight of the Lewis machine gun, the giant weapon now lying across a nearby table but not out of arms reach.

'Nice scar,' Bryson said, looking at the back of Donnie's hand. 'Short Strand?'

'I'd been wiping my brow when it happened.'

'Shit. Very lucky then.'

Conversation within the crowd resumed but at a much lower volume. So did the music but without the drum and pipe, the banjo gnome opting to fill the room with a dulcet tune, not to entertain the crowd but to calm his own nerves and hopefully keep Bryson's in check.

Sean returned with the drinks as Donnie and Bryson finished greeting each other. He noted Daniel was keeping quiet but kept a wary eye on the newcomer. The Australian stepped up beside Donnie and handed him his pint.

'*Sláinte* Sean.'

Bryson's eyes had watched Sean enter the group, knowing who he was. Not much got by him these days.

'Jim, this is...'

'Sean Doherty. The Australian right?'

'That's right,' Sean answered. He held out his hand.

Bryson took his hand after a long few seconds of staring into his eyes, reading the Aussie. His grip was strong but the handshake was short. 'Grab us a pint would ya.' It wasn't a question.

For a second Sean thought he was talking to someone else behind him, but the young crazed man's gaze held on him for a second more before returning to Daniel. Feared man or not, Sean Doherty was no waiter for this skinny fucker.

'I'm not a waiter, mate.' It was polite but assertive.

The small group around them couldn't believe their ears. Daniel's stomach turned. He looked at Sean and saw that the fool was staring straight back at Bryson, almost waiting for an apology.

Bryson himself was taken aback by the statement. To him the comment was like a slap in the face, something that rarely happened, *never* happened. He turned to look at this brazen foreigner here in *his* city, drinking in *his* bar, thinking *he* knew how things were run.

'I don't give a fuck if you're the Pope.' Now the whole room had gone quiet as the worst was anticipated. Some edged towards the two doors ready to make a quick getaway. 'I asked you kindly for a pint.'

Sean, who ignored the looks given to him by Daniel and Donnie, smiled across at Bryson. 'That old gun must be pretty loud when it goes off.' He paused for a second. 'Because by the sounds of it, it's made you deaf.' Behind them several people exited, preferring the cold night over the tension filled room. 'So because of your disability I will say this one more time. I'm...not...a...waiter.'

No one in the room breathed for fear of attracting attention.

Beside Sean, Daniel was trying to think how to defuse the situation but was in shock. All his brain kept on coming back with was "*get the fuck outta there*".

He wasn't the only one that was shocked. In the few short years he had been a soldier for, first the IRA then the Provisional IRA after the split, Jim Bryson had never had to say anything twice. He had purposely built up a reputation and prided himself on his staunchness. He believed he was more of a soldier than any of the men here in this room and wasn't about to be put in his place by this "tourist soldier" who was here to get his kicks because he couldn't go back to Vietnam. Just looking at this Australian standing there, holding his stare, thinking he knew how this town worked, was boiling his blood. He held the stare but spoke to Donnie.

'Don, I think you'd better tell your boy here how things are run.'

Donnie didn't know what to say. He would never admit it to Jim but Sean was right. Sean however didn't know the lengths Jim would go to make a point.

Before Donnie could think of something to say Sean lifted his pint to his lips and began to drink. The crowd watched with apprehension as he gulped down the black stout, taking his time but making sure the full glass went down in one attempt.

Behind Bryson, Daniel had to force his hand to not move to the pistol in his waist band. But what he would have done with it once it was in his hand, he wasn't sure. Experience told him to grab it but fear stayed his hand.

As the last of the Guinness ran into his mouth, Sean lowered the glass. A moustache of creamy foam clung to his top lip. He licked it before holding out the empty glass to Bryson. He had been in many pub fights before but not with so many armed men around and he shocked himself when he finally spoke, ready for what was inevitably to happen. He glanced at his empty glass and then nodded towards the bar.

'While you're there…'

Daniel swore he heard the rage trigger in Bryson. Before he had a chance to react, Daniel was moving towards Sean faster than he had ever moved before.

Bryson's face seemed to instantly turn deep red as his fist shot out, punching the rim of the glass, shattering it while Sean still held it. All around them the room came alive with movement. People took off like gazelles seeing a lion. Donnie tried to step in front of Bryson but was knocked aside as he followed through on his punch, his fist hitting Donnie in the chest. Daniel had opted not to go for the gun but to tackle Sean back towards the other exit and out of there. Bryson had too many followers in the crowd, some of whom were moving in to control the site of the fight that was beginning.

Sean's hand let go of the broken glass and prepared to defend himself, his eyes on the lunging Bryson when Daniel grabbed him in a bear hug from his right side and pushed him back into the crowd. Behind them, Kieran had stepped in to block Bryson who himself was now being held back by his own men, the wet jumper being pulled out of shape as he tried to break free.

'Get him out of here!' Donnie yelled at Daniel as he climbed back to his feet. His sternum was tender but he had more things to worry about, praying thanks that no one had decided to pull a gun.

The door had been left open by other fleeing patrons worried the Lewis would come into play and Sean and Daniel were soon outside. He kept pushing his mate until they had reached the street, both too worked up to realise they were becoming wet from the drizzling rain.

'Are you fucken mad?' Daniel exclaimed.

Sean pulled his jacket collar up around his neck. 'What? You would have gotten him a drink?'

'It's *Jim fucking Bryson!*'

'I *don't fucking care!* Cunt doesn't talk to me like that.' Sean turned and began walking home. 'So, drinks at home then?' The tone of his voice told Daniel the matter was now over.

'You don't get it Sean,' he said trotting up beside him. 'There aren't many other soldiers out there that are as respected and feared as him. If he gets it in his head to get rid of you then you're gone. No one will question it!'

Sean stopped and turned to face him. 'Including you?'

'Don't put me in that position then!'

'Glad to see you'll back me up. Don't go thinking I'm gunna to go back in there to apologise. I'd say he knows where I'm staying so he can come and apologise to me.'

'He'd just as soon blow your knee caps off before he did that.'

'What would you have done?'

'I wouldn't have done what you just did.'

'Fuck him.' Sean's voice rose and his stance became defensive, shoulders back. 'I'm not over here to fetch him a cup of tea when ever he feels the urge to put his feet up. I'm a fucking soldier here just like you and Donnie and that prick. I don't even know what kind of soldier he is! All I've heard is he likes to take that big gun of his out for long walks. He wasn't with us at Short Strand, he wasn't with us in Dublin or South Armagh. From the look of it I've done more to help you lot than he has. I don't care if he is a fucking lap dog for the Army Council. If they don't appreciate everything I've done for them then maybe it is time for me to go.' Without waiting for a reply he trudged off into the rain.

Daniel's head felt like it was going to burst. What a shit of a night. If only they had left when Donnie had told them Bryson was looking for him then all of this bullshit wouldn't have happened. Now Sean was threatening to leave.

Fucking Bryson.

Behind him Daniel heard his name being called out and hoped it wasn't that madman. He turned, relieved to see Kieran in the lane way.

'What!?'

'Come back! You're going to want to hear this!'

Daniel recognised the man that stepped up beside Kieran. It was Ted, one of the men that worked closely with Padraig and a bit of a madman as well. He nodded acknowledgement to him and turned to halt Sean but he had slipped further into the dark, wet night. Daniel just hoped he was returning home…to his Belfast home.

FORTY

For the first time in months Sean had a nightmare about Joel.

It had jumped around in location with a rate almost impossible to keep track of. Newcastle, Belfast, Vietnam, over and over, with Daniel and Joel taking pot-shots at each other from behind rusted hulks of cars, from within a maze of rubber trees in the humid South Vietnamese flatlands, in and out of the houses in his old Wickham neighbourhood. Whole magazines were emptied as each called out for Sean to back him up and help him kill the other.

Standing in the centre of this jigsaw of a battlefield, directly in the line of fire, was himself with one of Chad's M16s and the ability to end it all by taking either one or the other out with what he knew would be a single perfectly aimed, calm and precise shot.

To his left screamed Joel.

To his right Daniel.

Their own rounds seemed to pass within inches of his body and face, the air moving around him, the heat of passing tracers almost searing his skin.

Unable to stop himself, he watched as he pulled back on the charging, the burnished round lifting into place from the magazine into the exposed breach.

Don't do it, he said to himself.

His hands however were not being commanded by his brain, working on their own. The slide released, the round slid home, the weapon now loaded. Around him the noise grew so loud his ears began to scream. His name rang out continuously from each side. Before he knew it he had reversed the rifle and placed the muzzle in his mouth.

Don't do it, he screamed at himself.

Neither Joel nor Daniel tried to stop him, rather they carried on with their own war while roaring out his name for help.

He couldn't stop himself when his thumb pressed the trigger.

Unfortunately he didn't wake up.

His body fell back through the hail of rounds being fired by his friends, each bullet now hitting him as he slowly fell backwards to the road outside his home, his body unbending, the fall akin to a toppling tree. Clothing and flesh exploded from his body as his jungle greens turned black with blood. No bullet seemed to miss him now. Despite having no skull from his brow up, Sean could feel every hit, his eyes wide open as he looked up to the perfect blue sky being criss-crossed by the bright red burning magnesium of tracer rounds.

Still he would not wake up.

Behind the never-ending crash of gunfire he could still hear his name being called…

His eyes finally opened after forcing himself to leave the hell of his mind. He had a choking sensation to scream but bit down hard on the blanket to hide it. Heavy tears had welled in his eyes and when he clenched them shut the tears ran down into the bedding. For a minute he lay there before he opened them again, a slim feeling of fear still with him as he did so.

Turning over, he was glad Max was not there to see him in this state. He had awoken many times to find the lad sitting there on his little chair looking at him, half the time near frightening him to death.

He realised it was beginning to turn light outside. Nobody was up. Checking the time he saw it was still early. Only milkmen and drunks were up at this hour. Not wanting to return to sleep he dressed and made a pot of tea, glad that he didn't have the familiar hangover to join him.

Glancing out the window he saw the rain had stopped. It had belted down heavily last night after he had gotten home. Melissa and Max had both been in bed and he had fallen asleep not long after laying down. Whether Daniel was home or not he wasn't sure. If he was, he hadn't heard him come in.

He slipped his jacket on and, taking his tea, he stepped out onto the balcony that ran the length of the building. Outside the air was cold but he welcomed it. Leaning against the railing with the warmth of the cup cradled in both hands he looked out over the sleeping city, a rare morning peace allowing its citizens some respite. The buildings and streets had been washed clean with the rain of the night but the clouds hung low, threatening to start again.

Then he allowed himself to remember what had happened last night. He hated facing people after an argument but it had to be done. What he would say to Daniel he didn't know. He'd play it by ear but would stick to his conviction that he would never bow down to someone like Jim Bryson.

Behind him the door opened and he was glad to see both young Max and Daniel. Max climbed up onto his milk crate beside Sean with Daniel on the other side. Stretching up onto his toes Max peered over the edge, not saying a word, still waking up.

Sean decided to break the silence.

'What time did you get in?'

'Not sure. Took a while to get home in that storm.'

Sean gauged Dan wasn't pissed off with him. Both of them had had a bit to drink.

'Bryson calmed down yet?' he asked with a small grin.

Daniel couldn't help but smile. In the time he had known Jim Bryson he had never seen anyone stand up to him the way Sean had. Deep down he felt a little admiration creep in. He wished he had the balls that his friend did.

'Don't know. He wasn't there when I got back.'

'He'll get over it.'

'You reckon?'

'Fuck him if he doesn't.'

Daniel laughed. 'You don't know when to stop do you.'

Sean just shrugged. 'He'll be just another man with a grudge.'

'It'll certainly make your life a bit interesting.'

'You don't think there's enough going on already?'

'I thought you looked a bit bored.'

They both laughed at that.

Beside them Max spied a target below. He climbed off his crate and picked up a stone the size of a match box, clambered back up and took aim at the mangy black dog on the footpath below. With a small flick of his wrist the stone fell in a shallow arc and the three of them watched it miss the dog by only inches, instead hitting an empty garbage bin beside it. The bin clattered hollow, scaring the dog which scurried off with its tail hung low.

'Oh, close one mate,' Sean said, rubbing the lad's bed hair.

'I thought I had him this time,' he replied, a big smile pasted across his face.

'You'll get that fucken dog one day,' Daniel assured him. 'Always shitting around here.'

Max pointed his finger at the retreating dog like an imaginary gun, closing one eye to take aim. 'Powwww.'

'Sorry for having a go at you last night,' Sean directed at Dan.

'Same here. I probably would have done the same if…'

'If it *wasn't* Jim Bryson.'

'Maybe. I've never been in his bad books. Hey, did Donnie leave his car keys here?'

'Yeah, they're by the stove.'

'Good. I have to go and meet someone this afternoon so I might get you to drop me off. Not in the mood for walking. Looks like it might open up again,' he said with a cautious look upwards. 'Beside, I think Mel's going to Bingo over at St Pauls. We can pick her and this one up after.'

'What's this meeting about?'

Dan smiled slyly and winked at him. 'Wait and see.'

Ten hours later, outside of the parked car in which Sean waited, Belfast was preparing itself for whatever the night would bring. Parents were bringing in their children for dinner, ensuring they weren't on the streets when whatever would happen happened. Blinds were drawn over windows to deny any crazed snipers out there a clean shot at husbands/fathers/sons. As the light began to fade off to the west, away from the apprehensive city, Sean knew the only people on the streets tonight were out to cause trouble, attempt to control it, or both.

At the end of the block he saw an eight-man British Army foot patrol enter the street, moving away from him, finishing the last of their day patrol and winding their way back to base. With four on each side of the road, they cautiously made their way in a staggered file with their SLRs sweeping back and forth as they watched the windows across and above their opposite team mates. They hurried from shadow to doorway, covering behind cars or garden walls, ever cautious about becoming a static target. The men at the rear turned every few steps to keep check on the back door of their unit to ensure no rear ambush.

From this distance Sean thought they could almost be mistaken for Australian soldiers; the SLRs, a forward scout at the lead of each line of men, the C.O. being shadowed by the radio operator with his antennae waving back and forth like a drunken metronome that had lost its beat long ago. Were they in a jungle instead of the darkening urban maze of Belfast he could almost be convinced. Only their camouflaged greens and the ugly helmets they wore (a necessity against rocks and pavers favoured by children as missiles) broke the likeness.

Sean looked at his watch. It was just after four. As the patrol disappeared down the street, Daniel appeared from the doorway he had entered only ten minutes prior. With hands in his jacket pockets he trotted up the footpath, jumping into the car with a grin wide across his face.

Sean looked at him and waited for the obvious good news but Daniel just kept smiling back at him.

'Well?'

'What?' Daniel countered.

'Why the grin?'

'I'm just trying to picture how you're going to make this up to me.'

'Make what up to you?' The Irishman just grinned back at him. 'For fuck's sake!' Sean snapped. 'What are you on about?'

Daniel looked up, pondering as he spoke to himself. 'How many pints is this worth. No, wait. Not pints. How much whiskey…?'

'Get out of the car.' Sean jokingly reached across him to open the door when Daniel pulled his left hand from his pocket and opened it, palm down, letting something fall and dangle from his thumb and forefinger. Sean instantly recognised the noise the object made as the two small discs clinked together. He looked in semi-disbelief at his Australian Army issued dog tags.

'Where…?' he stuttered as he took them from Daniel. He couldn't believe he was holding them again even as his fingers ran across the cold indentations of each stamped letter and number.

'They found Brian Reardon last night. Your pistol man from Galway. Idiot had them around his neck.'

'How'd they find him?' He looked up at his mate.

'Didn't ask that question of him. Ted, I mean. He's one of the men Padraig goes to when things have to get messy. He's a psycho but when he applies himself…'

'So Reardon's dead?'

'I'd say so. If Ted talked to him. He just gave me those, said to tell you to hold onto them better this time.'

The green army boot lace which had originally held them around Sean's neck had been replaced with a black lace. He slipped them over his head, finding them a bit tighter as the lace passed over his nose. As he tucked the discs in under his shirt a torrent of memories came flooding back, some good and some bad. Amongst the good was Joel. Then a second later he was amongst the bad memories, remembering his nightmare from last night.

Daniel said, 'Another thing. Padraig wants to see us both in the morning.'

'What for?'

'Didn't say. Ted was just passing on the message.' He pointed down the road. 'Come on then. Mel will be waiting.'

Subconsciously Sean patted his dog tags as he started the car and lifted his foot off the clutch. It only took a few minutes to arrive outside of St Paul's church in the Mid Falls area. There were quite a few cars lined along Falls Road and Sean had to park about one hundred yards from the recreation hall located at the side of the church. The hall was beginning to empty of mainly women and elderly folk as they left their afternoon Bingo to get home in time to cook meals for their husbands and before it got too dark. Sean and Daniel climbed out of the car and lit up a smoke each as they waited for Melissa and little Max to leave.

'Does she ever win?' Sean questioned.

'Aye. Mel's the Bingo champion of the Murph. On average every third week she brings home the winnings.'

As Daniel talked, Sean spotted Melissa and Max leaving the hall with the last of the crowd. Melissa chatted with other young mothers, some pushing strollers, as the young master splashed in the puddles that had formed last night, his right hand never letting go of his sole parent. Sean curled his tongue and whistled to get her attention. She waved back and began saying goodbye to her friends.

'Wonder what Padraig wants?' Daniel thought out loud as he watched the cars around him head home.

'You're in the shit again I reckon.'

'What do you mean *again*? More like a promotion.'

'Promotion?! Ha! You never…' Sean's words were then ripped from his mouth.

Eighty yards beyond Melissa and her son, a package hidden in one of the cities five foot high cylindrical public mail boxes, triggered a current to a crude battery-operated timed-ignition system. The electrical spike ran through two yards of detonation cord; the cord itself being wrapped tightly around two and a half pounds of stolen demolitions explosive. With the sound of one hundred simultaneous thunderclaps the terrifying detonation of the makeshift bomb first sent out a giant concussive shock wave, a wall of extremely high pressurised air that, for less than an instant, was visible as a rapidly growing bubbled hemisphere. It destroyed every window in a two block radius, pulverised nearby brick walls into dust and tore limbs and crushed internal organs of the few unlucky pedestrians that were within twenty yards of the point of ignition.

Following close behind the shock wave came the shrapnel of the mail box itself moving close to the speed of sound. The air was filled with pieces of the cast iron mail box as it was obliterated, the deafening noise echoing across the city. Parts of it passed clean through the walls of the brick buildings to its left while other pieces would later be found over half a mile away. Two cars which were driving past it at the time were destroyed, one rolling to a stop with shredded wheels, a peeled open roof and shattered windows and panels, the driver riddled with shrapnel, dead before his brain had time to register the blast. The other car had skipped sideways, almost rolling over onto its side but falling back down heavily onto its wheels. The driver was somehow still conscious although he was now bleeding from the ears and eyes.

Across Belfast people knew what had happened, a guilty few even counting down the seconds before hand.

Half falling, half diving, Sean and Daniel hit the pavement as a large piece of shrapnel passed them by within inches, skipping along the road before embedding itself into the front grille and radiator of an oncoming Hillman, steam bursting forward through the twisted chrome teeth like a metal dragon's breath.

All sound expanded with a roar for a few seconds until there was nothing but the high-pitched ringing in their ears that follows a close detonation.

As fast as he could, Sean scrambled to his feet, pulling Daniel up with him. Both their eyes strained to see along the street as dust and smoke filled the space between them and Melissa. Without waiting they both sprinted forward into the dusty silence.

Then the screaming started.

Sean felt his stomach tighten. The screams, the smoke, the ringing in his ears took him back twelve months. A woman to his far right shrieked in pain as her body released her from her state of shock, her panic directed to her legs. With bloodied hands she reached down to the trenches carved in her thighs and hip by the high velocity shrapnel. The cry of a child from up ahead somewhere cut through the haze and both prayed it was not Max, the howl being one of immense pain as the child struggled to breathe in to let the screams out.

As they reached the spot where Daniel's sister had been beforehand they could see six figures lying slumped on the footpath. No, five. The sixth was a gruesome sight. Beside one of the women, who only moments before had been talking to Melissa, was a pair of legs in blood soaked men's trousers torn clean from the torso just above the belt and twisted at crazy angles.

Sean reached Melissa first, dropping to his knees to roll her over. As he did so she sat upright, a confused look of being lost was pasted across her face. Daniel headed for little Max; his tiny body had been thrown a few yards to his mother's left to the base of the church's stone fence. He scooped the boy up into his arms, glad he saw only light grazing on him but terrified because he lay there unconscious. As he lifted him and held him close, Max's eyes opened. He did not cry nor scream. He had been shocked into silence.

Melissa looked at Sean, trying to work out what was happening but before he could say a word she spun her head around in search of her son. 'MAX?!'

'I've got him!' came the call from her brother.

Sean was about to hoist Melissa up in his arms when he saw the left side of her cardigan was covered in blood, some of it in her hair. 'Are you hurt?' he asked her, aware she may not be feeling any pain as yet.

'No...Oh sweet Jesus!' Her eyes widened as she saw what Sean was looking at. She tried to touch her hand to her side but pulled back in fear.

'Lie down, lie down,' he told her in a calm but assured voice. Disregarding any polite approach he ripped open her cardigan and pulled back the bloodied material. Her dress underneath was clean. He then ran a hand through her hair in search of wounds to her head. He breathed out. 'You're fine. It's not your blood.' Before she could respond he slid an arm under her knees and the other around behind her back and hoisted her up off the ground. She wrapped her arms around his neck as he carried her off the debris-covered road to the grassed area beside the church.

'Here comes Daniel. He's got Max.'

Melissa turned and saw her brother carrying her son towards them. Sean set her down on the cool lawn, as did Daniel with Max. He did not cry as his mother threw her arms around him, herself trembling with shock.

Leaving the family there Sean turned and ran back to the other victims still sprawled out on the street. He could feel the heat of the fire coming from the unrecognisable wreckage of a car which had been parked beside the mailbox. The building by the car had lost its front wall altogether and the smouldering dirty smoke of a fire yet to combust billowed from the inside rooms.

All around him came terrifying screams, some from the heavily inflicted and some from people too deep in shock to know, despite a few lacerations, they were quite capable of walking. In contrast to this he could see a man on the other side of the bomb wreckage trying to get to his feet despite a broken leg that made him look as though he had an extra knee nine inches below his left knee. Yet he struggled on.

The first person Sean came across was another young mother feeling blindly out in front of her as she crawled along on her bloodied hands and knees working her way towards the screams of her little girl of about six. Dust and building debris had filled her eyes, her tears cleaning tracks down her grey cheeks as she cried out for her screaming daughter, 'GRACE! GRACE!' Her hand found her crying child just as Sean reached them. He went down on one knee in front of her.

'It's alright love. I've got you now. I've got your girl. Come on Grace, climb on my back. That's the girl. Now hold onto my neck tight while I help your mummy. Okay give me your hand. That's it.' Her hands gripped his tightly as he lifted the mother up to her feet. 'I'm just going to carry you over to the church yard okay? We'll wash your eyes out.'

He scooped her up and trotted over, the mother in his arms, her daughter on his back holding on with all her strength, her crying now just a repetitive blubbering. He noticed the priest of the church had arrived on the scene, darting from one victim to another, weighing up the severity of the injuries like a nurse in a busy emergency room triage. 'Father, some water here, quickly!' Sean quietened his voice as he spoke again to the woman. 'Father's got your little girl okay?' The priest took hold of her hand as he lifted the child from Sean's back. She tried to say something but it just came out as a moan. A few yards away Daniel was making sure his family was safe before running after Sean back out towards the carnage. In the background the sounds of sirens began to grow in the fading light.

By now people had begun to converge on the sight and scrambled to help where they could, putting out spot fires here and pulling people to safety there. Cars used their lights to illuminate the scene as their drivers tried to administer whatever first aid knowledge they had.

Sean and Daniel tried to not look down at the shattered lower half of the man that was lying on the footpath, wondering where the top half had ended up, as they reached the next woman. Her eyes were shut but she had a pulse so they grabbed one end each, Daniel up under her arms and Sean at her knees and pulled her away from the burning wreck of a parked car over to the grass. Laying her down softly Sean checked her signs again. Her breathing was steady, her pulse strong. Daniel called to the priest and asked him to keep an eye on her.

Returning to the street once more Sean and Daniel split up to attend to separate victims. Wedged about a foot underneath the rear of a parked car was a child of no more than four years of age. The little boy's screams had been hard to hear over the approaching sirens and with the noise of the house fire that had finally ignited, Sean had almost run past him, only hearing him as one of the sirens died off. Lying down beside the boy Sean reached under and placed his hand on the boy's head. 'I've got'cha mate. It's alright.'

The boy's screams did not subside. His shoulders were pinned between the fuel tank and the road such was the force of his journey.

One arm lay above his head and fresh blood flowed in small waves down his forearm, his jumper torn from wrist to shoulder. Sean had seen enough open wounds to know those pulsing waves meant the boy's artery had been severed. It was too dark to see how much already lay on the road. He had to work fast. He turned around to get Daniel's attention but he was heading back to the churchyard with a man over his shoulders in a fireman's carry.

Seeing movement behind him Sean turned to see two British Armoured Personnel Carriers pulling up to block the street off. Soldiers spilled from the rear of them, spreading out as they ran towards the mayhem.

'OVER HERE!!' Sean screamed out to them. As three of them headed for him with weapons at the ready Sean rolled over onto his side out of view of the soldiers, slipped his pistol into his jacket pocket before undoing his belt and unravelling it from his waist.

'There's a kid underneath,' he yelled to them as they approached. 'Lift when I say!'

All three soldiers spread out across the rear of the car, each of them placing their SLR on the boot lid.

Turning to face the boy, Sean took hold of his tiny legs.

'Here we go mate,' he said softly to him. Then to the soldiers he ordered, 'LIFT!'

The wheels of the small sedan came almost a foot off the ground and instantly the hidden wound opened further as the pressure was relieved. Sean pulled the lad to his own chest and rolled back clear of the car. The car dropped behind them both as Sean threw his belt around the child's upper arm, looping it through and pulling it tight. The pulsing gash above the elbow slowed its flow to a trickle and he lifted the boy into his arms as he stood. One of the soldiers pointed Sean in the direction the APCs which were being strobed blue by the flashing lights of the late arriving ambulances.

Running through the growing crowd of soldiers, he made his way to the first ambulance he saw, itself not even stopped yet. He ran to the rear, forced his way past some BBC cameramen and photographers who had turned up to film and snap the horror and nearly wrenched the ambulance's door off its hinges before the medic could climb out to open them.

'He's got a severed artery. I don't know how much blood he's lost.' The medic took the lad and placed him in the back but not before Sean patted the boy on the head for luck.

Heading back to the churchyard, he could see the fire trucks trying to get through the traffic that had clogged Falls Road but were having a hard time doing so. He jogged past the twisted flaming metal of the destroyed car and the scar on the pavement that had once been the mail box, disgusted at the people which had built such a weapon, repulsed at the soft target they had chosen.

This was the cowards way to fight a war and it made him livid.

Daniel had returned to help his sister get out of there. She was limping heavily but they all wanted to be as far away from the Brits and the police, knowing they rarely handled situations like this with empathy.

Sean looked at the others he had removed from the bedlam. The woman who had been temporarily blinded was still holding her child closely. Her face was wet from the priest's water and the two of them sat silently as they watched the scene around them, now feeling violated and lost like a mugging victim after the crime. She gave Sean no notice as he passed her by, unaware he was the man that had pulled them to safety. Her daughter however looked at him. It was a look of recognition that lasted barley a second before she turned back to the fire. The unconscious woman was still out to it and was being tended to by several citizens that seemed to know what they were doing.

Picking up Max, Sean fell in beside them as they pressed on for the car. He placed Max on the back seat before holding the front door open for Melissa. She eased into the seat, taking her time bringing her feet up into the car. Sean climbed in the back with Max as Daniel took off, doing a u-turn and snaking his way back through the traffic and onlookers.

Max looked up at Sean as they sped back for home.

'Are you hurt Sean?'

'No mate,' he smiled back at him but noted Max had reverted his gaze to Sean's chest. His shirt and jacket were covered in blood.

'You're bleeding.' Concern and confusion showed in his eyes.

'It's someone else's blood.' He said without a smile.

'Are they going to be okay?'

Fucking cowards.

'He's going to be fine Max.'

He hoped it wasn't a lie. He had done all he could.

FORTY-ONE

A year earlier the news of what was happening in Northern Ireland would have made it into the few Irish papers and the British papers but it would have scarcely made press oversees. The world, as a whole, didn't hold much interest in Ireland's little civil rights group or the movement of British troops within its own borders. There were much bigger things happening around the globe in 1969. Newspapers would rather spend their money sending reporters to other paper-selling locations instead of a country in which Irish citizens cried poor.

There was still Vietnam and its sudden helical fall, the Biafran War in Africa which had caused, so far, almost a million casualties through starvation alone and the War of Attrition across the Suez Canal between the Egyptians and the Israelis. The Kray brothers gaol term had received more news than Derry's Battle of the Bogside. American Senator Edward Kennedy's mishap into the waters off Chappaquiddick Island was better known than the release from gaol of unionist militant Reverend Ian Paisley only five months earlier. John Lennon and Yoko Ono had refused to get out of bed in the Amsterdam Hilton. And with both the maiden flight of the Concorde and the success of the Apollo moon landing showing mankind was capable of great things (although conservative westerners watched with revulsion at the growth of both the gay and hippie movement) reporters had hastily withdrawn from the green isle to cover the real news, leaving Ireland to boil unattended on its own.

Now, with the IRA showing defiance to loyalist riots and the British troop build-up in the area escalating, reporters were flooding back with more stories and photo opportunities than they could handle. Few predicted it was about to get worse.

One independent photographer was about to add a missing piece to a question which had gone unanswered for several months. He was about to send an image around the world that would change the lives of a specific few, the effects to ripple back to Ireland, all the way to the man in the photo.

David Newell Smith, a photographer whom had become renowned amongst his peers, had been travelling in a British Saracen containing members of the 2nd Battalion Parachute Regiment (2 PARA), when the bomb on Falls Road had detonated. Being only blocks away their Saracen had arrived within minutes, his lens capturing the first distant shots of the shifting dust and smoke amidst the wreckage and mayhem.

In the forty depressing yet exhilarating minutes he was there he snapped off over five rolls of 35mm film from the three cameras he carried about his body 24 hours a day. That night in his hotel room his professional eye scanned the self-processed negatives of the 125 photos within these rolls. With the small frames held up to the harsh bulb hanging from his ceiling, and with an eye perfected by years of practice, he worked out which shots would work and which he had failed to capture correctly. He developed and enlarged twenty-eight photos and chose fifteen to be the standout shots, the shots that would keep him in pocket. He would eventually develop the remainder of the shots but not tonight.

Sending copies of the standout fifteen to his headquarters in London, here they would be offered to each of the British newspapers to run with a coinciding story about the bombing from one of the many journalists which had arrived after he himself had left. If Newell Smith was lucky a photo editor with a superior eye would select one of his over the photos sent in by other photographers which had arrived late with the journos and he would receive an agreed fee for the shot. If he was extremely lucky the photo would be picked up by the international press and this would earn him even more.

Of the fifteen shots he had submitted there was one picture which seemed to sum up the futility and the horror of the incident and with that shot he had faith in his aim, focus and composition.

The shot was beautifully composed. On the left of the black and white photo was a young man whose face wore a look of determination far beyond any David Newell Smith had ever seen. The young man was moving towards the centre of the frame. On the right was a British soldier. The soldier was moving forward, away from the camera, rifle raised and ready, his face in profile looking at the young man rushing past him. In the background the fire of the bomb zone raged, shrapnel and debris littered the ground with little pieces of car, building and pavement.

What sold the picture and tied it together however was the third individual in the photo. Held tightly in the arms of the determined young man was a child who would have been lucky to be five years of age. Around the upper arm of the child was a belt, a battlefield tourniquet pulled tight to slow the child's blood loss, a lot of which covered the front of the young man.

As Newell Smith had developed this photo he felt sorrow seep into his stomach as he looked into the eyes of that young man. He saw a father pulling his innocent son, too late, away from a war he may have supported but at that time wanted to be as far away from as possible.

Was this child still alive? Newell Smith didn't know. All he knew was the next day would bring more destruction and violence in this city and he would be there to capture it because it paid more, was more stimulating and more a part of history than photographing lazy, stoned beatnik celebrities in bed.

He was not to know however that the young man in the photo was not the child's father but an ex-Australian soldier, now a volunteer for the IRA.

The picture ended up running in a total of sixteen global papers much to the delight of the photographer. However no British publications had decided to run with it; they all had chosen his number two and three choices, close-ups of 2 Para in action cordoning off the area; photos that weren't as bleak and depressing as his first choice.

One of the sixteen papers that did choose to run with his first preference, one was an Australian newspaper.

FORTY-TWO

Like the cold, harsh wake-up that a drunk needs, seeing Sean carrying a screaming, bloody child in his arms was enough to pull Thomo from his semi-intoxicated state of mind. It was like a splash of ice water to his face. At first, he had looked at the photo on the seventh page of the paper without taking in any of the detail, not even the headlines. He was still tired and partially drunk. He had already turned the page before his mind had taken the picture in. Something in his brain clicked and forced him to turn back the page without knowing why.

There he was, Sean Doherty, his friend, in Northern Ireland.

He stared at the photo for several minutes, reading the caption and article three times over to see if it mentioned Sean's name but it hadn't.

A cold shower to wake him up more so, another look at the article to make sure he wasn't imagining it, then he dressed, gathered the paper and ran out to his Triumph, kicked it over and raced off to the Lass O'Gowrie.

The photo, although not published in the papers in Britain, was inspected by a special group of men and women who work for the Metropolitan Police Special Branch. It is their job to monitor and identify Irish terrorists. All photos pulled from the Troubles pass under the noses of these astonishing people whose job it is to put familiar faces into certain piles. These faces were tracked through photo surveillance obtained from the unit's own men and what passed through the press. Surreptitious photos of Sinn Féin members and rallyers, suspected auxiliaries that ran messages for the IRA, even photos of Civil Rights members and people whom met a certain female Irish Member of Parliament of Westminster passed through this unit. Keen eyes tracked and collated, recognised facial features like the eyes and ears (the distance between eyes never changes and ears are always overlooked by people attempting a disguise) and added to the pile of people that needed to be watched, questioned, arrested or gotten rid of all together.

It was here where the photo of Sean was recognised by a man who was chosen for this particular job due to his extraordinary talent of being able to recall such minute detail. He remembered a photo from months ago and, after searching through the file titled "YET TO BE IDENTIFIED", placed the two photographs side by side. No attempt at a disguise was evident in either photo. The press photo of the young man carrying the wounded child matched that of the nameless man shaking hands with the head of the Provisional IRA at the Hall/Brown funeral.

The young Special Branch man smiled.

'Gottcha Paddy.' He loved his job. 'Now to find out who you are…'

The third person to recognise the man in the photo had personally served with him in South Vietnam. Grant Brooks had originally planned to continue his military career after his tour but his actions in that rubber plantation which had resulted in the deaths of those children had made him want to lay down the rifle for good. He had never told his wife Mary about it and nor would he. Every time he looked at his daughter Molly...

They had fallen so quickly, quicker than if they were thrown…a cloud of pink following them…the red dust rising around them as their bodies impacted the ground…

Daily he fought them from his mind but it was futile. They would be back.

So when his time was up he had rejoined his father's company and tried to get back into civilian life.

Technically it was his wife Mary that had become aware of the familiar looking man in the photo but couldn't work out how she knew him. As Grant looked down on the grainy print of black and white he knew those eyes that looked back past the camera's lens.

'Holy shit, it's Spud,' he gasped as he stared down into the face he thought he would never see again.

Grant called Brownie, their corporal from Vietnam, to tell him of what he had seen. Brownie was still in the army, training recruits in radio and signals at the Singleton army base in New South Wales. After tracking down a copy of the newspaper he agreed it was Sean and said he would look into it. Word spread throughout the small community of the army base and it finally filtered back to a visiting Intelligence major that decided to follow up on how this Australian soldier came to end up in Belfast. A sergeant in charge of records told the major over the phone that the file showed this Sean Doherty as AWOL.

Alarm bells were triggered. A signal was sent to the GHQ of the Australian Armed Services in Canberra who, after checking their own history of this soldier, in turn sent their own signal to the London-based representative of ASIO, the Australian Security Intelligence Organisation. This classified signal detailed all they knew of PTE Doherty, Sean 2790400; from his Newcastle address and next of kin, to his tour of duty details and wounds received within. Included with this information was the summary of the ongoing police investigation on the murder of one Mansfield, Simon with Sean being the chief suspect. The London-based ASIO man was a heavy drinker and, in his own way of networking, had found a drinking companion that worked within Britain's Special Branch. As is the norm, the two talked shop over several drams. Brows were furrowed, interests piqued, so files were cross-referenced the following morning.

When the Metro Police Special Branch file was compared to Sean's ASIO file in an "under the desk" cooperative, the two men took an even keener interest in this colonial. What they were seeing was not just some tourist bumbling his way into the bloodiest streets in Europe, but a trained soldier with battle experience who was wanted for questioning over a murder and was also in direct contact with the head of the Provisional army of Belfast. He instantly went into the top twenty people to arrest in the province of Ulster.

Bursting through the doors of the Lass O'Gowrie, Thomo caught everyone's attention. He normally never moved that fast and the speed with which he approached the bar told James something was wrong.

'Thomo…?' was all he got to say before Sean's old mate slammed the paper down on the just cleaned bar. Thomo didn't say a word, just looked up at the barman. James looked from Thomo's searching eyes to the creased paper. He didn't need to look twice to know the man in the photo carrying the injured child was his younger brother.

'What the fuck is this?!' James searched for words as his eyes skimmed over the article, not being able, with all his excitement, to follow the printed story word for word.

'Your brother is in Belfast.' Thomo's words were calm, not quite rehearsed.

Suddenly anger folded over James. 'Northern Ireland?! You sent him to *fucking Belfast*?!' Part of James' mind suddenly searched for the angle that this was not his brother. He scanned the caption printed under the picture. 'His name isn't here.'

'You know your own brother. It's him James.'

James could tell. The man in the photo had longer hair but it was definitely him. Despite all the relief he felt in knowing where his brother was and the fact he was far from the Australian police, he was frightened for him. The photo had him running around a bomb site in Belfast covered in blood. From what he saw on the news lately he wondered which was safer; Belfast or Saigon.

Strangely enough the picture of Sean had a positive effect on his father's health. For the last month things for him had gotten so bad that Melanie usually found herself every afternoon sitting on the back verandah overlooking the garden with a wine in hand, crying more than her fair share of tears while her father slept inside. Her father slept a lot lately. Fatigue had hit him hard. He was hardly eating anymore and had the energy levels of a lethargic narcoleptic. The photo however, despite the pessimism it bore, told him to fight on and not let this illness ruin his life. He had to stay alive for his family.

FORTY-THREE

Walking the several blocks to Padraig's flat the morning after the Falls Road bombing, Sean and Daniel didn't speak much. Both were thinking things over in their minds on how yesterday could have turned out different for all of them. They both took the bombing as a personal attack on Melissa and Max although it was clearly a random attack. Had they been a few minutes late walking out of the hall or if they had parked their car further down the road then they all may have been dead right now.

Last night, not being able to sleep much, Mel had walked out to the kitchen to get a glass of water. Max had slept in with Daniel that night, curling up to him, safe in the warmth of his uncle's embrace.

Standing there in the moonlight Melissa had stared blankly out across the city asking herself if it may be time to leave Belfast; to move south and start afresh. However she had no money and came to the realisation she would never leave this depressing city and the violence it spawned continually. Max would probably be drawn into the same world her brother now lived and where would his future lie? The Kesh or Crumlin Road with a life behind bars, or the grave. In her heart she was a republican and was proud of all they did but she would not hesitate for a second to leave this hell if she could.

Her realisation that they were stuck there made her suddenly burst into tears. She had tried to muffle the sound to not wake Sean but looking over to his makeshift bed she saw him looking back, himself not being able to sleep.

I'm sorry, she had mouthed in his direction.

Sean silently nodded, thinking he should get up and comfort her. He didn't have to. Melissa walked over to his bed by the far wall of the lounge room, tears flowing down her face and climbed in next to him, hugging him tightly, crying into his shoulder.

He hugged her back, whispering to her, telling her it was all going to be okay; lying about how it all would be fine. But he knew it was all bullshit. He knew she would be holding onto anyone at this moment, looking for hope and comfort, wanting an explanation as to why they had to suffer. He didn't know why but he hugged her back and told her it would all be alright.

That was how he woke the next morning, with Mel's back to him, his arms around her and the blanket covering them both.

Daniel had not woken her when he came to get Sean once the sun was up and he hadn't asked what had happened. He knew she had had a rough night. She was never one to come crying to him. He had only seen her cry twice before; when her husband Craig was killed and again at his funeral. As they both walked in deep thought, Daniel was glad Sean had been there last night for her.

Padraig was sitting by the window reading the morning's paper and drinking a cup of tea when they arrived.

'How's your family Daniel?' he asked as he let them in, both hands coming up to rest on Daniel's shoulders.

'They've been better.' He patted Padraig's side and moved inside, taking a seat by the radiator. 'Max says his ears are still ringing but not as bad as last night. The sleep did him good though.'

Padraig waved Sean in, shutting the door behind him.

'Poor fellow. Other than that they're fine?'

'Some grazes here and there from the fall but that's it.'

They all sat and tea was offered and taken.

'I have a proposal to offer you both. It was originally to be only you Sean but I'm to put it to both of you.'

Neither of the two reacted other than a slight nod. Sean was sitting forward, his elbows resting on his knees. Daniel slouched back into the faded floral lounge, his tea balanced on his thigh.

Padraig continued. 'The Army Council needs a new Active Service Unit across the water. We need capable and trusted soldiers to carry out the purchase and transfer of guns from wherever they can be found. This ASU will be a free control unit of only a few volunteers. You make your own calls, carry out your own security, you live free of our command so you run your own show...to an extent.'

There was still no reaction from Sean although Padraig saw a look of realisation come over Daniel's tired face. This was what they had talked about all those months back at the training ground up in the Iron Mountains in County Leitrim. From the response it seemed as though Daniel had forgotten about Padraig's plan he said he would one day take to the Army Council.

It was a plan that was embarrassingly simple. With the English authorities stepping up their security concerning Irish citizens entering the mainland, anyone with either an Irish accent or passport, whether Northern or Free State, was seen as a possible security risk. The plan he had taken to the council would assure his ASU team would go unnoticed. None of its members would be Irish.

'We have two Scotsmen and one English woman, and...if you accept the position Sean, an Australian. All of you would have a lot more freedom operating in both of their countries and Europe. Some of the bosses are even talking about sending someone over to America to chase up more guns like Chad's M16s.

'You'll be set up with jobs or some sort of front so suspicion won't be aroused. Finances have been sorted out. Housing and vehicles will be supplied which will all be legal. One thing we looked at was we had to make sure none of you are known to the police. We checked in with our contacts down in Galway and they say nothing can be tied to you over what happened when you arrived here. The Garda and the hospital staff still have no idea of your true identity.'

Sean listened to all Padraig had to say. He looked down to his scarred hands, his fingers interlocked with each other.

Remember when you just wanted to go farming in Donegal? he thought to himself. He looked back up at Padraig.

'This will make a difference won't it? To stop the shit that happened last night?'

'I guarantee it, Sean. If you do your job right there's no telling how far we could take this.'

Sean saw Padraig truly believed in every word he had just told him.

'Okay. I'm in.'

Padraig breathed a sigh of relief. He had a lot riding on collating this team and Sean was the last to sign on. The opinion Daniel had had back in summer about Padraig wanting to include Sean in this had changed. He knew Sean was ready for such an undertaking and was glad he was to be involved.

'Now…for Daniel.' Padraig looked over at his friend.

He had first met Daniel as a wee lad when his own nephew used to knock around with him. After his nephew had died he still met this young boy when visiting his sister's house, the lad coming over to help the family, almost filling in for the chores Padraig's nephew had done. He knew he would one day become a volunteer and was proud to see he had risen far in their cause for freedom.

'You, my lad, are to work from this side of the water, making sure what comes over from England gets here and stays hidden from the Brits. Bring it in by trawler, by ferry, buried in a truck's chassis…I don't care. As long as what Sean sends over gets here, I'll be happy. This may mean a bit of running up and down the coast therefore you'll be away from here for up to a week at a time.'

'Mel and Max?' was Daniel's only reservation. The only thing that worried him was how they would handle it. He knew he had the option to turn it down but this was something too good to pass up.

Padraig knew what he was thinking before he had bought it up. 'Melissa and Max will be taken care of. If something happens, which it shouldn't but *there is a risk*, I won't lie, they will be set up, but don't think such shite. You run more risk here in the streets if you think about it. I'll personally call in to see them daily whenever you're away, bring them what I can. I'll make sure they'll have so many visitors that by the time she gets a moment to herself you'll both be home.'

That was all Daniel needed to hear.

'Fine.'

Padraig couldn't wipe the smile off his face. If all went well he would certainly begin his climb up the Army Council ladder, but first things first.

'So Sean, how's your German?' He couldn't help but laugh at that.

FOURTY-FOUR

All my life living in this town and I've never been in this pub, Grant thought as he climbed out of his '67 Falcon wagon outside of the Lass O'Gowrie. He tried to picture his lost friend sitting outside on a hot summer's day, leaning against the cool green and cream tiled wall with a beer in one hand, a fag in the other and the jukebox keeping him entertained through the open windows.

He noticed a boarded-up window before he reached the small doorway, the patchwork adding to the rundown working class feel the place had perfected without trying.

Passing through the narrow double doors into the dark and cool interior he felt an explosion of nervousness form in his stomach before spreading to his throat and mouth making it click with dryness. He wondered if this was how Sean had felt when he had visited his own house to drop off the doll for Molly's fourth birthday. Mary had told him of the big impact he had had with his daughter and how reassuring he had been to herself, telling her that her husband was fine and out of danger and dying to get home. He knew Sean had lied for her sake.

Letting his eyes adjust to the dark, he scanned the quiet drinking house seeing only a couple of early morning patrons which is how he'd hoped to find it. He took the few short steps to the bar wondering if he was doing the right thing but before he could change his mind he saw the publican look up from behind the bar. Grant could see this had to be Sean's brother James.

'What can I get you mate?'

Grant was suddenly tongue tied, not knowing how to begin.

'Umm. Schooner thanks,' he said, nodding to the nearest tap. He sat quietly at a stool as his glass was filled, placing his money on the bar in front of him. James handed over his beer and change and was surprised to see the customer holding out his hand wanting to shake it.

'James isn't it? My name's Grant Brooks. I was in your brother's platoon in Vietnam.'

'Kim! Thomo!' James suddenly called out, not taking his eyes off the man before him.

Behind him Kim appeared in the doorway. From the pool table came Thomo.

James was still looking into Grant's eyes. 'This is Grant Brooks. He served with Sean.'

It was like a switch was thrown inside of Kim as her face changed and she rushed to the bar to stand by her man, her eyes full of question. Thomo looked him up and down before moving in to sit beside him at the bar.

Right then James felt like closing the pub just to spend all day with this brave young man because they had so much to talk about. First he had to make some phone calls.

Sean was the first of the newly formed group to arrive at the well-kept middle-class house on West End Park Street in the leafy suburb of West End, Glasgow. Unpacking the small number of items he had bought with him, he checked out the remainder of the house, turning up the heat radiators as he found them.

The two-storey tenement was in a long line of dwellings, each sharing their neighbours wall which were double brick and, thankfully, quite soundproof. This particular one had been converted long ago into two separate one bedroom flats, one above the other, both being rented out fully furnished.

Sean put the kettle on, sat at the table and began to strip and clean his pistol as he waited for the remainder of his team to arrive sometime over the next 24 hours.

Just after five, to coincide with the flood of workers returning to their homes, there was a knock at the door. With the now reassembled and loaded Browning HP behind his back Sean opened it to see a young woman a good six inches shorter than he carrying a small suitcase and rugged up against the cold.

'How does our new home look?' she asked with a Liverpudlian accent. She brushed a lock of straw-coloured hair away from her face and smiled.

'Better than our last place in Edinburgh,' he replied.

'We could always move back to Liverpool,' she offered, completing the code.

He opened the door wider and stepped back to let her enter. Shutting the door behind them Sean led her down the hall to the kitchen. Here he shook her hand.

'Sean Doherty.'

'Brigitta Harnden,' she introduced herself as she removed her coat revealing a curvy figure wrapped tightly in a brown paisley skirt and tanned stockings. 'I guess I'm your wife?'

Sean smiled. 'Don't you hate planned marriages?'

Just before 10 pm a knock at the door announced the arrival of the last members of the active service unit. As the new members entered the sombrely lit hall, Sean thought the colossal Scot had grown larger since he had last seen him. A huge smile beamed from underneath the blonde beard and moustache of Chad Macintosh as Sean held out his hand in welcome.

'It's good to see you again lad! If you know what I mean.' Chad exclaimed as he turned the handshake into a hug.

Sean shook under the blows of several heavy slaps on the back but nothing could hide the fact he was happy to see this familiar and friendly face again. 'I thought you'd be on the other side of the world by now.'

'I'd have been shark shite by now if it wasn't for you.' Chad stood back, holding Sean at arms length to look at him. He had learnt of everything which had happened to this remarkable young man from Padraig and was clearly excited to see him still alive.

'What the bloody hell has been going on? What have you been up to?'

Sean laughed as he tried to break free of Chad's grip. 'Get off me you kilted git!'

'Hah hah! Sean, this is Bradley Archer.' Chad gestured to the other man beside him.

Bradley was the same height as Sean, but a lot bulkier. His upper arms looked the same size as Sean's thighs under his dark blue woollen fisherman's jacket which stretched across the shoulders. The sleeves, which hid over two decades of colourful tattoos, tapered to hands which looked like they could crush rocks. With his dark hair cut short and his ears and nose testament to a rough past, Sean guessed Brad was put on this earth to do nothing but fight.

'Pleasure to meet you Sean,' he said as they shook hands, his voice deep with not quite as much of the Scottish brogue as Chad's own tongue.

'Good to meet you, mate. Chad and Brad hey? Just like a real couple aren't yas? Come on inside. You've got to meet the missus'

Chad threw his arm around the shorter Australian and headed further into the house.

'You, married?! That had to be Padraig's idea. The man's a romantic, if you know what I mean.'

'Padraig a romantic? No, it was my idea. It's all in the details, see?' Sean held up his left hand to show him the gold wedding band he had purchased from a pawn shop in town. Brigitta's ring was a slender version of his, a matching pair.

The four of them sat talking for the next two hours, drinking whisky Chad had bought with him. Introductions turned into stories, stories that became laced with jokes and anecdotes as the drink took hold. They all seemed to get along just fine.

Chad had at first been sceptical of working with a woman but the more he got to know her the more he knew he should have never doubted Padraig. While she never went into detail of her reasons for joining the Cumann na mBan, the woman's volunteer council, Brigitta seemed just as passionate as them about Ireland's struggle.

'So what's our first job?' she asked.

'Our last weapons haul,' Chad explained, 'was stopped by the Brits before it took place. From what Padraig has told me there could be as many as four shipments to get across now. More than what was originally planned. So we have to re-establish a link with the seller in Germany. Then if all goes well we organise transportation of said weapons across to our lads, if you know what I mean.'

'How much cargo and what sort of transportation have we access to?' Sean raised the question. Already he was going over in his mind the various possibilities of what could go wrong and how they could counter these problems.

'The amount of weapons we won't know until we meet with the Germans. As for moving it, I have several options but it will depend on where we arrange for the stuff to come in. Obviously somewhere on the east coast.'

'Where on the coast?' This was from Brad.

With his jacket off Sean could see the mess of tattoos which covered his arms. It was almost a chaos of blue, white, green, red and black that made one icon or image indistinguishable from its neighbour. They began somewhere under his shirt and ended at his wrists. Sean had served in the army with a few men, mainly full-timers, that were living canvases but Brad's would put them to shame.

Chad removed a high school version of the atlas from his bag, flicked it to a marked page and placed it on the table.

'I don't want to use any British port more than once so we need to check out some of the smaller ones. I've worked out of most of the major ports and they could be an option but smaller ports would be in our favour. Each time we move the gear we re-plan and change everything, right down to the type of vehicles we use.' He ran a finger over the map in front of them. 'So we look at options for getting in and out of Germany, France and possibly The Netherlands. Transport across

Britain will depend on how and where we come in. We've got a lot of driving to do over the next couple of weeks...check things out. Find places where we can move it'

'Where abouts exactly are they coming in from?' Sean asked.

'Again, not sure where until we contact them.'

'And the money? How do we pay for all of this?' Brad asked from the bottom of an empty glass, his teeth crushing what ice was left.

'I have most of the money for the first shipment. So...' Chad smiled from behind his own glass, 'we have to start making withdrawals.'

Brigitta raised her smooth brow in expectation. She hadn't realised they were going to be hitting it off straight away. 'Counter jumping time?'

'Withdrawals?' Sean asked, noticing the gleam in the Scotsman's eyes. 'Withdrawals from where?'

FORTY-FIVE

'The army knows where Sean is.'

Grant had agreed to stay for lunch to be able to talk to the rest of Sean's family and friends about what he knew, shocked about what they had divulged to him about Sean killing some jerk who had gotten his girl up the duff. As well as Thomo, James and Kim they had been joined by his father, Sean's sister Melanie and her husband Joseph, and Sean's best mate Luke and his girl Leanda. They sat in a quiet corner of the pub so they wouldn't be interrupted.

'A mate of ours that served with us over there is stationed up in Singleton,' Grant explained. 'He knows a few blokes that have noticed reports going back and forth about Sean and his short stint in the green. Apparently the English are interested in finding out all they can about him. They seemed to have gotten it into their heads that Sean is working for the IRA.'

At first they sat in silence for a few seconds waiting for him to continue on with some more information. He watched each of them, waiting for the reaction he himself had come to when he had first heard the news.

'Ha! Piss off!' Luke scoffed. 'Sean wouldn't work for the IRA!'

'IRA?' Leanda was confused as to who they were talking about.

'The Irish Republican Army,' Grant informed her.

A look of bewilderment hit her with the realisation of what he was implying.

'But…they're terrorists!'

Grant nodded, his face unyielding. Around him he heard similar remarks and even a few laughs.

All except Sean's father.

'Go on,' was all his old man said.

After that no one laughed, each of them wondering what his father knew that they didn't. Grant took a sip of his beer. James had offered drinks to all with only Leanda, Melanie and Joseph declining, each of them taking tea instead. His father sipped at a port. Melanie hadn't protested.

'Apparently they have a photo of him; another photo of him shaking hands with some boss of the IRA.'

'Doesn't mean he's a terrorist,' opposed Thomo. 'He likes to meet people.'

'So far all they've got is the two photos. The one we've all seen placed him at the bombing of a Catholic area by a loyalist paramilitary group called the Ulster Volunteer Force…'

'Who the fuck are they?' interrupted Luke.

Grant shrugged his shoulders. 'I think they're the Protestant version of the IRA. I'm not one hundred percent sure though. Anyway, the other photo, which I *haven't* seen, is the one supposedly linking him directly with the IRA.'

'How long has the army known about this?' This was from Sean's dad.

'Two days after this newspaper photo was taken.'

Nobody could believe it. The army had known about Sean being in Ireland for over a week now and still they had yet to talk to his family about it. All this time the army and police had hassled them for Sean's whereabouts but when they had information they didn't reciprocate.

'This is bullshit,' Luke announced. He turned in his seat to address everyone. 'It's Sean we're talking about! He wouldn't do something like join those wankers. It's not like him. He wouldn't do it.'

'We didn't think he would kill Simon but he did.' It was the first thing Melanie had said since she had arrived. She had been mulling everything over in her head and despite wishing desperately that her youngest brother was safe in hiding, she didn't put it past the new Sean to be mixed up in the Troubles. She had seen a different brother come home from Vietnam, as she had expected, and despite the shock of hearing what he had done to Simon Mansfield she knew her little brother was gone. He had been replaced by something only war could create. He was a different man and would always be haunted by whatever had happened to him over there. She knew he would never tell her of what he had done and had seen done by others. All she did know was he would never be the same. So the possibility of him doing something like joining an Irish para-military group was not beyond her.

'The Sean that came home from that war was different to the Sean that left. Add the shock of finding out your fiancée is pregnant to someone else. Honestly, and this might sound harsh, but I wouldn't put it past him.'

Sean's father's thoughts seemed to be running along the same lines as his eldest's. He chose to voice them.

'When I came home from New Guinea it was hard to go straight back into civilian life. I was only a kid when I went over but I came back more mature than most people twice my age.' He looked across the table to their visitor. 'I'll put money on it you felt the same way when you came home. You felt different didn't you?'

Grant nodded and wondered if they knew of his terrible mistake in the plantation.

'Several times,' the Second World War veteran continued, 'I found myself almost pushing through the threshold of patience into raw anger. Fortunately I was able to keep myself grounded and, I'm sure, out of gaol.' He suddenly coughed harshly and noticed his daughter flinch at the tearing noise it seemed to make inside his chest. He turned to face her and James sitting by his side, his heart breaking that his third child (and secretly his favourite) was not sitting with them.

He went on. 'Your mother saw the change in me but kept it to herself. It must have been hard on her at times. Sometimes I think she suffered just as much as me. I almost left her. Didn't want to get married. The thought of starting a family after what I had seen…I just couldn't fathom it. Thankfully your mother was stronger than me and stayed with me no matter what kind of foul mood I was in or what rage I sometimes flew into for no reason. Used to snap just like that.' He clicked his fingers. 'However not a day goes by that I don't love your mother for giving me my family and you kids for the opportunity to be your father.'

His voice seemed to waver, pausing for a second. He had never been able to tell them any of this before.

He turned back to Grant.

'Are you a Catholic son?'

'Church of England.'

'Our family's Catholic. Not that we attend mass. Don't hold much stock in organised religion, whatever the denomination. I've always been a bit of a republican though. I've got no love for the queen. Reckon the RSLs should all tear down those pictures of her. I didn't fight for her German-loving father and Sean didn't fight for that inbred offspring bitch of his. If Sean is doing what they say he's doing then it's because of our heritage and the injustices they must be facing over there. He'll always step in for the underdog. But definitely not for religion.'

He looked at the remaining two members of his family, proud of the adults they had become.

'My grandfather came out here from Ireland. It was one of the last things we talked about, me and Sean.' He paused, deep in thought. A sudden wave of Irish patriotism hit him. He hadn't felt that since his own father had been alive. Nothing would take away the Australian pride which had pushed him through the toughest years of his life as he had fought, literally, for his country. Now he could feel the addition of a secondary pride; a pride he had almost forgotten. He was Australian *and* Irish. The combination made him smile.

'Guess it made an impression on him. If he is his father's son then he's over there fighting because deep down he has Irish blood in his veins. But that doesn't mean that I want him there, in another bloody war.'

For a minute the pub was quiet. In the background, beyond the walls of the old building, they could hear the sounds of the city, sounds which had given the Hunter Valley its riches. A coal train rattled the pictures on the walls as it headed to the docks; tug boats sounded their air horns as they manoeuvred giant ships into place to fill their bellies with coal from its mines or grain from its farms; fishing boats returned with gulls in tow, cawing for the scraps they knew would be thrown their way. The world was moving forward with or without them.

'I'm going to Ireland.'

Every face in the room turned to the individual that had voiced what most were thinking but had not the courage to say.

'I'll go. I'll go and find Sean.'

Several of the crowd thought it was a joke. Looking at the speaker they could see he was serious.

'And do what when you find him?' asked Melanie.

To be honest, Luke didn't know what he would tell him *if* he found him. Should he try and convince him to come home, back to face the police for killing Simon? He doubted he could talk him out of being a terrorist.

He's not a fucking terrorist! His mind tried to understand the logic that would even allow that notion. *Someone has to have fucked up there! It's Sean. He's not like that! The picture though... He was definitely over there in a war zone.*

Luke shook his head, still unable to comprehend what everyone was implying.

'I don't know what I'll do. But I can't sit here and do nothing now I've heard all this. I'll just have to find him and see for myself.' He looked at Sean's father and saw the pain of loss which already seemed to be growing in the old man's eyes. Should he tell him of his father's ailing health? Would that make him leave?

'He'll listen to me. Whether or not he'll pay any attention to it... He may be a completely different person by now. Look at how Vietnam changed him.' He looked back around the room at the others. 'If I don't try something then what sort of mate am I?'

'What about your job?' James asked.

'Fuck it.' Luke looked James square in the eye. 'I've got some holidays due but Sean's more important.'

Leanda opened her mouth to say something but the look she saw on her boyfriend's face told her nothing was going to change his mind. At that moment she had a terrible feeling her own love was not going to come home and she wondered if that was how soldiers' wives felt when they found out their men were going to war. She was about to say something…although she didn't know what, when a second statement shocked them all.

'If you wait 'til after Christmas I'll go with you.'

The words had left his lips before he had the chance to think it over. After just returning from a war Grant knew that what he was planning to do would cause a major rift between him and his wife that would probably take a long time to repair. She had been so glad beyond words he had returned from the war "unscathed" and it hurt him to know he had just committed himself to an unbelievable journey which just may cost him his marriage. If not more.

How do you turn your back on a fellow serviceman?

PART FOUR

"When the sword of rebellion is drawn, the sheath should be thrown away."

John Singleton Copely

FORTY-SIX

It took a couple of seconds before the young red-haired bank teller realised the people coming through the door were not the normal type of customer. Her high pitched scream assisted the robbers by drawing everyone's attention towards her instead of them, allowing them to cross the floor unchecked before the remainder of the crowd realised what was happening.

'EVERYONE ON THE FUCKING FLOOR!' bellowed Brad through his balaclava, his sawn-off shot gun directed out in front of him towards those that were slow to move and still in a state of shock.

Spreading left and right behind Brad, Sean moved towards the counter on his right while Brigitta, her hair tied up beneath her own shrouded cover, headed to the left. Each held their pistol out in front as they negotiated their way across the prone customers. If the terrified patrons had looked closely they would have seen the brandished pistols had their hammers closed and safety catches on (although their thumbs hovered just above in case they needed to use them). However no one dared raise their head up off the cold polished stone floor.

Sean hurdled the counter and aimed his pistol at the crouching staff, his free hand pulling a pillow-sized cloth bag from the inside of his jacket. With Brigitta landing over the counter at the far end, Sean began emptying each drawer as she covered them with her Smith & Wesson.

'Just keep your heads down and we'll be out of here in a second!'

Brad assured the crowd in his distinctive accent as his eyes shot from one person to the other.

Sean pulled the draw string tight on the bag and tossed it across the room towards the entrance. It was so full it landed with a thud and slid past Brad's feet, the Scotsman's eyes not even glancing in its direction as it skated by to stop just short of the front door.

Sean didn't watch the bag's journey. Instead, as it was travelling through the air, he was heading back to the main vault which was wide open in the back room. Here he filled a second bag with only fifty and one-hundred pound notes in half the time it had taken to fill the first.

'Done!' Sean called as he raced back into the main hall. He threw the second bag across the room just as he had done the first and vaulted over the large marble counter of Newcastle's Royal Bank of England. His heart was racing but not with fear. Here he felt the excitement and thrill of danger. And he embraced it. War for him had been nothing but fear. This was different. Inwardly he smiled.

Brigitta waited until the Australian was safely over before joining the other members of the active service unit.

'No one follows!' Brad yelled as he ushered the others out, each of them stooping on the run to pick up a bag. Taking a few steps backwards, Brad looked over the crowd one last times before he turned and ran out to the waiting Rover. In less than a minute and a half they had taken close to fifty thousand pounds.

The following morning Chad placed a long distance phone call to a house in Dublin. It was a brief call which made no sense at all to the recipient and hopefully to anyone listening in.

'Pa, the dog is barking. Put it out and come in for dinner'.

Nathan O'Hare, the seventy-two year old recipient of the message, was not meant to make sense of it. All he had to do was write down what the caller on the other end said and deliver it to a member of the IRA which lived one floor below him. The message on the small folded piece of paper was then phoned forward to Belfast where it was taken across town and handed over to an excited man.

Padraig couldn't stop smiling as he read the coded words, automatically translating them as '*Contact the German. We have money*'. He wrote down the coded reply, handing it back to his runner.

Exactly one hour after receiving the call, O'Hare dialled a long distance number; the location of where his phone call was going was a mystery to him but he didn't care. He was a true republican. He had taken part in the Easter Uprising back in 1916 alongside Pearse and Connelly who, unfortunately, had faced a firing squad with thirteen of their comrades at Kilmainham Gaol. Not being a ringleader in the Uprising, the then eighteen year old Nathan O'Hare had escaped the death bestowed upon his leaders and lived everyday carrying out their calling. He did his bit for the cause without question despite the crippling arthritis that had ended his soldiering career years before the Border Campaign of the '50s, but good hearing and a sharp memory had taken him down another path. It kept him feeling alive knowing the small details he passed on helped his Ireland.

It picked up on the second ring as it always did. He heard no greeting and, just as the many phone calls before, hadn't expected any so he read from the newly delivered piece of paper.

'The flowers in the children's bedroom look dry. Water them lest they wilt.'

Nathan then hung up, burnt the piece of paper and went back to his television; this time with a whiskey in his knotted hand and an ageing heart full of pride.

In Scotland, Chad walked the short distance from the phone booth to the Halt Bar in Glasgow's West End with his hands deep in his pockets and the collar of his heavy woollen seafarer's jacket turned up to fend off the cold. Normally he didn't feel the cold but today it felt like it could snow.

He crossed the street to the wooden panelled corner pub which beckoned to him like all public houses did to all Scotsmen and women during the latter months. His work was done for the day. The good news had been delivered to Padraig and he had received confirmation the Germans would be told things were back on; the IRA was coming to collect its weapons.

Inside the warm Edwardian inspired pub he found the other three sitting in a booth, each drinking in celebration. From the Juke box the publican had Neil Diamond singing about how red, red wine kept his mind off of his long lost love; nothing like a depressing drinking song to boost sales.

Chad's drink was waiting for him as he slipped off his jacket. He sat down next to Brad, smiled at the three of them and raised his glass.

'We're on.'

'If you know what I mean,' Sean added with a grin.

Two days later in the *Hamburger Zietung*, an advertisement appeared in the classifieds. It was a coded message from Belfast to the arms suppliers they had originally contacted months ago letting them know they were back in business. The code was read by one of the arms dealer's subjects whose job it was to do nothing other than study the papers for such codes from a variety of clients from around the world.

Just as it was in Ireland, the code was passed on to a handler who took it across the town of Hamburg. From here it was passed on directly to his boss, the arms dealer, but not before the handler copied it and dropped this second copy off along the way at a secret drop. For the handler this deception was a way out for his family.

Nine months earlier Dieter Wilhelm Brasch, an employee of the arms dealing Mark Muller, had made contact with an off-duty detective of the Bundeskriminalamt, the Federal Criminal Police Office, in his hometown of Hamburg. Brasch stated that he would roll over and supply the police with information on his much-wanted employer if they would in turn help him get his sister and her husband out of East Germany. The BKA detective casually told him that he would think about it but once Brasch had left the detective was jumping for joy. Muller was a major target that they had been trying to pin something on for years but the crime boss had slippery skin and lawyers to match.

They accepted Brasch's offer. Two days later the English became involved because they now had a link to the man that was believed to be supplying weapons to the IRA.

Since then Brasch had kept in touch with the BKA detective letting the authorities know of every illegal act his crime syndicate was involved in. At first it made him feel physically sick every time he betrayed his fellow Germans by letting the authorities know what they were up to. Each piece of information he gave to them made him wonder if his own comrades were becoming suspicious of him.

When he had informed the authorities of the arms deal that was to head to Scotland which resulted in the deaths of two men, the guilt that washed over him caused him to ponder for a minute the thought of suicide. How easy it would have been to place his gun in his mouth and end it all with less than an eighth of an inch of trigger movement.

However, killing himself wouldn't get his sister over the wall.

The last piece of information he had given had failed to net their prize catch with a fuck up on both sides of the channel. The English had jumped too early and the Germans too late. And they were now putting pressure on Brasch, keen to make up for the embarrassment their information had caused not only their own department but their British contemporaries in their own war against the IRA.

The crime boss Mark Muller had lived in agony all his life. Not physical agony (although when he drank and thought about how his family had died he swore he felt his heart being torn from his chest as the perpetrators laughed in his face) but the agony of loss and grief rolled up into a culmination of hate that demanded retribution.

Retribution against the English.

He was there, all those years ago, when his family had been killed and remembered it vividly. He could still hear his younger brother Ewald screaming as he was burnt alive under the fallen wooden beams of the floor above. His parents were crushed under the collapsed brick walls; moans from his semiconscious mother had come from within the smoking pile of rubble for what seemed an eternity before she passed.

When he looked at the photos he had of them now, the image of them dying always seemed to come to the fore.

On the 14th of February 1945, Muller's uncle and role model, Helmut Mittelstadt, made the perilous twenty mile journey west, despite his wife's protests, from the German town of Bautzen in the cold of winter to what remained of the city of Dresden. From his home town he had heard and seen the now infamous bombing raid on his sister-in-law's city and knew he had to try and help his family, or anyone left alive, in any way he could.

After a day of travel, Helmut had fought his way around the burning city which, at the height of the firestorm, had reached temperatures of over 1000 degrees Fahrenheit. A mini-hurricane had swept up the rapidly rising air drawing in fresh oxygen which had only increased the inferno's intensity.

Finally making it to the street he had visited many times before in peace time, he found it obliterated, merely pile after pile of burning debris and wreckage of the houses that had once stood so proud. The street had been spared the hell-like blazes of the inner city but had suffered heavily due to the high explosive bombs.

He had pushed on to the house of his kin, greeted with the smoking and crumbling remnants of its destruction. Digging his way through the detritus with a rage the likes of which had never consumed him before, he pulled, with bloodied hands, only one body with life still intact from the cellar of the destroyed building; the barely pulsing body of his nine year old nephew Mark.

Raised as one of their own, Mark Muller listened to every recount of his rescue as he grew up with more and more detestation of the people which had killed his family.

The firestorm which had all but wiped Dresden from the face of the earth had been started by 873 Royal Air Force bombers dropping incendiary and high explosive bombs for 24 hours straight in a deliberate attempt to burn the city to the ground in a conflagration not seen in the history of warfare. For over seven hundred years it had been a beautiful city. It held no industrial or military significance to the war and its destruction did not produce a single beneficial act in helping the Allied advance to Berlin; yet it had been wiped off the face of the earth purely because the RAF was running out of targets.

Casualties varied depending on who was telling the story but Mark believed his uncle's estimates that over a quarter of a million people had perished, many of these being refugees fleeing from other bombed-out cities.

He looked past the fact that 311 B17 bombers from the USAF had joined in the bombing by noon the next day, and ignored the other fact that the Luftwaffe had tried to do the same thing to London in the early years of the war. Instead, Mark had clutched onto the energy this hatred had created and swore the British government and its military would one day be held accountable for the murderous rampage they had allowed Bomber Command to go on. Anything he could do to make them suffer he would do. The deal he had organised with the Irish was just the start.

He was thinking about the time his father had taken his brother and himself fishing on the River Elbe on the outskirts of his former home when the man in front of him spoke up. Leaving the happy images behind, Muller looked up from the rear seat of the big sedan out to the cold and saw a car pull up across the empty snow-covered street. Muller's driver climbed out into the cold and prepared to frisk the approaching customer. He watched as the young man held open his jacket to allow his driver to remove a pistol from his belt before turning around. He could tell the driver's hands were obtrusively uncomfortable but thorough.

The door to the Mercedes opened and the man was quick to enter, pulling the door closed behind him to keep the warmth inside. Holding out his gloved hand Muller introduced himself with his heavy accented English.

'Welcome Irishman. My name is Mark Muller.'

'Sean Doherty,' the young Australian greeted him back in his best Belfast accent. It was good enough to fool some of his own fellow volunteers, the inflection having been finely tuned with help from

Daniel and Melissa. 'Thanks for seeing us on such short notice.' He gave a half smile through a heavy stubble that most would classify as a short beard.

'I'm sorry for what happened to your colleagues in Scotland,' Muller began, wanting Sean to understand he had nothing to do with the deaths of Chris Hall and Glen Brown at the hands of the SAS. 'The attack on them came as a shock to us. You have to believe me when I say I had nothing to do with that.'

Sean watched the German closely. If he wasn't telling the truth then he should have been an actor.

'You believe me?' Muller asked bluntly, wanting to be sure they had an understanding before they conducted any business.

Sean nodded. 'I believe you.'

Not really. You are *a criminal.*

The German crime boss smiled, glad he could continue on with his own little vendetta.

'Good, good. I didn't want to have to turn around and sell the weapons to the PLO. Such bad customers. They take far too long to come up with the payment, wanting to talk about end-user certificates so it can seem as though they are a legitimate purchasing country. Do I look like a legitimate arms trader?! And rude! Just because I am a German they think they can pay less by saying they are continuing on the fight which my people started.' His face screwed up with disgust. 'I don't care about the Jews moving in down there. I don't care where they move to. I'm no Nazi. Let them have the sand and the heat. Just pay me my money. Such bad customers. Besides…I want the British to hear these weapons, not the Israelis.'

Sean steered the conversation back on track. 'When we see our guns you'll get your money. I can promise you there will be no delaying from our side.'

The German smiled. 'You will follow in your autos. I'll take you to the guns.'

Twenty minutes later the four members of the ASU stood in the rear of a still-operating warehouse beside an old wooden workbench which contained a sample of what they would return to Ireland with. Each of them picked up a weapon and checked it over before placing it down and grabbing the next. Sean pulled back the cocking handle of an L1A1, similar to what he had used in Vietnam and the only one in the diverse range which lay out in front of them.

Recollections of the people he had killed with just such a rifle threatened to resurface so he asked a question to distract himself.

'How'd…' he caught himself at the last second, forcing himself to speak with his Irish accent. '…you come by this one?'

'Most bought from American soldiers in Deutschland,' replied Muller from the far end of the workbench.

It didn't answer his question but then again Sean didn't care. He placed the rifle down and picked up an AKMS; an Eastern European version of the AK47 that had had the rear folding stock removed. A nice concealable weapon.

'You like?' the German asked.

Chad placed down the weapon that was in his hand and picked up the cash-filled sports bag which had stayed close to his side for the entire journey. He opened the bag and asked back, 'You like?'

Muller stepped around the bench, slapping the giant Scot on the shoulder.

'Very good, very good. We will do much repeated business.' He looked around the table at the four. 'Tonight we eat as guns are readied. If you like we can get some women to celebrate. You like women?' he asked the three men. He wasn't sure what to offer the young pretty woman that said little. He had been surprised to see a woman amongst their ranks but had not commented on it. He would like a night with her himself but would not say so until they had concluded *all* of their business. That could be months away. So drawn to her staunch resilience was he that he didn't think he could wait that long to proposition her. But business must come first.

Muller looked across the wide work bench to the broad-shouldered Scotsman. 'You like women, yes?'

Brad grinned and nodded over the barrel of another stockless AKMS.

'And you Sean? You will party with our women?'

The Australian glanced across at Brigitta and winked before looking back at Muller.

'Not in front of the missus, mate.'

From the other side of the room Dieter watched the small contingent of Irish. The guilt he had felt last time on hearing about the deaths of their comrades had failed to resurface this time as he pictured these four dead. The love of his sister now overshadowed everything.

Looking from one foreigner to the next, he felt a small sense of power over them. None of them knew how lucky they were that he was unable to contact his handler in the BKA today. He had told them he didn't want to be shadowed by detectives or undercover officers in case his boss discovered them somehow. He told them he would call when he knew the place and time. It had been too risky today, however, to get word to them and they would not have had enough time to get things in place for a raid, so quickly was this meeting assembled.

Sure they would curse at him and threaten him with his sister's freedom when they found out a deal had happened but he could live with that. Thankfully for him, the Irish would be organising more exchanges in the near future. These exchanges would involve a lot more weapons than what was here today. Dieter had patience. His boss would be arrested and the Irish taken by the British. And this time next year, he and his sister would be celebrating the festive season in America.

FORTY-SEVEN

Sean waved at the ferry crewman as he guided them out into the sheeting rain of Portsmouth. The wheels of the Humber Hawk III he was driving dropped the couple of inches off the end of the ramp onto the docks and he gracefully accelerated towards the customs officials, effortlessly pulling the 18 foot caravan behind them despite the extra weight of the cargo hidden within its walls and floor.

Knowing he was now on British soil, this was the time security forces and the police would have pounced, arresting both him and his Liverpudlian "wife" after their return from a French winter holiday around Le Havre. But he heard no sirens surrounding him or guns being cocked because they were not being watched.

Somewhere ahead of him Chad and Brad had exited the cross-channel ferry in a Ford lorry with the majority of weapons they had received from the Germans. The truck would have received more attention from the customs officials than they themselves would receive but Sean had confidence that the truck's paperwork – insurance, permits, cargo manifest, duty paid, et al – would cause no suspicion. So far both his and Brigitta's fake passports had checked out. Sean had made sure they kept his fake documents as Australian. It was easier not having to rely on too many lies if questioned by authorities.

The caravan they were towing had been stripped down to its bare-frame skeleton, loaded with weapons and then had its walls rebuilt around them. This had taken a day and a half. The truck had been easier. It had been provided by the Germans and all the team had to do was hide the stripped-down weapons within the cargo of commercial weaving machinery parts that were a legitimate consignment going to Dublin. After travelling across France they were all glad to be nearing their goal.

Once inland of the English coast, the rain began to ease up. Sean settled in for a long drive. He couldn't wait to get out of the car. His lower back was sore and his injured knee was giving him hell. Brigitta was keeping his mind off of his injuries by singing along to the radio, doing a sultry version of The Animals' *House of the Rising Sun*. He didn't know why but she was in a good mood. Maybe she just liked transporting large amounts of illegal firearms across her homeland with the thought that if she were captured she would be seen as a traitor to the crown and could therefore receive a penalty of death by hanging if found guilty. Or maybe not. Whatever the reason, her singing relaxed him and allowed him think. He thought of Megan, wondering if he would ever see her again.

Both vehicles were to travel at their own pace up to Liverpool where they would catch separate ferries the next day to Dublin. Daniel and another provo were to meet them there and run the weapons north. Then the ASU would return to Scotland to plan the second shipment.

Not until he handed over the keys of the Humber did Sean feel as though he had succeeded. Daniel was happy to be reunited with his friend as it had been nearly a month since he had left to carry on the struggle from within Britain's borders. He was surprised to see his Australian colleague had found even more beautiful women to surround himself with.

'Oh yeah. Daniel this is Brigitta. *Bree*, Daniel.'

The two shook hands with one showing more interest than the other.

'It's hard having to put up with this colonial all the time, hey?' Daniel joked, trying to look suave.

'That's my husband you're talking about.' Brigitta was sticking to her alias. She had never met Daniel before and eyed him suspiciously despite the fact he was now in charge of the weapons they had brought over.

Daniel just rolled his eyes – when she wasn't looking – and continued talking to Sean.

'No problems getting through?'

'Not unless you were Irish,' Sean explained. 'English customs are definitely paying more attention to them than anyone else.'

'That's Padraig's plan in action. Trust him to realise something we all should have known. So, how long have you got until you have to get back to Scotland?'

'We're on the next ferry back to Heysham, via the Isle of Man. We'll catch up for a drink next time. Oh, there some Christmas presents on the back seat for your sister and Max.'

'Where's mine?'

'What, a van full of guns not good enough for you?'

Daniel wished his friend the best of luck as he felt jealousy creep back in again.

'Righto men. Shut up for a minute.'

Captain Fordham stood before the men of A Squadron as they all assembled in the mess hall. He could see the SAS men were restless and hoped it would work in his favour for obtaining volunteers for the two missions he was to put forward. He knew it didn't matter much. If no one volunteered then he would simply pick them himself.

'Because it is so boring here...'

Laughter from the group.

'...I'm after three men to volunteer for a holiday to one of the most sunny and glamorous places this side of the equator.'

No one moved. They all knew he was full of shit.

Captain Fordham waited, knowing the first person to speak up would be number one on his list. Everybody remained silent...except for a recently arrived young lad from Nottingham; a trooper recently transferred from the Royal Green Jackets who hadn't quite caught on as to how things worked around here.

The young trooper cocked his head sideways as he asked, 'Where'd that be, Boss?'

Fordham's façade didn't change but he laughed inside, knowing it was the rookies that got the ball rolling.

'Thank you Owens. You and two others will be seconded to the Military Reconnaissance Force, assisting with intelligence gathering in *sunny* Northern Ireland…'

A groan came from the newcomer, kicking himself for falling into the trap. Everyone else laughed.

'…*and* you will be under their command for six months so take it as gospel that you won't be home for Christmas.'

Despite being new to the 22nd, Andrew Wilton knew certain jobs were best steered clear of and hoped he wasn't one of the unfortunate "volunteers". Sure he would love to be there if something went down but six months of nothing but information gathering caused cobwebs to form at your elbows.

'No one else stepping forward?' Fordham looked from one side of the room to the other but no one batted an eyelid lest they attract attention. 'Very well. Owens will be joined by Anderson and Williams.'

For a second the Australian felt his stomach drop as he thought it was going to be his name read out last.

Poor Williams. Thank fuck for that!

Captain Fordham continued.

'We've received word Paddy has acquired yet another consignment of weapons. They have shown some balls by passing through this great country of mine completely undetected. Obviously someone isn't watching these bastards as they come and go. So you three will be departing in four days time. Check in with Captain Hodsen the day prior for transport details to ensure you don't miss your flight... *accidentally*! Make the best of it lads.' He waited until the hush of relief subsided before he continued.

'Secondly; some of you may have heard that two of our lads in D Squadron have been seriously wounded in Oman. Anybody wishing to have a stab down in the Middle East has twenty-four hours to place in their transfer. It will be a boots 'n all trip so I'm giving you all some time to think it over. The length of the tour has yet to be decided but I guess that's up to our Arab friends. And, of course, the Adoo.'

No thanks, Andrew thought as he brushed a strand of long hair from his face. *The Middle East isn't my idea of fun.*

Andrew saw the rookie Trooper Owens two hours before his departure four days later on Tuesday morning back in the mess hall. He was sitting over at the far end of the large room reading through a pile of information. With only hours until his departure over the water he had decided to hone up on his terrorist identification amidst a cloud of his own tobacco smoke.

'Owey. What'cha got there?' Andrew said as he passed the twenty two year old. He could see the short tour into Northern Ireland had gotten him frazzled and being one of the newest to make it into the sandy beret mob, Owens was dying to show all and sundry he was up to the job.

'Hey Wilto. Just going over some of the faces that we need to keep an eye out for. Fordham's being real pushy on the intel thing. Wants us to spot the players from a mile off.'

"Players" were how the Irish volunteers were being referred to of late.

He leant back and motioned to the 4 inch thick jacket he was studying. 'Fuck, Wilto, there must be half of Belfast in here.'

'Can't be half,' the Australian replied with a grin. 'Probably more like a third. That's not that many! Umm... how many people are there in Belfast?'

'Thanks for nothin' yah cunt!'

'You'll be right Owey. You'll be back here before you know it *and* wiser for it. Probably teaching us a few things about intel' gathering.'

'Why don't *you* volunteer to go in my place and find out for yourself?'

'Think of it as a learning experience.'

'Again; why don't *you* go for the experience?'

'Did a couple of years of that shit in a place much worse than Belfast mate.'

'Yeah I heard you convicts turned Australia into a shit hole!' the young man grinned up at Wilto.

Andrew just smiled back.

'Have fun Owey.'

'Piss off.'

The Australian laughed as he walked away, glad he hadn't been so inexperienced as to fall into Fordham's trap. It wouldn't have been that bad as a training exercise but he was beyond that sort of thing at this stage in his career.

As he reached the door, behind him Owens turned the page and tried to memorise the next name and face with its accompanying spied photo. Some text circled in red at the bottom of the page caught his eye. Something had been added to this particular file. This player had been placed in top priority. The picture was of an Australian soldier gone AWOL named Sean Doherty.

Owey couldn't believe it. He knew that Wilto wouldn't know him… *but wouldn't it be funny.*

'Hey Wilto! I've got one of you lot here!'

Andrew turned from the door, curious to what classified an Irish terrorist as "one of you lot".

'You mean a tall, dark and handsome Paddy?' he called back.

'Nah. He's Australian!'

Every instinct told the sergeant it was beyond being possible for an Australian to be a member of the IRA but he bought into Owens' joke, speculative as to what the punch line was going to be.

'Let me guess. That's where Harold Holt ended up? Waving a Tommy gun about and draped in a tri-colour?'

Knowing he had one up on the sergeant, Owens held up the page to him. 'Not exactly,' he said with a grin.

Andrew strolled back to the table and his eyes focused on the several black and white photos affixed to the full page of text. It only took a second for his brain to recall their first jungle encounter and the drunken night he had spent with the man in the images before him.

'Fuck off,' he uttered so quietly that Owens couldn't hear him over the noise of the mess hall.

This can't be right!

'Is this right?' Andrew demanded as he snatched the file from the rookie's hands. Even with the picture inches from his face he still couldn't believe what was before him.

'Says there he served in Vietnam.' The smile on Owens' face suddenly melted. A shiver ran up the young man's spine. 'You don't know him do you?'

Andrew didn't hear him. He was already running to Captain Fordham's office.

FORTY-EIGHT

It had been the third time that week that she had dreamt about him and like those other mornings she woke with a smile. It may have been months ago but their meeting had started something she knew God himself could not stop.

Megan O'Brien watched the sheeting rain against her window and remembered the feel of the Australian pressed up hard against her, enveloping her, inside of her. It had been weather just like this. Every time it had rained since, the memory of Sean Doherty returned to her. And being Galway in the winter it rained six days a week and snowed on the seventh so he was always there in the back of her mind.

Running her fingers over her smooth body, she thought back to South Armagh, wishing that she had not left in such a hurry. And she had regretted it from that day on. She lay listening to the sky weep with joy for ten more minutes before finally getting up to shower and wash the sweat from her body. After dressing and having a cup of tea, she rugged herself up and pulled on a rain coat before heading out to visit one of her Cumann na mBan comrades. She had promised to help her with some extremely late Christmas shopping.

As she lingered in the rain during the short four block walk, the recurring feelings that rolled around deep within her resurfaced and she could feel him on her again…in her again.

God what's wrong with you girl, she thought. *Anybody would think you're in love.*

She couldn't help but laugh as she knocked on her friend's front door.

So what are you going to do about it?

Major Purvis and Captain Fordham looked over the file in front of them. It certainly was something unexpected.

'Are you saying you know this man?' queried his superior officer. '*Personally* know him?'

The photo in front of them showed two young men greeting the head of the IRA. The one the sergeant was clearly rattled about was shaking the older man's hand.

'We first met during a contact with the Viet Cong. He was Infantry. Didn't know his name then but a while later I met him in Vung Tau and we ended up drinking together.'

The two officers seated on the other side of the desk returned to the file leaving the Australian sergeant in an uncomfortable silence.

'It was at the end of my tour,' he continued. 'A fellow Regiment lad and I were out celebrating my upcoming transfer and we ran into him again. Ended up sharing a table with this man and one of the men from his own platoon.'

After nodding for while, Major Purvis looked up and spoke, his distinctive deep voice filling the room.

'And you now wish to volunteer for the secondment to Belfast?'

'Yes Boss.'

Major Purvis looked to his left at the stockier Captain. Fordham's face gave away nothing.

'The reason for this?'

He hesitated briefly before saying, 'I know him sir. I believe I could...'

'What?' the Major interrupted. 'Have a word with him down the pub over a pint and get him to hand himself in? It says here he is wanted back in your homeland for murder. Do you think he would turn himself over to you just because you two once got pissed and sang *Waltzing Matilda* together?'

Andrew tried to control his frustration. 'No, but if I…'

'I'm sorry', Purvis stated, 'but things have already been set up for the three men going over.'

Andrew raged inside at the insult but bit his lip.

Fucken officers the world over…they're all the same.

'Just because,' Purvis continued, obviously aggravated at his having to explain his assessment, 'you may be able to identify one of their volunteers does not mean you are more suited to the job than the three men which are leaving today.' The major closed the file. 'You are needed here Sergeant Wilton. That will be all.'

Andrew saluted cleanly, about-faced and left the Major's office one unhappy soldier.

Despite not having his family and friends around him, Christmas in Scotland was turning out to be great. None of the four members of the active service unit living in their West End house bought each other gifts. Instead they had all agreed to have a big cooked lunch with plenty of grog. A few days ago they had juggled with the idea of going down to the Halt Bar once it opened but secretly everyone just wanted to relax and put their feet up for the day.

They had been so busy lately. Sean never thought an ASU would be on the go so often. He thought it was going to be more cloak and dagger stuff like some of the spy books he had read when he was younger, with passing of information to shady characters in lane ways and blink-and-you'll-miss-it brief case hand over's, but it was a lot more exciting than that.

The Newcastle-on-Tyne bank job had made headline news throughout Britain and Padraig had sent them a message of congratulations, over the moon at how his brainchild was roaring ahead. Once the banks opened up again after the New Year's holidays, they were going to hit one more bank in Newcastle. It would have been a lot easier robbing a bank in Scotland but Chad had forced the rule that no Scottish money would be touched. This final job would give them enough money to cover the last two purchases with ample spare funds remaining to acquire the vehicles needed.

Sean washed down the mouthful of roast turkey with a swig of stout, his mind here and now with his new friends, not thinking about the risks they were going to be taking next week. Looking around the table at the three of them amidst a cloud of tobacco smoke with Brigitta's Beatles album filling the warm room with its harmonies, Sean could see the others had been unselfish and had made the best of a hard situation.

Chad and Brad had spent the morning with what family they had in Glasgow but both had arrived back in time for the lunch preparations. Nobody knew if Brigitta had family back in Liverpool as she didn't speak much of her home town. Rather, it had been her idea for an afternoon party starting with lunch at one.

They cracked open the first bottle of scotch around noon as Chad arrived to cook the turkey but he kept forcing them back out of the kitchen into the living room, declaring himself chef for the day. The dishes they could clean when he was done but the preparation of the fowl was his.

They ate late, around three p.m., each of them wearing a shine from the early drinking. Everyone worked their way through a banquet of dumplings, boiled vegetables, hot herbed bread, golden roasted potatoes and a spice-stuffed bird so perfectly cooked after what Chad had claimed to be years of practice by his grandmother's side.

Laughing as he told the story, Sean enlightened them with the tale of his last Christmas lunch which had been two mouthfuls of condensed milk and some hard biscuits before contact had been made with the flank of a Viet Cong patrol.

'…So for the next half hour we had to push forward into Charlie to try and gain some high ground as we waited for another platoon to come in and cut them off.' He paused as he took another mouthful of beer before explaining what was so funny.

'After a while, I looked down and saw my leg just completely covered in ants…these little red fuckers that seemed to burn when they bit you. You see, when the contact started I'd quickly jammed the tube of condensed milk down into my pocket. But the cap wasn't on. I was sticky with cream from my balls to my ankle and the ants were having a field day. I started screaming for my mate to get them off me and started pulling my daks off. Everyone around me thought I had been hit and was trying to hold me down as I thrashed around. Idiots were holding me down *on the fucking ants nest!*'

His laughter became more uncontrollable as the others infectiously joined in.

'Ended up dropping my rifle as I jumped around naked from the waist down! My cock swinging in a war zone! That was my last Christmas! Twelve months ago today!'

They laughed and drank the rest of the day away.

Chad and Brigitta danced to a number of songs they knew they would have forgotten about in the morning. Brad fell asleep on the lounge as night rolled in. Sean just lay back in the arm chair, smoked his cigarettes, sipped his topped up Ballantines, felt its warmth in his belly and thought about what those other people in his life were doing today.

The first to mind was Megan. He thought about her often and wondered if she ever thought about him. Did he leave as much of an impression on her as she had done to him?

Fucking women will be the death of me, he joked with himself. He raised his glass and took a sip. *Merry Christmas Megan.*

Hearing some kids running by outside, braving the cold, made him think of young Max. In his mind he could see him playing with his new soccer ball, driving his mother mad kicking it around the tiny flat. He had also gotten him a Tonka toy dump truck for days like this when it was too cold to be playing outside. For Melissa he had found a shop in Le Havre which sold the latest fashions from Paris. He hoped he nailed her size with the bright skirt and jacket. They were summer clothes but he knew she was a patient person. She would probably wear them around the flat anyway.

He then thought about his family and friends back in Australia. James would have put on a good feed for them out the back of the pub. His old man would be there telling James how to cook the steaks like he did every year.

I cook the steaks every year dad!

You always cook them too much!

I know what I'm doing.

Bullshit! You only need to turn them once! And stop pricking the sausages!!

Melanie and Kim would be trying to run interference between them, offering his dad another beer to get him away from the barby. After lunch with his own parents, Luke would turn up with Leanda to carry on drinking.

Sean sighed. *The second year in a row...*

If there was ever a day to felt homesick then this was it.

By the time Sean was sitting down to relax after a big meal of turkey and grog, Christmas in Australia was all but over. James was closing the front door of his father's place behind him. Satisfied his old man was asleep and the house spotless after a much smaller celebration than previous years, he headed to his car parked out front. Kim was already in it, her head leaning against the pillar as she fought to keep awake.

They had arrived there this morning at his father's, deciding with his condition being how it was, it was better to have lunch at his home. Melanie and Joseph had cooked up a roast lamb and the five of them sat down for the smallest and quietest Christmas in a long time.

His sister had relented and allowed her dad a few beers which he just happened to have in the fridge already. She thought she could see some improvement in his health. Once they had news on Sean, and she prayed it would be good news, she hoped it would improve him further. They all agreed seeing the picture of him in the paper had done some good so they would all now hold their breath until they heard from Luke and Grant.

The two were not due to leave for a few days and none of them could imagine how it must have been for Grant's family to accept he was leaving them again, albeit for no more than one month. That was all his wife could come to agree to amidst a torrent of tears. He had to be home before their anniversary.

James had missed not having Luke and Leanda around for dinner as they had in previous years. Instead of music blaring and laying around drunk under the back yard sprinkler, the five made lamb, potato and gravy sandwiches out of the leftovers and watched the tele until his dad had fallen asleep in his chair.

With him now in his bed and the house cleaned up, James started the car and pulled out into the street. Despite it being close to midnight the night air was still balmy. He knew Sean used to love driving around on nights like this with the windows down and the radio keeping him and Anna compa…

He sighed, wound his window down and pulled Kim into him, his arm around her.

Hope you had a good Christmas brother.

FORTY-NINE

The passenger train rattled its way across the English countryside, startling the heavily fleeced sheep which grazed by the track's edge amidst clouds of their own heavy breath.

Grant Brooks looked out the carriage's window, drawn away from his newspaper by another passing train which blurred by in the opposite direction. He waited until it passed before surveying the lush green land which moved by outside. Smoke from so many chimneys hung flat in a ghostly thermocline across the partially wooded valleys. He knew the people in those warmed houses were probably still celebrating Christmas with their families, eating leftovers and getting drunk on whatever it was that warmed them up.

Luke Kennedy was sleeping in the chair beside him. Grant wasn't sure how because they were the most uncomfortable seats he'd ever had the misfortune to place his arse into.

During the first half of his tour in Vietnam he had been able to catch forty winks almost anywhere he had a few spare minutes. It didn't matter if it was in the back of a troop carrier or a stomach-churning ride in a Chinook; he could get some sleep anywhere. After he had accidentally killed those…after *that* contact, he had trouble sleeping no matter how tired he was or how comfortable the bedding. The nightmares were hard on him. Sometimes he would wake from one only to see the two kids go running past his bedroom door, still screaming from the torturous pain he had inflicted upon them. Nightmares within nightmares were the worst, never knowing if he was awake. In a way he had almost come to hate sleep and the terrible memories it bought. The dark circles under his eyes seemed permanent now. He couldn't help but wonder if Sean was acting out in reply to the horrors he himself had been dealt.

The ex-serviceman shifted in his seat. His arse was numb. He hoped the seats on the ferry to Belfast in the morning were better than these second rate milk crates they dared to call seats.

On the long flight from Sydney they had talked about the best ways to locate Sean. Neither of them wanted to involve the police for Sean's sake. And both were understandably apprehensive about how the locals would greet them.

Since seeing the photo of Sean they had been reading all they could about the Troubles to try and get an understanding on the type of world they would soon be entering; almost daily riots, gun battles between the Protestants and the Catholics, paramilitary groups probing at each others defences, civilians of both faiths being gassed out of their homes by the British army…They both knew it would be a total culture shock.

Because the photo of Sean at the bomb sight was taken in a Catholic area, they had decided to ask around in that neighbourhood. In the far background of the photo was a church which would help them locate the actual street in the Mid Falls suburb. Then they would cautiously "pound the pavement", asking people while trying not to behave like police themselves. The one big advantage they did have was there probably were not many Australians in Belfast. However, if Sean didn't want to be found then maybe they had no chance at all.

The train crossed a junction causing him to bounce uncomfortably in his seat.

God, how much further?

He looked around and caught the eye of the woman behind him.

''scuse us love. How much further to Liverpool?'

The mother of the sleeping child beside her looked outside for a second, getting her bearings before consulting her watch.

'No more than an hour.'

'Thanks.'

'I know what you're thinking. I'll be glad to get out of this seat as well!'

Grant smiled back politely before returning to his paper. He skipped the English football sports pages and went back to reread the article on the growing number of bank robberies with the latest being a job in Newcastle-upon-Tyne up north by a group of four which were extremely professional according to witnesses.

If only our *Newcastle was this exciting*, he thought.

Dieter Wilhelm Brasch awoke with a hangover. His New Year's celebrations had carried on for three days after and now he was feeling the effects. In fact he didn't know what day it was. He had planned to sleep most of the day to try and regain some form of normality but some swine was knocking on his front door. No matter how much he buried his head into his pillow, the person outside continued to knock.

'Shut the fuck up!' he finally screamed out, the knocking finally halting. 'I'm coming.'

Slipping out of his warm bed he dragged the quilted cover with him and, draping it over his shoulders, he shuffled his way through the cold flat to the front door.

'Good afternoon Dieter,' said the man who greeted him with a smile from both his thin lips and his bespectacled eyes. 'It's a lovely crisp day out here. You should be out here enjoying it. The sun's out.'

Dieter cringed at the optimistic banter he always had to put up with whenever a message was delivered for him to pass on. If only he could read properly then Dieter might have been able to do the job himself, but the thought of dredging his way through every German newspaper everyday looking for tiny messages which may not even be there…

He guessed he was glad Karl could read.

One day I'll be able to read, he thought. *Then I'll read every American magazine I get my hands on.*

'Get inside,' he demanded. 'It's fucking freezing out there. And not so loud.'

Not dropping his smile, Karl lowered his voice as he continued.

'Bit of a hangover, Dieter? I told you not to mix schnapps with vodka. One or the other but not both. Sure it may taste good but I'd wager that it's not so good coming back out...'

'What do you want?' Dieter snapped. He definitely wasn't in the mood for this.

Karl pulled a piece of paper from his overcoat pocket.

'It was in this morning's paper. It's from the Irish again.'

Dieter's hangover suddenly diminished as he saw his sister's face for the first time in too long. She was so close now.

Karl continued. 'I know I'm not meant to know who it's from but one group's codes are distinguishable from the next. I think it is because Ireland has a history of good writers. Their codes seem to have a bit more...flourish to them.'

'Thank you Karl,' he stammered, caught up in the excitement only he was feeling. 'Thank you. I'll be sure to tell Mark what a good job you are doing for us. I may even be able to persuade him into giving you an increase in your payments.'

Karl's eyes lit up from behind his thick lenses.

'You be sure to tell Mr Muller it is a privilege to be working for such a fine gentleman as himself!'

What sort of work do you think we do Karl? Dieter almost laughed. *We're not saving orphans from the winter streets.*

'He should be the one honoured Karl,' he bullshitted as he opened the door for the annoying man, ushering him out into the cold. 'And thank you again.'

Hurrying back to his bedroom caused his head to begin throbbing again but he fought through it. He dressed, took two swigs of vodka to prime himself for the cold and headed out to call his handler within the Bundeskriminalamt.

'Won't be long Elsa. We'll be together again soon.'

So it was on that cold peaceful morning in early January, Dieter Wilhelm Brasch yet again sold out his fellow countrymen and now a group of Provisional volunteers he had only met once were destined to die.

Only the thought of seeing his sister again kept the guilt at bay.

The hold of the *Boreal Beauty*, a 65 foot Norwegian designed and built Romsdahl class fishing trawler was being packed with all sorts of goodies. Some had arrived in wooden crates whilst some weapons, like the machine pistols, came in blue sports bags.

There were fifty-eight AK47s from East Berlin and sixty-three AKMs from Romania, twenty-seven used WWII-era MP40 submachine guns, one crate of sixteen American made M26 hand grenades, one Russian DShK fifty calibre machine gun complete with bi-pod, thirty Russian Tokarev semi-automatic pistols, fourteen English Webley revolvers and over forty-thousand rounds of ammunition to cater for the eclectic range of firepower.

As well as the guns there was a sports bag which contained forty detonators and state-of-the-art electronic timers and triggering devices made in Switzerland. The crew took extra care of the bag which contained these items, not wanting to break the fragile circuitry within.

The trawler rocked gently with the incoming tide as the fresh water of the River Elbe, which had originated in the mountain ranges of Czechoslovakia, battled the opposing waters of the North Sea. As it did so the vessel's port side rubbed up against the rubber tyre protected dock, groaning with the friction that was a common sound in the small German town of Brunsbuttel.

Around them the docks were not entirely quiet either with several other much smaller fishing boats carrying out late night repairs several hundred yards away. The men handling the deadly cargo preferred it this way. A silent dock was too conspicuous to prying eyes and a busy dock was just…well, too busy. It would have been impractical to try and keep track of all the human traffic in such an area. The light hum of work around them shielded them just fine which was their reason for choosing this location.

Of the IRA's active service unit only Chad and Brad had made the crossing with the trawler's crew of four, leaving Brigitta and Sean back in Scotland to await their arrival at the riverside village of Inverkiething. It was much further up the Forth and into the heart of Scotland than they had originally planned but much better suited to their operation.

Preparations had been made to transport the trawler's cargo by truck across to the western coast and then ferried to Ireland. Two small 4 tonne furniture removalist trucks had been modified to hide the weapons underneath the flooring. Each truck came with its own cargo of furniture that would make detection of the false floors, an air gap of only eight inches, almost impossible.

As the last of the crates were secured in the lower hold, the two Scotsmen shook hands with the German mobsters before each group went their separate ways.

Beneath their feet the twin General Motors diesel engines roared to life before settling into a steady idle, the dirty smoke of ignition mushroom-clouding its way up into the night,briefly the lights from the net cranes for several seconds. She slipped her lines and the dilapidated trawler unworthy of her name pulled out of the safety of the small harbour and into the heavier waters of the North Sea.

Captain Fordham of Her Majesties 22nd Special Air Service couldn't believe the ineptness of the British Intelligence network sometimes. Both MI5 and The Secret Intelligence Service (incorrectly known as MI6) seemed to stuff up some major opportunities from time to time. He knew nobody was perfect but these fuckers were meant to be protecting their country.

Get the fucking boy scouts in. They'd do a better job. Better still, send in the SAS.

He was standing just inside the open doorway to the helicopter hanger on the eastern helipad at their base in Hereford. His men – and some SBS (Special Boat Service) men – were assembled around him, checking their kit which was laid out in front of them. Each was dressed in black and around them lay all the necessary gear to fight a small war, which is what each secretly wanted. By sheer luck the SBS men had been visiting from Poole, their base of operations, to take part in some combined training and Captain Fordham had received permission to use them and their specific expertise over water in the upcoming mission.

The late phone call - which had sprouted the mission - from the Regimental Commanding Officer was at the end of a long line of quick calls all aimed at getting the SAS/SBS lads geared up for a fight. The captain knew they could not be called upon by just anyone. The call to their CO on a scrambled line had to have come from the Director of Military Operations who was acting on a call from the Permanent Under-Secretary of Defence. The PUS would have received a request from his opposite number at the Home Office who would be acting on the information supplied by Special Branch. That Intel would have told all and sundry that the task required could not be handled by Special Branch. And because, under the constitution, the SAS can only operate within the United Kingdom in direct support of the police, the first call made that late afternoon would have been from the head of Special Branch of the Metropolitan Police officially asking for help from further up the chain. The police may have instigated the call but they would now stand back and wait. What was to follow was out of their league. The conclusion from such speedy communications, so far, was the collection of the finest fighters in the world all standing here before the captain now.

Captain Fordham wanted to make an impact within the IRA. He wanted them to know messing around with his country meant messing around with the best. Today he wanted to hit them hard.

Behind him in the black as pitch night stood two brand new Aerospatiale Puma MKI helicopters, each powering up in the cold Hereford morning. These were the first to be built in England rather than France. The lads before him had had the privilege of carrying out a few training exercises out in the hills yesterday, getting to know what this new multi-million pound machine could do. Yesterday was a joy ride, much like one test driving a new car and pushing it to the limits, but news of what may be happening up north had forced the choppers to become involved in today's activities.

The wash from the giant 45 foot diameter rotors swept across the wet ground, the cold air hitting the soldiers but none seemed to notice. Soon the noise of their two Turbomea turbine-powered engines would be too loud for him to be heard so he tried to make it brief.

'We have received word Paddy is trying to get some more weapons over from Germany. As usual the news may have come through to us too fucking late! Now some of you were in on the op' up in Scotland back in June. We bagged ourselves a few Provos but not their gear. For reasons which are beyond our pay-grade we had been sent in a day early. Now it looks as though the deal has just happened or is happening right now. Gentlemen, we have a fishing boat and its cargo to find.

'Our brethren in the SBS are checking all records for a boat called something along the lines of the *Bonnie* or *Boring Beauty*. All ports in and out of Great Britain have been ordered to double check *all* cargos being passed through under Irish ownership and passport.

'Lieutenant Tuckwell will be leading the first group and Sergeant Wilton leading the second. We will give you more info as we are inbound. Let's go get 'em men!'

The only Australian in their group, Sergeant Andrew Wilton, led his small contingent of men to the furthest Puma, the lights of the hangers reflecting off of its gleaming new skin. The side doors slid open as the dark metal machine waited to swallow up the hardest men in Britain.

Wilto, as his men called him, counted off the party of SBS and SAS soldiers as they climbed in, himself the last of twelve on board. He slid the door shut behind him and gave a thumbs up to the co-pilot before settling down in his seat. Placing his rifle, a Colt Commando, down between his legs with the barrel on the floor, he took the headset from the hook beside him and greeted the two pilots as they all felt the ground drop away from beneath them at an amazing rate.

'Gazza, Neil.'

The SAS have a semi-relaxed view on addressing people by their rank. Most are simply called by their first name or nick-name.

'Morning Wilto,' Flight Lieutenant Garry Marshall said. 'I've got the Captain and Tucky on for you.'

Picking up the headphones Andrew glanced at his watch. So it *is* morning, he realised, seeing the time at ten past midnight. He felt the nose of the Puma drop as they raced off, the two helicopters in a line as they passed over the outer buildings of Stirling Lines. They had a lot of ground to cover and, unfortunately, a lot of last minute planning to do on their way.

FIFTY

It was still dark when Sean woke up. He was lying in bed next to Brigitta (Her idea. She refused to have him sleep on the lounge or floor) with less than two hours until they had to head out.

'Cant sleep either?'

He rolled over to see his "wife" looking at him, her eyes reflecting the streetlight which had found its way through the curtains.

'Bad dream.'

Her mouth curled into her cute smile that he had become quite fond of. It reminded him of his missing Galway girl.

'I thought so,' she said in a whisper. 'You've had a few of those since we've been here.'

'Do they wake you up?'

'Sometimes. I'm a light sleeper.'

'Sorry.'

She smiled again. That bloody adorable smile. *It* had crossed his mind but he didn't want to start something with her when there was so much responsibility riding on his shoulders. He hadn't picked up any flirtatious signals from her indicating she wanted anything sexual from him which was fine in his opinion. When she was at work she was the most focused of their group. The drive for her doing what she was doing seemed stronger than anyone else's. When she relaxed she almost turned off that soldier's mask that she wore day in, day out.

Almost.

On the first night in their Glaswegian house, after they had planned the Newcastle job, Brigitta had convinced him the lounge was too cold and the floor too hard and they didn't have the blankets to go around. Sean didn't know upstairs Brad *was* sleeping on the lounge and he would sleep right through with no worries at all, nice and toasty.

The "husband and wife" had agreed on underwear and t-shirts and, as he was climbing into bed on the first night, he was just about to tell her he would be gentlemanly about the sleeping situation and not try to cop a feel during the night when he glimpsed the dark shape of her Smith & Wesson pistol underneath her pillow's edge. That alone told Sean that although she was almost naked and about to sleep next to him, part of her was still a soldier, still turned on (in the soldierly way) and tuned for conflict. He fell asleep that first night next to, but not touching, her warm body and dreamt about that other strong woman which had come into his life recently; Megan O'Brien.

'Don't be sorry,' she said bringing him out of his thoughts. 'Half my dreams are nightmares. I guess it's our lot in life. Doing what we do. Our experiences are a little more heavier than your average person on the street.'

Our experiences! Suddenly he was exceptionally angry with her. *I spent nearly a year of my life in a fucking Asian hell hole watching my friends die for no fucking reason and you think your dreams can compare with anything I've seen!*

He spun around and planted his feet on the carpet, trying to get control of a temper which had almost gotten the better of him. The clouded thoughts in his head began to clear as he stood up.

'I'm going to have a tub; get something to eat. I'll wake you when it's time to go.'

Brigitta watched him close the door behind him, not knowing if she had just said something to piss him off or if he was embarrassed about his nightmares.

He woke her at two. His anger to her stupid comment had abated and he had a light breakfast now ready for her. Fifteen minutes later they climbed into the Renault and headed north, crossing the Firth of Forth at Kincardine where they travelled down river. They arrived at the machine workshop in Inverkiething where the modifications had been carried out on the removalist trucks. Leaving the Renault in the workshop along with the decoy furniture, they each drove a truck down to the wharf where they awaited, in silence, the arrival of the *Boreal Beauty*.

With an hour and a half of darkness remaining, the trawler made its way in beyond the home of the Scottish Fisheries amidst a scattering of early working vessels. Her small crew, sheltered up behind iced-over windows, was edgy but no one payed them any more attention than a sounding of an air horn or the wave of friendship as other boats passed by. On their port side the lights of Edinburgh, Granton Harbour and the Leith Docks lined the shore a mile away. Towering above them, the Forth Road Bridge carried a light scattering of early morning traffic.

Fighting the outgoing tide they finally reached the docks of Inverkiething as the blue light of morning drew itself in a fine line across the cold south-eastern horizon. They headed for the northern bank as the skipper bought her around in a wide sweeping arc, pointing her bow back out into the river and slipping in sideways beside the long pier on its port side. Glad to be out of the cold wind which had begun to build as they finished crossing the North Sea, the crew readied itself top-side, eager to swiftly empty her deadly consignment. Two of the crew scrambled over onto the wooden dock, caught the hawser lines at bow and stern and secured the bobbing vessel to the bollards.

Brigitta backed her truck down first. It was a five year old L47 Volvo with the exterior of the rear compartment proudly painted in the Scottish colours of blue and white. She pulled up just short of the pier and climbed down to assist in loading.

Each weapon crate had been opened on the trip across from mainland Europe and the contents laid out for packing individually. The crates had then been weighted and thrown overboard. The lack of crates allowed them to pack the secret compartment of the trucks as tightly as possible with rifles stacked in side by side and end to end.

One of the fishermen delicately passed Sean the next bag. 'Careful with this one,' he advised the Australian.

Curious to this bags fragility, Sean unzipped it and was puzzled by what he found.

'What's this shit?' he was genuinely confused as he asked Brad above him, his arms out waiting for the bag.

Craning his neck to see in the dark, he recognised the electronic pieces.

'Electronics. Timers, detonators.'

Alarm bells rang in Sean's mind.

'For what?'

'For bomb making.' Brad sounded like he was stating the obvious.

Sean felt a flush of blood surge across his face. This isn't what he had signed on for. He had told Padraig he was doing this to help stop cowardly acts like the one Melissa and Max had almost been killed in. He didn't want to be part of anything as indiscriminate as bomb making.

'Come on Sean,' Brad urged. 'Pass it here.'

Sean hesitated.

'What's wrong?' Chad called down from the truck. 'What's the holdup?'

'Bombs Chad?' he asked, pointing at the bag at his feet. 'We're making fucking bombs now?' His tone had changed and everyone stopped and turned to him, aware he was not happy.

'It's going to be a different war, son. We have to be ready for everything.' He motioned for him to carry on. 'The bag, Sean.'

Still Sean hesitated. He had no problem at all in supplying the IRA with guns. Bombs however...he had seen the effects first hand, from two wars, and knew it was a dirty way to fight. Unless a civilian has picked up a weapon then they were not a target. Even if they were planning to use bombs on the loyalist paramilitaries, how would they know no innocent people, Catholic or Protestant, had wandered in range of the device? They simply couldn't.

Before he could decide on what to do about it, Brigitta stepped over and grabbed the bag, passing it up to Chad.

'We're wasting time,' she snapped, giving Sean a suspicious glance.

Watching the bag disappear into the floor of Chad's truck, Sean went back to work, but in the back of his mind he was working out what to say to Padraig when next he saw him. He wanted no part of a bombing campaign. If it meant leaving his responsibilities of his ASU then so be it. He would return to the streets of Belfast at greater risk as a soldier armed with a gun; not a terrorist with a bomb.

After fifteen minutes the first truck was done and Chad left with Brad driving, heading back to the workshop to load in the furniture.

Sean, Brigitta and the boat crew filled the compartment in the second truck; a 67 Austin cab-over with a plain white body with two fine red stripes down its length. Giant red lettering up the side declared it a "Cameron Removalists" truck. The remaining weapons, including the grenades which had been repacked into shoe boxes, barely fit under the floor boards.

With the timber floor back in place, the boat crew bid them farewell, removed the empty fuel drums that had allowed the crossing, untied and headed back out into the cold open waters to fish (in case they were questioned later on they would have a record of sale for their catch of that day), leaving Sean and Brigitta to race off to the workshop to fill up its own quota of furniture.

Reaching the workshop they pulled up beside their other ASU members as they were departing.

'I've just put the call through channels to Daniel…' Chad said to them, his breath forming in the cold. '…to tell him everything's on track and to expect us. Let's hope it all goes well. Good luck. See you when you get back.'

Sean just nodded as he pulled away, still upset about the cargo in Chad's truck.

It only took them twenty minutes to load the truck and secure it, padding out the furniture to make it look like a professional job and then they themselves were on the road. To lessen the chances of the Brits getting their hands on the illegal freight, each truck was to travel to different locations on the western coast of Scotland. Brigitta and Sean would take the remainder of the day to drive back through Glasgow, northeast into Argyll on the A82, through the beginning of the Scottish Highlands and finally down the A83, to the peninsula of Kintyre where they would catch a ferry first thing tomorrow morning from Campbelltown. They hoped to be having breakfast the next day across the North Channel in Ballycastle; a small, quiet and predominately Catholic village sixty miles north of Belfast.

Brad and Chad were to head south to Cairnryan on Loch Ryan in the southwest of the Scottish Lowlands. A lot closer than Campbelltown, they would be there by lunch to load the truck onto a Larne bound ferry. Daniel would meet them in Larne today, the drive being only twenty-five miles north of Belfast.

Neither truck would be in contact with each other. The next time they saw each other would be back in their Glasgow flat in three days… if Sean decided to return to Glasgow.

FIFTY-ONE

With nothing else to go on yet, the SAS/SBS laden Pumas had had to land at RAF Prestwick, home to the Scottish Air Traffic Control Centre (Military) several hours ago to await instructions; instructions which looked as though had just come in.

The base's Scots Gaelic motto "*Faire Agus Gliocas*" translated as "Watchfulness and Wisdom", two things Andrew thought seemed to be lacking with British security at the moment.

Despite the slow start he was excited. This was the sort of thing you wouldn't get to do in the Australian SAS. They had no land borders and even more boring neighbours. There was no chance New Zealand would ever launch a covert attack by invading Bondi Beach.

Standing with his group at the far end of the hanger complex, away from the prying eyes from their RAF contemporaries, the Australian Sergeant was listening to an update from Captain Fordham.

'Okay! Listen up! Here's what we've got to go on. The SBS lads currently scouring the water - call signs Charlies' One, Two and Three - have located a fishing trawler called the *Boreal Beauty*. It fits the description intel' had passed on and it is currently trawling eight miles out off the mouth of the Firth off the east coast of Scotland. Pilots, here are your grid references.' He handed over a sheet of paper to each of the jump-suited men beside him.

'The SBS are keeping their distance and will continue observation until we arrive. Winds are from the north west but mild so we will approach from the south east. Alpha team is under Lieutenant Tuckwell. Alpha's Puma will stop the boat by crossing its bow. You are to act as snipers in case anyone decides to have a go at the boarding crew. Bravo team, which will be led by Sergeant Wilton will then fast-rope down onto the deck and detain the crew. At this point Charlies One and Two will be alongside to assist Bravo team and pull anyone out of the water if they're stupid enough to try a Jesus and walk on water.

'Remember gentlemen that this is an "arrest option", I repeat an "arrest option" but treat everyone on board as armed, even if it turns out we've got the wrong boat. Expect anything from Paddy. He may even be stupid enough to even try scuttling the boat once we've been made so we have to move fast. Once everybody on board has been detained I want a thorough search for the weapons. Our source in Germany says the quantity is quite substantial so it shouldn't be too hard to find. If they have already made the drop-off then I want the location fast, so don't be afraid to break a few bones to get it. Oh, and some of the goods they have taken on include grenades gentlemen, so eyes peeled please!'

It was a rushed plan but it was better to take them while they were still at sea and without their own ground support. As for the rest of the plan they would just have to play it by ear. They prided themselves on the perfection of their training but sometimes decisions had to happen on the run and they had to be ready for such eventualities. That's what they got payed for.

'Any questions?' There were none. 'Okay. Let's go.'

The two Puma helicopters held an altitude of one thousand feet above the choppy water. With a full load on board they were not racing near their top speed of 151 knots, but still they pushed hard into the head wind, one behind the other. They estimated the trawler crew would have less than half a minute before they realised what was happening.

The pilots were in contact with the Special Boat Service men on the surface who were holding off over half a mile east of the target in small sea-faring rubber boats; three of them with four men in each. Once they got the call from the birds they could be alongside the trawler within two minutes.

On his radar, the Alpha Puma pilot, Flight Lieutenant Al Barr, could see the fishing boat. He could not make out the SBS men running parallel to the trawler so low was their profile in their own boats.

The Australian sergeant behind him tapped his shoulder. It was time. Without knowing exactly where the men on the water were, he gave the call.

'Charlie One; Alpha. Copy?'

'*Alpha; Charlie One receiving.*'

'Charlie One, go for target.' His voice was controlled despite the rush of his job.

Flight Lieutenant Barr could just imagine the small vessels now racing in towards their mark. Why on earth anyone would volunteer for the Special Boat Service had him fucked. They spent half their lives splashing about on the freezing waters of the Northern Sea, the English Channel and the Atlantic getting hypothermia. And secretly he thought that because of the conditions they put up with, the SBS men were just that little bit tougher than the Airborne lads of the SAS. But he would never tell either that. He much preferred it up here in his heated cockpit knowing the only water that would touch his skin today would be a hot shower and maybe a scotch and water if they succeeded.

Fuck it, he thought. *I'll have one anyway.*

He dropped the machine to the deck, skimming the white stippled black sheet of water. Watching his altitude and radar at the same time as keeping an eye on the ocean below and forward of him, he counted down the seconds.

'Alpha moving in to block.'

'*Bravo breaking away.*' The voice in his earphones was unwavering.

Ken Casey, the eldest and longest serving crewman on his brother-in-law's trawler, the *Boreal Beauty*, yawned as he was about to start up the port crane winch and begin taking the slack out of the net line. Just as the electric motor of the winch began to whine under tension, he thought he heard something that shouldn't be. He shut down the crane, his ears pricked. The fatigue which had begun to take hold after dropping off the cargo instantly vanished as he became alert once more. The world around him was still dark with the faintest hint of blue growing in the south east and it threw an eerie ghost-like illumination over the cold choppy waters around them. He looked to their south and forced his eyes to focus towards the source of the noise.

It grew over the racket of the twin diesels and the slapping of chop against the hull. Fading in and out as the wind raced by, he finally recognised the growing, growling, thudding sound.

Helicopters.

His stomach dropped as he located the two silhouettes less than a mile off their port bow. Turning to the bridge he screamed out a warning to his brother-in-law but he knew it was pointless. Unless the most amazing miracle blessed the undermanned fishing crew, he knew he would be in gaol before the day was done.

Or dead.

The Bravo Puma braked hard less then thirty feet above the still moving trawler, the tail dropping to pull them up before overshooting. A large spotlight fixed to the side of the Puma came on, illuminating the deck of the boat with its bright beam. Downwash from the now hovering machine almost pushed the boat further down into the water as the crew on the deck scurried inside. From within the new bird's belly, two thick ropes unfurled like dead pythons out of each side.

After being pissed off with the Major's decision not to send him to Belfast, Sergeant Andrew Wilton, at that exact moment was glad his CO had held fast.

I wonder what Owey and the boys are doing now in boring old Belfast. Nothing like this I bet!

The Australian SAS sergeant gripped the fast rope and pushed himself out of the Puma, chasing the rope as it continued to unfurl beneath them. Of the two men that had slid down, he was the first to hit the deck, bringing his slung Colt Commando around from his back. He aimed it towards the door the crew had escaped into and wondered if they were going to put up a fight. He swiftly led his growing group forward as more men dropped to the deck behind him.

The trawler eased down both engines, not having a choice as the Alpha Puma pulled up in front of their bow, giving them no room to manoeuvre. The men by the chopper's doors which were aiming their automatic weapons at the bridge saw the panic painted on the fishermen's faces.

As the captain of the *Boreal Beauty*, bought the engines back down to idle, he had no idea he and his crew would be tortured over the next fifteen minutes for what they knew. The crash of the door behind him being splintered to pieces and the mind-numbing explosion of stun grenades told him they meant business.

FIFTY-TWO

A blotched sunrise of slate grey and rose yellow appeared behind Sean and Brigitta as they travelled around the banks of Loch Lomond on the A82, west of Glasgow. It was going to be an overcast day and a cold one at that. Wind raced down from the mountain ranges ahead of them, slowing the Austin truck as it tried to climb the hills surrounding the loch. Sean hoped the wind would abate soon to ensure they had enough fuel to reach Campbelltown.

Beside him Brigitta attempted to tune in the radio but was met with nothing but static. For almost five minutes she had climbed the frequency band in search of something to break the silence which had developed between them. When she reached the end she came back down the width, stopping at the recognition of a voice. She danced the dial back and forth as she tried to fine tune it but eventually gave up and continued the long search back down.

Lighting up a cigarette, Sean knew it was going to be a long drive.

Bravo team was airborne and on the hunt.

It hadn't taken the trawler crew long to crack, giving them the location of the drop and a vague description of two trucks which had taken on the cargo.

There had been a time when Andrew was far from proud at the methods they used to gain information but time had taken care of the guilt. It was now simply a utilitarian approach they had all agreed to use to get what they needed.

Two removalist trucks of unknown make had been loaded in Inverkiething. Four people had met them, three men and one woman. The crew had claimed it as too dark to describe the trucks in detail but one of them recalled the colours of each. One was white with "Cameron Removals" in red lettering and the other was white on blue. Mid-sized trucks wouldn't be scarce this time of day but he hoped they were on the move right now. If they had gone to ground they were fucked. The terrorists had an hour head start and may have used this time to park up already or even switch the load to some other form of transport.

Alpha and Bravo Pumas were now racing in to the heart of Scotland. Each would take a different motorway to search while staying at a high altitude. The most probable direction would be to the south west so it cut down on the number of roads they had to scan. The police had been notified to report all trucks resembling the two described but under no circumstances were they to approach. That was to be left to the six cars of SAS men that were now racing north from Carlisle in their high powered sedans.

Looking out from behind the plexiglass window of the bird, Andrew scanned the growing traffic of the roads below. Commuting traffic was increasing. Already there had been four possible sightings with each Puma being assigned two to check out, but the size of each had been all wrong. Still, each truck had been assigned to an SAS car and would be pulled over for inspection when they arrived within the next twenty minutes.

'I think I got one.' It was Neil, the co-pilot.

Andrew could feel the tension in the cramped cabin grow as he leant forward between the two pilots to get an eyeball on the ground. Two miles below and three in front of them he saw a blue truck with white markings.

'Call it in and take us down for a closer look.'

The more they watched it the more he was certain this was one of them. It was staying within the speed limit, indicating every time it merged lanes and keeping its distance from other vehicles. The Puma pulled along side of the truck a mile out to its left. Andrew pulled out a pair of binoculars and focused in on the cab. There were two men inside.

'They're certainly doing everything by the numbers,' Neil said.

'So would you if you didn't want to draw attention.' Andrew replied. 'Where's Alpha?'

'Alpha's thirty miles east of us.'

Andrew weighed up the situation. His gut screamed at him that it was them. Everything was pointing in that direction. So he made the call.

'Okay. Let's get them over here. What about our cars? Any of them on the A75 yet?'

'We've got three cars west of Dumfries.'

'Inform them of our target. We'll need a road block at the last minute. Stage an accident or something. Their ears will be pricked but we can't help that. Once we box them we move in.'

As he sat back in his seat and turned to face his small group, he could feel his heart beginning to pound away.

'Right lads! Here's what we do.'

The London Bach Choir came in through the scratchy speakers as Chad chased the last few drops of coffee, sucking in the few lingering spheres from the lip of the mug. It was a batch Brad had put in a thermos on the boat during the crossing, a hot and milky blend.

Chad had found The Rolling Stones on the radio and the slow rhythm of the song didn't help his alertness any.

I saw her today at the reception

A glass of wine in her hand

They had been awake a long time and the adrenalin charge of the job had worn away after just an hour on the road. They didn't dare stop to grab a feed, only regretting now not bringing even just some fruit with them. It was something they would rectify on the next run. But Cairnryan was less than an hour away. They would get something to eat on the ferry.

They had left the coastline ten minutes ago and now followed the road south into the land which was typical of the Lowlands. Rolling hills off to the sides of the road rose and fell in shallow undulations. Farmable paddocks were being turned over in preparation for the next crop. Trees sat in tight groups at the corners and intersections of each farm, hunched together as if in protection from farmers looking for that extra yard to make money from. Those paddocks which weren't carrying livestock or being worked due to the rock bed just under the soil were covered in a mixture of harsh spine-grasses and patches of heather. At times when the geography allowed, they could sometimes see the water just beyond the hills. The smell of salt water was calling to Chad.

We're nearly there love, he said to the sea, his mistress, as the song continued.

I knew she was gonna meet her connection

At her feet was a footloose man

Turning his attention back to the road, Chad reasoned the few cars travelling south with them were probably heading to Cairnryan for the first boat out or to Stranraer for its ferry to Belfast. There wasn't a lot of traffic on this road, a hell of a lot less than they had imagined. A few more cars may have meant blending in but it also led to accidents on patches of black ice and therefore more police.

No sooner had the thought merged in his mind did he see the brake lights of the few distant cars come on.

The lyrics teased him, dared him to be pessimistic.

You can't always get what you want

You can't always get what you want

Immediately their threat radars were scanning the distance for trouble. Chad could have sworn he felt his heart shoot up his throat when he saw the flashing lights a mile ahead.

'Fire truck,' Brad said in a short grunt.

'Could be an accident. Black ice.' But he couldn't be sure.

There were no police vehicles and only one car blocking the lane. It was nose in against the outer guard rail, perpendicular to the other cars.

With no road to turn off and divert, Brad went down through the gears as he made his approach to the scene as drawn out as possible. In between him and the crashed car were two other vehicles, both sedans. Behind him, a single car closed in the group. If needed he could throw the removalist truck around onto the other side of the road but this would draw attention. With such a big turning circle it would need to be a three point turn.

'What do you want to do?'

The elder man strained to look ahead.

Something's not right. What is it?

Then it dawned on him.

'TURN! TURN! TURN!'

Without questioning Brad heaved the wheel hard to the right, the truck understeering slightly as it crossed the wet dividing lines of the road.

Chad was still looking ahead to the "accident". There was no one out of their cars. Even the small fire crew had yet to emerge from their vehicle. It may have been cold but it wasn't *that* cold. And the car which had nosed into the barrier showed no signs of damage.

'Fuck!' he cursed as he pulled his pistol from his belt. 'How the fuck did they find us?!'

Beside him Brad fought to keep the truck in a tight turn as the high centre of gravity nearly lifted the inside wheels clear off the ground. As he held the steering wheel at full lock with his foot forcing the accelerator through the floor, he felt the truck shudder as both front wheels exploded, ripped to shreds by automatic gunfire. The heavy vehicle lurched and skidded off the edge of the road, the front left wheel running off the bitumen and ploughing, sinking into the soft shoulder of dirt, buried up to its axle.

Their run was over.

You can't always get what you want

But if you try sometimes, well you just might find

You get what you need

'Head for the cars!' Chad shouted to his fellow Scot over the sound of Mick Jagger's vocals and was out of the truck before it had settled into place, his eyes darting left and right as he looked for their ambushers, his ears picking up the sound of a descending helicopter too late.

From his left he saw several figures leap from the open doors of a giant helicopter that seemed to have appeared from nowhere, hovering over the black top. Each was just a shadow of darkness with a rifle pointed at him as he ran back towards the stalled traffic.

Without hesitation his pistol came up as he kept moving along the side of the truck. He crabbed sideways as he aimed in on the closest assailant and fired two quick rounds, the sound muffled by the chopper as it climbed back into the sky. He knew he was outnumbered and outgunned but hoped he to at least keep the ambusher's heads down as he hijacked one of the cars behind him. The odds were so overwhelmingly stacked against him but he refused to go quietly.

Gunfire rippled behind him and he heard the distinct noise of sheet metal being peppered and torn. Despite the years of training he was shocked to see it was all happening much faster than he had hoped it would. It was hard to focus as the fear of the situation began to sink in. So he turned and ran.

Coming around the back of the truck he chanced a look to the driver's door. He saw Brad sprawled face down out on the road amidst a pool of blood and shattered glass, one foot caught on the step, his leg up in the air. His pistol lay by his side and the mess in his back showed a multitude of exit wounds.

From around the same front corner of the truck came two of the black-clad figures; one with his rifle pointed at Brad, the other bringing it up to Chad only twenty yards away. Chad fired three shots at him without aiming, his training now worthless under the pressure. The aiming figure opened fire.

It hit him hard in his left shoulder, left chest and stomach and he fell sideways, cracking his elbow on the road. The gun went off in his hand as he hit the ground and it was answered with more automatic gunfire. Chad's body was screaming in pain as momentum rolled him over onto his shredded belly. With his forehead flat on the ground he could feel the cold of the bitumen but it was nothing compared to the searing pain coming from within his stomach and chest. It was as though he had swallowed red hot coals. His legs felt as though they were on fire and his breathing now felt like his chest was in a giant vice.

His body was going numb.

Realising it was over he tried to look past the distant hills to the coast beyond. He just wanted to see his beautiful country one more time, just one lasting vision of his Scotland and her commanding waters to take with him wherever it was he was going.

He tried but couldn't turn his head. His neck muscles wouldn't respond. Heavy coughing bought forth a spattering of frothy blood. His entire vision was that of the road under his nose. The grey pebbled surface of the A77 began to blur and gradually fade to black.

As the sound of the gunfire continued to dissipate away and the area fell into a ghostly post-engagement calmness, Mick still sang on in the background from the radio in the destroyed truck…

You can't always get what you want
You can't always get what you want

It had taken a bit of shuffling around but they had been able to isolate the truck and surround it with the other SAS cars without the terrorists becoming aware. The men in the cars had been told to hold their positions but keep their weapons ready should they need them. The fire truck had also been Andrew's idea; commandeered from the nearest town by a pair of troopers on the ground. A police car blocking the road would have alarmed the terrorists. Unfortunately for the driver and his passenger they had realised the trap a little earlier than hoped. The box-in hadn't quite worked.

There was no going back. It was done now. It had been an intense seconds and now it was all over. He would have preferred to take them alive but the decision to use deadly force is always decided upon by the other side. Well... almost always.

No one from the public had witnessed the shootout which had

been a major priority. They didn't want the other truck, wherever it was, to find out through the media that they had lost their partner. There was still a chance to take them out.

Andrew lowered his still smoking Colt Commando from the passenger he had just dropped. He had gotten halfway to the line of cars, not knowing they were full of armed men which would have killed him just as assuredly. These soldiers were now exiting their cars and approaching the scene to assist. Andrew signalled them to hold position as he and three of his men approached the rear of the truck. Each man had his weapon trained on the rear door as one of them lowered his assault rifle and bought up a pistol-gripped shotgun and aimed it at the heavy padlock. As soon as the padlock was shredded to pieces they threw open the doors, glad to find no threat inside but worried by the contents they did find. Furniture.

Had they just taken out two furniture removalists by mistake?

But removalists don't try to dodge road blocks and they definitely don't shoot back, he thought. There was a chance they were nothing more than criminals in a similar truck to the one they were hunting with a load of stolen furniture in the rear. However, the odds of that happening were slim. If it was, there would be hell to pay. It had been his call and he would take full responsibility for the two deaths.

As calls were put out via the helicopter's radio to the powers that be, he prayed they would find something which linked them to the republican movement.

Sitting in the smoke filled interview room of the Bundeskriminalamt headquarters in Hanover, Dieter Wilhelm Brasch could taste the freedom he and his sister would soon be granted. More importantly he could already feel his sister's embrace.

He had been "arrested" with the other members of his group barely an hour after the Scotsmen had left on their gun-laden trawler. For a while there, he thought the authorities were going to miss their chance, again, at catching them.

So inept sometimes, he thought.

Sipping his coffee he waited for the new group of officials which had just come in to begin with their round of questioning. He hoped these were the ones that were to organise his sister's escape over the wall. He knew they already had enough on his boss, Mark Muller, and that was all he needed to hear. The deal was for his boss's conviction and they had that all sealed up, taking him in an early morning raid on one of his estates just outside the city.

'Just one last thing Dieter,' the detective began. 'Once you do this we can see about getting you and your sister to America.'

'And her husband,' he corrected.

The detective smiled and nodded. 'And her husband.'

Stepping forward to the table was a well dressed gentleman. That was how Brasch saw him, as a gentleman. The way his suit fit him and the command and attention that his presence required was not like the other unshaven and baggy suited men in the room. This worried the now ex-criminal.

'Mr Brasch,' began the suited man in a near perfect German tongue (with a flawlessly inflected Bavarian accent) that had been perfected interrogating senior *Wehrmacht* and *Schutzstaffel* prisoners during the big push of 1944/45. 'My name is Mr Craft. I am a member of Great Britain's Home Security and I believe you can help us.'

The Englishman placed a thick leather folder on the desk in front of them and opened it. Brasch could see it contained hundreds of portraits, mug shots and surveillance photos. He hoped he didn't have to read it.

'The people within this folder are terrorists. Enemies of my country. What I need you to do is identify the ones you have communicated with over the last few months.'

'And then we get my family out.'

Mr Craft's smile was so trusting; again, something that had worked wonders against Hitler's finest.

'It will be the next thing on my list.'

It was around three in the afternoon and Sean could see the seaside village of Campbelltown ahead. He was tired and looking forward to a stiff drink and a shower. He knew he would probably have to settle for a bath but that would do just fine. Although he was getting rather sick of baths.

Why can't these people just have normal fucking showers! Even in Ireland most had baths. Relaxing it might be, but every fucking time?!

Beside him Brigitta slept. She had been going on about getting herself new clothes for winter after discovering a tear in her jacket. Sean, however, wasn't interested in what sort of jackets Jenner's carried for women and had tuned out of her spiel. With her damaged jacket now rolled up as a pillow against the window after declaring she was "just resting my eyes for a while", Sean enjoyed the remainder of the journey in peace.

The countryside they had driven through had been some of the most breathtaking he had ever seen. Colossal mountains either side of them had commanded the sky, the bulk of their mass now covered in snow. A single Scottish mountain would dwarf an entire mountain range back in Australia. Rivers of ice cold water cut their way through valleys of granite forming pools and high waterfalls which cascaded over cliffs further downstream.

It pleased him to see several fishermen out in the rivers, fly-fishing in the near frozen waters for what he guessed were trout. He had never been keen on fishing himself but watching these Scotsmen whip their lines back and forth made him envious for the relaxation they were enjoying.

A holiday would be nice…

Driving across the mountain ranges he kept himself amused by trying to pronounce the tongue-twisting names of the Scottish towns they passed through. Then seeing a town called "Rest and be Thankful" made his mind wander.

Maybe I could go and check out Donegal once I get a chance to get back over there. I still would like to find some family. Maybe I could head down to Galway, look up Megan first…

He chased the dreams from his mind and pushed on.

Once in Kintyre it had been mostly a down-hill run. Traffic was almost non-existent. Pulling into town they found their way to the accommodation they had booked in advance. Sean disabled the truck's engine so it couldn't be stolen and doubled-checked the locks on the rear door before heading into the Seafield Hotel.

FIFTY-THREE

A wave of relief filled Sgt Andrew Wilton as he went over the details that had been uncovered. For once their intelligence had been right. After towing the truck out of the dirt with the fire engine and dragging it a half a mile down a farmers' lane-way and out of sight of the main road, they had gone at the truck with crow bars, prying open every panel and compartment big enough to hide a bullet. It hadn't taken long for one of them to realise the flooring in the storage area was higher than the walls told outside.

'Both men were Scottish,' Captain Fordham told the Australian and Lieutenant Tuckwell as they stood before the impressive amount of arsenal at their feet which was now being photographed. 'Passports are fake but very convincing…top quality. We have photos of them in the file but no names to go with them.'

'And,' the Australian Sergeant joined in, 'nothing on them or in the truck to lead us to the second truck.'

'But we do know how they're getting them over there,' the Captain concluded. 'Tucky, I want every boat big enough to carry a truck this size under surveillance right now. From Glasgow to Liverpool for a week. I'll call up and see about getting us deployed along the coast. Keep them undercover. Anything spotted is to be surveyed only. Don't worry about Major Purvis. I'll talk to him myself.'

'Don't forget Boss,' Andrew said to the captain, 'the other truck isn't necessarily being driven by an Irishman. There's a good chance they may be Scottish.'

Fordham nodded and added, 'Looks like you'll be getting your wish after all. We all may be in Belfast by tomorrow if those guns get across. You may get to chase your Aussie mate just yet, once we're done with these bastards.'

The idea came like a flash. The Australian's brow furrowed as he tried to picture the man he had met in that tiny, hot bar back in Asia behind the wheel of the other truck. Up until then the Australian SAS Sergeant hadn't thought to place another Australian amongst an ASU team working in Britain. He felt a shiver run over him.

'What's up?' asked Lieutenant Tuckwell, noting the change in his sergeant's form.

'Fuck, I would if I was them,' Andrew was saying to himself, lost as he played it out in his head.

'You'd what if you were who?'

Andrew looked up at his two superiors, his brain trying to map out the bizarre web of ideas he had just come up with.

'If you were an IRA commander...' he began, thinking out loud as he thought it through, '...and you had an Australian within your ranks that had a cool head then wouldn't you plant him over here to do this sort of job?' A small grin appeared at the corners of his mouth. 'It fits in with the two Scotsmen. While Special Branch, Customs and Port Security were busy looking for Irishmen, they had the balls to plant an Australian.'

Fordham mulled it over himself and realised the Sergeant had a point.

'It's worth a try,' he agreed, turning to lead them back to the awaiting Pumas. 'I want a team at any port that has checked in a male fitting his description with an Australian passport. If there has been then I'm recommending you join up with our Recon lads over there.'

Climbing down from one of the Pumas, Flight Lieutenant Marshall met the Captain.

'This just came through, sir. Says they've identified all four of the gun runners from an informant in Germany. Two Scots, and English woman and, believe it or not...' he turned to look at Andrew, '...an Australian!'

Captain Fordham grinned back at his own Australian soldier.

'By fuck, you're earning your pay today lad.' He turned back to the pilot. 'You tell those slow bastards we're already two steps ahead of 'em. We know who the Australian is and we're going in to get the prick.'

It had been years since Daniel had felt physically sick. Even now standing on the pier in Baile an Chaisil (Ballycastle) he still felt ill. Twenty four hours ago he had been in Larne, anxious about the first truck's arrival. He had watched vehicles of all sizes disembark from the mouth of the Cairnryan ferry. As the minutes ticked by he could feel a heavy, sickly feeling cultivate in his stomach as he realised the truck driven by Chad and Brad was not on board. He himself had taken the call from Chad in the early hours of yesterday morning. Everything had been on track. It had been going better than they had planned.

However, now they were missing two men and a truck full of guns.

Fearing the worst, Daniel had left one of the other Belfast brigade men in Larne to await an explanatory phone call from Chad (if it came) while he had driven north to Ballycastle to await the arrival of his Australian friend.

He hadn't gotten much sleep last night and tried not to think about all the possible explanations as to why the first truck had not turned up. The night then got worse when he projected those fears onto Sean. What if his friend was arrested? Would they extradite him back to Australia for the murder he had committed over there? Could he be tried for treason against the crown because he was a Commonwealth citizen? Or had they already been mown down by an SAS ambush and were at this moment lying as cold corpses on even colder stainless steel gurneys?

Please be on the ferry.

With his jacket collar pulled up to deny the wind, he smoked anxiously, sucking back deeply as he stared out to the horizon. Even the gulls cawing above him seemed to get on his nerves.

Halfway into his seventh he saw the vessel appear and grow as it cut its way towards him across the choppy waters. The stress was nearly killing him as he impatiently waited, watching it take a lifetime to come in and tie up to the dock. He knew trucks exited first – for time is money to them – and silently waited as they took their time coming down the ramp of the ferry like newborns from a mother's womb.

Then he saw him. Never before had he felt such a weight lift off his shoulders as when he saw Sean's face grinning from over the steering wheel as he drove out of the ship's belly into the morning light. It was the slightest nod of his head but it was all Daniel needed to see. Sean was indicating everything, as far as he knew, was going to plan. For a second Daniel thought that maybe Chad had aborted the Cairnryan ferry and had followed Sean but no truck followed him down the ramp as his was the last to debark.

Once customs were happy that all was in order, Sean followed Daniel's car to the edge of town. Here the two friends finally shook hands.

'Happy New Year,' grinned the Australian.

'I wish it was Sean.' Daniel took in a breath before continuing. 'Have you heard from Chad because he didn't arrive in Larne yesterday?'

Sean thought he was joking. Chad was one of the biggest men he had ever met. Nothing could stop him. The look in Daniel's eye, however, told him he was serious.

'He wasn't there? No mate, we haven't been in contact with him. Could he have missed the boat? It could just be that.'

'We've got a man down there waiting for either a phone call or the next ship across…' he looked at his watch, '…which should be in an hour and a half.'

Sean let out a long breath as he looked across to Brigitta. Both of them thought everything had been going so smoothly. None of them had picked up any surveillance that they knew of and if they *had* gotten him then why not themselves?

'Nah,' he said shaking his head. 'He'll be across. It'll be something so simple we couldn't have accounted for. Mechanical failure or the weather could have closed their port. Ours was pretty rough. He'll be 'right. Two Scots aren't going to raise any eyebrows.'

He watched his Irish friend nod his head but Sean could see his hopes had gone long ago.

'I hope you're right Sean. If you're not though then it means this is the second time we've been jumped. Which means someone within this operation is talking and the Brits could know everything we're doing.'

'If they knew then they would have grabbed us already,' Brigitta stated.

Sean agreed with her. 'Seeing as how they haven't then there's no reason to think otherwise about Chad. He *will* be on the next ferry. You'll see. Anyway, I'm starving! Let's get to a roadhouse. I'm gunna have the full breakfast.'

Daniel nodded before looking at his watch. If they left in half an hour they could be in Larne in time for the next ferry from Cairnryan. Hopefully they would have some good news. If not then it may mean the end of this active service unit.

'How's Max and Melissa doing?' Sean asked interrupting his pessimistic thoughts.

'Ah!' exclaimed Daniel. 'I forgot. You have a visitor back at my place. Someone I'm sure you weren't expecting to see again for a long time.'

'Who?'

Daniel just winked. 'They asked me to keep it a surprise.'

Sean nudged Brigitta. 'He always does this to me.'

Depression set in. No one said much on their trip back into Belfast. They had watched the ship in Larne regurgitate all the vehicles it had taken in at Cairnryan but none of them were Chad's truck. The man who had been left in Larne to await the call said none had come. Unless some miracle occurred, the ASU was definitely over.

They had to assume Chad and Brad were done. Arrested or dead… it didn't matter. They had to assume if the Brits had the Scots then they had their safe-house and possibly even the identities of the remainder of the ASU. All of their gear in their West End townhouse would remain there. It would be suicidal to return and besides, there was nothing there to link them to the IRA. Word would come through of the two Scotsmen but all knew it would be from either the British army or their media.

The man in Larne took command of the Sean's truck and headed south, following Daniel as he drove the couple back to see Padraig. The organiser of the ASU was yet to find out about the possible fate of the first truck and none of them wanted to be there when he did. This was meant to have been Padraig's baby. This was the plan that was going to show the Army Council the type of leader he was.

This was not going to be pretty.

They reached the outskirts of the Northern capital. It had snowed in Belfast the night prior but the white-capped rooftops of the city weren't worthy of the serene Christmas-card scene it erroneously portrayed due to the few heavy black columns of smoke that blemished the purity implied.

Finally sick of the silence, Sean bought up the topic of the bomb making equipment which was now lost.

'Did you know about it?'

'No I didn't.' Daniel's tone was neutral.

'You *do* remember the bomb that nearly killed your little nephew?'

'There's no need to get facetious.'

'What the fuck are we doing bringing shit like that over!'

'Look... they plan to start a bombing campaign against economic and commercial targets. The idea is to cripple the British economy in Belfast. We're not going after people but buildings, infrastructure...'

'This *will kill* innocent people!' Sean snapped. 'You can't believe for a second that only buildings will be targeted. Even if you do this on a weekend when businesses are shut, there are still people around who've nothing to do with this shit. Can't you get that?! You've seen what happens to people anywhere near these things. Your own sister was nearly killed! I'm not in this to help you bring in weapons which could just as likely kill me or you if we happened to be in the wrong place at the wrong time. Rifles are what wars like this are fought with! Not bombs!'

'For fuck sake Sean!' Brigitta piped up from the back seat. 'Do you even know what…'

'SHUT UP!!!' he bellowed back at her, his finger pointing at her face. Both Brigitta and Daniel jumped at the unexpected outburst. Sean had finally snapped from the tension. 'YOU SHUT THE FUCK UP! I'M TALKING TO HIM, NOT YOU?!' He held her blushed gaze in silence until she turned her eyes away, unable to face him any longer. For ten long seconds he glared at her, daring her to look back at him before finally turning back to Daniel in the driver's seat.

'I don't want to fight this way Daniel.' Sean's tone was calmer now, almost sympathetic. 'This isn't being a soldier. You know they call us terrorists the world over? This is going to cement that image in their minds for generations to come. You won't be seen as rebels or freedom fighters any more.' He tried to look into Daniel's eyes but the Irishman kept them on the road ahead.

Because of how Sean had reacted to the bombing in Mid Falls, Daniel had feared the Australian finding out about the upcoming bombing campaign of both Northern Ireland and the British mainland. The load of detonators and time triggers that had been in Chad's truck was to have been trialled first in the financial district of North Belfast in the coming weeks. The outcomes of the trials would have been valuable lessons for the bomb makers to take into police stations, army barracks and the heart of the Empire itself.

'There's not many left that do see us that way Sean. Other than ourselves.'

Despite turning deathly grey, Padraig took the bad news better than they had anticipated. Not that he welcomed it at all but he did think long and hard after listening to all Daniel and Sean had to say.

Brigitta had said nothing. She just sat at the end of the table, her small travel bag by her feet and her mind set on returning to organise another active service unit. She knew Sean would not be included. Not if she had anything to say about it.

'If they *have* been caught,' Padraig mumbled with his eyes shut, the colour returning to his round face, 'then this whole operation will have to start again. New members, new house…we'll need more money for that. Christ, we still have another shipment to pick up!'

'Not if it contains bomb material,' Sean declared calmly.

Padraig opened his eyes at the young Australian across the table.

'What's that?'

'If you're bringing in stuff to blow up civilians with then you can count me out. I'll go back to guarding intersections with a .303. Fuck, I'll walk the streets with Jim Bryson if I have to.'

This, more than anything, had surprised Padraig. He had personally pushed for Sean to be involved because of his professionalism. He had assured the bosses he would see things their way, but now Sean was getting all judgmental on him?

'Sean, this war is going to change soon. There's no need to get all high and mighty…'

The Australian held up his hand to silence him.

'I don't care Padraig. I'll bring in every rifle on earth if you could buy them. But I will never smuggle in bombs to blow the arms and legs off of some kids playing nearby. That's the end of it.'

Daniel had half expected him to snap like he had in the car, but he didn't. He watched him pull the gold wedding ring off of his finger and place it on the table.

Nodding to Padraig, Sean rose, turning to Brigitta.

'Sorry I bit your head off.' Then he walked out the door.

'What the fuck Danny?!' Padraig barked once Sean had gone. 'How did it all fall apart so fucking quickly?!'

Daniel wasn't sure if he was talking about the loss of two more ASU men or the change in Sean's mindset. He could see Padraig wasn't in the mood to be clarifying which, so Daniel took a stab.

'Someone who knows must have talked.'

'There's not many that *do* know, son.'

'It only takes one,' he retorted, not liking Padraig's implicating tone.

Padraig rubbed his eyes and kept his hands over them as he breathed in slowly. The Army Council was going to shit glass when they found out, if they didn't know already. He got up and walked over to his lounge room window to look out across the rooftops down into the city in the distance. Between the taller buildings of the city centre and the sea beyond, the two giant yellow gantry cranes of the Harland & Wolff ship yards stood out against the dreary urban colours surrounding them. The Titanic had been born there nearly sixty years before when it had been the most productive shipyard in the world and despite the luxury cruiser's tragic sinking it had been the greatest thing to come out of his city. The shipyards were also where, as a teenager, Padraig's knowledge of sectarianism had been unfurled. At the age of fifteen he had approached their offices with the hope of securing a job, any job, within. At first the tall solidly built foreman seemed to begin to nod as though he was thinking of a position fitting for the stocky but strong young lad before him. Then the man asked for his name. The naïve fifteen year old temporarily forgot that in Northern Ireland your religion dictates your job.

At first the man stared at him like he had spoken with an alien tongue. Then he began to laugh; a laughter which rolled into a fit of hysterics and tears. Padraig smiled along with the unknown joke and waited uncomfortably for the man to explain what was so funny. The foreman however turned and bought someone else into the joke, the two of them laughing and pointing at Padraig. It was the first and last time anyone ever called him a Taig, the derogatory name for a Catholic Irishman.

He ran from the shipyards in shame and tears, the foul word repeating in his head over and over. He could not understand why a Catholic would not be allowed to work there. But over the years he saw the hatred played out onto his people and understood that the only way to communicate with men like the Harland & Wolff foreman was through violence.

The knot in his stomach seemed to get worse as he recalled the birth of his hatred for the unionist. For so long he had planned to hit them so hard it would be heard the world over. And now this Australian, that little prick whom he had helped evade the law in Galway, whom he had given the greatest opportunity by striking a blow for a united Ireland, was quitting?! Months of planning had gone to waste because this colonial bastard had gone moral on him right when he was so close to achieving the goal of a life time!

You don't quit on me you fuck! YOU FUCK!!

Both Daniel and Brigitta sat in silence, not wanting to interrupt a man in mourning at the death of his great scheme. They saw him take a deep breath and nod to himself. Crossing the room to his phone, Padraig made a quick call, summoning a runner.

'Ted will be here in a minute,' he said looking at Brigitta. He seemed calmer. 'He'll get you to a boat for home.'

'I'm sorry Padraig,' she said in her English accent. 'I thought Sean would have been stronger than this.'

He just shrugged his shoulders, holding his rage.

'We will be organising another team won't we?' she asked. 'I mean, we still have guns to bring across…'

Padraig shook his head. 'It took a lot of convincing from me to put you lot in and look at how that turned out. Granted we did get a lot of guns in but they won't see this as a sacrifice. In their eyes it'll be a fuck up they'll deny once word gets out. They don't want the Brits knowing that we are building ourselves up. No... I doubt they'll let me in charge of a bunch of snot-nosed Fianna na hEireann kids when it's all over.' A knock came from the door and Padraig's runner Ted entered. 'You take care over there,' Padraig said as he shook hands with Brigitta.

The female soldier smiled back.

'Please let me know when I can be of use again. Goodbye.' She picked up her bag, turned and left with Ted.

'So when do you go and see the Council?' Daniel asked when they were alone.

Padraig sighed. The Brits had gotten their hands on the much needed electronics *and* the Russian .50 cal they were hoping for. He knew the Army Council would tear strips off him.

'I guess the sooner the better. I know Joe Cahill will be happy. He was against sending Sean over in the first place…'

Suddenly there was a hurried staccato of rapping on the front door before it flew open. It was Donnie.

'What's wrong with you lad?' Padraig demanded with his normal harsh tone.

Donnie fought for breath before delivering the news they all knew would come one day.

'We just found out through our intelligence sources. It was the SAS. They killed your two Scotsmen.'

Padraig nodded, knowing it had be them. Just like Scotland last year. Someone had definitely talked. One of these two. At that moment Sean seemed like the obvious one but there was a niggling feeling that Brigitta may have turned. Had she taken the Crown's gold? She seemed too calm. Too calm...

So Brigitta's first.

Although it allowed him to accept his rash decision, he knew he would not sleep tonight. Not until he had made sure that those involved would never destroy his plans again. Just as the Titanic had been the greatest thing to come out of Belfast, Padraig was determined to be the greatest republican leader ever to set foot in the northern capital. The Army Council would understand and see his loyalty was with the cause. They would see that he could take the responsibilities of a true leader.

He looked at Daniel and hoped he would understand when it was all over. It was nothing personal, just a utilitarian decision leaders sometimes had to make.

The cold winter's air rubbed at Sean's ears as he walked the few blocks back to Daniel's. Looking around the streets, parks and lane-ways he could see nothing had changed since he was here last, other than fewer people being outside. He hoped Melissa was at home. He didn't want to have to wait outside for Daniel to come home. With the way he had just talked to his Irish friend that could be hours away just out of spite. Then he remembered there were people there waiting for him.

To keep warm he jogged up the flight of stairs with his hands in his jacket pockets and headed for Daniel's front door. He could hear Max playing inside. Hearing his voice made him realise how much he had missed playing with the little fella. As he reached for the door handle he could hear Mel's sweet voice as she entertained this surprise. Then he heard the other person's voice as he turned the handle. Daniel was right; he had never expected to hear that voice again.

'Sean's home!' Max screamed as he scrambled to his feet, tripping over the toy truck Sean had given him as he rushed to hug him.

Squatting down, he caught the little man in a great bear hug and laughed with him.

'Yeah mate, I'm home now. How was your Christmas? I see you got my present!'

'Yeah! And the ball! Do you want to go and kick it? Mum can we go outside and kick the football?'

'Not now love,' she said as she stepped forward, hugging Sean herself. 'Welcome back Sean. Thank you for my gift. It was beautiful. I hope everything went well over there.'

'Things could have been worse,' he said as he kissed her cheek. 'They're better now I'm back here.'

'You have a visitor,' Melissa declared as she let him go.

'I can see,' he said with a smile he couldn't wipe off. 'Didn't think I'd see you again for a while.'

Megan O'Brien moved into his arms and hugged him tightly.

'Didn't forget me, did you?'

Her voice and her embrace took him back to the summer night in South Armagh. He honestly never thought he would see her again and now he was here holding her. It wasn't fair for a woman to make him feel this way all over again. The first time he held Anna after returning from war was so similar. He knew the feelings inside him now shouldn't be, but how do you convince yourself you're not falling in love again.

'I couldn't if I tried,' he whispered to her. Bringing his hands up to her cheeks, he held her stunning face for a second, looking into her eyes before kissing her hard on the lips.

He was glad she kissed back just as hard.

Taking her cue, Melissa grabbed two jackets and, with Max's hand in hers, she dragged the wide eyed boy outside.

'We're just going down to see Wendy for a while.'

As soon as the door had shut behind them Sean was lifting Megan up in his arms and moving her over against the wall. His body pressed into hers as they kissed passionately

'Why did you leave?' he said into her mouth as their lips parted briefly.

This time her hands found his face and held him back, just inches away from each other.

'I don't know…' she finally breathed.

The colour and clarity of her blue eyes seemed so much more vibrant than they had all those months ago. He never thought he would ever get to look into them again. She moved in slightly, her mouth open but still out of his reach.

'…but I'm here now.'

Their lips met hard again as their tongues brushed against each other. Reaching down to her backside, Sean pulled her pelvis tightly into his.

She had missed him as well. It was all she had been able to think about over the last few months. He came to her dreams almost nightly and distracted her when she was awake. Her closest friends could tell she had met a man whilst in Dublin but she had not revealed a thing to anyone. All winter she had ached to be with him again, angry at herself for treating him the way she did, both before and after she had slept with him. When she had returned home she tried to convince herself it wasn't anything, but the more she dwelled on it the more she knew she had to see him again. She had to know if he felt the same way about her. If he didn't then she would leave him alone.

She could tell he did.

She gasped as Sean's cold hand slid its way up under her shirt, his fingers like ice against her skin. She bit his bottom lip softly as he cupped her breast in his coarse cold hand.

Feeling himself growing harder still, Sean's hands moved around to her back and lifted her free of the ground once more. Not wasting anymore time, he moved them to Daniel's bedroom, shutting the door behind them.

Ted, the quietest of all Padraig's "muscle", had told Brigitta the last boat to Liverpool was in half an hour and she had plenty of time. Taking a peripheral glance at the young girl beside him, he knew it was a waste of a fine body and wished he had more time to have a bit of fun with her before the court martial began. It was freezing out and he didn't particularly feel like raping her on the cold back seat of his cramped little car. He contemplated getting something bigger so if a situation like this arose again he could take his time in comfort.

Maybe a Rover. Or a Jag. They have big back seats. Nah, they're too expensive.

He took a left and pulled up outside an alley behind one of the pubs. Brigitta was just about to ask what was going on when her door was opened and she was pulled suddenly from the car by two men. Before she had a chance to scream she was hit hard in the stomach and all the wind was knocked from her. Her knees buckled as she struggled to breathe through the pain but she was held upright and thoroughly frisked, her handgun taken from her. She was thrown back into the rear of Ted's car and bookended by the two men before her shoes were removed.

Ted pulled back out onto the street and headed toward the burnt out warehouse they used for court martials. But he wasn't thinking about the hours of torture that would be inflicted on her. That wasn't his job. His would be to question the tout bitch and then dispatch of her. But he was not thinking of that either. Instead, he was wondered if he would be the one sent to make sure the Australian was seen to. He would welcome that challenge.

PART FIVE

"What ill-starr'd rage
Divides a friendship long confirm'd by age?"

Alexander Pope

FIFTY-FOUR

Belfast had as much charm as a hung-over whore with the shit kicked out of her. At least that was how Trooper Owens had described it when Andrew Wilton arrived at the debriefing room a day ago. The Australian thought it an unfair assessment but he had only just arrived so reserved his own judgement for later. Right now all he cared about was locating the other Australian soldier in Belfast.

Had they pushed their search in Scotland further north than they had when looking for the second truck then they may have caught them red handed. They had discovered an Australian man and an English woman had passed through the town of Campbelltown on the Kintyre peninsula. Major Purvis had near blown a gasket when he heard about how close they had come to stopping the guns going in. Plus they had no idea how many detonators had been in the second truck. Guns they could deal with but not bombs.

The order had been given; find this IRA active service unit no matter what the cost.

Now dressed in his civvies, Andrew sat beside Owens as they drove the streets of the deadly city in an armoured-plated Vauxhall in the darkening afternoon light. Down beside both of them, out of sight, were their primary weapons, their Colt Commando carbines; each able to be brought to bear in a second flat. They also carried on their person a Browning Hi-Power 9mm pistol tucked into the front waist band of their pants.

With the heater going hard they battled the condensation inside as they traversed in and out of streets along the edge of The Falls.

'Been through Ballymurphy yet?' asked the newcomer.

'Yep,' replied Owens. 'It certainly has an atmosphere about it. The locals call it the Murph for short. You can feel thousands of eyes on you as soon as you turn in there. Makes you wonder if they know who's in every car.'

The Australian looked at the time. Soon it would be too dark to take in detail. They weren't out here to pick anyone up; Andrew just wanted to get the "lay of the land" as it were before going in the next morning.

'The other bloke in the photo with this Sean Doherty; do we know who he is?'

Having memorised every name in the file, Owey pictured in his mind the photo in question. Doherty was shaking hands with Sean MacStiofain. The other young man in the photo they believed to be one Daniel Carragher but it hadn't been confirmed as Owens explained it to the Sergeant by his side.

'And we're not yet sure where he lives. Somewhere in the Murph. He's not rated highly on the list so they haven't bothered tracking him down yet.'

'He's standing next to the IRA's head man!' the Sergeant exclaimed. 'He's obviously got to be someone more than just a go-fer. Whose decision was that?'

'That's the problem with this fucking job. We answer to the Army over here and their Intelligence is calling the shots.'

'Yeah, well fuck that. We need to start acting on our own initiative and instinct. Fuck 'em if they see things differently. We need results. You feel like a beer?'

Owens was stunned at the change of topic, not liking the sound of the idea.

'Why?'

'Take us to a republican bar.'

The Private felt his stomach tighten. This sounded like suicide.

'Are you fucking mad, Wilto? We wouldn't last five minutes in there!'

'Maybe not you with your King's English, but I bet I can with my inflection.'

Walking in to Collins' Bar just off Falls Road, Luke Kennedy and Grant Brooks could feel the room look them over in an instant. This was only the fourth pub they had been into today. Having arrived in Belfast the night before, they had been too tired to go searching, opting to bed down for the night at a hotel in a quieter part of the city in the south.

The other three pubs had given them the same reception but had ignored them as the time passed, with no one offering any conversation. Luke spoke to the publicans of each pub. He had known Sean longer and the pictures he carried with him proved they had been mates their whole lives. Knowing he was looking for someone who would probably be protected around here, he chose his words carefully and was always ready to leave straight away should the attitude of the barmen or the crowd become obvious that they were not welcome.

So far nobody knew of Sean. Or so they had said. He thought the last publican had changed demeanour at the mention of Sean's name. When Luke presented the photos the man lost interest and went back to serving his other customers. They obviously knew but no one was talking. Taking the cue to get out, they had moved on to Collins' Bar.

After serving the two men the publican asked them, 'So where you boys be from?'

'We're from Australia,' Luke began. 'A town called Newcastle, just north of Sydney.'

'Australians hey!' he said with seemingly genuine surprise. 'So what brings you to Belfast lads? I hope your tourist bureau didn't sell you a ticket here because you got cheated if you did!' He chuckled at his own joke.

Seeing the fat man was in such a positive mood, Luke decided to ask straight away instead of trying to build up a rapport as he had tried at the other pubs.

'We're trying to locate a friend of ours,' he explained as he pulled one of the many photos from his jacket pocket. He placed it down on the bar and pointed to Sean. 'This is me and my best mate. His name is...'

'Sean,' cut in the publican. 'Sean Doherty.'

'You know him?' questioned Grant, his eyes lighting up.

'Not as well as the two men standing behind you.'

The Australians turned and saw two men positioned closely behind. One was tall and lanky, the other just as tall but bulked up with muscle. Each wore a jacket that barely covered the pistols hidden in their belts. Both were looking dangerous right about then.

'Been following you for an hour since you left Robinsons,' explained the publican.

'You boys want to come and have a seat with us.' the tall one stated, not asked. He made to move but saw the look of unease on the Australian's faces. Both were still weighing up the situation; seeing if they were in any danger.

'It's fine,' the tall one said and motioned to an empty table on the other side of the crowded room. 'I know Sean.'

Sitting down at the table Luke and Grant could feel every eye in the room drilling into them. The tall one held out his hand.

'I'm Kieran, this is Liam.'

'Luke Kennedy.'

'Grant Brooks.'

Both of them still didn't know where they stood.

Two pints arrived for the Irishmen and Luke tried to remember if they had even ordered any. Then he was wondering why he cared. Right at that moment he was scared shitless.

'So Luke Kennedy and Grant Brooks,' Kieran said with a grin. 'How do you know Sean?'

Walking back to his house, Daniel felt uncomfortable at the tone of questioning Padraig had delivered at him. After knowing the older Irishmen for so long it surprised him the way he had insinuated that

Sean had something to do with the failure of his beloved ASU. The more Padraig went on the more stupid Daniel thought it sounded. He knew Padraig was upset but to imply that Sean was responsible was stupid…wasn't it?

Stop thinking like Padraig, he ordered himself. The days of being jealous were over.

He chuckled to himself. If there was anything to be jealous about it was the amazingly gorgeous woman that had been waiting back at his house for his mate. He wished he could have been there when Sean saw her again but knew he would have only been in the way.

As soon as she had turned up at his door two days before he knew whatever had happened between them down at the border had made the girl mad for Sean. He could see it in her eyes when he told her he was working out of town for a while. When he said he was due to visit soon she almost begged to stay until he returned.

The lucky fucker.

He stopped walking and thought about where to go instead of home. He didn't want to walk in on them tangled together. Mel had said she would give them some time alone and he hoped they weren't doing anything on his bed. If they were doing what he thought they would be doing then he had a few hours to kill.

He considered going to one of the illegal drinking halls but didn't relish the thought of running into Bryson again. Collin's Bar wasn't too far away so he set off around the cemetery. It wasn't closer than the shebeen but better a crowded bar than one with that mad man and his Lewis gun.

Kieran and Liam kept the two Australians entertained as they talked about their mutual friend. They had to be sure these two were authentic before they made any move to reunite them with their long lost mate.

Luke told them of his childhood growing up with one of the toughest kids in the suburb while Grant told them unbelievable accounts of his time in Vietnam with him. One topic Sean had remained quiet about (at least with them) was some of the things he had encountered in that war and it had genuinely enthralled Kieran and Liam.

As Luke sipped at the red beer he had been handed by Kieran, he wondered if his mate was near. Was he even possibly watching this meeting take place, curious to see who was asking for him all over town?

Where are you Sean? We need a translator. I can't understand half the things these blokes are saying!

Growing more relaxed as time went on, Luke felt more at home sitting here in the packed pub. It was not unlike the Lass O'Gowrie on a busy Friday or Saturday night. Except for the four piece band by the end of the bar which was filling the room with inspiring folk music, it could have been the same pub.

Grant on the other hand was thinking about what these men did as a profession. As someone not of the Catholic faith he was more concerned with them getting down to details and finding out he was not one of them. He knew they were men that used force to get their way and several times during their seemingly jovial drinks did he feel somewhat uneasy. At one point he felt the hairs on the back of his neck stand up. Last year he had trusted that instinct with his life but here he wasn't sure how he would fare.

Both of their Irish "hosts" noted the arrival of one of their own.

Standing at the bar, Daniel ordered a pint of Guinness. As the publican placed it down in front of him he nodded towards the table across the room.

'See the two with Kieran and Liam?'

Turning to see the mentioned table, Daniel could tell straight away they didn't belong. Not only were they clothed differently but the way they held themselves was completely dissimilar to everyone else in the pub. These people were definitely from out of town. Fuck, they were from out of the country!

'Who are they?' he enquired with genuine interest.

'Believe it or not, they're friends of Sean Doherty.'

Daniel was stunned and his mouth almost dropped open.

'What the fuck are they doing here? How did they track him down?'

The publican just shrugged.

'Going from pub to pub. Lucky they haven't gotten themselves killed!'

Daniel shook his head in disbelief.

'Fuck, when it rains it pours.'

'What's that?'

'Nothing. *Sláinte.*'

Before going over to them he stopped by the ceili band and put in a request for the next song. It would be a little surprise for the Australians; sort of a welcome song from him. Patting the fiddle player on the shoulder he walked around the room as he took in the faces of the two friends of Sean from afar, putting Luke's face into the many stories Sean had told him. He was different than he had imagined. He certainly looked like he could pull the ladies as Sean had declared of him.

A worrying thought suddenly hit him. *Would Sean leave with these two? Would they persuade him back to his homeland, somehow making him feel homesick?*

Daniel knew Sean was certainly disheartened enough. It would only add fuel to Padraig's paranoia if he did leave.

Behind him the band finished their rendition of *The Wearing O' The Green* as the crowd clapped and whistled. He sipped his pint once more unaware of the new man which had come in off the street, this one looking as though he did belong.

The Australian SAS Sergeant forced himself to remain as calm as possible as he weaved past the rock-filled oil drum barricade and entered Collins' Bar; one of the most dangerous places for a member of the British Armed Forces to be in. He knew going in alone was not how the SAS did things but one man would not cause as much suspicion and he needed Owey ready to cover his exit and be ready to roll. He also knew that every person in the pub, male and female, could be a member of the IRA. He knew he was an unfamiliar face in a place where everybody knew the next man.

He prayed being Australian would be his ticket to remaining alive.

Approaching the bar he saw that not too many people payed him any attention. He was dressed exactly the same as every person under thirty in the bar with jeans, a denim jacket, hair too long to be a soldiers and two healthy side burns that ran almost to his jaw from under his woollen beanie.

As he waited for the barman to serve him he cast his eye over the crowd, trying to see if Sean Doherty was here or not. He doubted the fugitive Australian would recognise him in his current guise but leant on the bar anyway as he tried to hide his face by resting his chin in his hand, his fingers stroking his stubbled top lip.

What if he is in here? he thought. *Do I talk to him?*

There was still a part of him that believed if he sat down with Doherty and told him what the Brits had in store for him then he may just disappear on his own accord. The fact they were both Australian and had both served in the same war did bring forth some feelings of patriotism.

In the end he's made a choice just as I have. Nobody forced him into this.

He stayed close to the door, knowing that Owey was outside with the car idling over with the Colt Commando in his grasp but out of sight. At a full sprint he reasoned he could be back in the car in less than five seconds.

If five seconds was enough time.

Straight away he recognised at least seven people from the files he had studied over the previous day but no Australian. There was no way he would do something as stupid as act on it. At this stage all he wanted was to find out, if he could, if Sean Doherty was in town.

The barman came his way.

'You right lad?'

'Just a pint of Red thanks mate,' Andrew said in his own accent.

Hearing the client's inflection but not reacting, the publican began pulling the pint, thinking, *three Australians in here in under an hour is a bit too much of a coincidence and this one wasn't at the last couple of pubs with those other two.*

As the beer flowed into the glass he searched for Daniel and hoped to get his attention. He turned to a patron sitting further down the bar and quietly asked in Irish, '*Feighany, a fháil Danny. Go ciúin.*'

Paul Feighan, one of the regulars, scanned the crowd, and calmly set off to get Danny.

'I know every accent that this island has ever produced,' the publican said as he topped off the head of beer and bought it over. 'And that's not one of them son. Where be you from?'

'Australia mate. Cheers.'

Taking the money back to the till, the publican looked around for Daniel.

Danny, where are you! Something's going on.

Andrew placed his beer on the bar and turned to face the band. He could see the crowd was relaxed, primed by their grog and enjoying inspirational and therefore dangerous music. As he listened to the band carrying out a quick tune up of their fiddle and banjo, he allowed himself a moment to relax. It had been a long day; first in the intelligence centre listening to information which may or may not have been true. Then the boring city tour with Owey looking for a man who may not even be here.

As he took his first gulp of bitter he was suddenly aware of someone standing next to him. Trying not to look like he cared, Andrew turned his head slightly and noted a young man drinking next to him.

'Fockin great band hey!' the Irish local said. 'Me uncle plays the fiddle did ye know?'

Andrew thought about ignoring the drunk but then realised he could use it to his advantage in locating the wayward Australian. 'Yeah mate. You never hear bands like this where I'm from.'

The drunken Irishman cocked an eyebrow. 'Yeah? Where might that be then?'

'I'm from Australia.' *C'mon mate, spill your guts.* 'This is my first time in Belfast.'

Placing his empty pint down on the bar, the Irishman took a step back. 'Get the fock outta here! I know an Australian!'

Andrew smiled internally.

'What's his name?' he asked the drunk in a casual tone, turning to face the Irishman for the first time. For a brief moment he saw the young man cast his eye across the room as though he was looking for someone. Something wasn't right, thought the SAS sergeant, his instincts beginning to kick in. Years of on the job training told him to beware.

Behind him in the corner, the fiddler introduced the song.

'This one's for our guests from half way 'round the world.'

It was an up-tempo tune that was as recognisable as the man beside him was suspicious. As the lyrics of the song raised above the din of the crowd, Andrew felt his stomach drop.

'Once a jolly swagman camped by a billabong,
Under the shade of a Coolibah tree,
And he sang as he watched and waited for his billy t' boil,
"Who'll come a waltzing Matilda with me?"'

Hairs stood up on the back of the Australian's neck. He looked into the drunk's eyes and suddenly realised he wasn't drunk at all.

'His name's Ned Kelly,' the Irishman continued. 'Maybe you know him. Betrayed by his own country. Betrayed by the crown…'

Andrew recognised him too late. He took two steps back as he went for his pistol, realising the man he had been talking to was Daniel Carragher. His plan now was to cover himself as he got the fuck out of there as fast as he could. Reefing his shirt up high, he pulled his Browning clear of his belt and was bringing it up but saw at least three others had beaten him to the punch and were drawing their own pistols. He knew he could have his gun out, aimed and be firing in under a second so they had obviously been watching him. He felt so stupid for getting made so soon.

As he moved backwards towards the door, both his pistol and another from somewhere on his right fired at the same time.

FIFTY-FIVE

'Have you thought about what you're going to do?' Megan asked Sean. 'I mean, have you thought about living here for good?'

They were lying on the top of Daniel's bed amidst a pile of their own clothes. There hadn't been time for them to get under the blankets. Both were naked and still wrapped around each other's clammy body.

'Here with Daniel?'

She brushed his fringe out of his eyes.

'No I mean Belfast. Are you going to get a flat of your own or will you move to somewhere not so crazy.'

'Like Galway?' he smiled. 'Become a herring gutter?'

'That's Donegal. I'm not saying Galway, but there are other places you could be where it's not so dangerous. Maybe Dublin?'

'Are you worried something might happen to me?' He felt flattered that someone cared for him.

'Yes,' Megan said bluntly. The time for jokes was over.

As she looked into his eyes she knew she didn't want to waste anymore time. The last few months had been heart achingly terrible for her. While it had taken her a while to admit it to herself, she loved this man with every ounce of her soul. It had never hit her so hard before. Yes, there had been other boyfriends before but never someone like this. It was a feeling of joy so complete that nothing else in the world mattered. For the first time in her life she was experiencing true love. Sure, she knew it sounded corny but she couldn't care less; she loved Sean Doherty and she wanted to tell him before the weight of the words crushed her.

'I love you Sean.'

Sean felt his entire body flutter as she it. He hadn't been expecting her to say something like that so soon, but was glad that she had, because he felt the words build up from within him and before he knew it he had said the same.

'I love you too.'

Her arms around him griped tighter and she kissed him hard. His hands spread wide on her back and pulled her in tighter still. After a minute without a breath they stopped and looked deep into each others eyes once more, each knowing their lives would intimately involve each other from now on.

Smiling as he looked at this beautiful creature which had just declared herself his, he thought about their future. Would they stay in Belfast or would he follow her back to Galway? The last few days had thrown a lot of doubt at him so maybe living in the republic wasn't going to be that bad.

Do I still want to be a member of the IRA? He knew she was so much more committed to the cause than he was now. *But I don't want to turn my back on these people…*

He touched her soft cheek with his fingertips, gently stroking it as he pondered what was to come. He had come so far and endured so much to finally meet the love most never find.

Remember when you just wanted to go to Donegal?

'So now what do we do?'

As soon as he heard the first gun shots, Trooper Owens was moving the car forward towards the door knowing his partner would be the first out. After three more muffled reports from inside the pub the door flew open and he saw Wilto backing out fast, gliding past the barrier of oil drum bollards. Once he was out of Owey's line of sight, the younger SAS man bought up his Colt Commando and rested it on the door frame, the barrel sticking out of the open window.

Andrew ran across the street as fast as he could run and threw himself in through the opened door. 'GO, GO, GO!' he screamed at Owey.

The tyres squealed on the cold road surface as he launched the sedan down the road. Training the rifle towards the door of the pub as they drove past, Owey saw it open and two pistol waving figures appeared in the frame. Not having time to aim it perfectly he let rip with two long bursts of fully automatic fire. Impulsively the two silhouetted IRA men ducked as the car disappeared down the street.

'Fuck me Sarge!' Owens exclaimed as he placed the rifle back down by his side so he could control the car better. 'What the fuck happened? You weren't in there five minutes and you come out guns blazing?'

'They made me before I opened my mouth. Met Daniel Carragher though. Nice bloke. Tried to shoot me.' He held onto the dash as Owens slid the car around a corner. 'No choice but to take out some of them and shoot my way out.'

'Did you kill him?'

'No I don't think so, but I'm pretty sure I killed his mate.'

'You've only just arrived in Belfast and already you go to war! Doherty? Was he in there?'

'Nup. He's somewhere around here though. I can tell. Come on. Let's get the fuck out of here.'

Daniel and Liam carried Kieran's lifeless body out of the main bar and placed him onto the back seat of a waiting car. They didn't have long before the place would be full of English soldiers.

Kieran had gotten off the first shot but they were unsure if the SAS man (there was no other explanation for who he could be) had been hit. Unfortunately Kieran had taken two rounds centre chest and had died within a minute. Paul Feighan, the regular at the pub and not a member of the IRA, had also been hit. He was being rushed to the hospital with gunshot wound to his right hip, an injury caused not by the SAS man but by a wayward shot as Kieran fell.

As they watched the car speed off, Daniel allowed himself a

brief moment to think about the young volunteer's family. This would devastate Kieran's mother. It was almost three years since his brother had been killed. Now the family had another son to bury.

The pub was empty. Everyone had taken off and headed for home; all excluding the two Australian friends of Sean who stood around in shock, waiting for a chance to talk to Daniel.

'I guess you two had better come with me,' he said as he walked past them. 'I'll take you to Sean.'

They followed quietly through the cold night. Behind them they could hear the sounds of garbage can lids and saucepans hammering on the ground announcing the imminent arrival of the armoured vehicles out the front of the pub. Daniel knew the soldiers they carried would be spilling out into the street and creating a cordon around the area. He had studied their deployment so many times he was sure he could have done their job better than most of them. Somewhere else behind them they could all hear the sounds of yet another riot beginning. Not even the cold could keep hatred indoors.

They wound their way through the maze of alleys and cul-de-sacs, crossed through the dark cemetery and up the road into Daniel's neighbourhood. The previous days' snow had all but vanished and the ground under them was wet and soft from the thaw of the day. Each trudged on quietly through the small puddles of mud. Neither of the two behind Daniel said a word when they passed two men standing at an intersection in the shadow of a dead street lamp; one was armed with an AK47, the other with an M16. Luke looked across at Grant. Both knew what the other was thinking; if they hadn't been in this Irishman's company then they would probably be just as dead as young Kieran back there.

Far off in the distance there came the sound of rifle fire. Grant knew it was the British. The sound of an SLR had been tattooed onto his brain many times over.

Suddenly Daniel stopped. Looking ahead of them he saw Jim Bryson come out from a narrow laneway. He was rugged up in a heavy jumper and carrying his infamous Lewis machine gun. He made a beeline straight for Daniel.

Fuck, not now Bryson!

'Are the Brits down on Falls Road?' he demanded as he stormed in towards them.

Daniel could see the rage in his eyes. He was after a fight.

'I'd say Collins' Bar is surrounded by them right now,' he conceded.

'Is it true? They kill the young Hough lad?'

'Killed him they did. There was some bastard undercover in there. He pulled a pistol and got Kieran before we could stop him.'

Bryson spat. 'Fuckers.'

Daniel began leading the others up the road when Bryson called back out to him.

'Hey Danny!'

The younger Irishman stopped and turned.

'That Australian bastard…'

Christ Jim, just let it go, Daniel almost said out loud.

'…tell him he did good…with the guns.' Bryson didn't wait for a reply and turned and ran off in the direction of the Brits.

If it wasn't for the grave atmosphere, Daniel would have cracked a smile. He turned and looked at Luke and Grant. He could tell they were both feeling lost and even more uncomfortable with everything which had happened and was still happening.

'Not far now.'

After a further five minutes Daniel opened his front door and saw that his sister and nephew were home. Max was watching TV and his mother held a cup of tea in both hands. The expression on her face told him she already knew about Kieran. Sitting with her at the table were Sean and Megan. Sean looked up and was about to ask how it had happened when he saw the two behind Danny come walk in. It took several seconds for their faces to register with him.

As Luke and Grant stepped into the warm flat they were shocked at the appearance of their friend. His long hair and short stubbly beard threw them off for a second but the brightness of his eyes would never belie his identity.

Sean stood and walked over to them in silence. He looked at Luke then Grant. For a long while his brain scrambled the mixed images of his past meshing with his present. A flood of memories flashed by in an instant and he didn't know if he was in Belfast, Newcastle or Nui Dat. For a second he was taken back to his last nightmare.

'Luke? What the fuck are you doing here?' The question sounded harsh, like they were unwanted but that wasn't his intention. He just couldn't believe they had tracked him down.

'Sean?' Luke began. 'I…what are…?' He couldn't bring the words he was feeling to the surface. He had never believed he could feel so lost. So he stepped forward with his arms out and grabbed his best mate, hugging him. Luke tried not to cry as he felt Sean hug him back.

With his face turned away from everyone bar Grant, only Sean's fellow ex-serviceman saw the tears roll down his face in silence. Quiet with embarrassment, no one spoke for almost a minute as they held each other. Finally Sean pulled away and held him out at arms length.

'How did you find me?'

'You're picture was in the paper!' he said, unable to hold back a laugh.

'My picture?'

'You carrying a little boy from a bomb sight.'

He remembered. Many times he had thought about the little boy and wondered how he was doing now. He let Luke go and stepped over to Grant and hugged him.

'Brooksy. It's good to see you brother.'

'You too Spud.'

'Good to see you got out of there alive.' He looked into Grant's eyes to make sure it was him. 'What about everyone else? They all come home okay?'

'Sergeant Lynch copped a land mine a week after you left. Lost a leg and his genitals. But other than that we all came home.' He didn't have to add none of them were okay.

'Fuck. Steve hey?' He shook his head as he pictured his blasphemous Sergeant. *Poor bastard.* 'So how did you get dragged into this?' he asked.

Grant half grinned. 'Long story mate.'

'You know I went and saw your kid. For her birthday.'

The grin grew into a smile that he couldn't wipe from his face.

'I know. Thank you.'

Sean recovered some composure and introduced his mates to the Carragher household.

Then Luke got serious. 'Sean we need to talk to you.' He waited to see if anyone was going to take the hint to give them some privacy but Sean decided for them.

'You can talk here. These people are my family.'

Luke felt a pinch of rejection at this comment. Would he still feel this way when he told him everything which had happened back home since he had left?

'Okay then.' He took in a deep breath. 'Sean, you're dad's sick.'

Everyone saw Sean's face go slightly paler as the blood drained from it.

'What's wrong?' he demanded.

'He's got asbestosis. Some type of lung infection from his work. He's short of breath all the time and he's lost a lot of weight. He's not good. The doctors say it's usually fatal.'

He asked the next question with his eyes shut. 'How long has he got?'

Luke shrugged. 'I don't know. The doctors say it's hard to judge. They reckon they've seen blokes go for years. Some…months, maybe. I don't know, mate. I'm sorry.'

Sean sat quietly for a moment as he worked things over in his head. Whatever his dad had it had to be bad. In Sean's whole life he had never seen his old man get sick. He was tough. He was tougher than anyone he knew, including himself. What could he do from here though? He realised it might have seemed selfish but what good would returning home do.

Oh dad. Please don't die. Not just yet.

'What else?'

'What do you mean?' Luke asked.

Sean nodded to Grant. 'You two just didn't bump into each other down Hunter Street and decide to come over here and tell me that. What else are you here for?'

Grant leaned forward and looked his platoon mate in the eyes.

'The army back home knows you're fighting with…the IRA.'

Sean would have let out a laugh if this had come from anyone else, but he could see they were serious. He shook his head in disbelief, his mouth open in bewilderment.

'How the fuck do they know this? I hardly know what I'm doing from one day to the next?'

'It's not just them,' Grant continued. 'Brownie is stationed up in Singleton now, working in signals. He's chummy with the intelligence captain up there. He says our brass handed over your service record to the Poms. They know you're over here. If you're with these guys then it makes you a target for them. If I were a British officer and knew one of the men I was fighting had your military experience…Spud, I'd want you removed from the problem before you became one. Every pair of eyes I had would be out there looking for you.'

Grant stopped to let the words sink in. He wasn't sure if Sean would believe the exaggeration but he would do anything to get him away from these people. He knew he wouldn't be able to persuade him to come home because of what was waiting for him back there, but if he could at least get him away from the violence that this place spewed out in abundance then he could live with that.

'Listen to him Sean,' Luke pleaded. 'You have to leave this place.'

'Fuck! The SAS man in the pub,' Daniel interrupted. His mind began running through the answers which now seemed so clear.

Is that why Chad and Brad were dead? Because the Australians had people looking for Sean? He felt a chill course through his body. *Do they know he's been staying here?*

'The one who shot Kieran…' Daniel paused for a second, allowing Sean to interrupt and finish his sentence.

'…was Australian?' Sean was still struggling to take all this in. Not once had he ever felt like he was being watched. But that was what they were taught in the army. If you are doing it right then they will never know. He closed his eyes and took a deep breath. The time for survival had come.

'I need to get out of the city for a while.'

Sean's comment stunned them all.

'*We* need to get out of the city for a while,' he corrected, turning to look at Megan.

His eyes told her he would only go if she was with him. A small nod of her head was her only reply. She would follow this man where ever he went.

'But,' he continued, looking to Luke and Grant, 'I want you to know I won't be going home. I know that might not be what you want but this is my home now. Believe it or not but I love this place. What I'm doing here has more meaning than anything we ever did in Vietnam. Over there we had no idea what we were fighting for. Here...' he waved his hand around the room indicating not just his new family but the city and country beyond the drab walls. 'Here I have a reason to fight. I can't turn my back on that.' He turned to Daniel. 'The Brits can't enter the republic can they?'

'No.' He knew what Sean was getting at.

'Then I'll do what I can from across the border.' He felt Megan squeeze his hand in approval.

Luke could see his friend slipping further out of reach once more.

'Mate you don't have to do this. You can't be a fugitive…'

'Remember what you said to me that day in your car?' Sean asked, cutting him off. 'You said I had to stay away or I'd get caught. Remember? I can't go back. I know it's fucked up with dad being crook but what other choice do I have? I'm not going to sit in gaol while he dies. He'd want me out here being alive while I still had the chance. I'm alive *here* Luke. I can make a difference here. I already have.'

Both Luke and Grant could see there was no way they could make him change his mind.

A silence fell over the small dining room.

Daniel looked at Sean and studied his friend. He thought back to the day on those rough seas out beyond the Kerry Peninsular at their first meeting. He remembered thinking this Aussie had some balls just coming on board a boat he knew full well could have been the last place he would be seen alive. Padraig had told Danny later he wasn't far off putting a bullet in Sean and dropping him over the side. If Chad hadn't stepped in then that's what might have happened. Thinking back to that moment he could now see that Sean would have fought to the end.

'When are you leaving?' Daniel finally asked.

Sean turned to Megan.

'Have you got a spare helmet?'

'Too cold for that this time of year. I've borrowed a car.'

He nodded. 'First thing in the morning we're heading for the border. These riots tonight will have every Brit trigger happy so we'll wait for dawn.' He looked at their two guests. 'We can give you two a lift to Dublin if you want. I'm sorry it has to be this way but it just does. This is where I've ended up through no one else's decisions but my own.'

Neither Luke nor Grant said a thing. They didn't have to; Sean could tell they weren't happy with his choice.

FIFTY-SIX

Standing on the landing outside Daniel's front door, Sean pulled his leather jacket tight around himself as he sucked in the remnants of his last cigarette. Out beyond him, in the freezing darkness, he could see the fires which had started some time before midnight. He guessed they were over by Springfield Road.

As much as he thought it might sound ridiculous, he knew he was going to miss this city. Despite all the hatred and violence which came to the surface so often and so readily, this place had welcomed him when his own hometown, no, his own *country* had seemed to reject him. The hearts of the people here had opened to him and that was going to be hard to leave behind. Something which, so he was told, was rare to an outsider. Maybe he would end up living permanently in Dublin or Galway or even his elusive Donegal, but Belfast would always open its arms to him and for that reason alone he accepted that he loved the dirty, violent, unwanted and forgotten bruise of a city.

His glowing ciggie butt spiralled down to the ground below, his eyes following it until it popped in a small shower of sparks on the pavement far below.

The door behind him opened and he expected to see Megan but it was Luke.

'Watcha doin'?'

Sean smiled and looked back out to the random surviving street lamps and glowing fires whose pulsating glow was mirrored on the low clouds above.

'Just looking at it one last time.'

Luke leaned up against the railing and surveyed the chaos of the distance. In contrast to Sean, he felt revulsion to this place and couldn't wait to be free of its cloud of poverty and violence.

'Is it always like this? The riots I mean.'

'Not always. Sometimes it can be as peaceful as home but then she can turn around and explode the next day.' He laughed quietly to himself. 'The riots are entertainment for these people. Sure they're serious and get deadly but even you would get a kick out of watching the crowd call out points scored for a direct hit from a flying rock or the cheers when a copper catches it like he's playing cricket. You can pick out the ones that play cricket.' He laughed and shook his head in bewilderment. 'A riot anywhere else on the planet would cause fear but here it's a spectacle… it draws the crowd like a footy match. It's a good laugh. At the least it keeps you alert and on your toes.'

Luke feigned a smile. He couldn't see what the attraction was. He changed the subject.

'I heard Max talking about Christmas and he said you weren't here. What did you get up to?'

'I was in Scotland.'

'Doing what?'

Sean shrugged. 'I'll tell you about it one day. What about back home? James put on a big one at the pub?'

'Nah. Your old man doesn't get out that often now so James and Melanie cooked up a feed for him over at his place. I had a quiet one with Leanda's folks.'

Luke didn't know what Sean would say. He hadn't meant to make him feel guilty but if he wanted to know what was going on then he wouldn't polish it over. He would tell him things as they were.

Sean just nodded, eyes still off to the city.

In the distance a siren started up and weaved its way through the brick and concrete sprawl. Neither of them spoke until it faded out in the breeze.

'You know, Anna…'

'I don't want to know mate,' Sean cut him off. He didn't want to hear what that bitch is up to. She was dead to him.

'Sorry.'

'It's alright,' Sean conceded. 'That part of my life is over now. I'm done with all that. All of it,' he said quietly.

'Fair enough. So what about Megan. Can I talk about her?'

There was more than a hint of sarcasm in the comment and Sean relished the friendly dig at him. He realised he had missed talking to his mate. It seemed so long since the two of them had talked so openly. His return home from Vietnam had been too short for them to pick up where they had left off so long ago. If anything, Luke was one who could keep him grounded with a few simple words and he did miss it.

'For one, she's taken, and two, I seem to remember you having a girlfriend. I think Leanda was her name. Remember her or is Megan's beauty making you stray?'

'She misses you, you know?'

Sean laughed. 'I bet she does!'

'Piss off. Remember when she saw you naked down the beach? She says she still has nightmares about it.'

'No need to get jealous mate.'

They both laughed. For a while neither said anything, each preferring to watch the glow of sectarian violence in the distance. They silently wondered what it would be like if Australia ever got herself into a predicament like this. Neither could picture neighbour fighting neighbour like they did here. It just seemed impossible. To accentuate the fact, they both looked over in the direction of a cackle of gunfire.

'You know, if we were businessmen we could open a scrap merchants here and clean up. You've seen the amount of torched cars and buses there are around here. Or a glaziers. You know how to install windows?'

Luke chuckled and shook his head.

'Oh, the footy…' Sean said with a start. 'Who won the Grand Final?'

'Souths beat Manly twenty-three to twelve.'

'Good. Fucken hate Manly. What about local?'

'Wests got up over Maitland.'

'Fair dink'? Maitland did it easy last year. And Bathurst?'

Luke laughed. 'Fuck mate, if you're that hard up for Aussie news then maybe you should come home.'

Sean just grinned. 'Come on. Did a Torana take it out?'

'Alan Moffat. Falcons first and second. Holden came in third.'

Sean nodded. He had missed some good memories. Part of his adolescence had been watching the race first with his father then later with his friends as he grew up.

'Third hey? Not bad for a six potter. They say those Falcons are putting out some serious horsepower.'

'They just got lucky.'

Sean pondered something for a moment and then decided he would. He stuck his hand down inside his shirt and pulled his dog tags up over his head. Looking at the two small discs one last time and remembering the places he had worn them, he finally held them out to Luke.

'Here. I want you to give these to my old man when you get home.'

Taking them, Luke looked over them himself for the first time, running his thumb across the indentations. He nodded before saying, 'He'd like these.' He pocketed them, adding, 'You know, when he saw your picture in the paper it picked him up some…made him look a bit healthier for a while. It was a grim picture but as long as you were alive that was all that concerned him.'

Sean didn't know what to say to that. He thought Luke might be trying to make him feel guilty again. Who could blame him?

'Listen,' he turned to face his friend to be sure what he was about to say was taken in sincerity. 'When you get home, I want you to tell them that it's not all the media makes it out to be over here. The big paper's here are owned by men that are loyal to England and what they print is biased beyond belief. I know that they're…we're seen as terrorists but the only reason that all this has happened is because we have no choice.

'Luke, the vast majority of blokes I talk to over here have sought alternatives to war but it has gotten to the point where they have to defend themselves and their families. The police wouldn't help, the government wouldn't help, people are getting burnt out of their homes, teenage kids are being tortured by the authorities after being illegally arrested by the army without being told what charges are against them…and if this ever happened back home I know you would be leading something similar. The armed struggle in Northern Ireland is a last resort.'

Luke turned from his mates gaze to the city in chaos. Somewhere beyond the fires in the distance came another crackle of gunfire. For him it was such a surreal experience. It seemed like the world's largest movie set not a city in which people fought for their lives. He did try to picture his own home town in such disorder but couldn't fathom having to take up arms to keep your neighbours on their side of the road. But here in front of him was just that. Any last ideas he had about making Sean feel guilty had vanished.

They way Melissa and Max had taken his goodbye the next morning had made him feel like they were thinking permanently. Mel hadn't cried but her hug seemed to be one that said "thank you for coming into our lives". She acted like he was never going to return.

'Please take care Sean', she begged of him. 'We'll miss you.' She didn't have the guts to say she had had a terrible nightmare about him last night.

Max's hug felt even stronger. The little guy had let a few blubbers of tears flow but wiped them away in embarrassment as he tried to remain brave in front of his mum.

'Why do you have to go Sean?' he stammered.

'It's alright mate,' Sean said, trying to console him. 'I'll be back for your birthday. We'll have a party and play footy…the time will fly by just like that.' He snapped his fingers.

'It'd better. Or I'll kick your arse back to Australia myself.'

Everyone laughed except for Sean. He just squeezed his little mate even tighter.

'I promise I'll be back.'

Then Sean tried to deny Daniel's offering.

'We'll be 'right. We've got pistols if we need 'em.'

But his Irish mate wasn't having a bar of it.

'Take it. You never know. If what they say about them having someone on your arse is right then you may need it.'

'He's got *me*, Danny,' Megan said with a smirk.

'Granted, but there are quite a few people out here that wouldn't mind claiming your boyfriend as a trophy.'

Daniel held out the AKMS assault rifle and waited until Sean had taken it. He then passed him a cloth shopping bag with three extra magazines, each fully loaded.

'You never know,' he repeated as he shook his hand. 'Then again you might never fire a shot.'

'I know I'll never fire a shot!' Sean affirmed.

Daniel held out his hand.

'*Slán mo chara ... agus a bheith cúramach.*' Goodbye my friend… and be careful.

Sean gripped his friend's hand. He had done so much for him. By all rights he should have been arrested in Galway and extradited to Australia last year. Right now he could have been sitting in a stinking hot gaol in Long Bay or Maitland watching what constituted a life fade away. Despite all that had been afforded him still he could not fathom the generosity of the Irish people.

'*Ná bíodh imní ort. Beidh mé. Beidh mé ag glaoch ort nuair a rachaidh mé go Baile Átha Cliath.*' Don't worry. I will be. I'll call you when I get to Dublin.

Luke kept quiet as his mate spoke in Irish. They had been mates so long and the last couple of years had separated their friendship so far that he now seemed like a stranger. But he hid the jealousy he felt at his mate experiencing new things without him. First the war in Vietnam and now the companionship he shared with this weapon-toting Irishman. He had nothing personal against Daniel for he knew he had gone far out of his way to help his mate but he was quietly glad that Sean was distancing himself from this wretched violent city and the men that had created it.

Looking over from the driver's seat to Megan by his side as they passed through the southern suburbs of a waking Belfast, Sean recalled young Max standing on his milk crate, looking down on them from the landing as Sean drove off with his girl by his side and his two friends behind him. The little man had not wanted to come down to the street, opting for a distant goodbye.

See you soon Max.

They headed south on the A1, passing through Lisburn before they chanced a stop for breakfast. It wasn't a long stop. Since leaving the safety of the Catholic ghettos of West Belfast Sean felt uneasy. It was like he was being watched. Every twenty seconds he found himself looking up at the rear vision mirror. He wasn't sure if it was just the talk from Grant about the Brits knowing where he was or what Daniel had said about the Australian SAS being the one which had gunned down Kieran... Whatever it was, he felt as though he was now out in the open.

After passing through Newry they crossed from County Down into County Armagh and took Forkhill then Drumintree Road with the plan to wind their way through the laneways to the borders. Here there would be less of a chance at being seen. And it was one place where he should have felt safe. The IRA in the south of this county had a reputation of being tougher than their comrades further north. He should know. He stayed in one of their houses the night he had first slept with Megan.

As he drove down through the geographical feature known as the Ring of Gullion he began to feel better about his situation. If what Grant had told him was true then the authorities had come close to finding him. Never did he think they would track him down. He was on the other side of the world! To think such a humane act as helping to save a child from the horror of a terrorist's bomb had been the start of it all.

Little bastard better grow up to become a millionaire!

Subconsciously his hand found its way down to the AKMS down by his side between his seat and the door of Megan's Rover. Its folding rear stock had been removed and it fit snug down beside him. He wondered if this was one he had bought into the country.

Lifting his fingers from the cold metal of the assault rifle, he rounded a corner and realised the hills in the distance were the lightly snow-dusted caps of the Cooley Mountains situated in the Republic. He could almost see the invisible line. In the north the land was over-farmed with every scrap of usable land seeded or turned. At the border paddocks became less tamed with agriculture not being so forceful in the Republic. The landscape of South Armagh around them was of lush paddocks; some tilled, others left for the winter months. Each field was surrounded with either stone walls or hedges which intersected with neighbouring properties in an untidy criss-cross fashion. They could see some farmers braving the sunny but cold day to tend to their flock or herd or crop.

We're nearly at the border. We're nearly there…only another two miles…

Along the road the hills were slight, almost flat with farms, but in every direction they could see high hills and mountains which made up the Ring. Behind them was the white top of the great hill of Slieve Gullion; probably another observation post for the Brits by now. Megan said it had once been used by the legendary folk hero Finn MacCool as a hunting ground and his own observation post during…

Oh God no…

The border was one mile away but suddenly that distance may as well have been one hundred miles. Sean's brain went into a frenetic overload as he tried to work out his next move. He only had seconds before the randomly placed British checkpoint saw his vehicle approaching down the laneway.

Megan saw him tense and looked ahead.

'Sean?'

'*Sea, tá a fhios agam.*' Yes, I know.

'What's wrong?' Grant asked from behind him, his own eyes now darting about in search of danger.

'*Cas timpeall.*' Turn around, Megan advised as she placed her hand on the grip of her pistol beneath her coat.

'Ró-dhéanach, tá siad le feiceáil dúinn.' Too late, they've seen us. Sean sighed.

'What's going on?' Luke demanded, himself now worried by everyone else's manner.

'Vehicle check point up ahead,' Megan explained.

Neither of the two back seaters knew what that entailed but from the reactions of the two upfront they now feared for their lives without knowing why.

'I.D.s out boys,' Sean recommended as he began to go down through the gears.

As he neared the roadblock he saw several of the British soldiers looking directly at him.

Have they already spotted me? Do they know I'm in the car? Do they know who I am?

'What do we do?' Luke snapped, his face flush, his blood pressure suddenly rising.

'Relax, stay calm and smile,' Megan replied. 'They'll call in the licence plate but it's fine.'

On the road ahead, the Brits had placed two portable A-frame barricades similar to those used on work-sights. These formed a sharp chicane which cars had to slow down dramatically to pass through. This was to give the soldiers ample time to aim and take out the car or driver if the need arose.

Off to one side was parked an armoured 6 wheel drive Saracen, its crew sitting by its opened rear doors enjoying a hot cup of tea. The Browning .30 cal up in the top turret did not rotate as they approached which told Sean no one was mounted up in the turret. Scattered around the checkpoint, spread out to give cover, were five other members of the platoon, each with faces of green and brown camo paint. Eight soldiers in total. To the left and right stone fences gave them no chance of escaping in the car through the paddocks. On foot they had next to no chance.

Look for an option Sean, he thought to himself as he went down through the gears. Ahead of him two of the soldiers were standing either side of a car in front while a third inspected the contents of the boot. The soldier at the rear shut the boot lid after seeing nothing of interest and nodded to his khaki bereted colleague by the driver's door. After handing back something to the driver he gave a short wave and sent them on their way. The soldier which had been inspecting the boot of the car turned around and waved Sean forward. He could see the soldier talking into a radio clipped to his shoulder, talking to base, forwarding the car's licence number, waiting for a reply of clear or detain. They couldn't be arrested by the army unless the RUC was present to invoke the Special Powers Act so who knew what brutality they would endure at the hands of these soldiers while they waited for the law to arrive. The soldier paused briefly as he waited and nodded to himself as the clear reply came back.

Just talk calmly, Sean said to himself. *But be ready…*

As he coasted down the road to them he saw there were no cars heading north. All attention would be on him but it did allow an open path through the barricades. If he decided to run for it he wondered how far they would get before the Rover was shredded with lead and the four of them turned inside out. With his left foot holding down the clutch as it idled in gear and his right leg raised slightly to hide the AKMS between his leg and the door, Sean felt his heart near explode with every pulse as the British soldier, a Lance Corporal, leant over and tapped on the glass. Heart racing, it took every muscle and effort to wind the window down with a smile.

'Morning sir. Heading across the border are we?' His accent was unmistakably Liverpudlian. The badge on his khaki beret made him a member of the Royal Anglians.

Sean noted the other soldier on the left of the car had not approached. If he did take a good look in through Megan's window there was a chance he would see the barrel of the rifle down by his foot. Turning to look up at the Lance Corporal under his khaki beret, Sean nodded slightly, trying to look innocent as he replied, but fearing the white eyes that shone back from within the mottled green face above him.

'Off to Dublin.' He didn't want to go using his perfected Irish accent in case they were asked for identification. An Aussie passport and an Irish accent wouldn't go down well.

Leaning down further, the Brit looked at the others in the car.

The girl's a bloody nice bit of gear, the Brit thought *but the lads in the back look worried. Better check them out.*

Sean could sense the moment coming.

'ID please.' The breath behind the soldier's dreaded appeal clouded in the cold air.

How up to date are these border patrols? Sean wondered as he reached for the documentation in his jacket pocket. *Have the SAS sent out a communication or are they still as secretive as mute mice?*

Off to his left he saw the second and third soldier now walking up beside the car. One stopped by Megan's closed window as the other headed for the boot. The soldier outside tapped on Megan's window as Sean handed over the passport which contained his fake identity. His eyes didn't know which way to look; to the right, the soldier was about to find out he was Australian; to the left, the second soldier was leaning down to get a better look in the car as he wrapped his black gloved knuckles on the side glass.

'Could you wind your window down please Miss?'

Megan was nodding as she fumbled for the handle, stalling as she reached for her documents.

'You're Australian?' The words came out as half statement, half question from the soldier with Sean's ID.

Sean nodded but he could already see the LC's pudgy face had creased slightly as he began to concentrate.

'Australian...' he said to himself again.

Sean shifted slightly in the seat, his foot hovering over the accelerator.

Then it happened. The soldier outside Megan's window saw the AKMS's barrel by Sean's foot.

'GUN!!'

FIFTY-SEVEN

Daniel had just poured himself a cup of tea when a knock came from the front door. He opened it thinking Sean had forgotten something but saw Donnie instead.

'Is Sean still here?' he asked as he stepped inside before being invited. His tone worried Daniel.

'No,' Daniel said as he shut the door behind him. 'He's gone. He and Megan were taking his friends down to Dublin so they could catch a boat to England. They were going to call once they got there.'

'What's wrong Donnie?' Melissa asked from the kitchen table.

Donnie didn't say anything straight away. He thought over his words before speaking. 'Danny…this might be hard for you to hear but…it's Padraig. He's ordered the members of Sean's ASU to be court martialed. Brigitta's already dead, she was found out on the edge of the Lodge just now and he's told Ted this morning to take care of Sean. Ted's getting a team together to go after him.' He looked from brother to sister with eyes of remorse for having known of such a treacherous act.

Danny smiled as he stood in the centre of the room. 'You're having a go aren't you?'

'No Danny. The Peelers found Brigitta's body. Tortured and shot. I heard it over their band. He think's they're touts. He's cleaning up his failed idea. He's trying to show off to the big lads.'

Daniel's face went white then quickly reddened. While he knew Sean was on his way to safety, he was now furious at the betrayal by his lifelong friend. 'Padraig…' The words came calmly despite the rage that boiled within him. 'I'll kill the cunt. I'll fucken shoot the cunt myself.' He grabbed his jacket from the hook on the wall and made for the door but Donnie stepped between him and it.

'Leave it for now Danny! Sean will be fine. He's safe for now!'

'Like hell he is!' the younger man declared as he pushed his older friend aside. 'Padraig knows too many of the wrong people on this island. I should know! He's introduced me to half of them.'

'You can't do this Daniel!' Melissa warned. 'He'll end up hurting you if you go over there!'

He glared at his sister. 'Let the cunt try.'

Donnie understood nothing he could say would talk him out of it. Reluctantly he stepped aside. If only he had known Sean had already left then he wouldn't have come over here with the news which was probably now going to get Daniel killed.

Both of the British check point soldiers reacted simultaneously, cocking their rifles while springing back several steps, their SLRs coming up into their shoulders. But Sean was already away. The Rover's tyres gripped perfectly, launching him forward, punching his way through the first wooden barricade as the engine screamed in protest.

'GET YOUR HEADS DOWN!' he screamed to his mates in the back seat but they were already down.

Either side of them he saw soldiers scrambling into action. None of them had expected the Rover to bolt but their professionalism kicked in sooner than Sean had hoped.

The second barricade collapsed as he shifted into second and he heard the first rounds being fired close behind him. Grabbing third gear, the car was gaining some distance just as the rear window exploded in sending glass flying throughout the sedan. Three rounds punctured the front windscreen in the centre as a fourth found its way high, taking out the rear vision mirror. With the glass now crazed with cracking, Sean's vision was almost gone.

Still he pushed forward.

He could hear Luke and Grant screaming obscenities at him from down by the floor but he didn't have time to listen to them. If he could make the bend in the road ahead which was less than two hundred yards away then they would be out of the Brit's line of sight. There was no way the Saracen would catch them.

Then a back tyre was shot out.

He felt a shift in the car's handling as it began to track left but he clutched into top gear and pushed on. Like trying to run in a dream, Sean felt as though the car was going nowhere. Everything moved in slow motion. Several more bullets chewed their way through the car and he watched tiny cubes of shattered glass float around like they were in zero gravity. A tracer round passed them by on the right and it seemed to Sean he could have just reached out and plucked it from the air like a firefly buzzing by on a balmy spring afternoon. The steering wheel shuddered hard and tiny droplets of blood climbed in an arc, reaching the inside of the ruined windscreen and splashing across it in an abstract pattern.

A scream from Megan and the sight of blood finally bought him back to reality.

'Are you hit?!' he yelled at her. Looking across he could see her hair forward over her face with her head on her knees. *Oh fuck no!* 'MEGAN!' he bellowed over the noise of British gunfire. 'MEGAN!!'

She finally turned and her eyes looked back in fear. 'Are you hit?' he demanded.

'NO!' she hollered back, fear in her voice. She had been shot at before but never like this.

The tearing noise of metal was interrupted by the bursting of the front left tyre. Instantly the car lost all but the smallest amount of steering. With the view of the road ahead just a shattered opaque blur and an unresponsive wheel in his hands, Sean held it straight for as long as possible before the car worked its way off the road and into the culvert. He tried to correct but the mud bogged down the car and spun them into the stone fence with a terrifying crunch. The front shattered windscreen finally blew out with the impact as all four of them were thrown hard across the inside of the car. The Rover lifted at the rear and spun around on its nose in a flat arc. It spun around 180° and slammed into a wooden gate within the fence.

Having slammed his left knee into the steering column, Sean's injury from Vietnam wrenched at his nerves, making it feel as bad as it had on the day he had woken up in the Vung Tau hospital. Then, as the noise of the impact dissipated, Sean realised the gunfire had stopped. Looking back the way they had come he realised the road block was out of view. They had made the blind corner by at least one hundred yards. The revving of a distant Rolls Royce engine though, told him they were bringing the Saracen around.

Looking around at his friends for the first time since their short run to freedom began, he saw that Luke had split his forehead open during the collision. It was bleeding heavily and his head ached. Other than that they were unharmed. Both however were furious at him.

'WHAT THE FUCK ARE YOU DOING?!!' screamed Luke as he sat back up. 'THEY COULD HAVE KILLED US!!'

Sean was about to tell them to get out and run when Grant began dragging Luke out the side door. The Novocastrian knew what was happening and his soldier's instincts were pushing him on to survive.

Sean and Megan both slid out the passenger's side of the car but not before he grabbed the AKMS. Limping, he tried to keep up with Megan. 'Through the paddocks! The border! Use the fences for cover!' he yelled at them.

'The tree line!' Megan screamed. 'The border's at that tree line!'

Luke and Grant didn't need to be told twice. Both climbed up over the boot of the car and jumped the gate with a newfound energy as they tried to put as much distance between them and the oncoming armoured vehicle.

With the bag of additional magazines, Sean followed Megan over the car and into the paddock. They crossed the open field, running perpendicular to the road until they reached another field-dividing stone fence. Megan sprinted along the southern edge of the fence for almost fifty yards before she realised Sean was not behind her. She stopped and turned to see him down on one knee, crouched behind the end of the stone wall, the rifle aimed back up the road. Fear gripped her hard as she began running back to him.

'SEAN!!' Her shoes sank into the soft earth as she ran. The cold air burned her lungs as she filled them deeply with each gulp. 'SEAN!!' she bellowed again. Her words were cut off by the deafening clatter as he futilely emptied a full magazine at the oncoming heavy green vehicle.

Sergeant Andrew Wilton wasn't looking forward to the chewing out he knew was coming. His CO had ordered him down to the British army HQ at the Thiepval barracks outside of Lisburn. He was not impressed with the Australian's decision to go "bar hopping on his own little sleuth tour of Belfast" as he had put it.

Andrew knew there would be disciplinary action for sure, even the threat of taking back the coveted sandy beret, but he doubted it would go that far. Or maybe he would be sent back home. He tried to get out onto the streets for the day with Owey until the CO cooled off, however they had been tracked down and ordered back to meet the chopper which was inbound.

Having just come in from a surveillance run they were both still kitted out in their civilian apparel and fully armed when the small Westland Scout came in to land. Holding their Colt Commandos by their sides, they ran over to the bird and climbed in. Within a minute they were heading south over green fields, a refreshingly welcomed sight compared to the brown and grey sprawl of the city. Andrew grabbed a set of headphones and introduced himself and Owey to the two man crew. He didn't say they were SAS and he probably didn't have to.

'So what's in Thiepval for you two?' the pilot asked. He didn't think he would get an answer from the "special boys" but his flying colleague had a hangover and wasn't saying much so why not try with these two.

'An arse kicking by the sounds of it,' Andrew replied. 'I'm not looking forward to it either.'

The pilot grunted a short laugh. 'You sass boys not been making your beds in the correct military fashion?'

'You just can't keep some officers happy,' he admitted.

'Belfast does that to people. You an Aussie or a Kiwi?' the pilot asked, glad for the conversation.

'Aussie mate. Don't go getting the two confused.'

The pilot grinned. He knew either hated being referred to as the other. 'Met a Kiwi a few years back. Pilot. Fixed-winger. He was one of the most clumsiest people in the world when he got drunk. So how long you been out here?'

'I'm at the wrong end of an indeterminate tour.'

'I've been here almost a full year,' stated the pilot as he levelled off at their designated altitude, 'and I can't wait to get back to London.'

The four settled into the flight, the two crewmen doing their job while Wilto and Owens peacefully enjoyed the lush environs below them. When they were only a few minutes out of Lisburn and about to begin decent, everything changed.

'Shit,' the co-pilot interrupted. 'Someone's having a good time down on the border. There's a VCP under fire.' Without being asked to he switched the radio into everyone's earphones to listen in.

'...in the field on our left...there by the wall. Near the wall!'

'Yeah I see him. Get back and come in from his right. Come in from further down the road.'

'Say again?'

'Can we come in from...FUCK!...'

Andrew heard the distinctive sound of gunfire in the background. 'Where's this happening?' he asked.

'South of Newry,' the co-pilot explained. 'Right on the border.'

'Who's under fire?'

'Not sure. I didn't catch the start of it.' The voices came through again.

'Cunt's got a Kalashnikov!'

'The Saracen's bellied out! And Macca says he's blind without the front periscope!'

'How many are there in the field straight ahead?'

'We think four. Yeah, four. He's...' more gunfire *'For fuck sake! Get someone around his flank!'*

'I've lost sight of him...'

'What about the others. Can you see the woman? Is she armed?'

'Negative. She was by the Australian. Near the wall.'

Andrew nearly jumped out of his seat. He leaned forward. 'What?! Did he say she was Australian?!'

'No,' Owey corrected. 'They said she was *by* the Australian.'

Andrew couldn't believe his luck. Sometimes you just had to be in the right place at the right time. 'I need you to get me down there.'

For a second no one answered.

'Where?' the pilot finally asked. 'To this?'

'Yes! Right now! I'll take responsibility. Don't worry about that. Just get us down there.'

The crew looked at each other briefly before calling in their new destination. Banking slightly and accelerating to their top speed of 130 mph, the Army Air Corp Scout raced towards South Armagh.

The eleven tonne Saracen hit the disabled car in an attempt to ram the Rover through the gate and allow it access to the paddock. The blunt nose ploughed into the b-pillar square on, but the Rover buried down into the soft earth as it wedged itself against the stone fence. The driver accelerated, hoping to make the machine climb over the car but the wheels spun in the mud underneath. He stopped, reversed and was looking for a weak spot in the fence to push through when rounds began to clang off the front of the APC. Naturally he flinched. As he shifted into forward gear he saw the glass of his viewing prism crack in a blinding flash. Then another round hit it and the glass went completely crazed with cracks. His forward viewing periscope was gone. There were two more viewing prisms but these faced front-left and front-right. Using what he had left, he aimed for what he thought was a shorter part of the wall. The noise of impact was almost deafening within the machine and all inside felt the front wheels ride up and over the now destroyed wall. Almost up and over the wall. Without perfect vision, the driver had not hit the best spot. Here the stone fence was shorter but thicker at the base and the belly of the Saracen scraped hard, it's engine revving high as three of its six wheels spun free of the ground. Now flustered, the driver shifted into reverse. The APC groaned as it scraped across the stones underneath but the only wheels with purchase dug its way down into the mud. One more attempt at forward and he stopped, knowing he was stuck.

Sean smiled to himself. A fluke of a shot and the Saracen now stuck belly up on the fence. His main problem now neutralised, he pulled the empty magazine out, dropped it on the ground in front of him and had to look twice as he saw blood on the metallic banana-shaped object. Looking down at his left hand he saw he was missing his little finger and the last two knuckles of his ring finger hung by a small sliver of skin. All that was left were torn and bloody stumps. As soon as his brain realised it had been the source of the blood in the car, the searing, stabbing pain followed. There wasn't a lot he could do about it now so he grimaced and tore the dangling finger off, stuffed it into his jacket pocket and reloaded as best he could whilst looking between a gap in the thick stone wall for the next threat.

Several of the soldiers that had not given chase in the APC were moving down through the paddock just off the road. They were trying to use the cover of the ancient stone fence but had mistakenly chosen the wrong side of it. They were still at least four hundred yards off, a lot further than the Saracen which had got to within two hundred yards of his position. For Sean to hit any of them from here would be hard but he needed to keep their heads down for a little while longer. He took aim on the first soldier who was moving forward in a crouched jog and squeezed off half a dozen rounds.

Pain now stabbed into his hand as the rifle bucked with recoil. The forward hand grip of his Romanian AKMS was vertical like the old American gangster's Tommy gun and it was slick with blood so he had to tighten his grasp despite the pain it caused. Not having a rear butt on the rifle made it even harder to aim but he was pleased to see he at least peppered the wall in front of them, forcing them to the ground. They were clearly now in a state of confusion, having thought he was on the other side of the wall they were traversing along.

'Sean!'

He heard Megan calling out from further down along the stone fence. He looked up and saw her running back towards him, her pistol now in her hand. 'Get down!' he yelled back at her, waving his hand to motion her to the ground.

Chips of stone exploded just behind her on the top of the four foot high wall and she dove for earth. She landed hard but looked back up at him and nodded she was alright. Above them rounds from the Saracen's .30 calibre turret gun pounded the wall. The noise of its rapid firing disheartened them but he knew it would not be able to follow them. They were blind to it and just had to stay on this side of the stone fence.

He glanced back through a gap in the stones to see if anyone had dared to venture outside of the Saracen down to his left. He swore to himself as he noticed the rear doors were open. Soldiers had exited but he had not seen them do so. He had no idea where they were. Time to move.

A quick glimpse south revealed Luke and Grant still jumping fences, each racing through the knee high grass the next field over. They were out of accurate shooting range of the British SLRs and were not far off from the tree line where the border ran.

Stuffing the remaining two full magazines into the right-hand pockets of his jeans, he scrambled along the base of the wall to where Megan lay.

'We have to keep moving,' he said as he wiped sweat out of his eyes. His body was reacting to the pain causing him to overheat. It also didn't help having a dozen blokes trying to blow his head off. Looking around he could see the route taken by Luke and Grant was now too open for a straight run by himself and Megan with the Brits so close. He looked up the incline of the small hill to the east along the stone fence they now crouched behind. Fifty yards up a second four-foot wall ran south, perpendicular to the one they were now behind. It didn't go all the way to the border which Sean guessed was maybe three quarters of a mile away. His plan now was to make it to the other side of the wall alive. If that went well then they would head back down the hill on the other side of the wall whilst using it for cover.

He didn't wait around to tell Megan the plan. Grabbing her by her elbow he pulled her to her feet and began running as fast as he could while remaining as low as possible. They hadn't gone two yards before clumps of dirt and chips of stone began exploding around them. Sean could hear the gunfire from back down near the road. It was the men which had exited the armoured vehicle.

'KEEP GOING!' he ordered Megan as he spun and dropped to one knee.

His aim was inaccurate at this range. The troops were taking cover behind the stone wall at the edge of the road over one hundred yards away. He spayed the remainder of the half empty mag in their direction, giving Megan enough time to reach the stone wall.

Now it was his turn. Pushing himself up, he pumped his legs as hard as his injured knee would allow and ran for cover. He knew at any moment their rounds would be coming back in answer.

Forty yards to go and no gunfire…

Thirty yards and rounds cracked as they passed close to him…

Twenty yards and it hit him hard, knocking him sideways to the base of the thick stone fence. The rifle fell from his grip as he tried to control his fall. He landed on his left side but it was his right side that worried him. His right hip rang with a dull pain and he feared the worst.

FIFTY-EIGHT

As Padraig had predicted, he had not slept well. His anger and half a bottle of whiskey had refused him a deep sleep. The news from Ted that Brigitta had been disposed of had done little to settle him down. He knew it had to be done to show the Army Council he took responsibility in his role seriously and he could clean up his own mess even though he had not been asked to do so.

He had chosen her personally. He had seen her at work once before and knew she was good at what she did. But had she been the cause of the failure? Had her English blood, despite her Celtic heritage, seeped to the surface? Had she done something to let his side down…to destroy all that he had worked for?

Where the hell is Ted? He should have been here by now?

He turned his thoughts to Sean and was thinking of how he had shot down any chance of him succeeding when the expected knock at the door finally came. He moved to open it.

At least Ted can be trusted to get the job done…Fuck you Sean. After all I've done for you. How could you go and…

He hadn't opened the door half an inch when it was suddenly kicked open. The heavy wood smashed into Padraig's face and he staggered back against the wall, barely keeping himself upright. His eyes flashed over white for a second as the pain began to drill inward. When they began to refocus he saw Daniel standing in the doorway with his 9mm Browning aimed at the bridge of his split and bloody nose.

'Were you going to kill me too Padraig?' Daniel asked in a tone Padraig had never heard from him before. 'Was that part of your climb to the top? I was involved in your little plan as well remember? Was I to die after Sean?!' He slammed the door shut behind him and grabbed his once mentor by the shirt collar and drove the pistol into his eye. 'You killed that girl? After the risks she took for you! And Sean?' He threw him down on the lounge and took a step back, his pistol still aimed at Padraig's face.

'You don't understand. He should never have become one of us…' Padraig began but Daniel wasn't having any of it.

'Don't you dare give me some internal political shite or I'll kill you before you take your next breath you lying cunt!' His words were clear and exact but his heart rate was pounding faster than it ever had. 'Did you have her killed?' he asked as he held back his fury.

Padraig thought about lying but could see Daniel wouldn't buy it. He nodded.

'You sent someone after Sean?'

A pause this time but then he nodded again. It was like he couldn't bring the words forth.

Daniel closed his eyes for a second as the truth of the betrayal hit him. He didn't understand how two people fighting for the same cause could see things so differently. 'And me?' he asked, fearing the response.

For a moment Padraig seemed to be confused as to why his protégé would ever ask such a question but he reasoned the last two days warranted some doubt. He shook his head, defiant of the situation.

'They failed me, Danny. We should never have trusted him.' His face was turning red, anger at the thought of failure rising up again. 'He wasn't one of us. We were stupid to help him out. I can't afford to make mistakes like that again so I did what had to be done…for our cause. One of those two betrayed Ireland, betrayed the cause! They had to go!' His face suddenly turned solemn, empathetic. 'But I would never harm you Daniel. You're closer to me than my own family.'

Daniel almost squeezed the trigger at the gall of his once inspiration but held off. He realised that he had been so wrong, so misled to follow this creep for so long. 'And you wonder why your family won't talk to you.'

Off to his right a shadow appeared at the front door. With his pistol still on Padraig, Daniel turned to see Ted walk in, his eyes instantly taking in the hostile situation. One hand held the front door knob; the other the morning paper. The man that relished the jobs no one else would touch didn't move. Nothing moved but his eyes as they surveyed the two and the threat involved.

Daniel still had his Browning aimed at Padraig, but he could see Ted weighing up his chances. 'Don't do it,' he warned.

It seemed like ages they stood there looking at each other.

It had to end.

Without warning Daniel took the upper hand, turned and fired once. The shot hit Ted in the face, his squinting face imploding in on itself, collapsing into the rear of his skull as he fell in a crumpled heap to the floor on top of his newspaper.

Returning his aim to the traitor on the lounge, Daniel looked at him with resentment.

'Sean left this morning. He's safe now. You'll never see him again. And if I ever see you or any of your Gestapo goons within ten blocks of my place, you know who I'm going to tell about your betrayal? Not the Council. Fuck them. I'll tell Jim Bryson and Paddy and the "Toddler". Men like them…men no one can control will be told of how you killed our own. There will be no place in Ireland safe for you.' He lowered his pistol. 'You may as well be a Brit.'

With that he walked out of Padraig's flat and never saw him again.

Somewhere ahead of him Sean could hear Megan calling out to him with worry. He lay there listening to her voice for a few seconds before turning his attention to where the bullet had struck him. Looking down at his hip he could see the magazine in his pocket had taken a glancing blow from the British bullet. Thankfully none of the rounds had gone off with the impact. He pulled the useless and buckled mag from his pocket and saw the jagged tear which ran horizontally across the centre of its black metal skin. Dropping it, he retrieved his rifle and looked back down the hill.

No other shots had followed it as he now lay in a blind spot in a shallow recess. Not wasting time, he scuttled along the wet ground until the hill's curve began to fall away, then shot up and bolted once more for the stone fence as the Brits fired after him again. The ancient wall was peppered as he launched himself over the top. Landing heavily next to his girl he joked, 'This is getting a bit intense now.' He loaded in his last mag, puffing with exertion as he did so.

'Oh shit Sean! Your hand! You've been hit.' She moved in to look at it.

'Hurts like hell but no one ever died from losing a couple of fingers.'

Her composure returned as she explained their situation.

'There's three soldiers down on the road and three more are moving around to our right just north of this wall. We've got to go now!'

'You've got my vote, love.'

Megan made to move but Sean lifted his head to locate the soldiers to their north. They weren't as far away as he thought. He made out two of them moving up the hill using the few trees in the field for cover. He knelt back down and looked towards the tree covered hills off in the distance. The Republic of Ireland. It was so close. Another shot rang out from down near the road but it hit the top of the wall, the bullet whining as it raced by overhead. The British were shooting at shadows now.

'Okay. Lets…'

The sound which cut off his words sent tremors through his body. So many times he had heard the sound before but in the past it had once meant help was coming. Here it meant the exact opposite. Here it meant death.

The helicopter skimmed above the trees to the southeast. It was only small and carried no side mounted weapons. However, even five hundred yards away, Sean could see two figures in the back, each with a rifle.

He and Megan were about to be boxed in.

As the Scout came in low and fast Andrew already had a good idea of where his target was from talking to the troops on the ground via radio. Approaching from the north he had seen both groups of soldiers trying to encircle the small rocky tree-spotted hill. Their men had been taking fire from about half way up on the other side of the stone fence which ran latitudinally dividing the hill in two.

After convincing the apprehensive pilot he would be well out of range of the gunmen, Andrew had directed him to come in as low as possible and in a wide turning arc aiming for the south of their target. Making sure not to cross the border, the Scout slowed down but kept moving forward as the two SAS men dropped the six feet to the soft ground. As soon as they hit, the bird accelerated and gradually climbed to a safe distance from where it could be used as another set of eyes.

Bringing up his shortened assault rifle, Andrew judged the wanted Australian on the hill to be at 12 o'clock; dead north. The area they had to cover was wide and because there was a chance that he may slip past them they agreed to spread out. Owey set out across the paddock on a direction of 11 o'clock while Andrew went uphill at 1 o'clock. They would cut off his escape and wait for the two groups of regulars to flush him their way.

Andrew heard the distinctive report of British SLRs firing from the other side of the hill and wondered what they thought they were firing at; there was no way they could see Doherty from where they were.

As the Sergeant trotted forward through the small clump of oak trees the hill came into view. Dropping to one knee he focused on the stone wall at the top, straining his eyes to make them out. There were two of them up there. It was hard to tell but one looked like a woman. She was moving south along the longitudinal stone fence which ran perpendicular to the wall bisecting the hill laterally. The man beside her – presumably Doherty – fired off a series of rounds down hill before he moved east along the wall, heading further up the hill towards a copse of trees.

Where are you going Sean?

'Fuck,' Sean simply said as he watched the small helicopter skim above the ground. As it went behind some trees it slowed before taking off again and climbing high sans passengers. He chanced another quick look over the wall to the men north of him. The three Brits were ready this time and showered the wall with rounds. Ignoring them as he dropped back down behind the safety of the ancient stone fence, he directed his attention to the sight of the helicopter drop-off.

For a second he thought he saw a local IRA volunteer in civilian attire and scruffy hair running west, away from the helicopter, possibly a local coming to help. Then it hit him like slap in the face; the man was SAS not IRA. No other British troops dressed like that. If they weren't in the shit before then now they definitely were.

'SAS.'

Megan turned and looked at the fear on his face. It was the first time she had ever seen him like that.

'What is it? Sean? What is it?!'

'Down there. There's an SAS soldier coming across to cut us off. You have to run straight down along this wall. I'll get his attention and draw him off you.'

She didn't budge. 'We go together Sean or not at all!' Her hand reached out and gripped his shoulder. She looked into his eyes with determination, telling him she would not let him sacrifice himself for her.

'Megan,' he explained as he placed his good hand on her cheek. 'These are the types that killed Chad and Brad. They don't fuck around. I'll get their attention so you can cross over. They can't shoot into the Republic so when you make it to the edge of those trees I want you to get their attention with this,' he gave her his pistol. 'Fire off everything you've got from both your pistol and mine. You won't be in range but the noise will get their attention. I'll head that way,' he nodded east, 'before coming in around behind them. They won't see me cross the border from over there.'

'No Sean…' she tried to argue but he cut her off.

'Listen. If you don't go now neither of us is getting out of here alive.'

She tried to protest but she knew he was right. She knew this was their only chance. They had to spread themselves thin. She moved in and kissed him forcefully.

'*Is breá liom tú. Ná bheith ró-fhada.*' I love you. Don't be too long.

He winked. '*Feicfidh mé tú ar an taobh eile, babe.*' See you on the other side, babe.

Letting go of her was one of the hardest things he had ever had to do but it was their only choice. If they were to both get out of there it had to be now.

He didn't tell her the second SAS soldier was not with the first. Where he hid was anybody's guess. He would just have to take his chances with that one. All that mattered now was getting her safely across the field.

He watched her begin to sprint down the hill before he headed up along the ragged stone wall towards the nearest tree twenty yards away. He slid down behind the base of the wide trunk and took aim on the figure heading across the base of the hill. It was a long shot and without a rear stock he was unsure of a hit but he drew a bead on him anyway. Giving himself enough lead to allow for the SAS man's running speed, Sean flicked the selector to single shot and breathed in and out several times before squeezing off his first round. With the ground so soft and wet, no dirt or dust kicked up to assist him with his aiming. All he saw was the SAS man still moving forward. Sean re-aimed and fired off three quick single rounds. This time the SAS man dropped to the ground but Sean could see he was only taking cover.

Still Megan ran on.

Sean fired single shots now to keep the SAS man's face in the dirt. He knew it would be a fluke if he hit him but the man was not heading towards Megan or himself and that had been the plan.

Still he couldn't see the second man from the helicopter.

'Run babe,' he said as he watched her peripherally while keeping an eye on the first man he had forced to ground. The tree that was his cover took several hits at least a foot above his head. The sound of the gunfire finally rolled up the hill to him a second later and he could see the SAS man he had forced to ground now taking well aimed shots back towards him.

Sean fired back with three more. 'Go, go, go…' he urged her on.

Somewhere out there he knew Luke and Grant were watching this knowing they were beyond range of all weapons being fired. He was angry at them for turning up but if they hadn't…would he be in a prison or morgue right now? Might they have raided Danny's house to get him?

Ducking back behind the tree, Sean removed the magazine and pushed down on the round at the top of the stack with his thumb. The spring tension and the weight of the mag itself told him he had, at most, half a magazine left. A quick look around the tree earned him several close shots from the first SAS man but the risk gave him good news; Megan was too far away from the Brit for him to hit her. She was going to make the border. All he had to do now was wait until she began her avalanche of cover fire and he would then leg it over the top of the hill and then southeast around the trees to the border. In three or four minutes he would be safe.

Being sure to keep the tree between him and the SAS man at the base of the hill, Sean crawled up to the stone wall and looked over it. Bad news. The trio of Brits from the vehicle check point were less than fifty yards away.

He had to move now. He aimed the barrel of the AKMS over the top of the rocky fence and fired off seven blind shots. All he wanted was to make them take cover to give him time to begin his own escape. With, at most, eight rounds left he made his move. He pushed on up the last incline and into a small copse of trees, still wary there was a second soldier down there somewhere. He darted in and out of the thick trunked trees until he passed over the crest and began his decent. Dropping to his backside he slid in to the base of the first tree. With barrel up, he looked out over the ground ahead. It was clear. All that remained was a cluster of trees not two hundred yards off at the base of the hill and then an open run across two stone fence-divided fields to the border at the east.

At that moment on the other side of the hill came a different sound of gunfire. It was Megan and her Walther giving him cover fire. He pushed off once more, running as fast as his injured knee would allow down the slippery slope.

His head began to ache from breathing in such cold winter air and his left hand was throbbing painfully but these were far from his mind. He just concentrated on running.

Sweat soaked his shirt and jacket.

Blood soaked his left sleeve.

His lungs burned from the cold.

His knee, injured in another war…another life, felt like it was going to crumble under his weight.

He ran despite the pain, passing through the trees out into the open.

Megan's gunfire changed tone. She was now firing the Browning pistol Daniel had first given him when he had become one of them, a soldier for a united Ireland. She had thirteen rounds available and he hoped she wouldn't rush through them. He needed more time.

Keep going babe. I'm nearly there. Just over this fence then another hundred yards or so.

Never in his whole life had he run like he was at that moment. Knowing at any moment a 7.62 mm round from a British SLR somewhere behind him could slam into his torso was reason enough to push through and beyond his pain threshold.

He slowed slightly as he approached the stone fence and, with the near-empty rifle in his bad hand, vaulted over the wall cleanly and landed on the other side...just five yards away from the second SAS man.

His assault rifle was aimed at Sean's face.

FIFTY-NINE

Sean froze. He couldn't believe he had gotten so close. There was no way of bringing up his own rifle. It hung from his bloodied hand, each now as useless as the other. For a second he almost closed his eyes to await the fatal shot which would end it all but he didn't. Instead he looked down the aimed barrel to the eyes of the soldier behind it and... *I know you*...recognised him.

He was back in Vung Tau... drunk on scotch... laughing with the man now before him.

'You?' Sean's voice cracked as he searched his memory for a name. 'Wilto?' He looked at him in confusion and disbelief. He never thought he would see the man again and here he was about to kill him. Here was the man he had met in the jungles of a far away land... now standing on the Irish border aiming a rifle at his face??

As he fought to catch his breath, Sean looked into Wilto's eyes, trying to understand how he could do what he was about to. Sean, mouth agape, was shaking his head slightly.

Why?

Andrew had been watching him come down the hill through the gaps in the stone wall. At first he hadn't been sure this was Doherty but the closer he got, the more he recognised him. He could have picked him off, dropped him with a well aimed shot long before he made it to the stone fence but for some reason he had waited.

Had the recognition of his enemy been the reason? He knew he had enough justification and authority to shoot him and should have dropped him long ago. However now seeing the man that looked so different from when they had first met…he couldn't. Suddenly, in that split second, he wanted to tell him to run. *Keep running and never come back. Get out of Northern Ireland. Just disappear and never come back. Never come back.*

He realised why. As he looked at the sweating, bleeding and breathless young man before him he saw the Sean Doherty which had gulped down shots of scotch with him. He saw the same Sean Doherty that had laughed with him as their mates danced in a drunken stupor. He saw a natural leader that had stood ground *with him* against the Viet Cong. He saw a fellow Australian soldier…a fellow digger.

Sean's eyes briefly moved from Andrew to the hills beyond, looking into Ireland itself. In the distance he could see Megan five hundred yards off amongst the trees. Beside her were his two mates from two different worlds. He knew he would never see any of them again. He smiled at his love one last time and then turned back. In the time it took him to look back at the death he knew was coming, Andrew had lowered his rifle.

Sean had only landed over the fence not twenty seconds ago to what he had believed would be his final demise and now the soldier that could have ended it all was letting him go.

Andrew wasn't sure if the question in Sean's eyes was '*why let me go?*' or '*why are you here?*' but he never got to explain. And he never heard the shots which hit his own body.

Sean, however, certainly heard and felt the rounds which hit him.

One hundred yards away two out-of-breath British soldiers had taken aim and fired a total of nine rounds along the stone fence at what they thought were two IRA gunmen. The sound of Megan's screams rivalled the echo of the gunshots as they rolled throughout the valley.

Sean was hit squarely in the chest by two rounds. He dropped heavily to his side as his legs went numb under him. A groan left his mouth, the noise visible in the winter air. Beside him he could see Wilto sprawled out face down, not moving. His face and neck were covered in blood. His eyes were shut but his back was rising and falling with unconscious breath. His right hand still gripped the now splintered and smashed rifle.

Sean tried to talk but nothing came out. As his brain cried out for oxygen it began to overlap past memories with reality and he was taken back to that hot and dusty blood filled gully in South Vietnam… back to Joel's side.

Even though his body was shutting down, Sean's twitching, shattered left hand reached out for his mate, grabbing Andrew's left hand, squeezing it tight in a weak attempt to pull him closer.

I'm with you Joel.

I've got you mate, I've got you...

Sean turned his head and looked up to the sunny Irish morning sky above him. Thin sparse cirrostratus clouds stretched out high in the atmosphere above him, each one failing to veil the bright winter sun. No wind stirred in the valley around him.

It was going to be a nice day.

When the soldiers cautiously approached him a minute later they thought he was still alive. His eyes were still open but all life was gone.

Sean Dominic Gordon Doherty died just after nine in the morning on the 8th of January 1971…within sight of freedom.

SIXTY

Andrew was rushed to the Military Hospital at Musgrave outside of Belfast for emergency surgery. Here a team of three specialists removed a bullet and pieces of shattered rib from his shredded right lung and repaired the terrible and near fatal damage another had done passing through his neck.

After coming out of the anaesthetic the following night he was told by a visiting Army officer of how he had been mistaken for an IRA soldier due to his civilian attire. Before the officer could tell him the details of his injuries Andrew asked if his fellow Australian soldier had survived.

On learning Sean Doherty had been killed, Sergeant Andrew Wilton of Her Majesties 22nd Special Air Service Regiment and 3 Squadron Australian SASR, decided he no longer wanted to be a part of any armed forces. Before he could walk again the once career soldier had quit the military.

The piper moved to the centre of the ancient stone building. His shoes were polished so deeply the crowd could be seen in the crisp, black reflective surface. The national tartan of Ireland which hung about his waist as a kilt had been pressed and brushed clean; the yellows and whites bold against its mossy green background. The sgian dubh sheathed within his sock was razor sharp and gleamed as brightly as the polished metal buckle of his wide kilt belt even though no one would see the hidden blade. His gaze did not waver from the end of the aisle as he lifted the mouthpiece of the bagpipes to his lips and began priming the bladder with several deep breaths.

He was ready. With over three decades of playing, he summoned all his skill, squeezed the bag by drawing in his elbow and began. The familiar underlying drone sounded. The tune *Mist Covered Mountains* would lead the body of Sean Doherty down the isle of the church and out into the street where over a thousand people were waiting to walk with him to his final resting place.

Daniel tried to stop his eyes from watering as the song began. The notes sounded crisp and echoed in the ancient hall, the tune bringing forth tears from many.

Behind the piper, at the head of the coffin, Daniel lifted the fine timber casket from the bier to his waist. He was to lead the way with Sean's best friend from another world. Luke held his mate's coffin in his right hand. He had come here to warn his friend of the trouble he had gotten himself into. Too late, he was now carrying him to his grave. Yesterday he had managed to get a phone call through to his home town. James had answered the phone by the bar. Never had Luke heard such pain. He was glad Sean's father hadn't answered. He didn't know how he would have handled that.

The piper stepped forward and began the long march.

Behind Daniel and Luke were Donnie and Grant. Carrying the rear of the casket were Coen and Roger. Both had come up from Dublin once they had heard the news. Each followed the piper down the isle towards the door.

Sean's love Megan and Daniel's sister Melissa fell in behind them. Little Max walked between them, one hand in each and tears enough for all of them.

From the darkness of the church the piper stepped out into the light of a bright winter's day, the skirl of the pipes being heard for miles around. He made his way down the steps to the street and into the passage which the massed crowd had forged. Here he waited as the bearers made their way out into the daylight.

Even today it is not known whose idea it was. Neither Daniel nor the other members of the IRA claimed responsibility. Whosever idea it had been, it was greeted by the crowd with reverence. Draped over his oak casket was a modified Australian flag. The Union Jack which had originally made up the top left corner of the southern continent's standard had been cut out. An Irish tricolour had been sewn in its place.

The six lifted their comrade to their shoulders, linking arms to create a platform as the procession of more than a thousand began to make its way to the Milltown cemetery. They shuffled along in silence listening to the tune which had sounded at John F Kennedy's funeral just over seven years earlier across the Atlantic.

The piper turned onto Falls Road, the road that would bring them to the vast graveyard. Daniel tried hard not to cry when he saw the windows of several tenements up ahead. He gripped Luke's shoulder and although he couldn't see his face he knew the Australian had seen them. They were impossible to miss.

Hanging from a dozen or so second storey windows were Australian flags, each floating in the light, lazy breeze. Where they had been sourced from was anyones guess.

With the mass of people behind them and their country's flag hanging over the cold streets of Belfast, Luke and Grant were only now realising the impact their good friend had had on this dark, hate-breeding but hopeful city. Since returning to Belfast they had been told of everything that Sean had gone through since meeting that bald and bearded Scotsman on their own Newcastle docks. Daniel had told of how their friend had been kidnapped, tortured and crucified; of his plea to help them in their fight and of the task he had undertaken in Dublin to exact revenge. His fearless defence of Short Strand, his meeting with The Farmer, his work in Europe…they now knew it all. In knowing all this they now understood why he had loved this neglected, war torn, despised, blackened and unwanted land so much.

It was because its people, unlike their own, had welcomed him with open arms and had loved him selflessly.

He had found home.

EPILOGUE

Not that he understood the Fourth of July celebrations but Dieter Wilhelm Brasch certainly liked the party atmosphere the Americans got into around that time. While they may not have partied like his fellow Germans back home, he enjoyed the fact American women would use any opportunity to strip off to next to nothing once the summer months rolled around. And the hippie women! Why did they not have more of these back home. They were so open to suggestion. The drugs and the sex were the high point of his new life here.

Stepping out of his Fairview, New Jersey home, he made sure he had the list his sister had carefully written out (in large and easy to read words) and given him before she had walked to work. It was just going on eight thirty in the morning and he wanted to get the shopping out of the way as soon as possible. First he had to go to the liquor store and get some beer and schnapps for the barbecue they were having. He hated the dog's piss they dared to call beer so he would always buy the imported stuff when it was available or if he could afford it. It was so expensive to drink what he could get for next to nothing back home. Then he had to pick up the groceries and finally stop in at the butchers for the meat they had pre-ordered. The preceding Fourth of July had caught them unprepared and the butcher had run out of the best meats.

He climbed into his Oldsmobile and looked down the street. It was quiet out. Those that were unfortunate to be working today had already set off and the remainder of his neighbourhood were still waking up.

As he was turning the key in the ignition, he stopped. There, stuck into the padding of the dash of his car, was a little paper flag attached to a tooth pick. It was no bigger than the face of a match book but it caught his eye. He leant over, plucked it out and looked closer at it.

Three vertical stripes, one each of green, white and orange were painted on both sides of it. He tried to remember where he had seen those colours but couldn't recall which country it belonged to. At first he thought maybe his sister had put it there when she had borrowed the car two days ago, but he remembered he had driven it since then.

Then it came to him. It was an Irish flag. He remembered it from the festivities and parades that had taken place back in mid March.

'*Ich hab die Schauze voll von diesen Irren*,' he muttered in his native German as he realised who had placed it there.

Those shitty kids.

There were a large collection of Irish families on the next block over. Their kids were always playing their noisy hockey games on his street because it was a quieter road. Twice he had warned them about hitting his car with their ball but they would just laugh at his accent, call out "I know nothing! Nothing!" and "HOGAN!" in a mocking German brogue and run before he had the front door open.

He cursed them for breaking into his car as he kicked the Detroit V8 into life, dropped the lever into drive and lifted his foot off the brake pedal thus re-closing a recently fitted non-factory two stage earth-activated circuit.

Standing on the hillside cemetery which overlooked the suburb below half a mile away, Daniel and Donnie were surprised at how big the explosion was. They watched the car turn inside out from a huge shockwave that carried almost no flame.

'Fuck me,' Daniel remarked. 'Think he saw the flag?'

Donnie grinned. It had cost them a lot but the information obtain from a turned clerk within British Intelligence had been worth it. A year and a half of searching for the infiltrator whose information had killed Sean and his active service unit had just culminated in him being vaporised.

'If he did, it would have been the last thing to go through his mind.'

'Literally.'

Below them people began to come out of their homes to look for the cause of so many broken windows. The two Irish lads returned to their car, Daniel pulling out into the light traffic at a steady pace. Heading north to Massachusetts towards a meeting with their new American arms dealers and away from the mayhem, Daniel and Donnie began to sing.

'There was a wild colonial boy,
Jack Duggan was his name.
He was born and raised in Ireland,
In a place called Castlemaine.
He was his father's only son,
His mother's pride and joy.
And dearly did his parents love
The wild colonial boy'

Sean Doherty is buried next to Kieran Hough in the County Antrim Memorial Plot which was set aside for IRA soldiers for the years 1969 – 1972 in the Milltown Cemetery, West Belfast.

To this day his head stone is still attended to by the Carragher family.

Sean is survived by a son, Sean Seamus O'Brien, born nine months after his death. Today he lives in Dublin with his own family, close to the home of his mother, Megan.

Andrew Wilton returned to Australia and currently lives in the small northern Victorian town of Corryong with his wife. After running a successful paper mill he retired in 2002. They have two daughters and three grandchildren.

He has never held a firearm since that day on the border.

Luke Kennedy went on to become an engineer for the Newcastle BHP Steelworks and stayed with the company until its closure in 1999. He died in a road accident two years later. His true character was applauded when over eight hundred people attended his funeral. He is survived by his widow, four sons, one daughter, nine grandchildren and a great-grandson.

Sean's father visited the final resting place of his little soldier boy and met his first grandson in 1972, giving him Sean's dog tags.

In August the following year he succumbed to his illness and passed away at the Newcastle hospital.

His other son James and his eldest, Melanie, travel to Ireland once every few years when funds permit.

They are still close friends with both the Carragher and O'Brien families.

Lightning Source UK Ltd.
Milton Keynes UK
UKHW01f0940060518
322140UK00001B/43/P

9 781925 08649